Refrigerator Full of Heads

REFRIGERATOR FULL OF HEADS

RIO YOUERS WRITER
TOM FOWLER PENCILLER
TOM FOWLER & CRAIG A. TAILLEFER INKERS
BILL CRABTREE COLORIST
ANDWORLD DESIGN LETTERER
SAM WOLFE CONNELLY COLLECTION COVER ARTIST

BASKETFUL OF HEADS CREATED BY **JOE HILL** WITH ART BY **LEOMACS**
REFRIGERATOR FULL OF HEADS CURATED FOR HILL HOUSE COMICS BY **JOE HILL**

REFRIGERATOR FULL OF HEADS

PUBLISHED BY DC COMICS. COMPILATION AND ALL NEW MATERIAL COPYRIGHT © 2022 DC COMICS. ALL RIGHTS RESERVED. ORIGINALLY PUBLISHED IN SINGLE MAGAZINE FORM IN *REFRIGERATOR FULL OF HEADS* 1-6. COPYRIGHT © 2021, 2022 DC COMICS. ALL RIGHTS RESERVED. ALL CHARACTERS, THEIR DISTINCTIVE LIKENESSES, AND RELATED ELEMENTS FEATURED IN THIS PUBLICATION ARE TRADEMARKS OF DC COMICS. THE STORIES, CHARACTERS, AND INCIDENTS FEATURED IN THIS PUBLICATION ARE ENTIRELY FICTIONAL. DC COMICS DOES NOT READ OR ACCEPT UNSOLICITED SUBMISSIONS OF IDEAS, STORIES, OR ARTWORK.

DC COMICS, 100 S. CALIFORNIA STREET, BURBANK, CA 91505

PRINTED BY TRANSCONTINENTAL INTERGLOBE, BEAUCEVILLE, QC, CANADA. 9/9/22. FIRST PRINTING.

ISBN: 978-1-77951-690-9

LIBRARY OF CONGRESS CATALOGING-IN-PUBLICATION DATA IS AVAILABLE.

PEFC Certified
This product is from sustainably managed forests and controlled sources
PEFC
PEFC/01-31-106
www.pefc.org

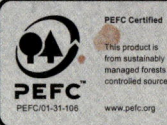

ANDREA SHEA & CHRIS CONROY EDITORS – ORIGINAL SERIES
ANDREA SHEA EDITOR – COLLECTED EDITION
STEVE COOK DESIGN DIRECTOR – BOOKS
AMIE BROCKWAY-METCALF PUBLICATION DESIGN
SUZANNAH ROWNTREE PUBLICATION PRODUCTION

MARIE JAVINS EDITOR-IN-CHIEF, DC COMICS

ANNE DePIES SENIOR VP – GENERAL MANAGER
JIM LEE PUBLISHER & CHIEF CREATIVE OFFICER
DON FALLETTI VP – MANUFACTURING OPERATIONS & WORKFLOW MANAGEMEN
LAWRENCE GANEM VP – TALENT SERVICES
ALISON GILL SENIOR VP – MANUFACTURING & OPERATIONS
JEFFREY KAUFMAN VP – EDITORIAL STRATEGY & PROGRAMMING
NICK J. NAPOLITANO VP – MANUFACTURING ADMINISTRATION & DESIGN
NANCY SPEARS VP – REVENUE

REFRIGERATOR FULL OF HEADS #1 COVER BY SAM WOLFE CONNELLY

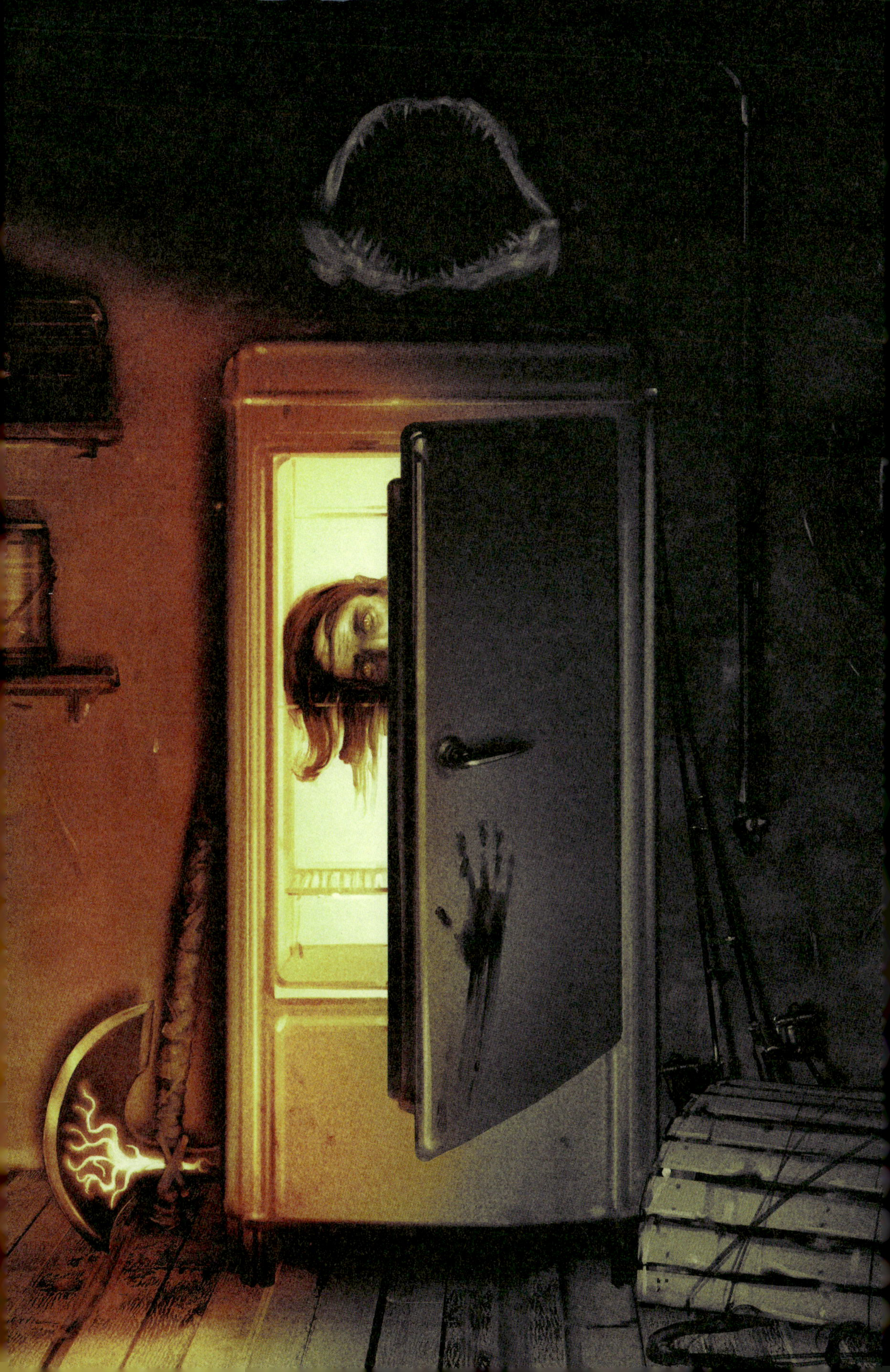

REFRIGERATOR FULL OF HEADS #1 VARIANT COVER BY LEOMACS

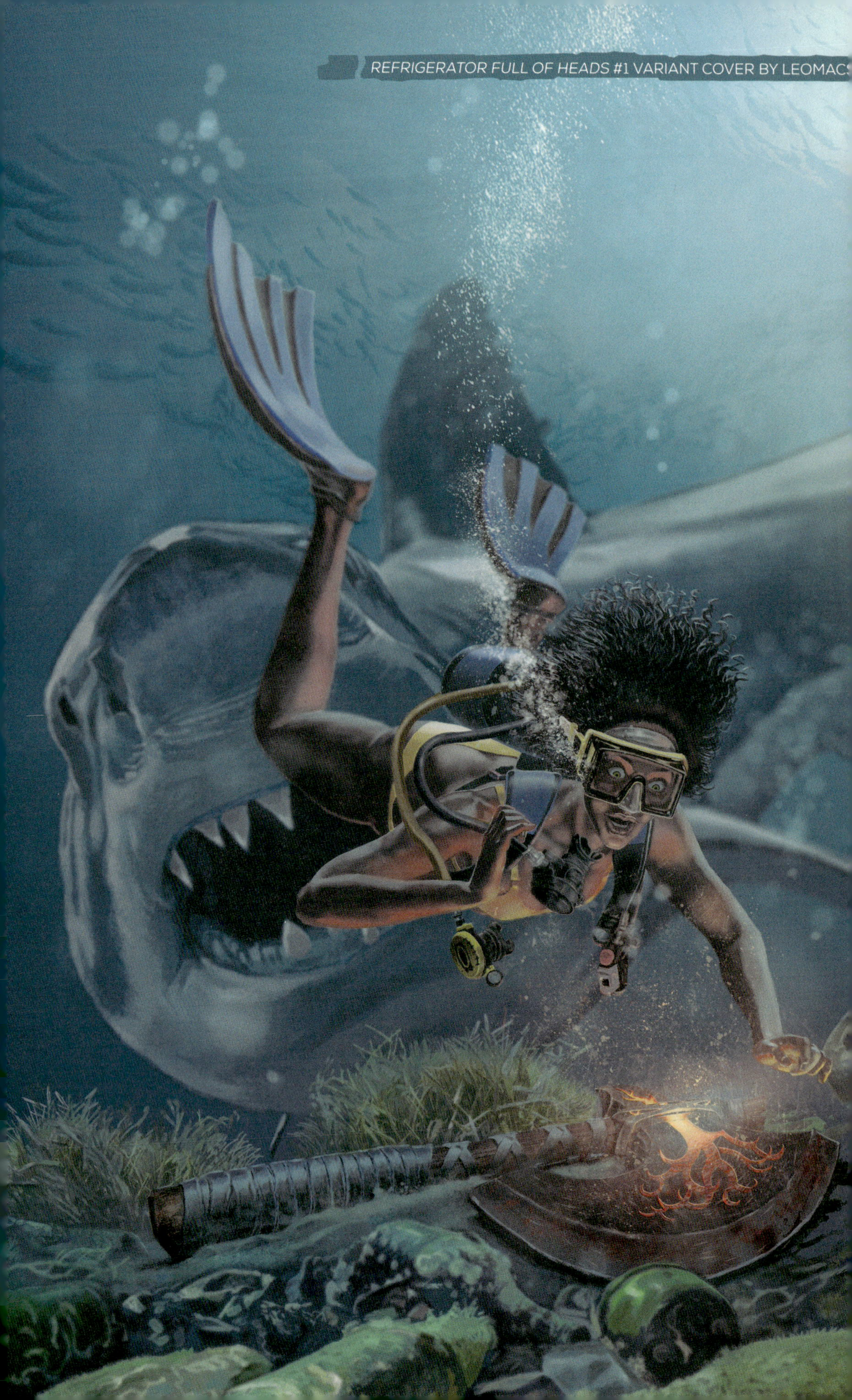

BEFORE.

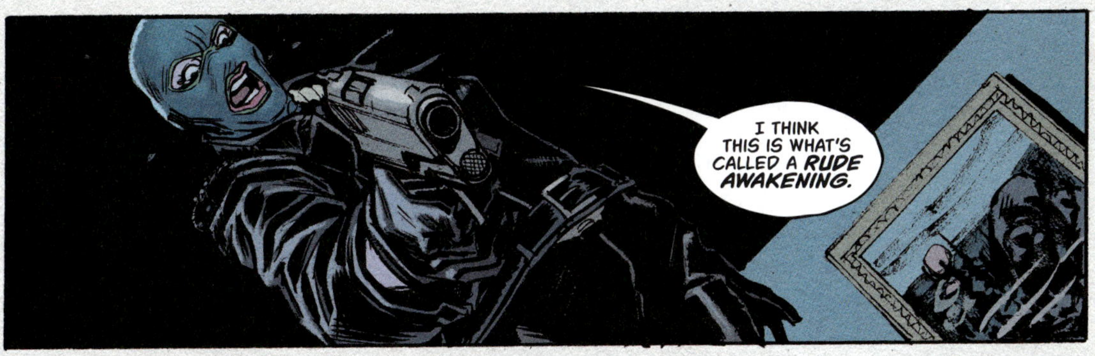
I THINK THIS IS WHAT'S CALLED A *RUDE AWAKENING*.

LAUREN VALLEY, CALIFORNIA.

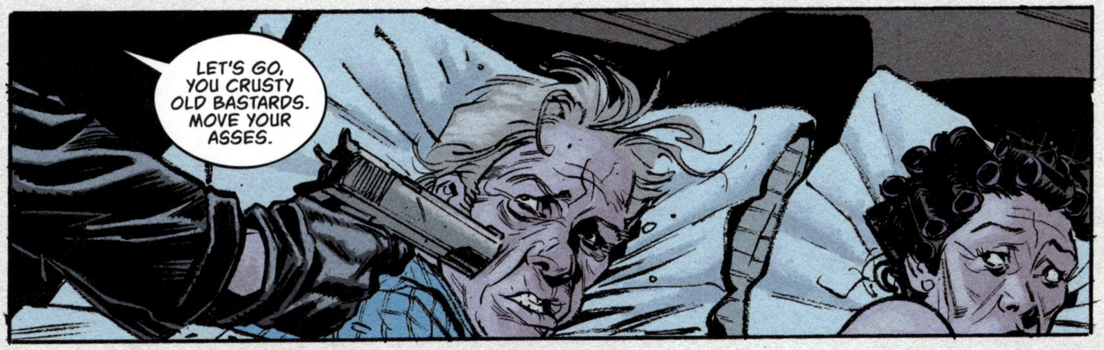
LET'S GO, YOU CRUSTY OLD BASTARDS. MOVE YOUR ASSES.

NOVEMBER 1983.

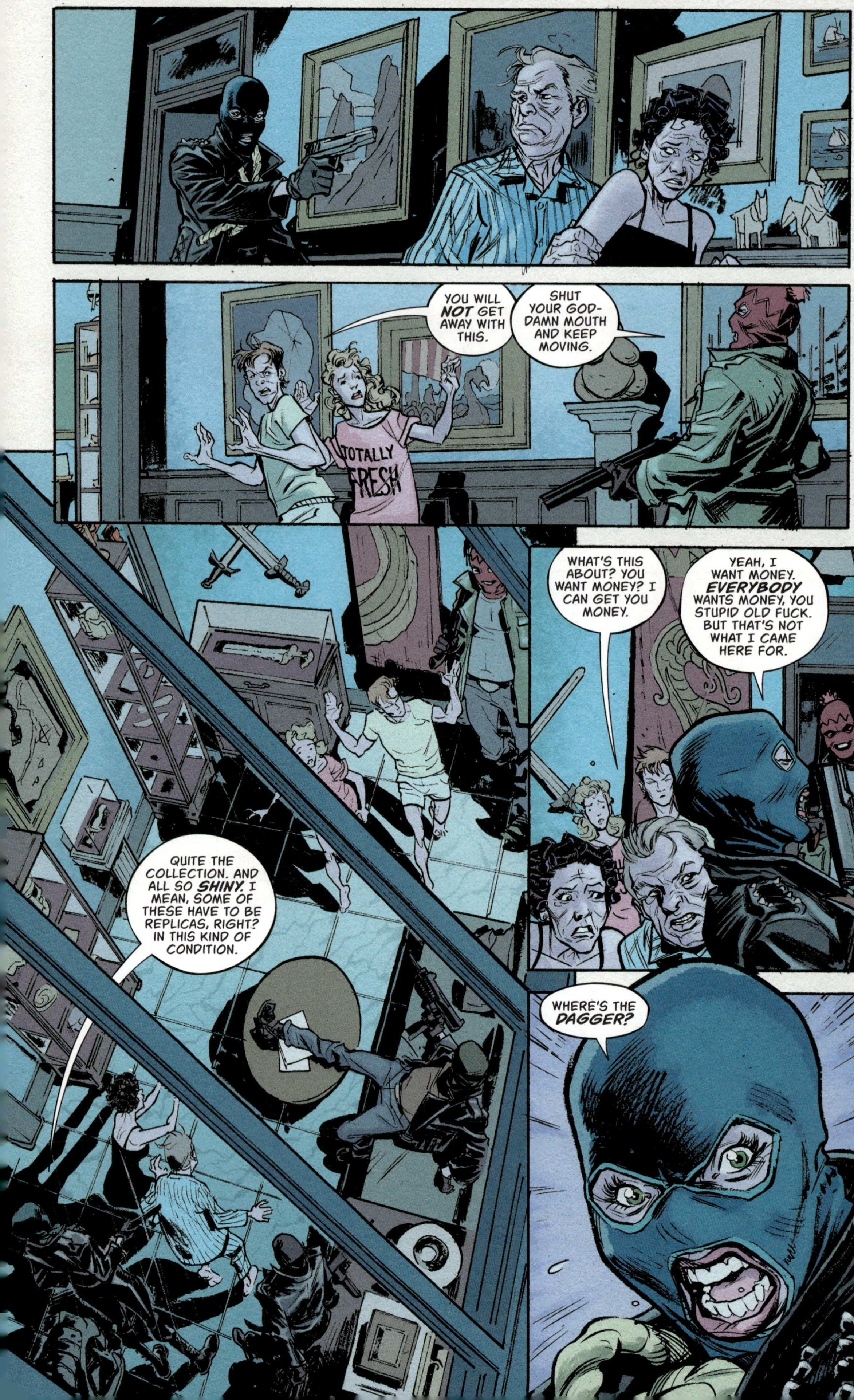
YOU WILL NOT GET AWAY WITH THIS.
SHUT YOUR GOD-DAMN MOUTH AND KEEP MOVING.
TOTALLY FRESH
QUITE THE COLLECTION. AND ALL SO SHINY. I MEAN, SOME OF THESE HAVE TO BE REPLICAS, RIGHT? IN THIS KIND OF CONDITION.
WHAT'S THIS ABOUT? YOU WANT MONEY? I CAN GET YOU MONEY.
YEAH, I WANT MONEY. EVERYBODY WANTS MONEY, YOU STUPID OLD FUCK. BUT THAT'S NOT WHAT I CAME HERE FOR.
WHERE'S THE DAGGER?

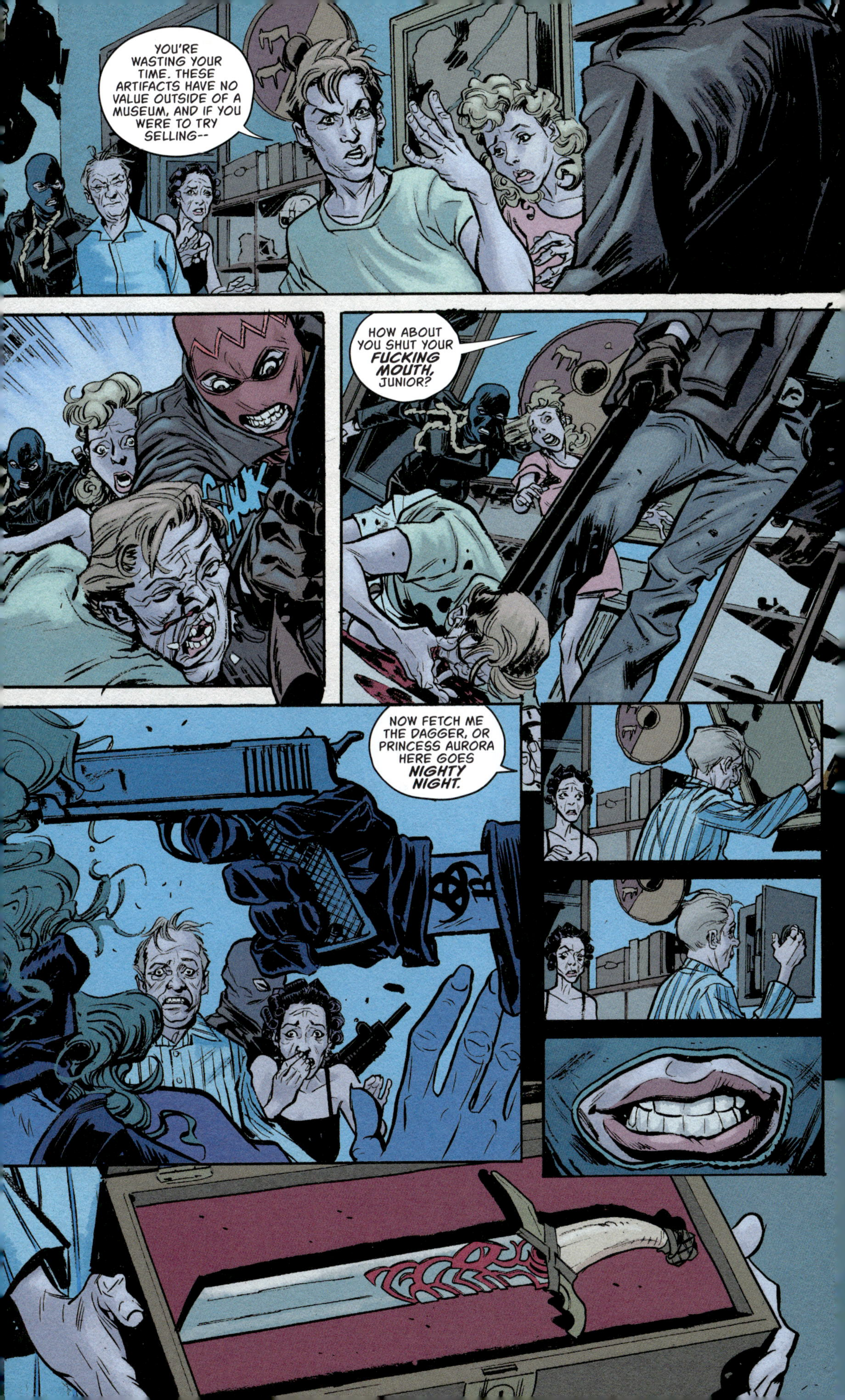
YOU'RE WASTING YOUR TIME. THESE ARTIFACTS HAVE NO VALUE OUTSIDE OF A MUSEUM, AND IF YOU WERE TO TRY SELLING--
SHUK
HOW ABOUT YOU SHUT YOUR FUCKING MOUTH, JUNIOR?
NOW FETCH ME THE DAGGER, OR PRINCESS AURORA HERE GOES NIGHTY NIGHT.

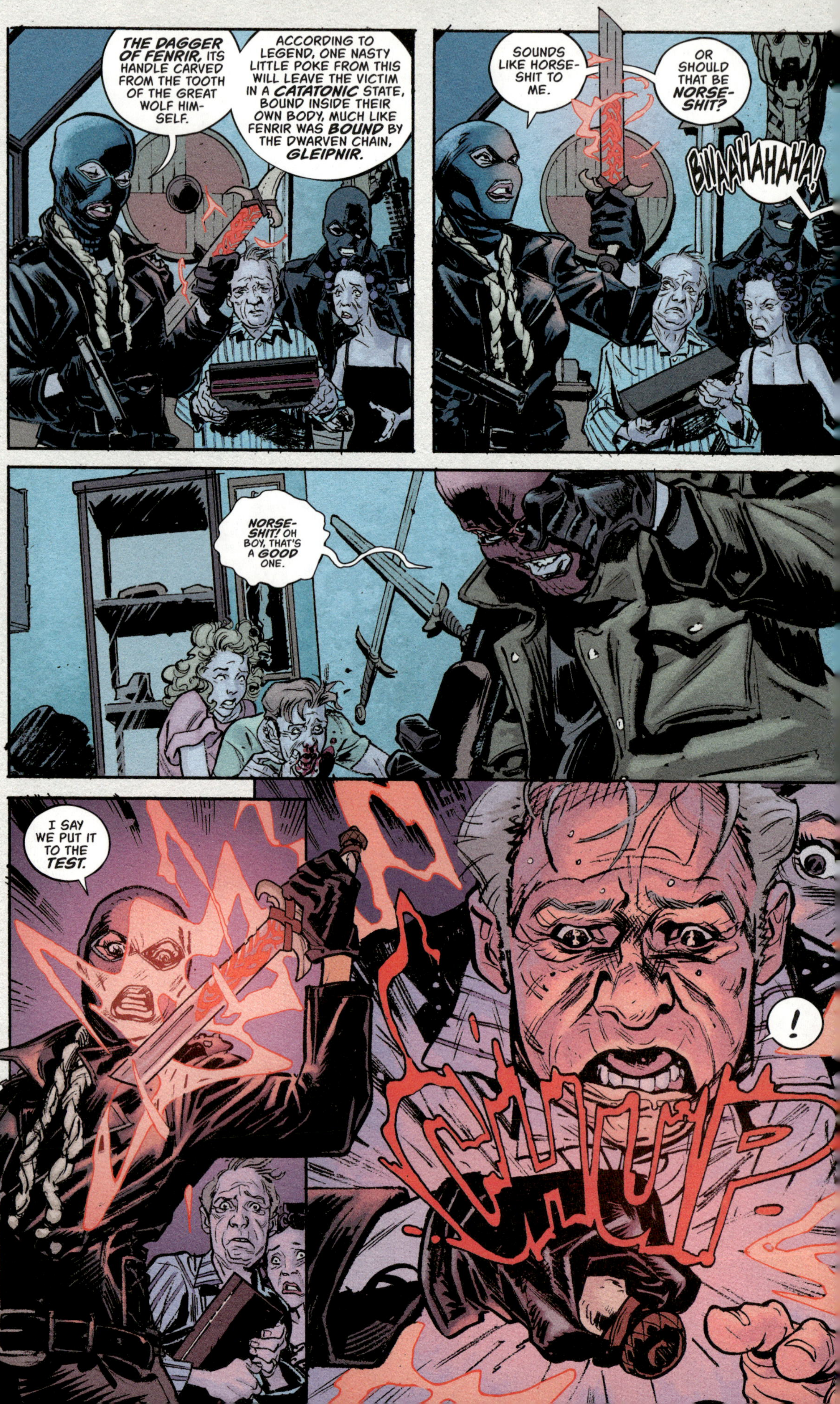
THE DAGGER OF FENRIR, ITS HANDLE CARVED FROM THE TOOTH OF THE GREAT WOLF HIMSELF.
ACCORDING TO LEGEND, ONE NASTY LITTLE POKE FROM THIS WILL LEAVE THE VICTIM IN A CATATONIC STATE, BOUND INSIDE THEIR OWN BODY, MUCH LIKE FENRIR WAS BOUND BY THE DWARVEN CHAIN, GLEIPNIR.
SOUNDS LIKE HORSE-SHIT TO ME.
OR SHOULD THAT BE NORSE-SHIT?
BWAAHAHAHA!
NORSE-SHIT! OH BOY, THAT'S A GOOD ONE.
I SAY WE PUT IT TO THE TEST.
!
CHUNK

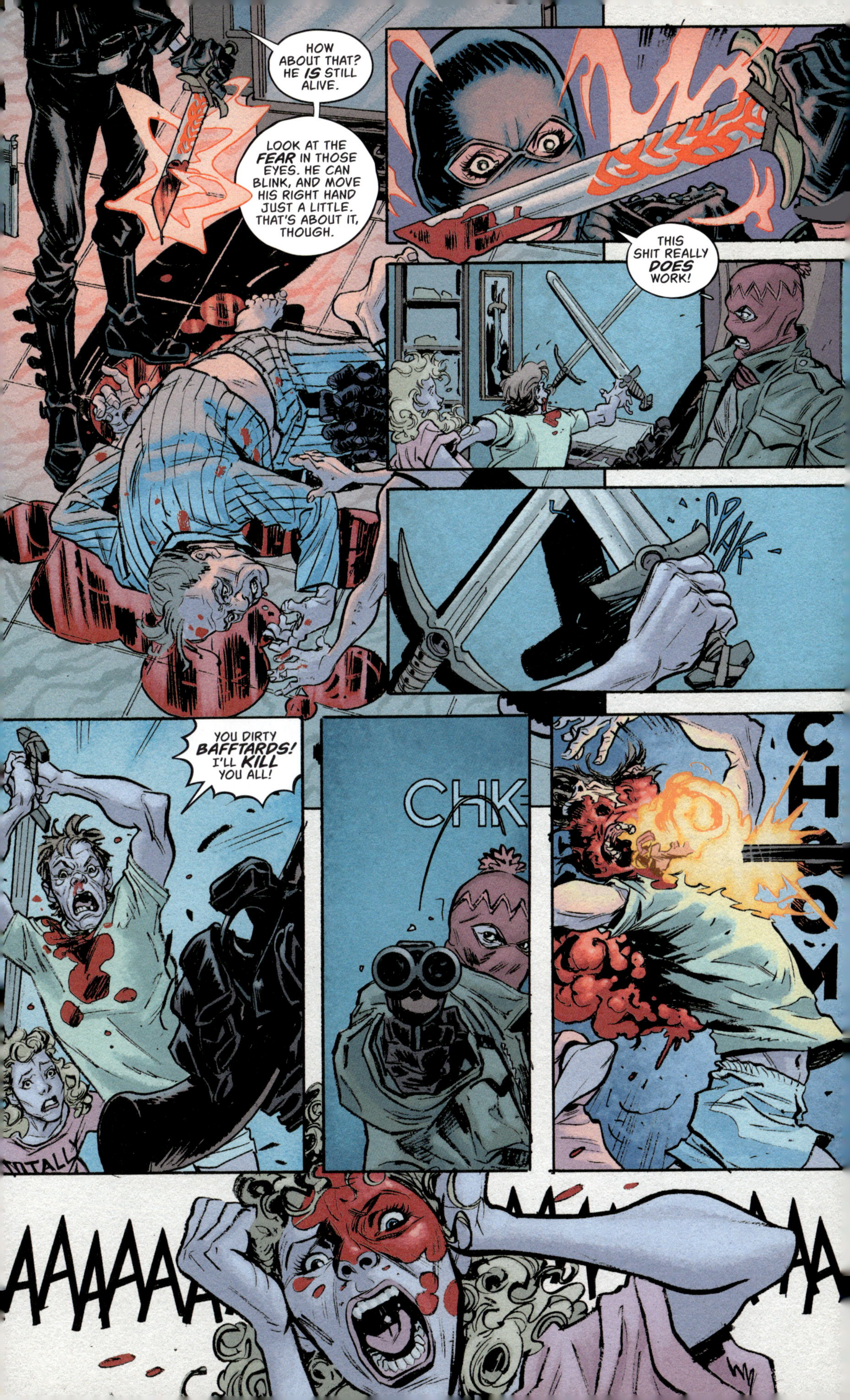
HOW ABOUT THAT? HE IS STILL ALIVE.
LOOK AT THE FEAR IN THOSE EYES. HE CAN BLINK, AND MOVE HIS RIGHT HAND JUST A LITTLE. THAT'S ABOUT IT, THOUGH.
THIS SHIT REALLY DOES WORK!
SPAK
YOU DIRTY BAFFTARDS! I'LL KILL YOU ALL!
CHK
CHOOM
AAAAAAAAAAAAAAAA

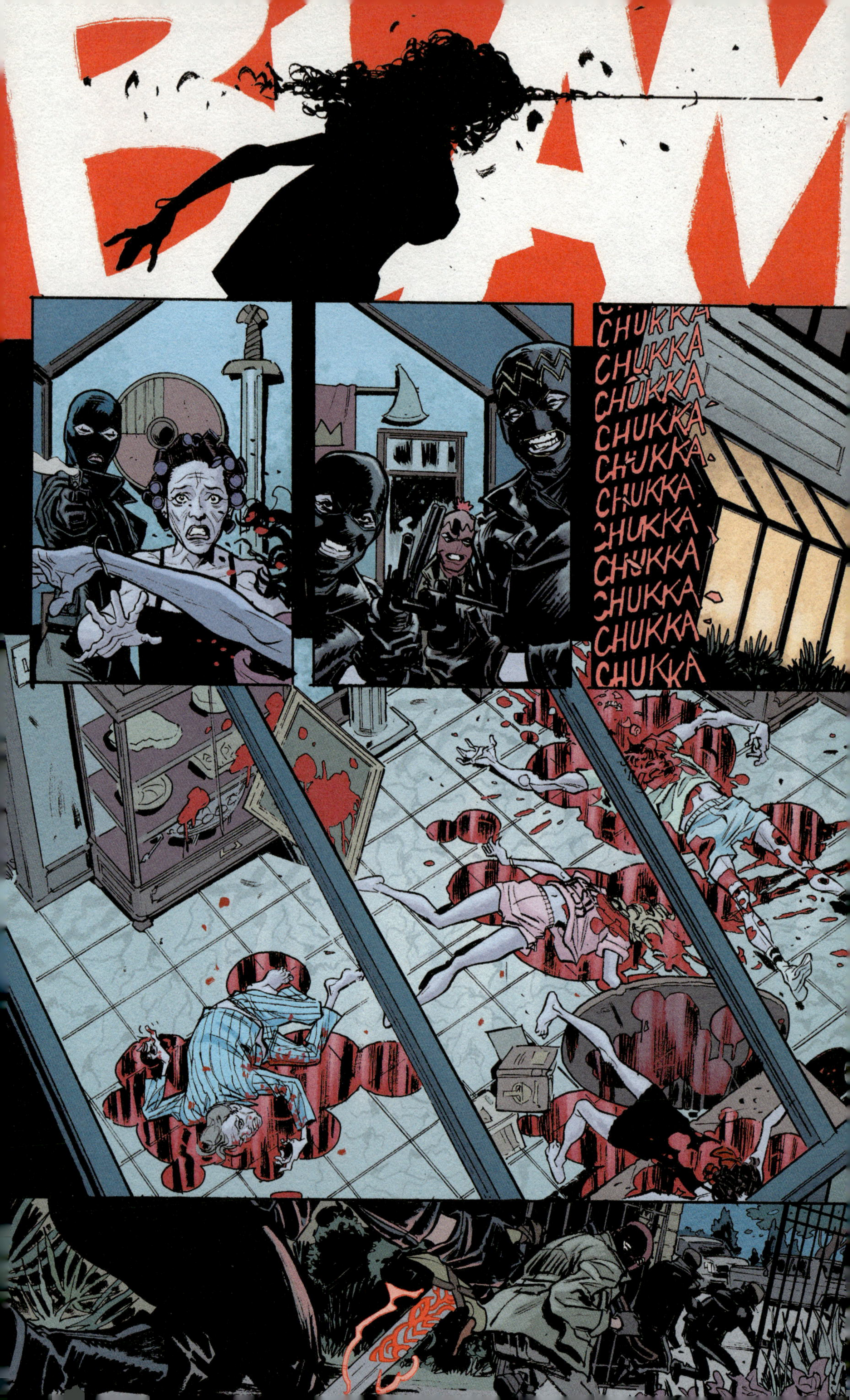
CHUKKA
CHUKKA
CHUKKA
CHUKKA
CHUKKA
CHUKKA
CHUKKA
CHUKKA
CHUKKA
CHUKKA
CHUKKA
CHUKKA
CHUKKA

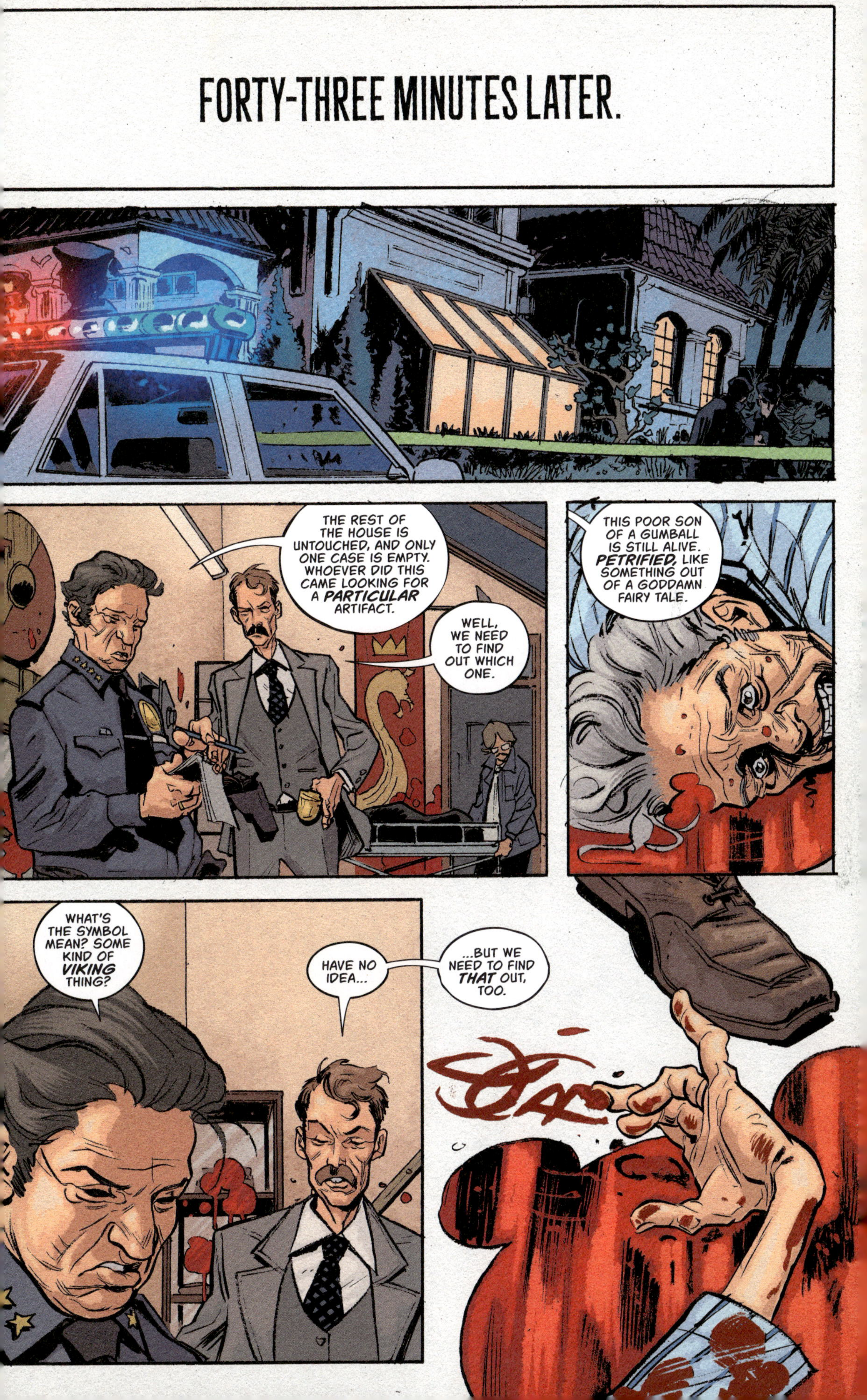
FORTY-THREE MINUTES LATER.
THE REST OF THE HOUSE IS UNTOUCHED, AND ONLY ONE CASE IS EMPTY. WHOEVER DID THIS CAME LOOKING FOR A PARTICULAR ARTIFACT.
WELL, WE NEED TO FIND OUT WHICH ONE.
THIS POOR SON OF A GUMBALL IS STILL ALIVE. PETRIFIED, LIKE SOMETHING OUT OF A GODDAMN FAIRY TALE.
WHAT'S THE SYMBOL MEAN? SOME KIND OF VIKING THING?
HAVE NO IDEA...
...BUT WE NEED TO FIND THAT OUT, TOO.

NOW.

BRODY ISLAND, MAINE.

JULY 1984.

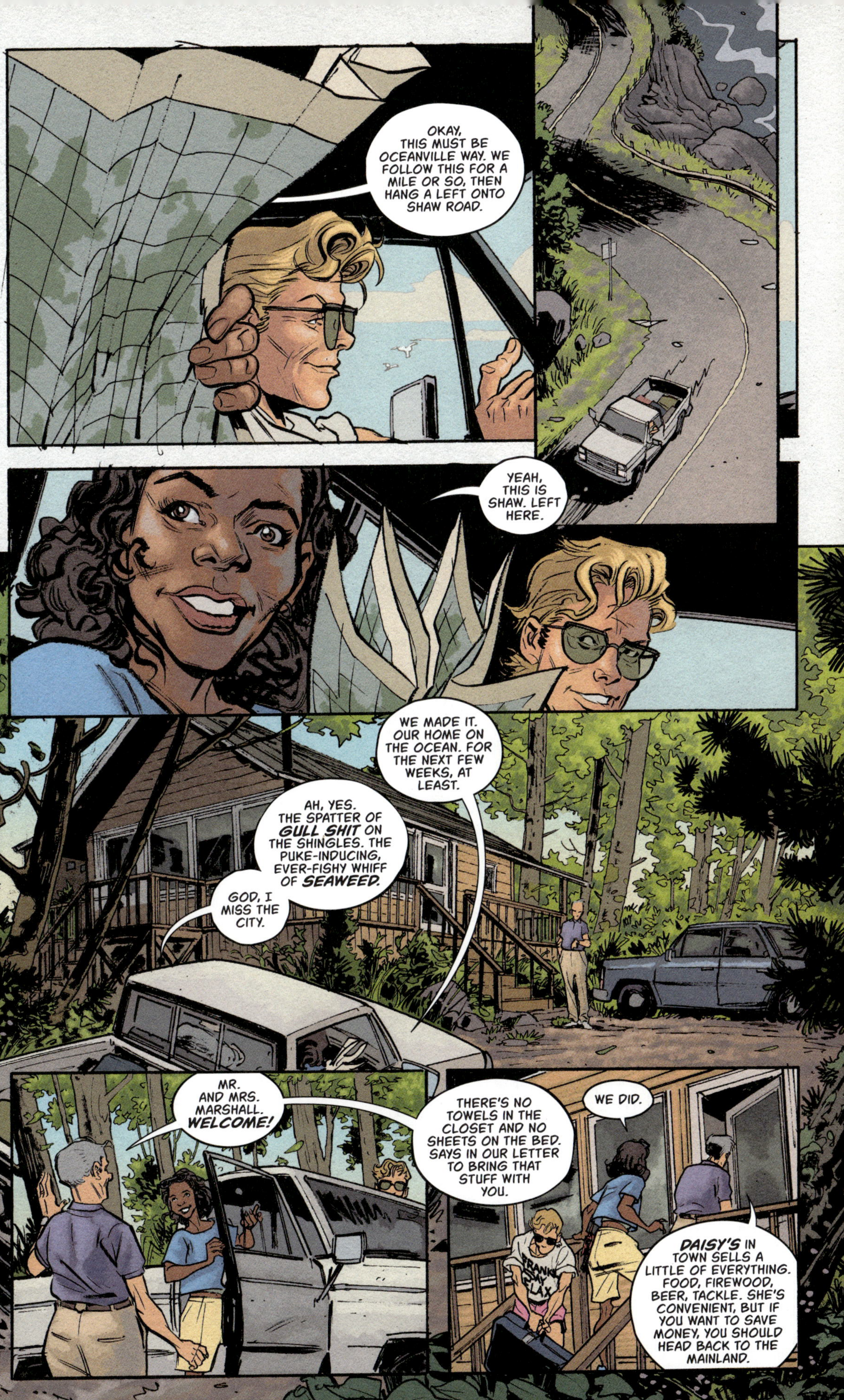
OKAY, THIS MUST BE OCEANVILLE WAY. WE FOLLOW THIS FOR A MILE OR SO, THEN HANG A LEFT ONTO SHAW ROAD.
YEAH, THIS IS SHAW. LEFT HERE.
WE MADE IT. OUR HOME ON THE OCEAN. FOR THE NEXT FEW WEEKS, AT LEAST.
AH, YES. THE SPATTER OF GULL SHIT ON THE SHINGLES. THE PUKE-INDUCING, EVER-FISHY WHIFF OF SEAWEED.
GOD, I MISS THE CITY.
MR. AND MRS. MARSHALL. WELCOME!
THERE'S NO TOWELS IN THE CLOSET AND NO SHEETS ON THE BED. SAYS IN OUR LETTER TO BRING THAT STUFF WITH YOU.
WE DID.
DAISY'S IN TOWN SELLS A LITTLE OF EVERYTHING. FOOD, FIREWOOD, BEER, TACKLE. SHE'S CONVENIENT, BUT IF YOU WANT TO SAVE MONEY, YOU SHOULD HEAD BACK TO THE MAINLAND.

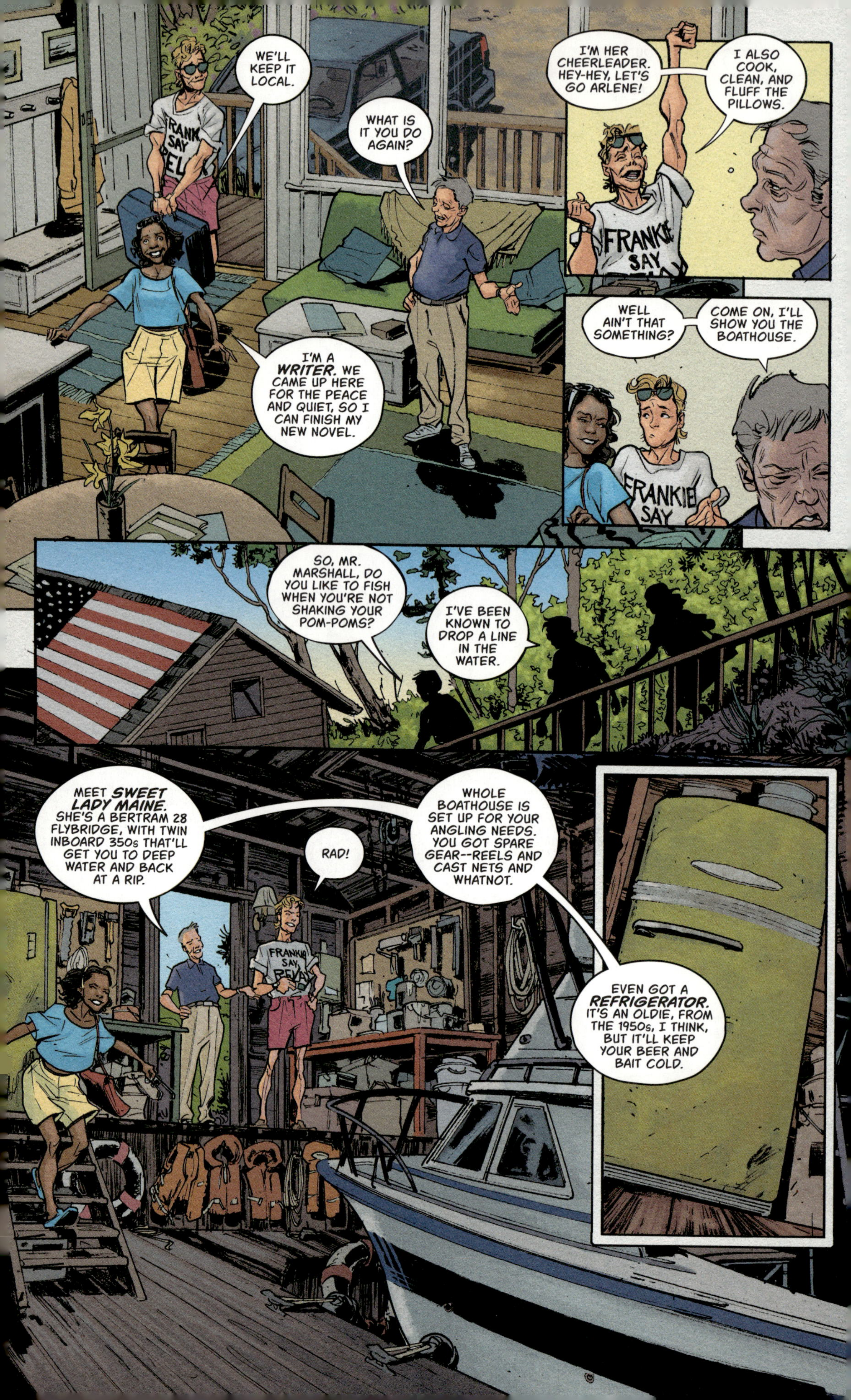
WE'LL KEEP IT LOCAL.
WHAT IS IT YOU DO AGAIN?
I'M A WRITER. WE CAME UP HERE FOR THE PEACE AND QUIET, SO I CAN FINISH MY NEW NOVEL.
I'M HER CHEERLEADER. HEY-HEY, LET'S GO ARLENE!
I ALSO COOK, CLEAN, AND FLUFF THE PILLOWS.
WELL AIN'T THAT SOMETHING?
COME ON, I'LL SHOW YOU THE BOATHOUSE.
SO, MR. MARSHALL, DO YOU LIKE TO FISH WHEN YOU'RE NOT SHAKING YOUR POM-POMS?
I'VE BEEN KNOWN TO DROP A LINE IN THE WATER.
MEET SWEET LADY MAINE. SHE'S A BERTRAM 28 FLYBRIDGE, WITH TWIN INBOARD 350s THAT'LL GET YOU TO DEEP WATER AND BACK AT A RIP.
RAD!
WHOLE BOATHOUSE IS SET UP FOR YOUR ANGLING NEEDS. YOU GOT SPARE GEAR--REELS AND CAST NETS AND WHATNOT.
EVEN GOT A REFRIGERATOR. IT'S AN OLDIE, FROM THE 1950s, I THINK, BUT IT'LL KEEP YOUR BEER AND BAIT COLD.

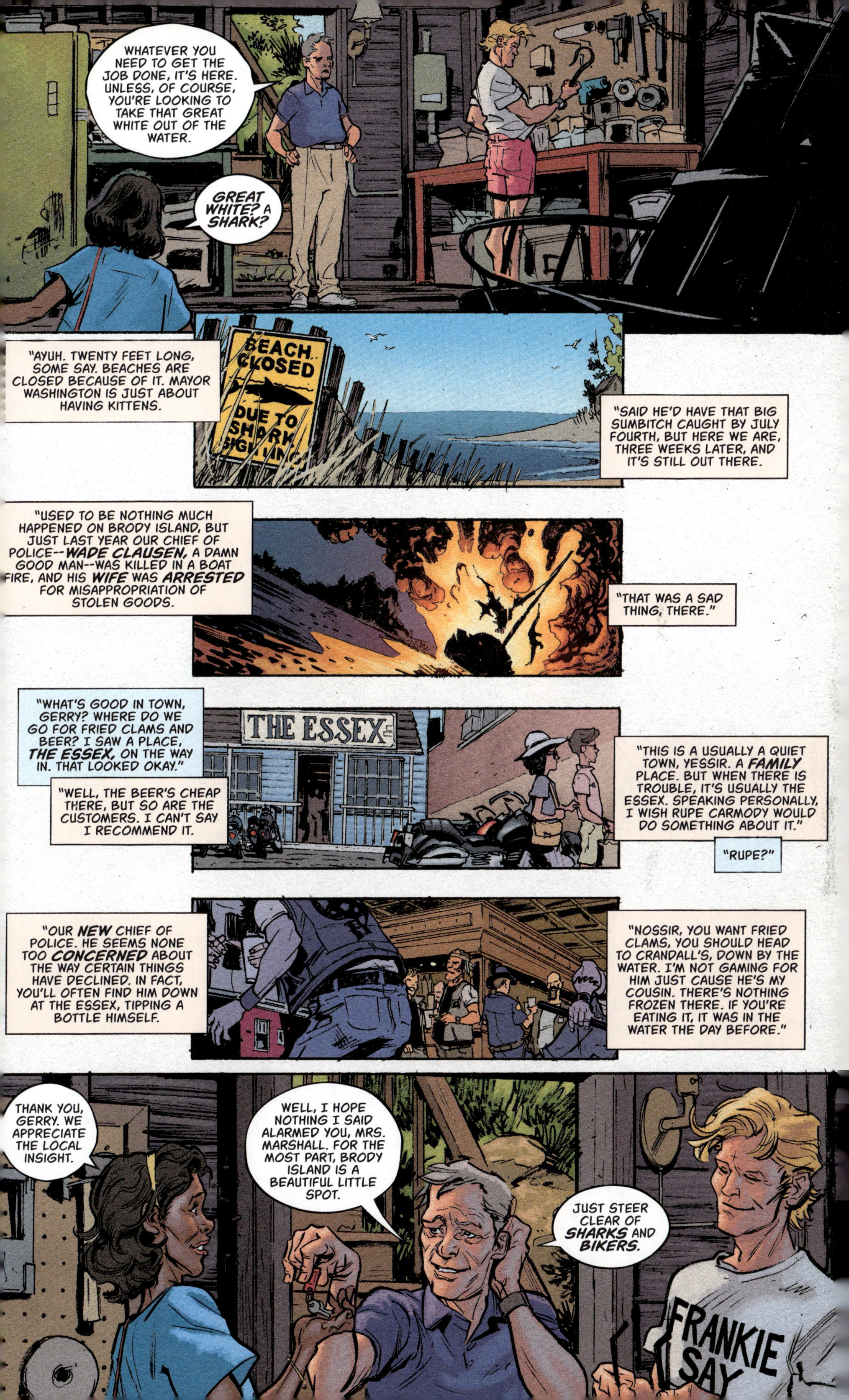
WHATEVER YOU NEED TO GET THE JOB DONE, IT'S HERE. UNLESS, OF COURSE, YOU'RE LOOKING TO TAKE THAT GREAT WHITE OUT OF THE WATER.
GREAT WHITE? A SHARK?
"AYUH. TWENTY FEET LONG, SOME SAY. BEACHES ARE CLOSED BECAUSE OF IT. MAYOR WASHINGTON IS JUST ABOUT HAVING KITTENS.
BEACH CLOSED DUE TO SHARK
"SAID HE'D HAVE THAT BIG SUMBITCH CAUGHT BY JULY FOURTH, BUT HERE WE ARE, THREE WEEKS LATER, AND IT'S STILL OUT THERE.
"USED TO BE NOTHING MUCH HAPPENED ON BRODY ISLAND, BUT JUST LAST YEAR OUR CHIEF OF POLICE--WADE CLAUSEN, A DAMN GOOD MAN--WAS KILLED IN A BOAT FIRE, AND HIS WIFE WAS ARRESTED FOR MISAPPROPRIATION OF STOLEN GOODS.
"THAT WAS A SAD THING, THERE."
"WHAT'S GOOD IN TOWN, GERRY? WHERE DO WE GO FOR FRIED CLAMS AND BEER? I SAW A PLACE, THE ESSEX, ON THE WAY IN. THAT LOOKED OKAY."
"WELL, THE BEER'S CHEAP THERE, BUT SO ARE THE CUSTOMERS. I CAN'T SAY I RECOMMEND IT.
THE ESSEX
"THIS IS A USUALLY A QUIET TOWN, YESSIR. A FAMILY PLACE. BUT WHEN THERE IS TROUBLE, IT'S USUALLY THE ESSEX. SPEAKING PERSONALLY, I WISH RUPE CARMODY WOULD DO SOMETHING ABOUT IT."
"RUPE?"
"OUR NEW CHIEF OF POLICE. HE SEEMS NONE TOO CONCERNED ABOUT THE WAY CERTAIN THINGS HAVE DECLINED. IN FACT, YOU'LL OFTEN FIND HIM DOWN AT THE ESSEX, TIPPING A BOTTLE HIMSELF.
"NOSSIR, YOU WANT FRIED CLAMS, YOU SHOULD HEAD TO CRANDALL'S, DOWN BY THE WATER. I'M NOT GAMING FOR HIM JUST CAUSE HE'S MY COUSIN. THERE'S NOTHING FROZEN THERE. IF YOU'RE EATING IT, IT WAS IN THE WATER THE DAY BEFORE."
THANK YOU, GERRY. WE APPRECIATE THE LOCAL INSIGHT.
WELL, I HOPE NOTHING I SAID ALARMED YOU, MRS. MARSHALL. FOR THE MOST PART, BRODY ISLAND IS A BEAUTIFUL LITTLE SPOT.
JUST STEER CLEAR OF SHARKS AND BIKERS.
FRANKIE SAY

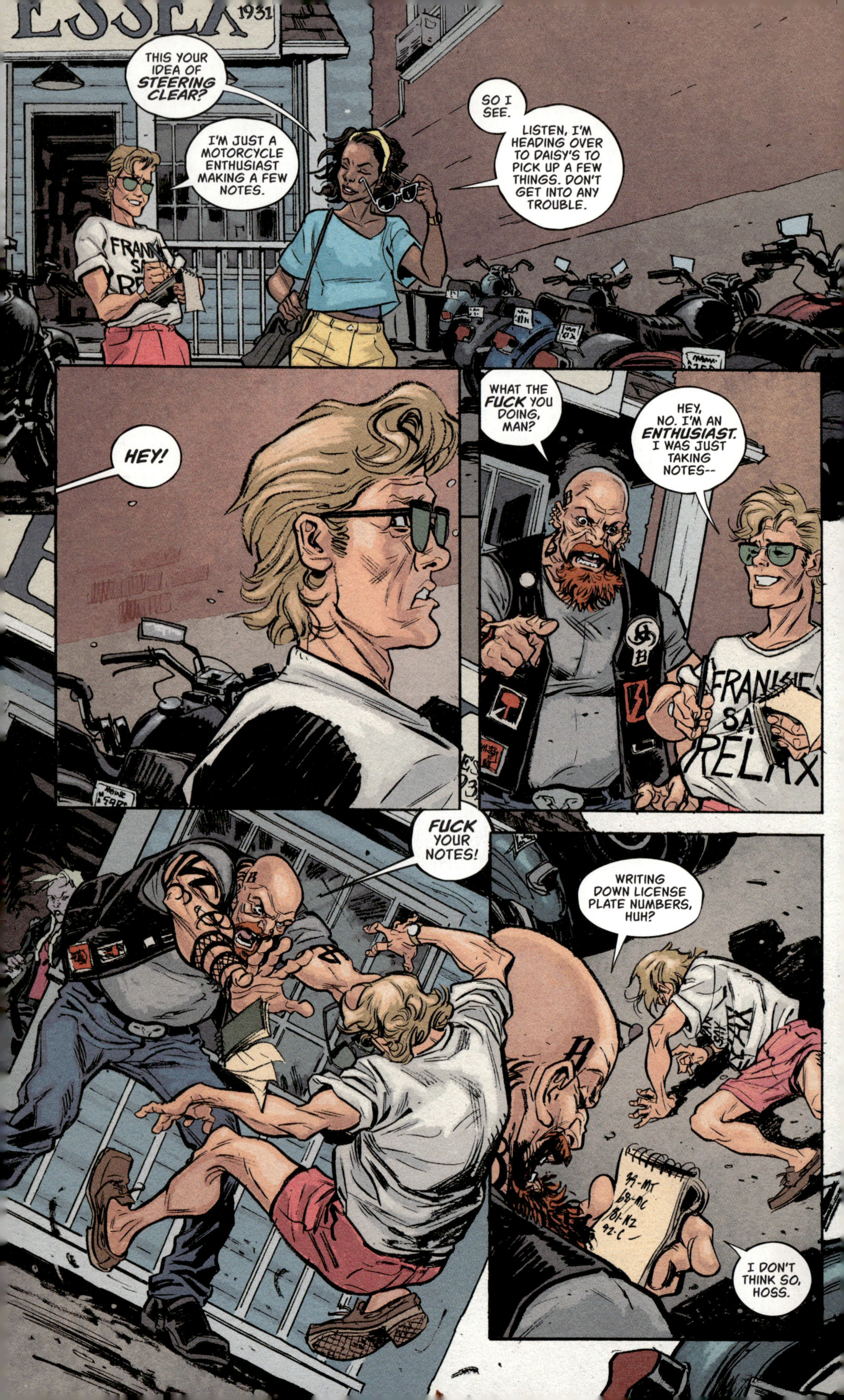
ESSEX 1931
THIS YOUR IDEA OF STEERING CLEAR?
I'M JUST A MOTORCYCLE ENTHUSIAST MAKING A FEW NOTES.
SO I SEE.
LISTEN, I'M HEADING OVER TO DAISY'S TO PICK UP A FEW THINGS. DON'T GET INTO ANY TROUBLE.
HEY!
WHAT THE FUCK YOU DOING, MAN?
HEY, NO. I'M AN ENTHUSIAST. I WAS JUST TAKING NOTES--
FRANKIE SAY RELAX
FUCK YOUR NOTES!
WRITING DOWN LICENSE PLATE NUMBERS, HUH?
I DON'T THINK SO, HOSS.

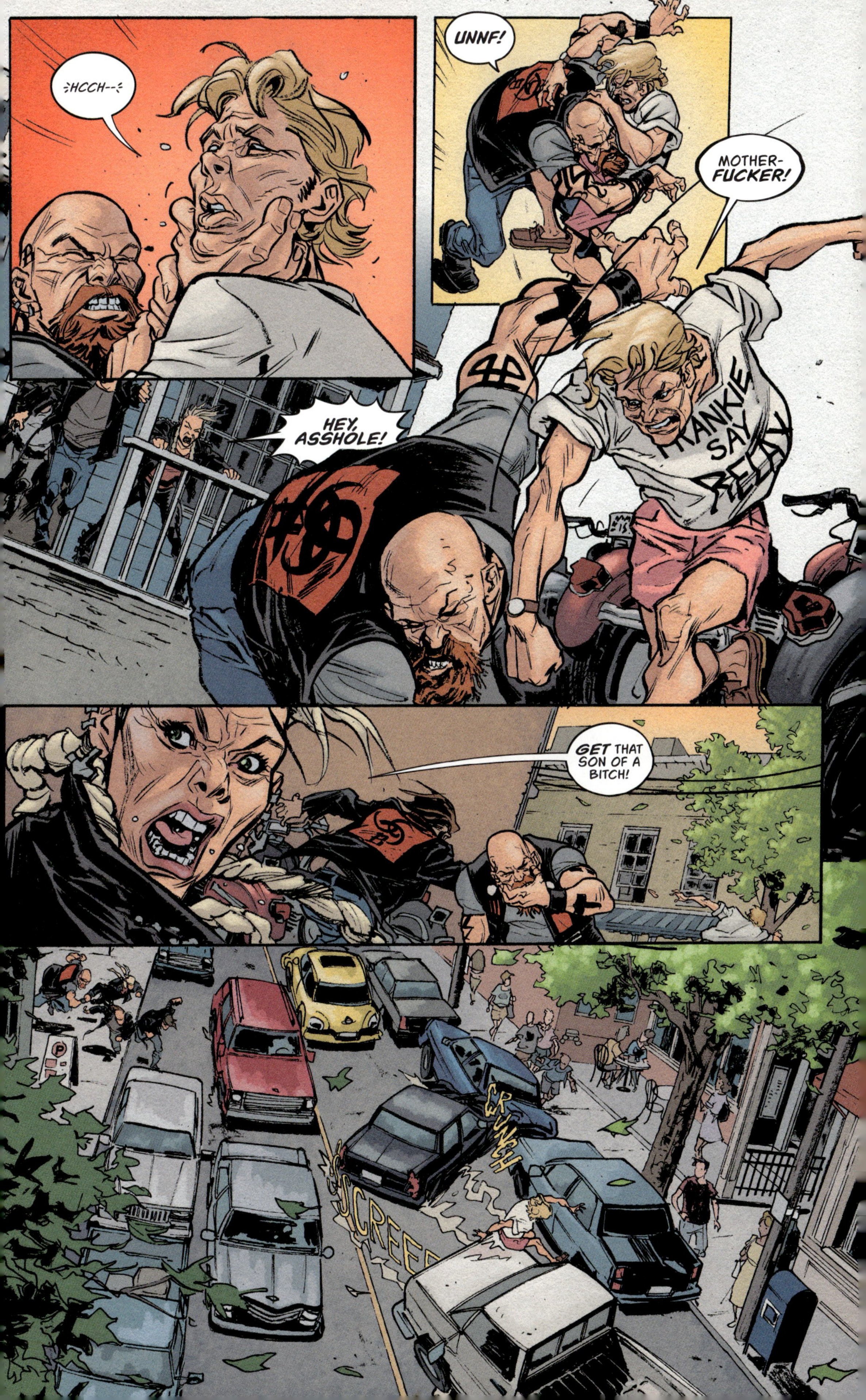
HCCH--
UNNF!
MOTHER-FUCKER!
HEY, ASSHOLE!
FRANKIE SAY RELAX
GET THAT SON OF A BITCH!
CRUNCH
SCREEE

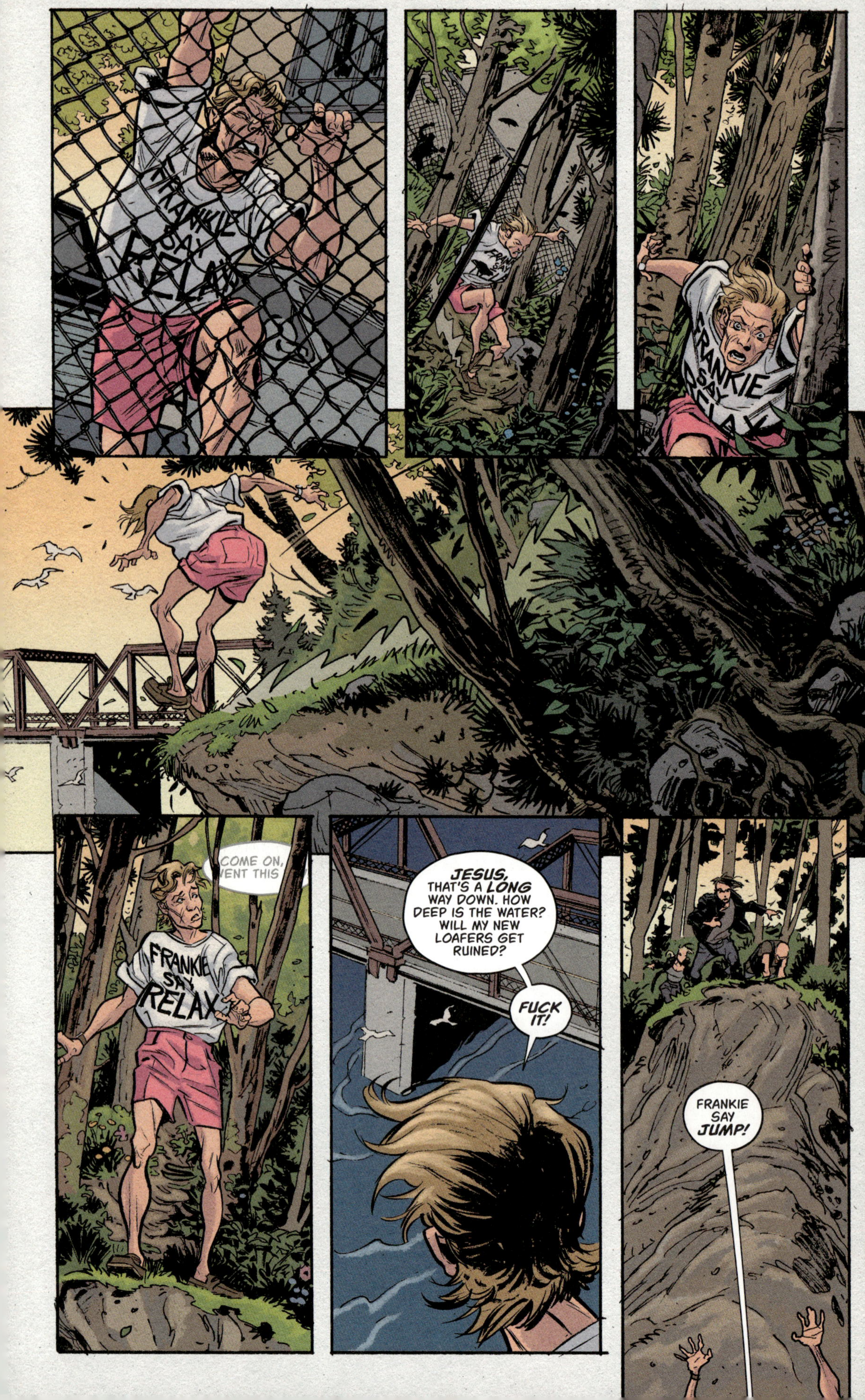
COME ON,
WENT THIS
JESUS, THAT'S A LONG WAY DOWN. HOW DEEP IS THE WATER? WILL MY NEW LOAFERS GET RUINED?
FUCK IT!
FRANKIE SAY JUMP!

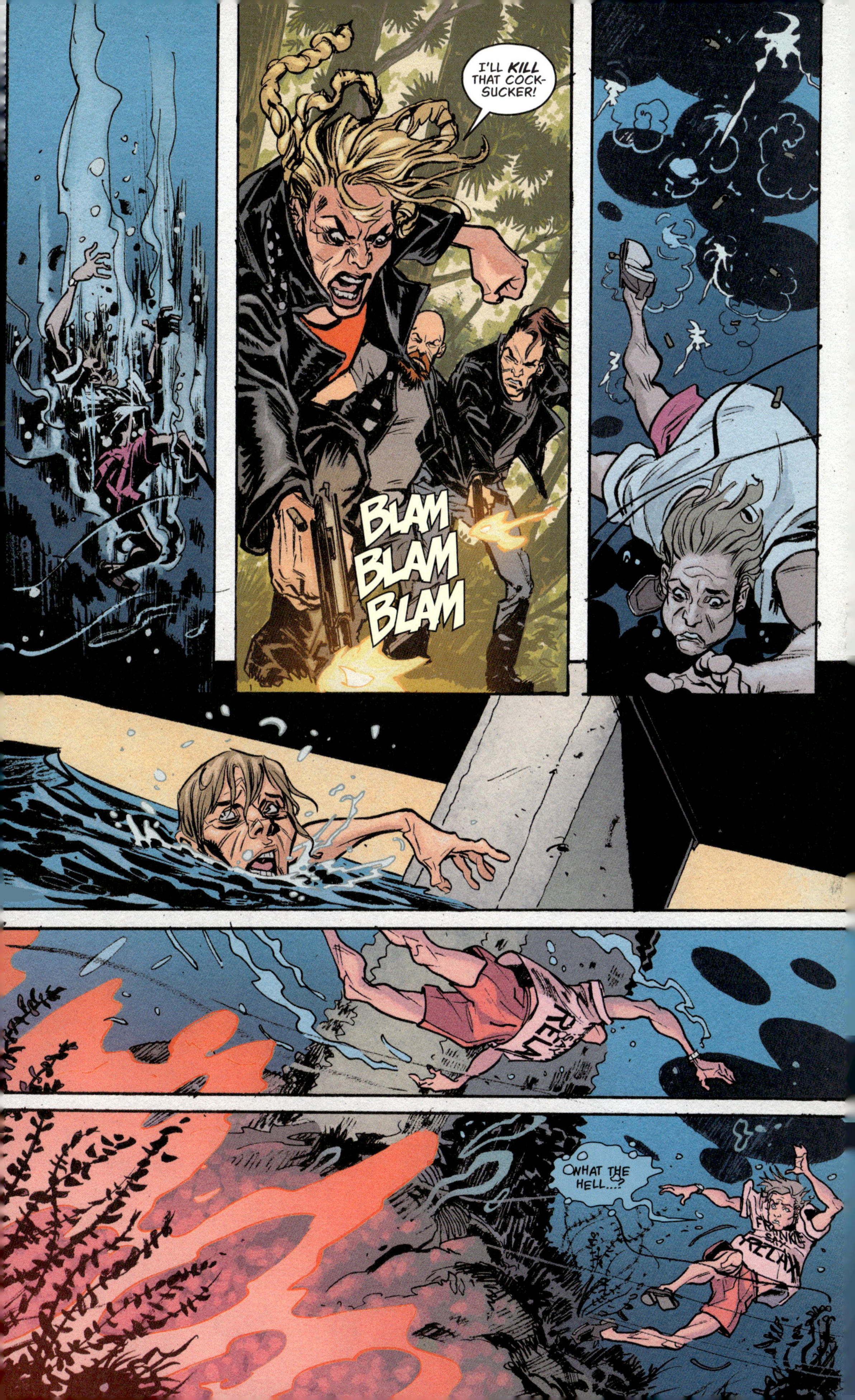
I'LL KILL THAT COCK-SUCKER!
BLAM BLAM BLAM
WHAT THE HELL...?

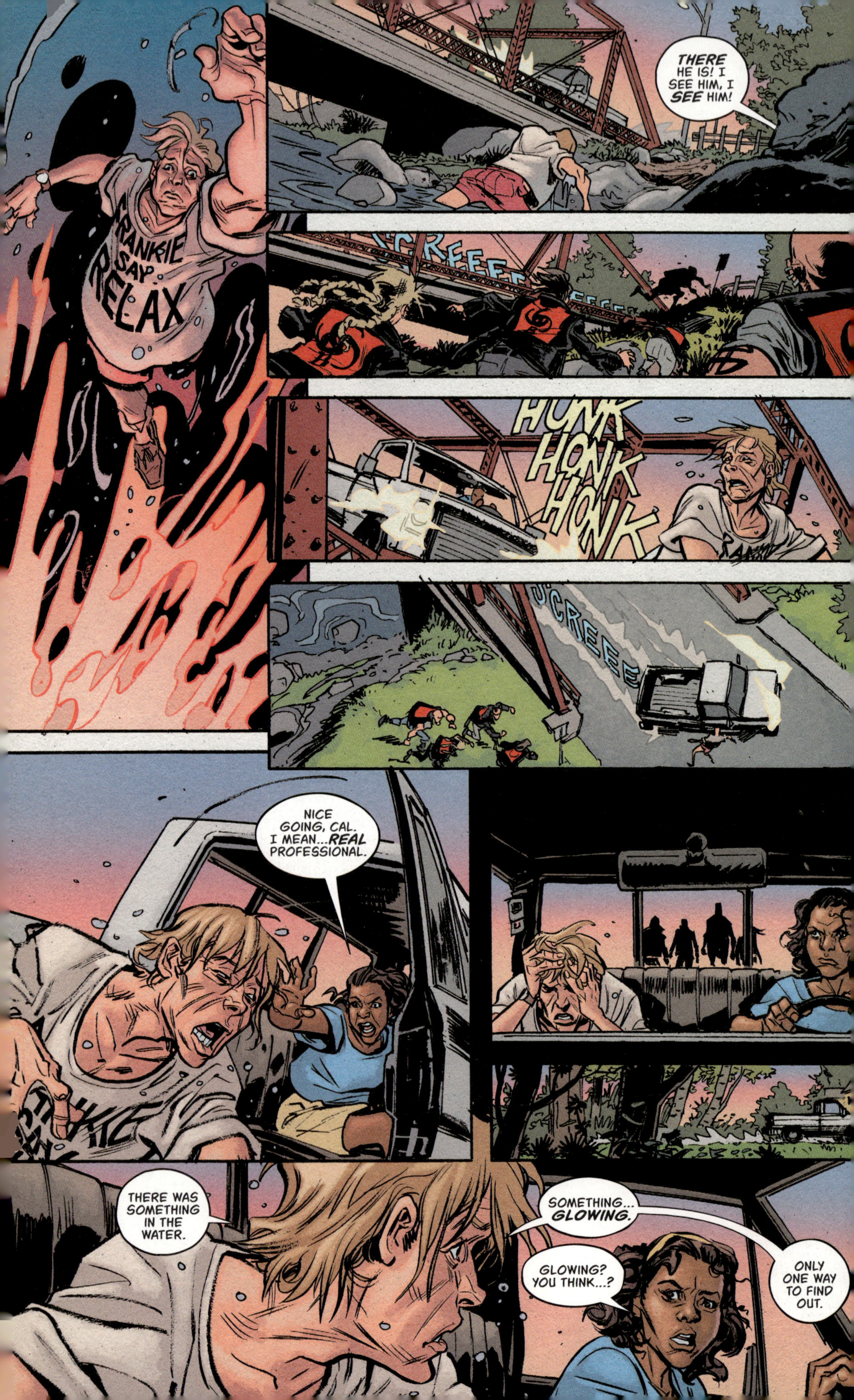
FRANKIE SAY RELAX
THERE HE IS! I SEE HIM, I SEE HIM!
SCREEE
HONK HONK HONK
SCREEE
NICE GOING, CAL. I MEAN...REAL PROFESSIONAL.
THERE WAS SOMETHING IN THE WATER.
SOMETHING... GLOWING.
GLOWING? YOU THINK...?
ONLY ONE WAY TO FIND OUT.

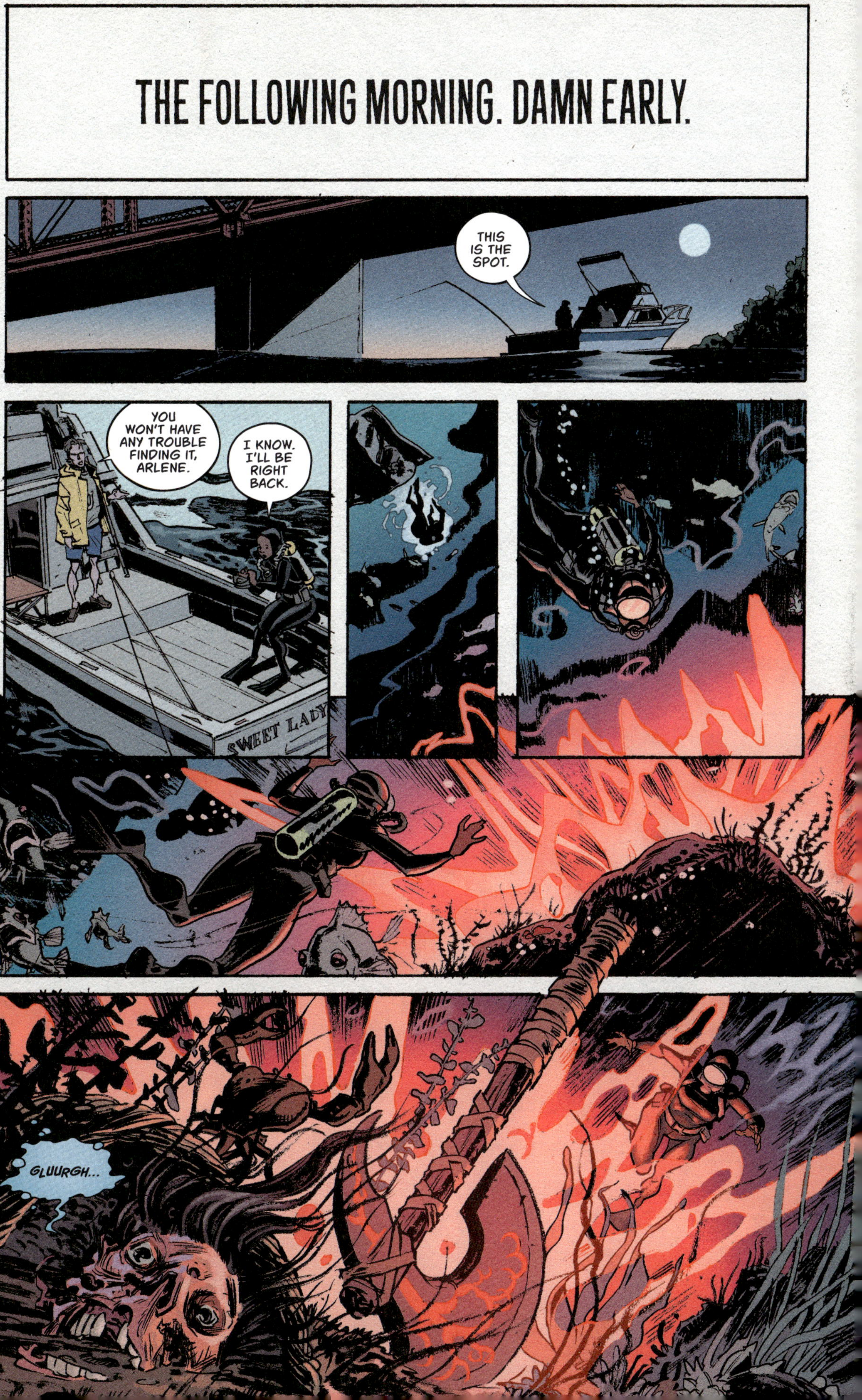
THE FOLLOWING MORNING. DAMN EARLY.
THIS IS THE SPOT.
YOU WON'T HAVE ANY TROUBLE FINDING IT, ARLENE.
I KNOW. I'LL BE RIGHT BACK.
SWEET LADY
GLUURGH...

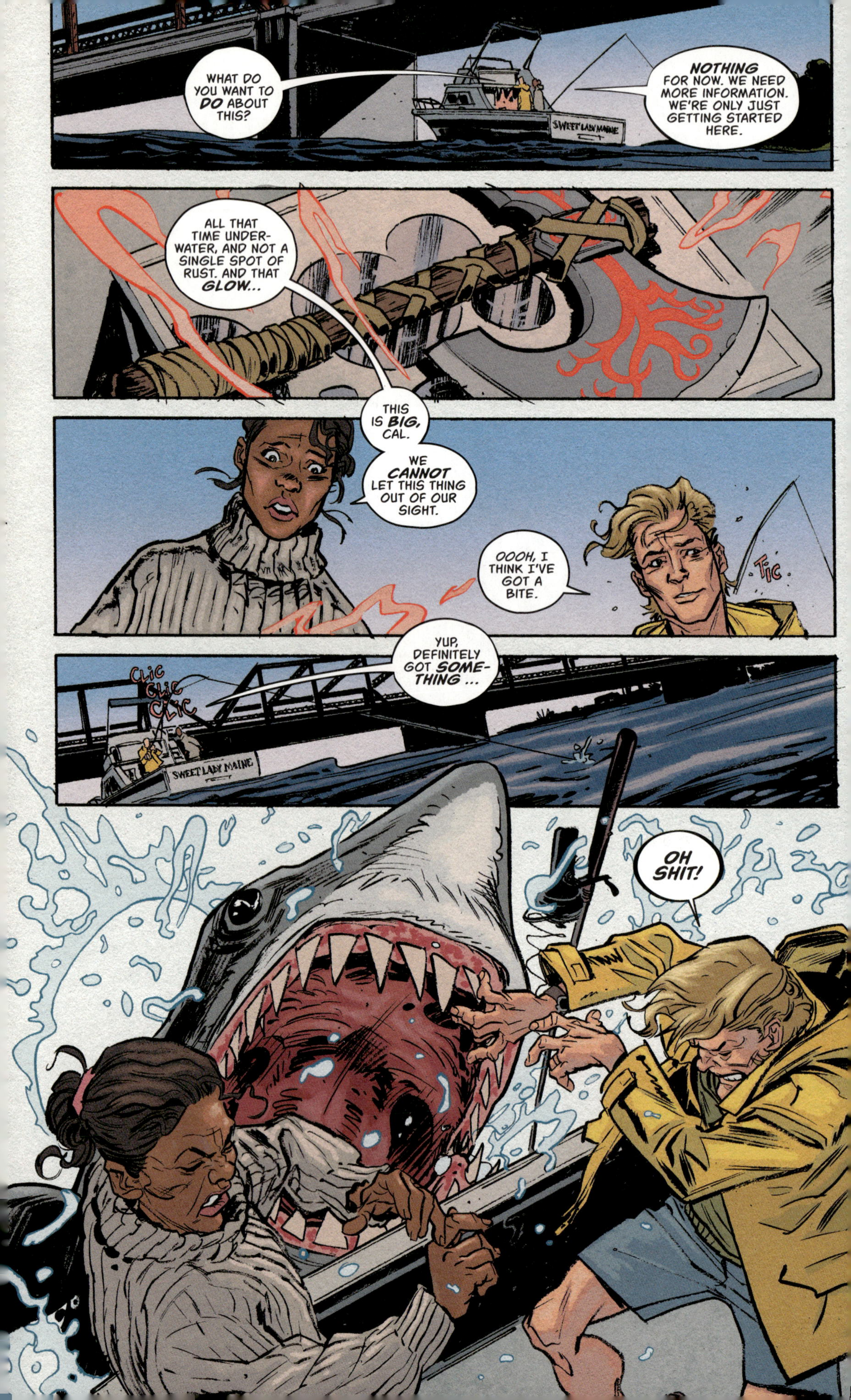
WHAT DO YOU WANT TO DO ABOUT THIS?
NOTHING FOR NOW. WE NEED MORE INFORMATION. WE'RE ONLY JUST GETTING STARTED HERE.
SWEET LADY MAINE
ALL THAT TIME UNDER-WATER, AND NOT A SINGLE SPOT OF RUST. AND THAT GLOW...
THIS IS BIG, CAL.
WE CANNOT LET THIS THING OUT OF OUR SIGHT.
OOOH, I THINK I'VE GOT A BITE.
TIC
YUP, DEFINITELY GOT SOME-THING ...
CLIC CLIC CLIC
SWEET LADY MAINE
OH SHIT!

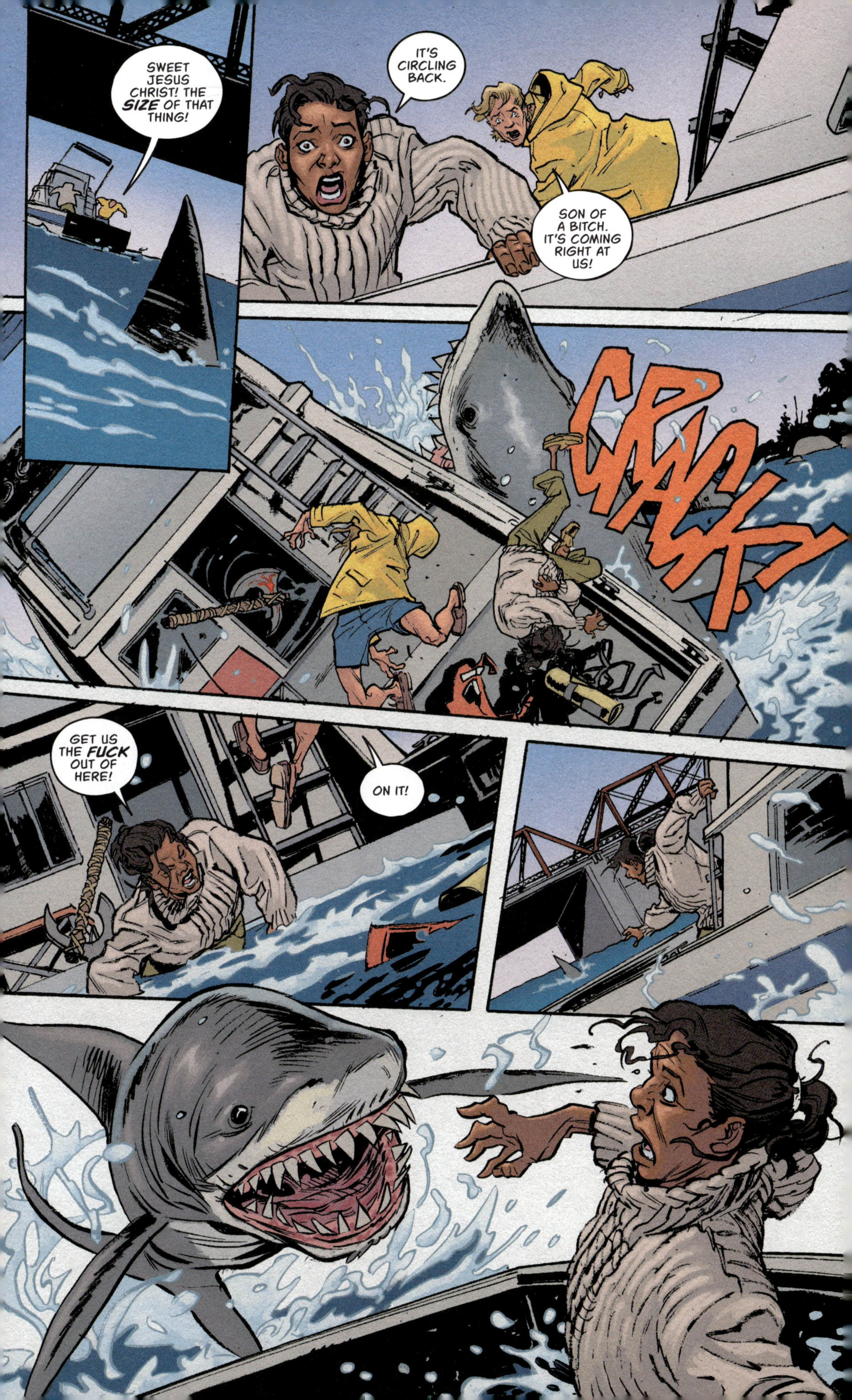
SWEET JESUS CHRIST! THE *SIZE* OF THAT THING!
IT'S CIRCLING BACK.
SON OF A BITCH. IT'S COMING RIGHT AT US!
CRACK!
GET US THE *FUCK* OUT OF HERE!
ON IT!

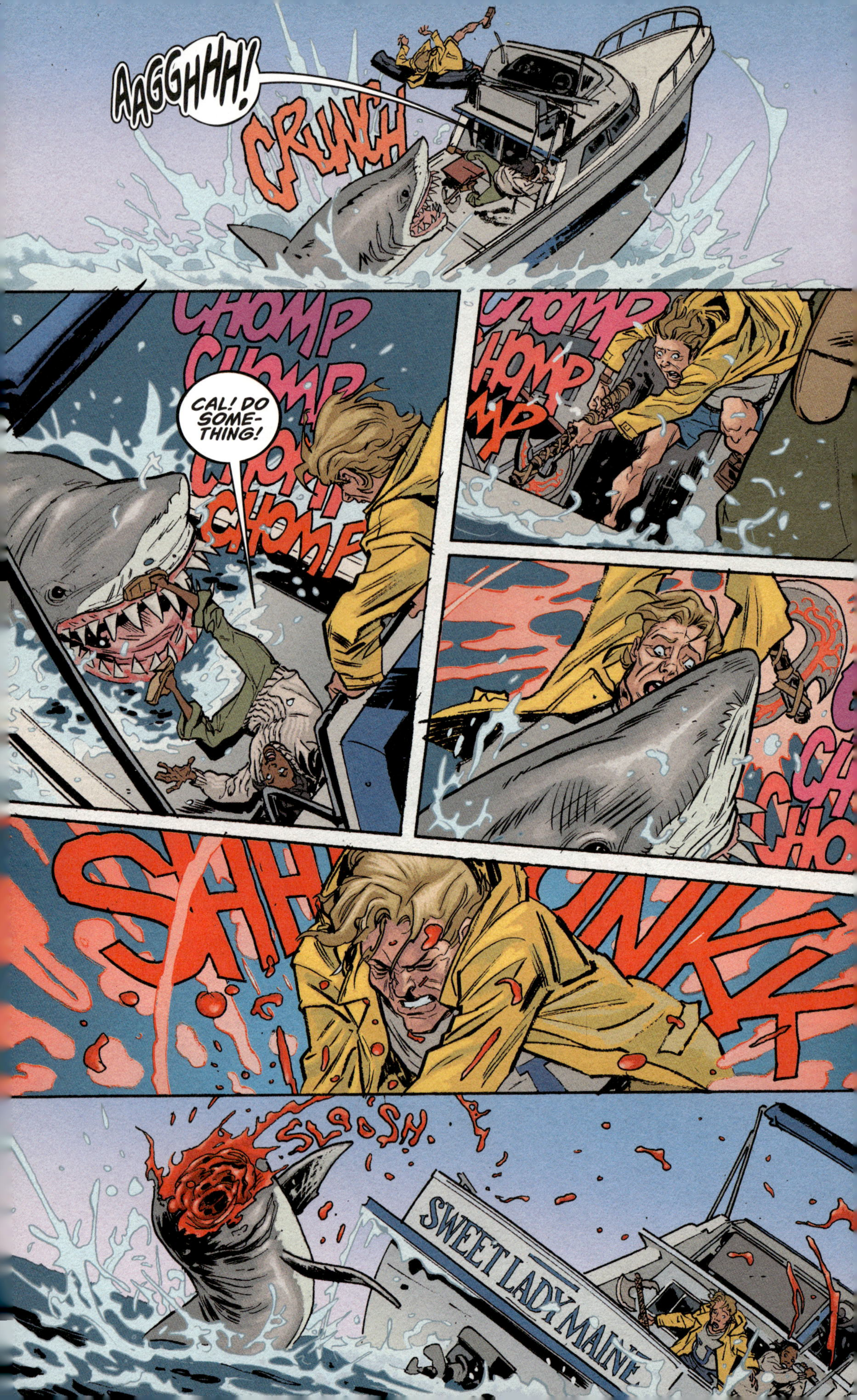
AAGGHHH!
CRUNCH
CHOMP
CHOMP
CHOMP
CHOMP
CAL! DO SOME-THING!
CHOMP
CHOMP
CHOMP
CH
CHO
SHHUNKK
SLOOSH
SWEET LADY MAINE

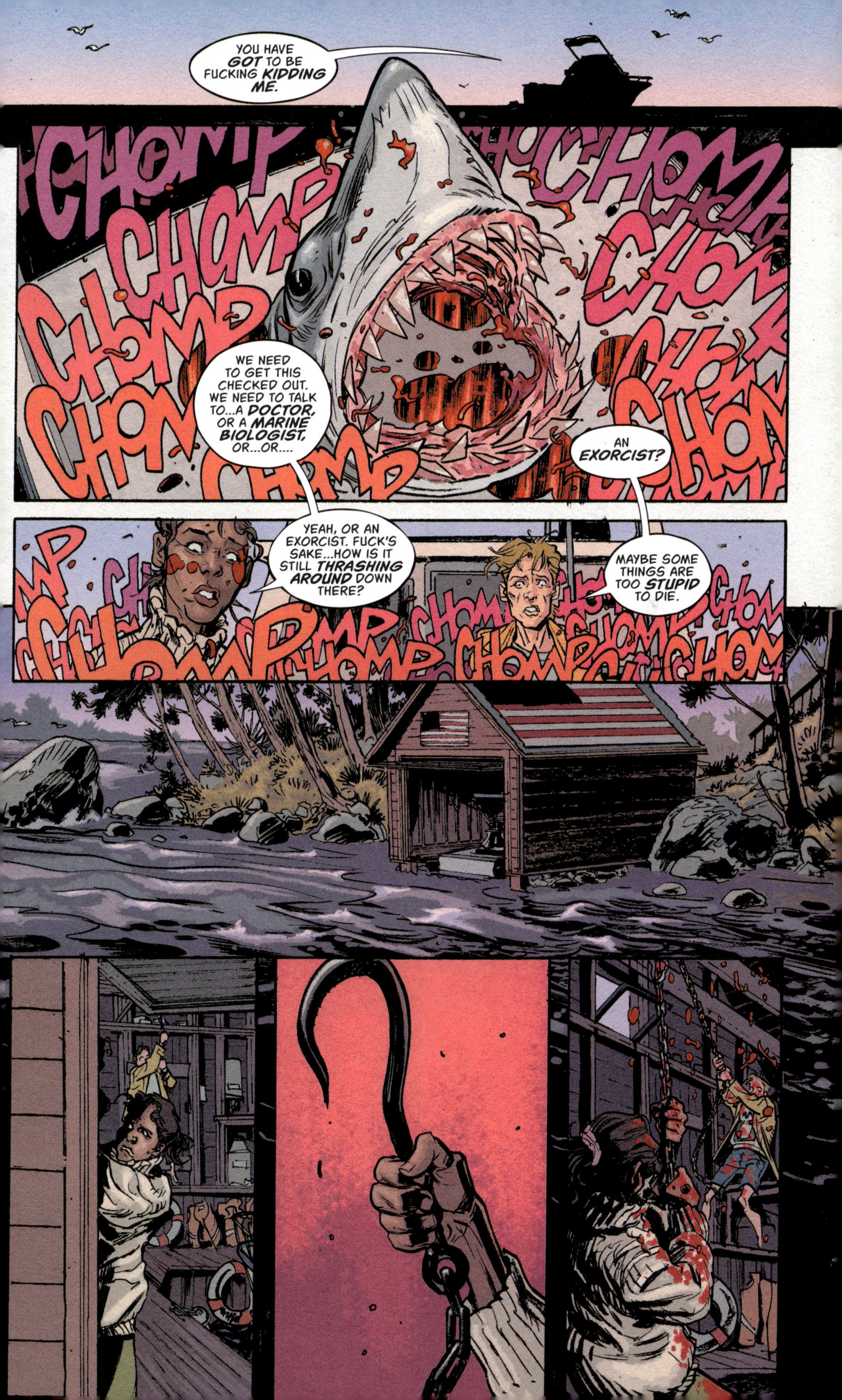
YOU HAVE GOT TO BE FUCKING KIDDING ME.
CHOMP CHOMP CHOMP CHOMP
WE NEED TO GET THIS CHECKED OUT. WE NEED TO TALK TO...A DOCTOR, OR A MARINE BIOLOGIST, OR...OR....
AN EXORCIST?
YEAH, OR AN EXORCIST. FUCK'S SAKE...HOW IS IT STILL THRASHING AROUND DOWN THERE?
MAYBE SOME THINGS ARE TOO STUPID TO DIE.
CHOMP CHOMP CHOMP

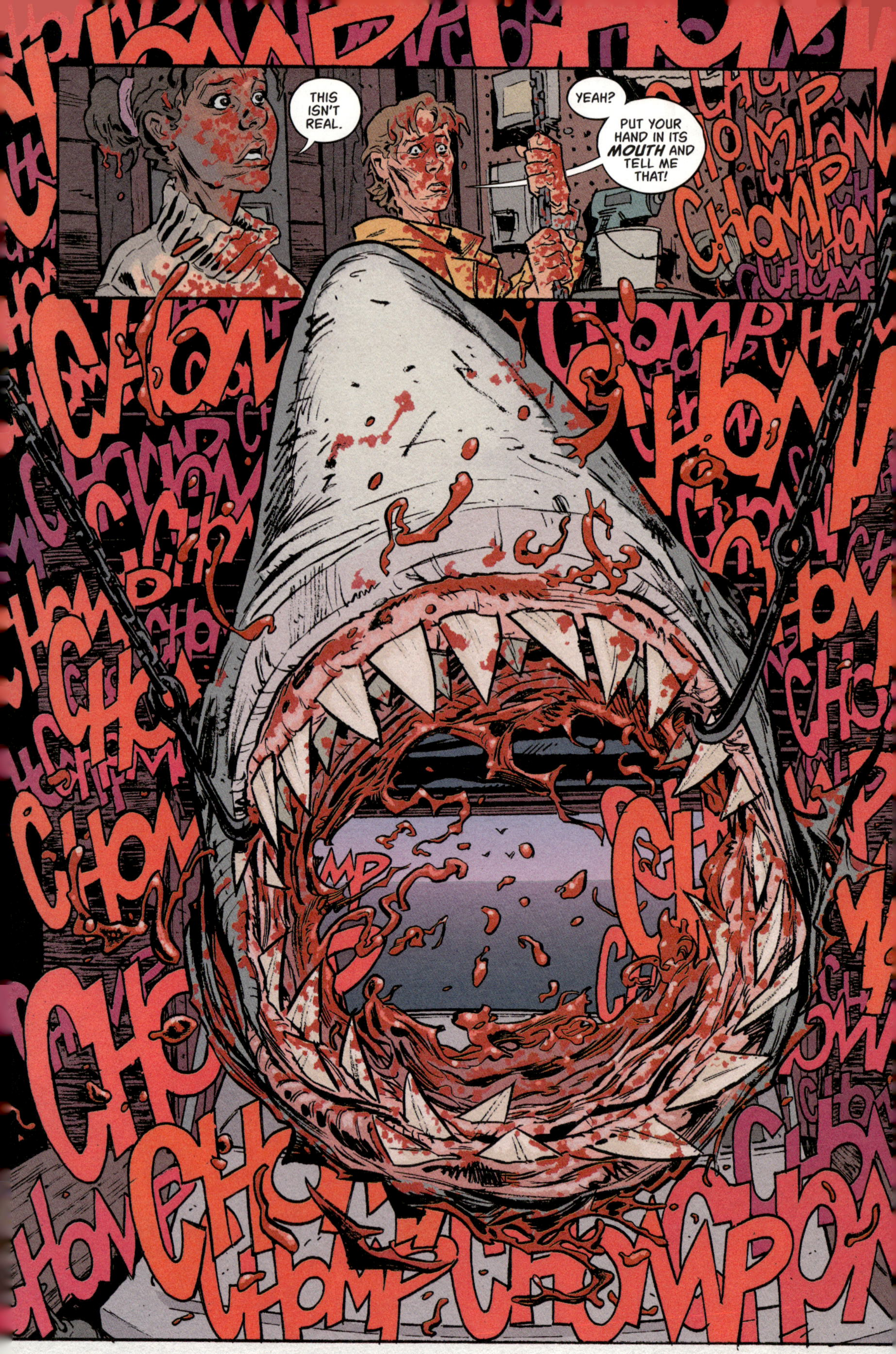
THIS ISN'T REAL.
YEAH?
PUT YOUR HAND IN ITS *MOUTH* AND TELL ME THAT!
CHOMP

IN THE NEXT ISSUE ...

HOW TO GET A HEAD ON BRODY ISLAND...

REFRIGERATOR FULL OF HEADS

Written by RIO YOUERS Drawn by TOM FOWLER
Colored by BILL CRABTREE Lettered by ANDWORLD DESIGN
Cover by SAM WOLFE CONNELLY Variant cover by LEOMACS

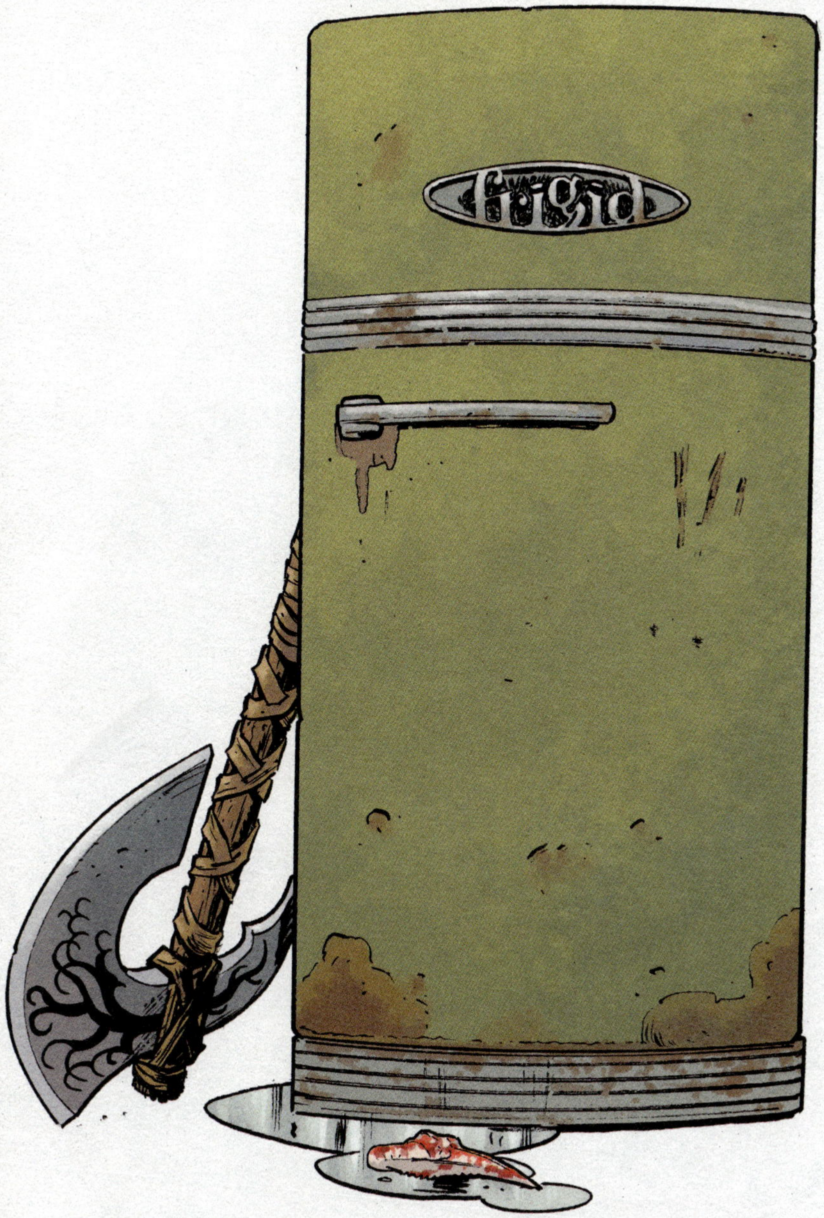
frigid

CHRIS CONROY Editor
MAGGIE HOWELL & ANDREA SHEA Associate Editors

BASKETFUL OF HEADS created by JOE HILL with art by LEOMACS
REFRIGERATOR FULL OF HEADS curated for HILL HOUSE COMICS by JOE HILL

"THERE WAS SOMETHING IN THE WATER. SOMETHING...GLOWING."

REFRIGERATOR FULL OF HEADS #2 COVER BY SAM WOLFE CONNELLY

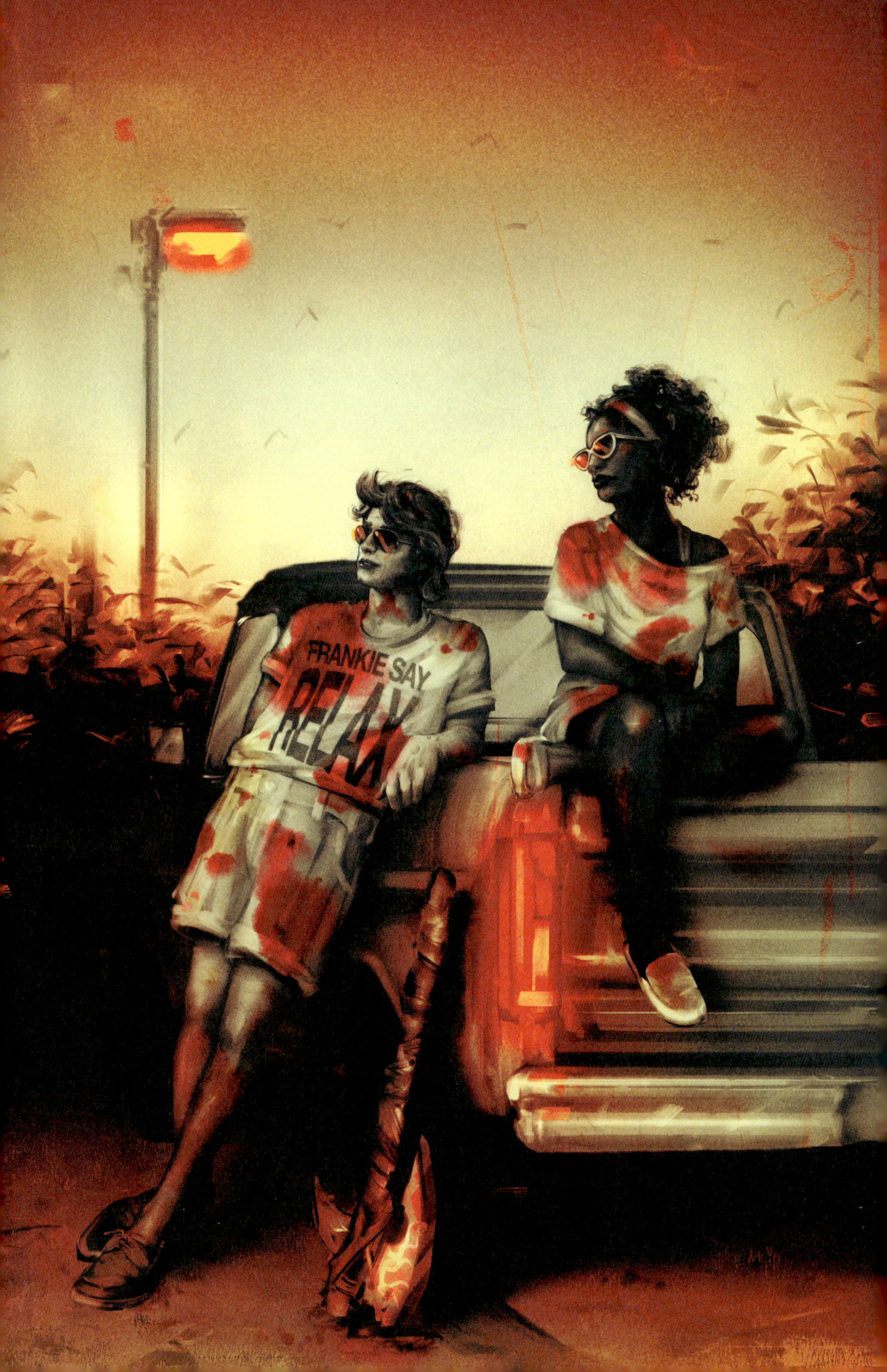
FRANKIE SAY
RELAX

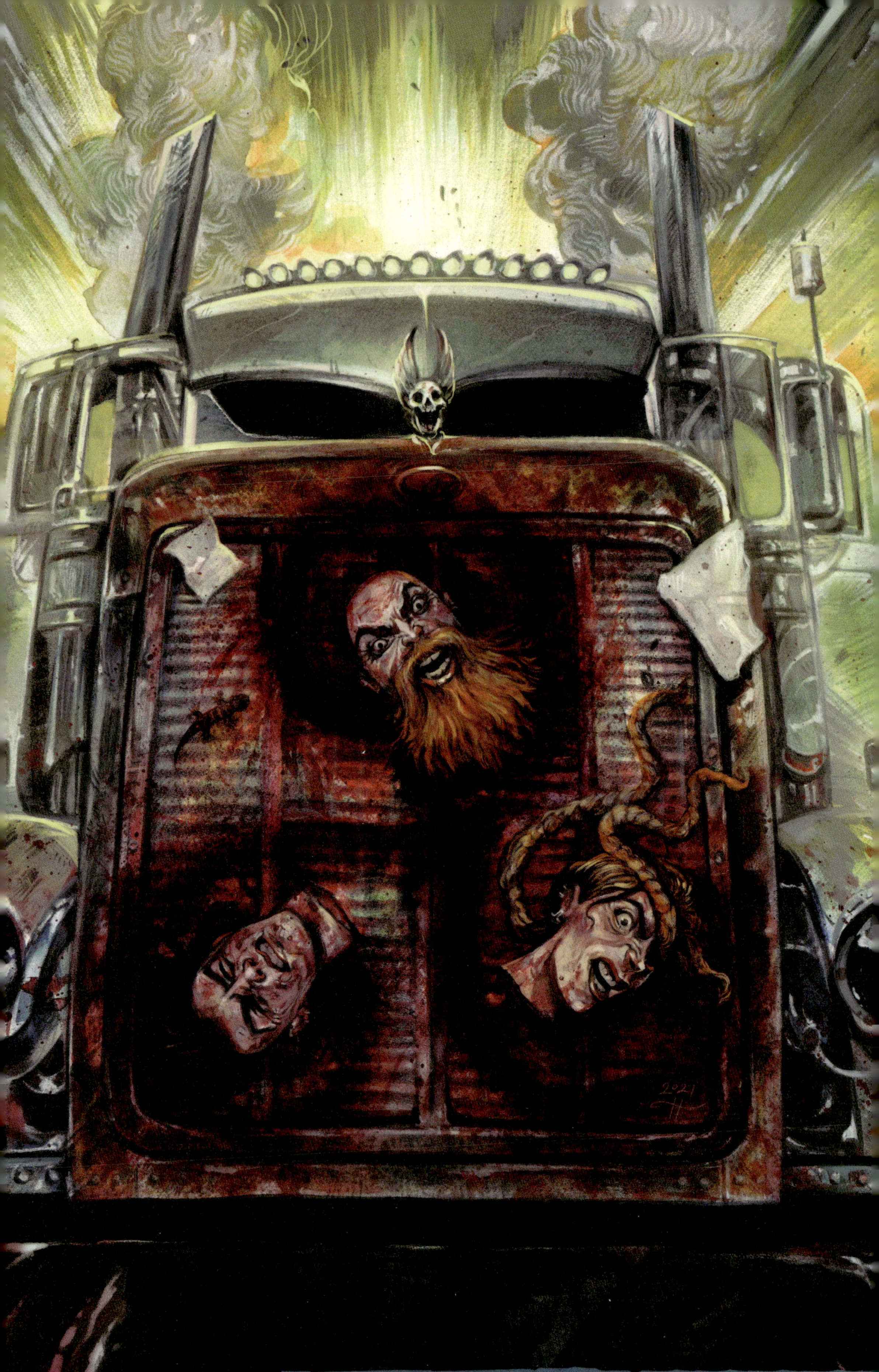

REFRIGERATOR FULL OF HEADS #2 VARIANT COVER BY TIFFANY TURRILL

MEANWHILE...

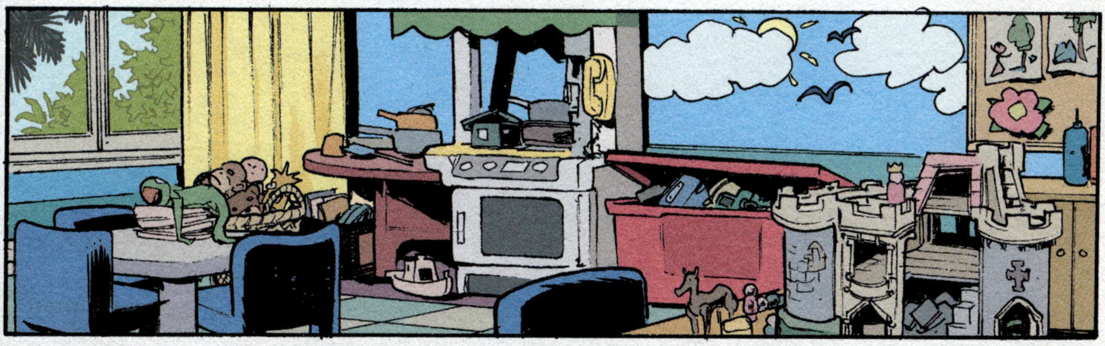

MOTHER DUCK'S DAYCARE.

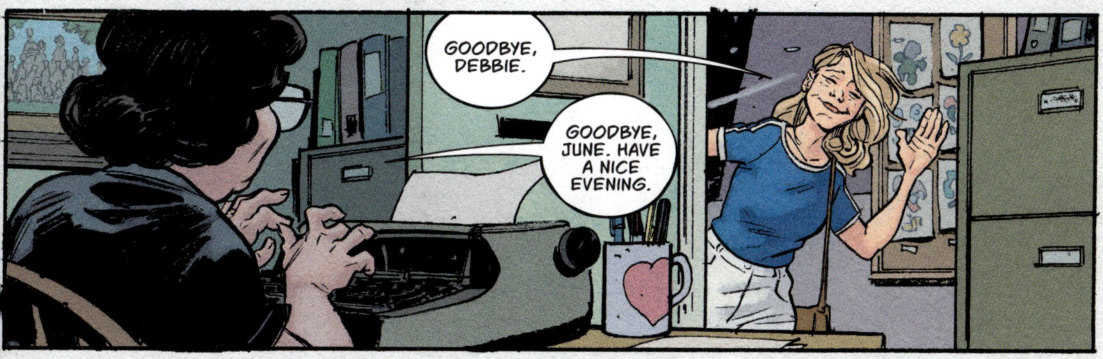
GOODBYE, DEBBIE.
GOODBYE, JUNE. HAVE A NICE EVENING.

GREEN RIDGE, NEW JERSEY.

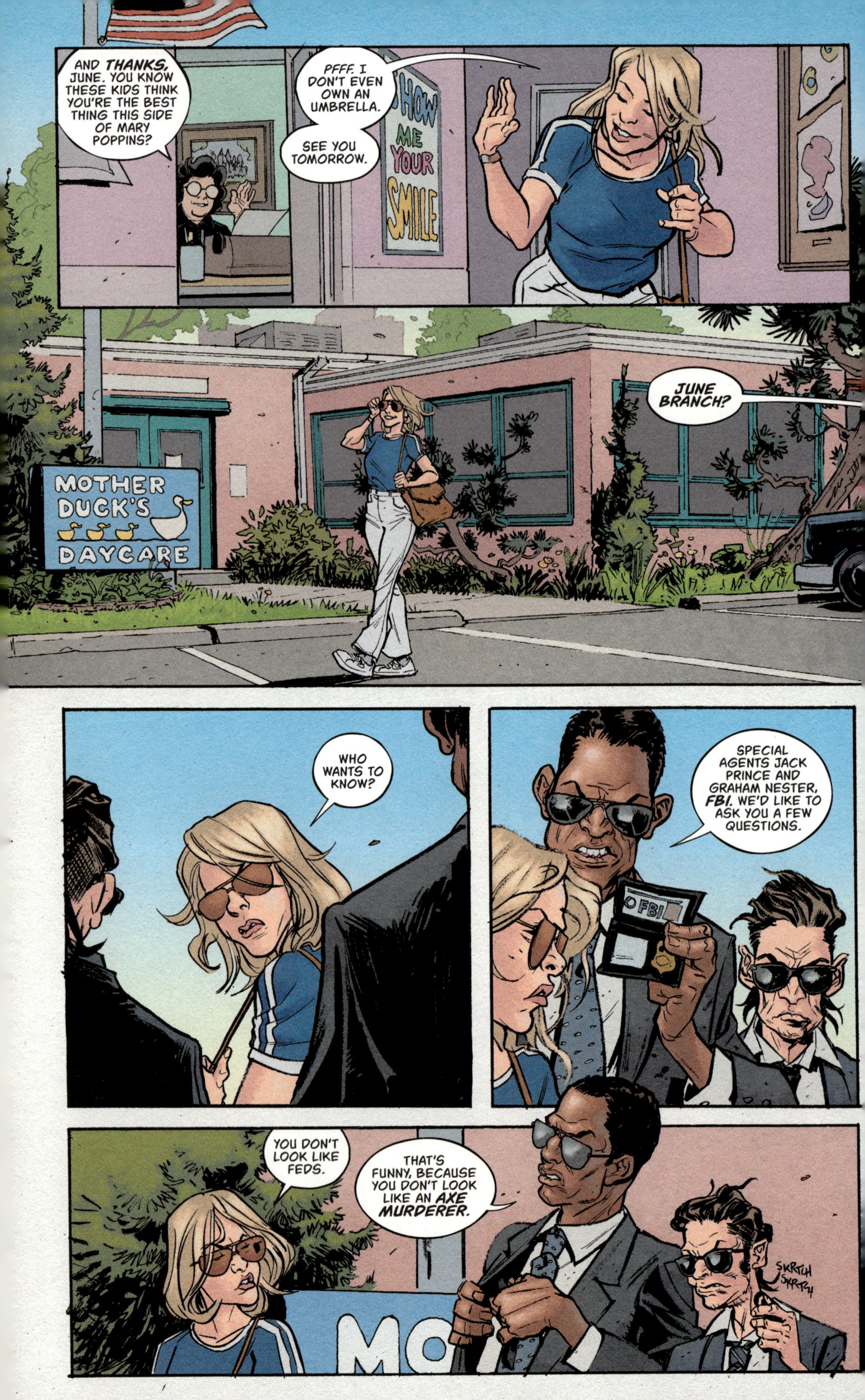
AND THANKS, JUNE. YOU KNOW THESE KIDS THINK YOU'RE THE BEST THING THIS SIDE OF MARY POPPINS?
PFFF. I DON'T EVEN OWN AN UMBRELLA.
SEE YOU TOMORROW.
SHOW ME YOUR SMILE
JUNE BRANCH?
MOTHER DUCK'S DAYCARE
WHO WANTS TO KNOW?
SPECIAL AGENTS JACK PRINCE AND GRAHAM NESTER, FBI. WE'D LIKE TO ASK YOU A FEW QUESTIONS.
FBI
YOU DON'T LOOK LIKE FEDS.
THAT'S FUNNY, BECAUSE YOU DON'T LOOK LIKE AN AXE MURDERER.
SKRTCH SKRTCH

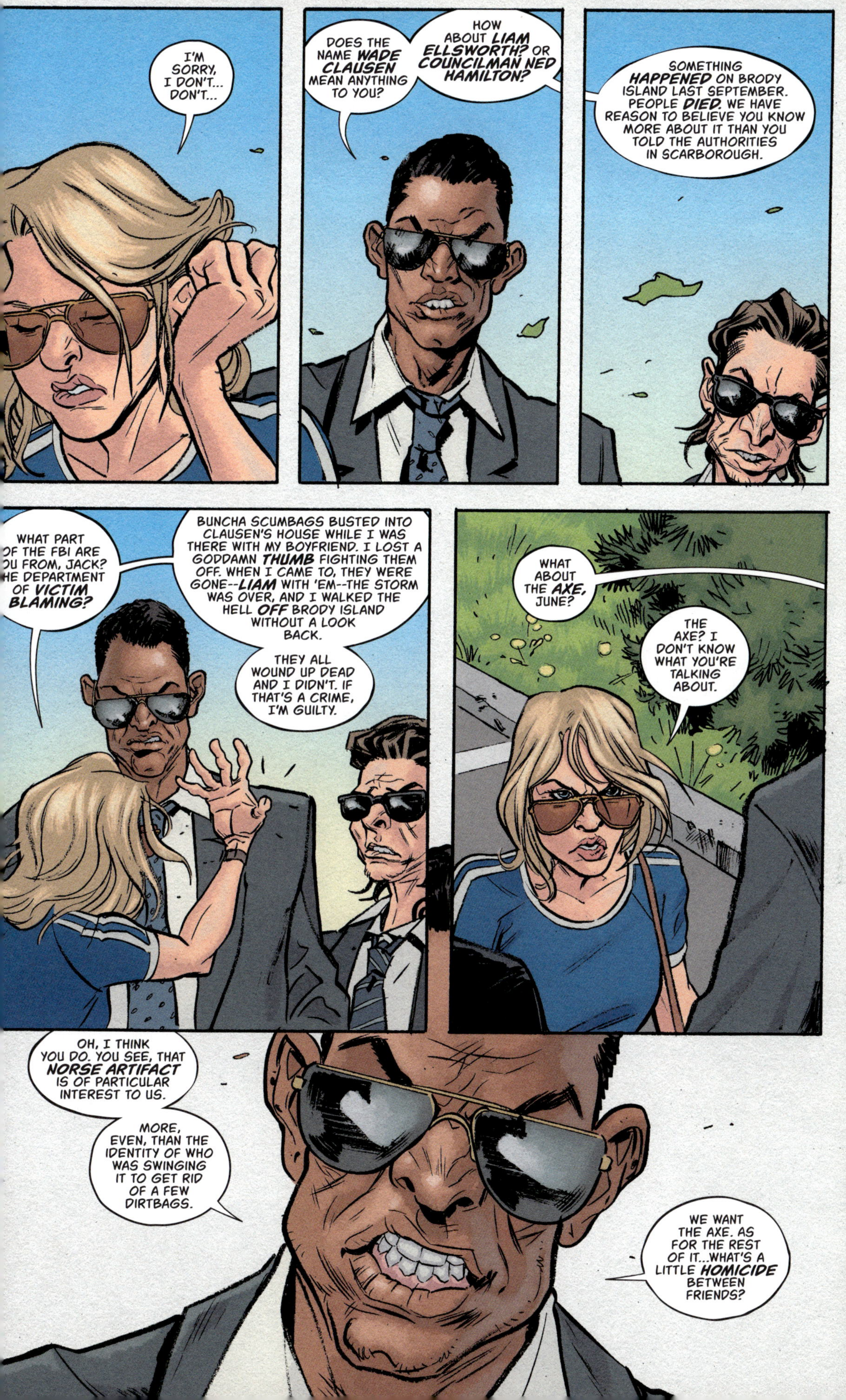
I'M SORRY, I DON'T... DON'T...
DOES THE NAME WADE CLAUSEN MEAN ANYTHING TO YOU?
HOW ABOUT LIAM ELLSWORTH? OR COUNCILMAN NED HAMILTON?
SOMETHING HAPPENED ON BRODY ISLAND LAST SEPTEMBER. PEOPLE DIED. WE HAVE REASON TO BELIEVE YOU KNOW MORE ABOUT IT THAN YOU TOLD THE AUTHORITIES IN SCARBOROUGH.
WHAT PART OF THE FBI ARE YOU FROM, JACK? THE DEPARTMENT OF VICTIM BLAMING?
BUNCHA SCUMBAGS BUSTED INTO CLAUSEN'S HOUSE WHILE I WAS THERE WITH MY BOYFRIEND. I LOST A GODDAMN THUMB FIGHTING THEM OFF. WHEN I CAME TO, THEY WERE GONE--LIAM WITH 'EM--THE STORM WAS OVER, AND I WALKED THE HELL OFF BRODY ISLAND WITHOUT A LOOK BACK.
THEY ALL WOUND UP DEAD AND I DIDN'T. IF THAT'S A CRIME, I'M GUILTY.
WHAT ABOUT THE AXE, JUNE?
THE AXE? I DON'T KNOW WHAT YOU'RE TALKING ABOUT.
OH, I THINK YOU DO. YOU SEE, THAT NORSE ARTIFACT IS OF PARTICULAR INTEREST TO US.
MORE, EVEN, THAN THE IDENTITY OF WHO WAS SWINGING IT TO GET RID OF A FEW DIRTBAGS.
WE WANT THE AXE. AS FOR THE REST OF IT...WHAT'S A LITTLE HOMICIDE BETWEEN FRIENDS?

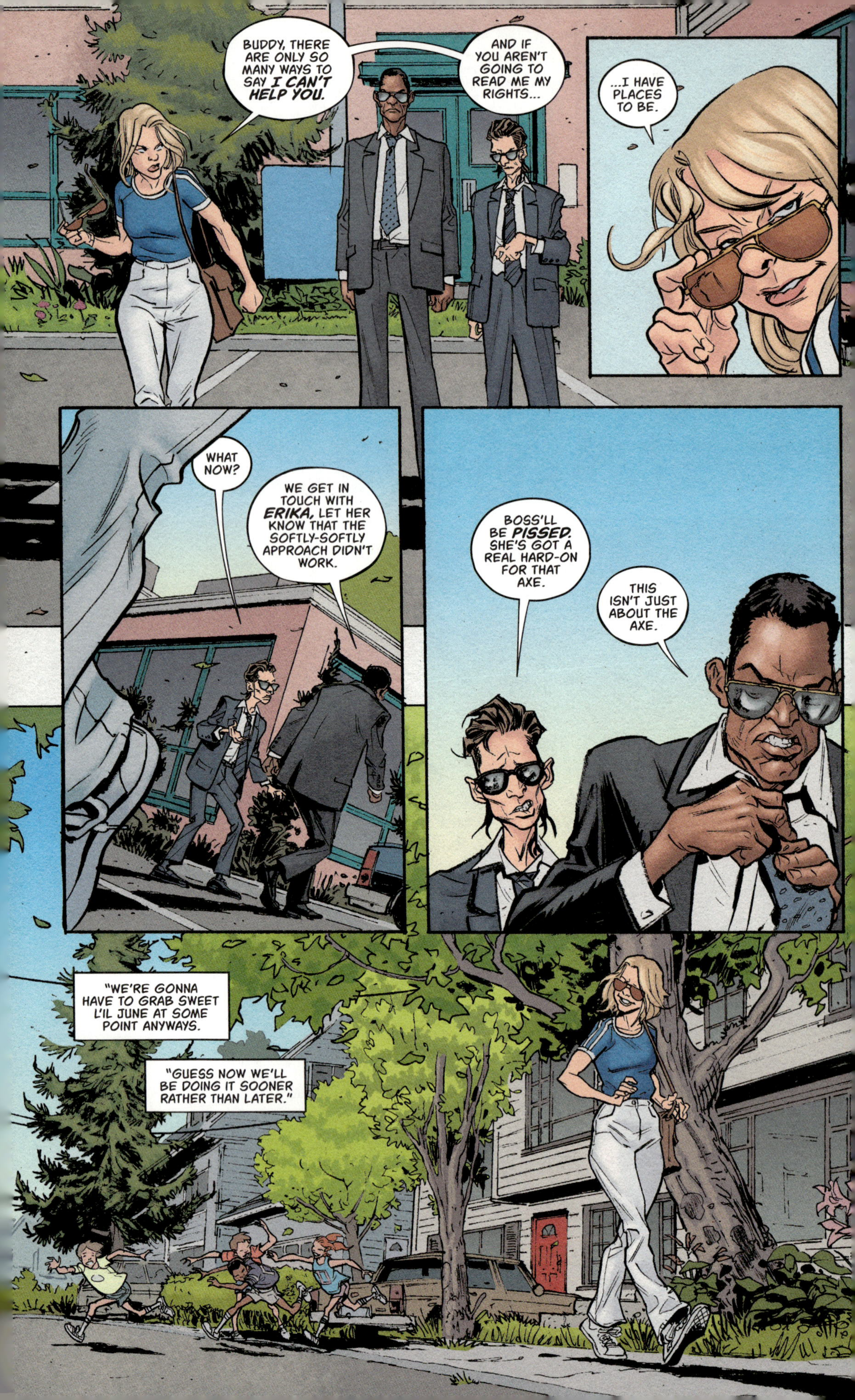

BUDDY, THERE ARE ONLY SO MANY WAYS TO SAY *I CAN'T HELP YOU.*
AND IF YOU AREN'T GOING TO READ ME MY RIGHTS...
...I HAVE PLACES TO BE.
WHAT NOW?
WE GET IN TOUCH WITH *ERIKA,* LET HER KNOW THAT THE SOFTLY-SOFTLY APPROACH DIDN'T WORK.
BOSS'LL BE *PISSED.* SHE'S GOT A REAL HARD-ON FOR THAT AXE.
THIS ISN'T JUST ABOUT THE AXE.
"WE'RE GONNA HAVE TO GRAB SWEET L'IL JUNE AT SOME POINT ANYWAYS.
"GUESS NOW WE'LL BE DOING IT SOONER RATHER THAN LATER."

BRODY ISLAND, ONE DAY LATER.

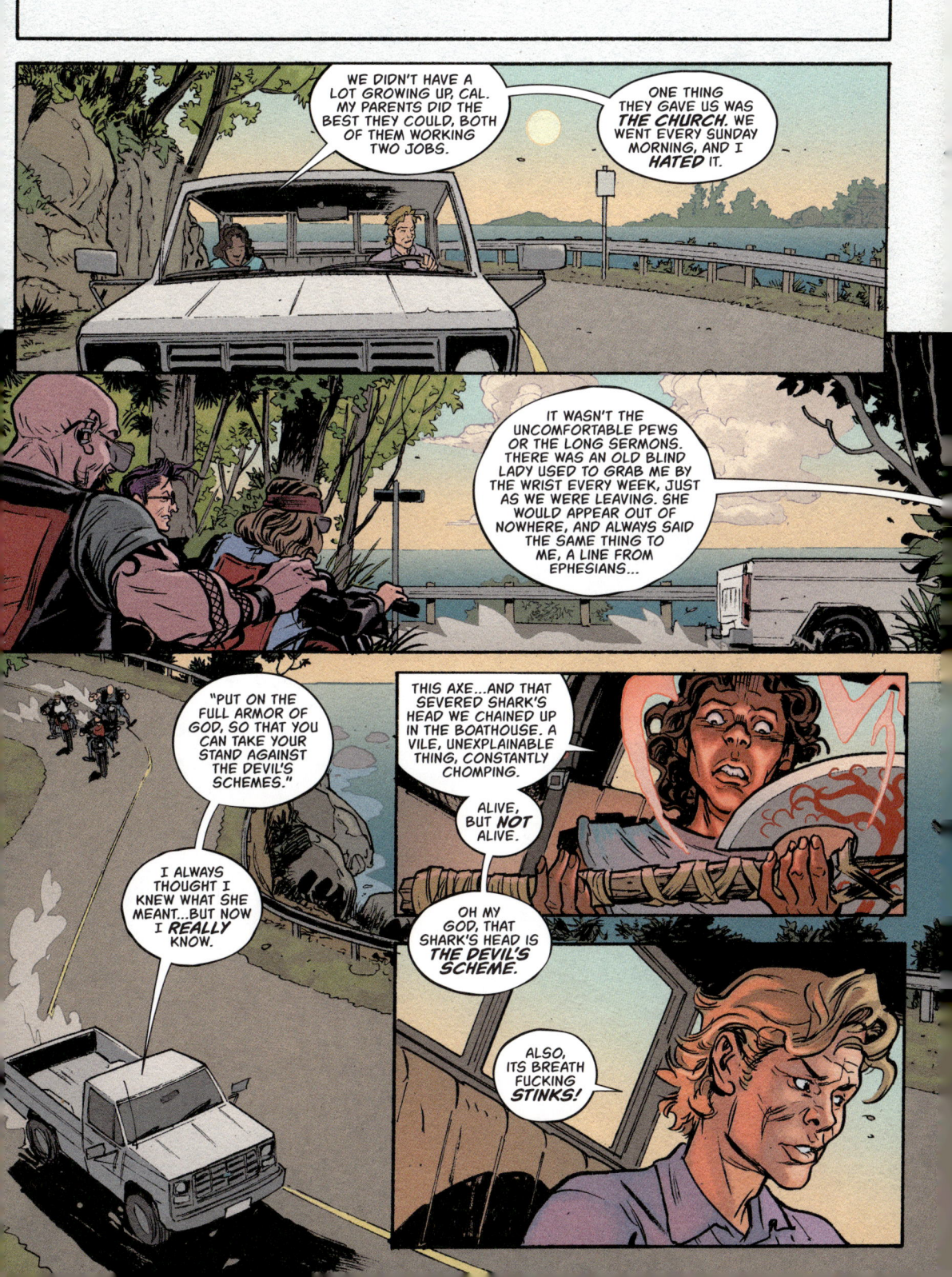

WE DIDN'T HAVE A LOT GROWING UP, CAL. MY PARENTS DID THE BEST THEY COULD, BOTH OF THEM WORKING TWO JOBS.

ONE THING THEY GAVE US WAS *THE CHURCH*. WE WENT EVERY SUNDAY MORNING, AND I *HATED* IT.

IT WASN'T THE UNCOMFORTABLE PEWS OR THE LONG SERMONS. THERE WAS AN OLD BLIND LADY USED TO GRAB ME BY THE WRIST EVERY WEEK, JUST AS WE WERE LEAVING. SHE WOULD APPEAR OUT OF NOWHERE, AND ALWAYS SAID THE SAME THING TO ME, A LINE FROM EPHESIANS...

"PUT ON THE FULL ARMOR OF GOD, SO THAT YOU CAN TAKE YOUR STAND AGAINST THE DEVIL'S SCHEMES."

I ALWAYS THOUGHT I KNEW WHAT SHE MEANT...BUT NOW I *REALLY* KNOW.

THIS AXE...AND THAT SEVERED SHARK'S HEAD WE CHAINED UP IN THE BOATHOUSE. A VILE, UNEXPLAINABLE THING, CONSTANTLY CHOMPING.

ALIVE, BUT *NOT* ALIVE.

OH MY GOD, THAT SHARK'S HEAD IS *THE DEVIL'S SCHEME.*

ALSO, ITS BREATH FUCKING *STINKS!*

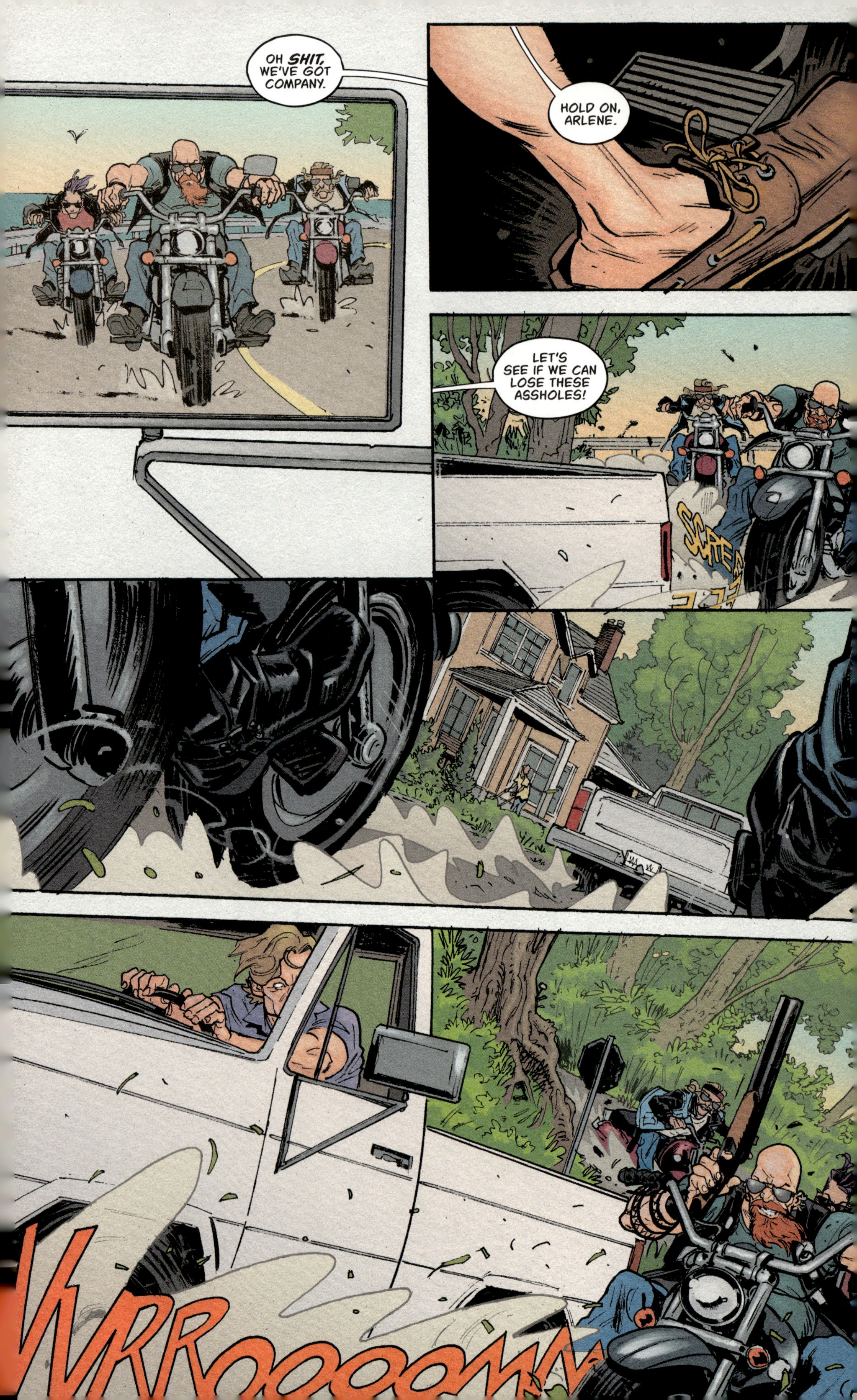
OH SHIT, WE'VE GOT COMPANY.
HOLD ON, ARLENE.
LET'S SEE IF WE CAN LOSE THESE ASSHOLES!
VRRROOOOM

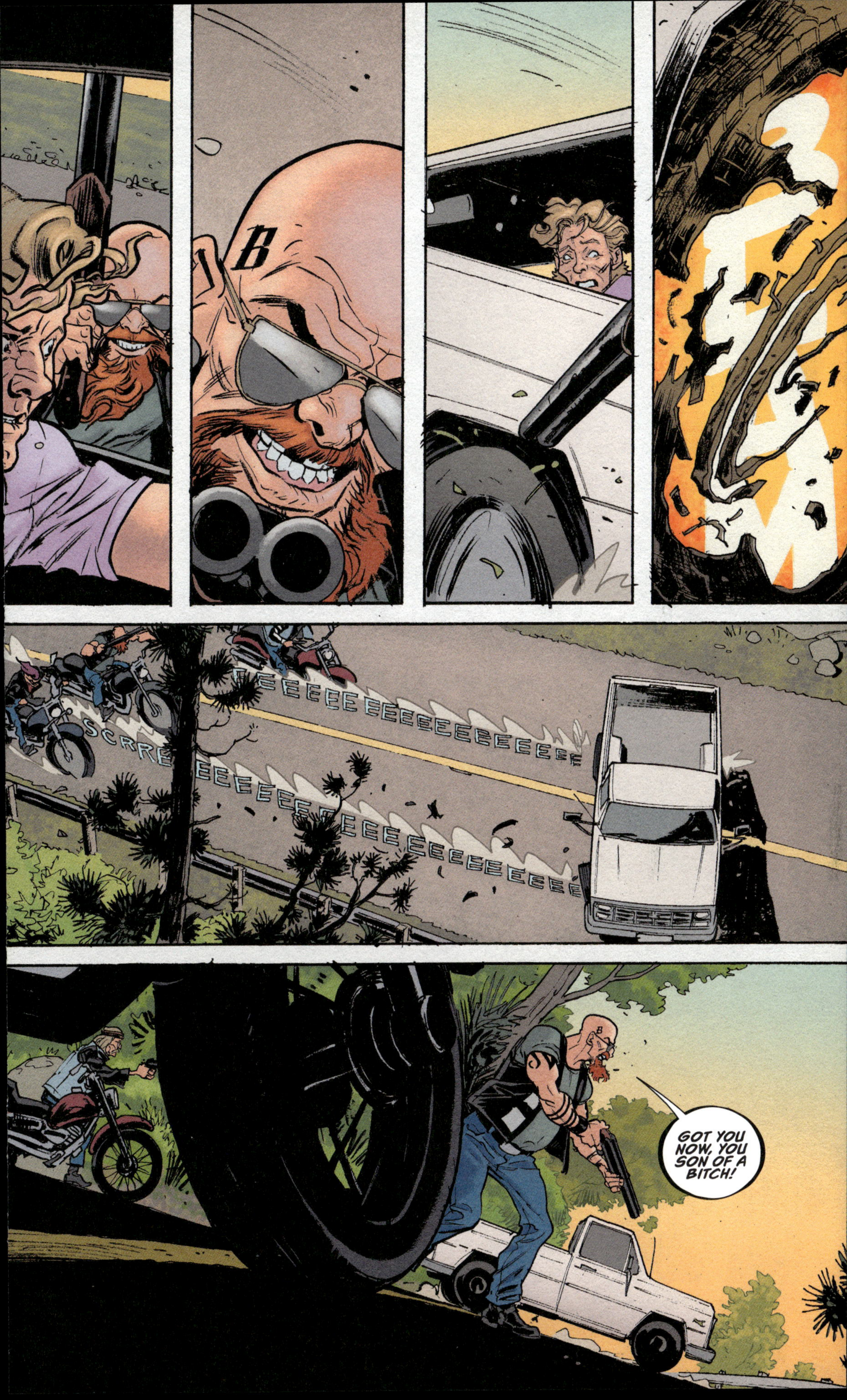

SCRREEEEEEEEEEEEEEEEEEEEEEEEEEEEEEEEEEEEEEEE
GOT YOU NOW, YOU SON OF A BITCH!

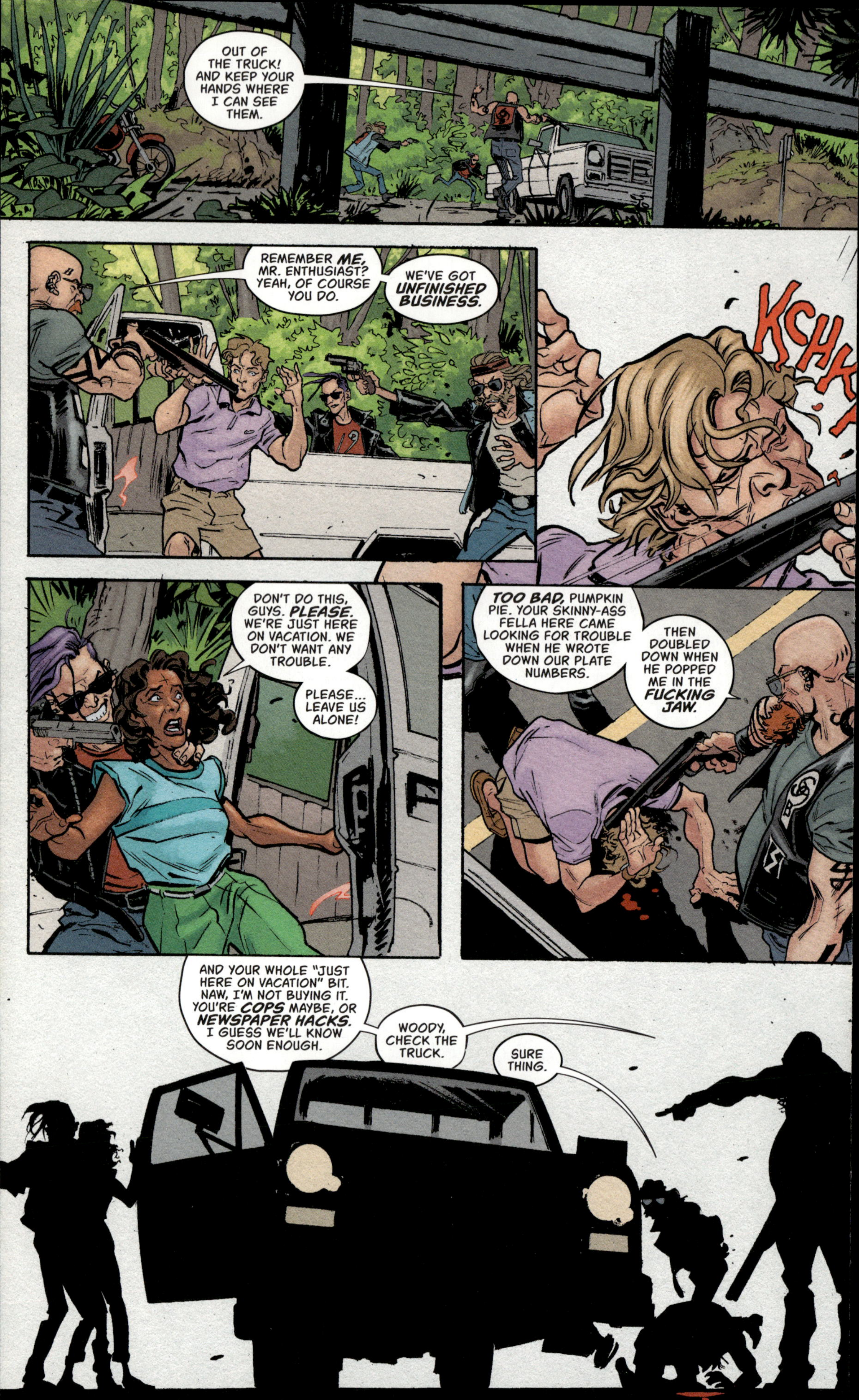
OUT OF THE TRUCK! AND KEEP YOUR HANDS WHERE I CAN SEE THEM.
REMEMBER *ME*, MR. ENTHUSIAST? YEAH, OF COURSE YOU DO.
WE'VE GOT *UNFINISHED BUSINESS.*
KCHK
DON'T DO THIS, GUYS. *PLEASE.* WE'RE JUST HERE ON VACATION. WE DON'T WANT ANY TROUBLE.
PLEASE... LEAVE US ALONE!
TOO BAD, PUMPKIN PIE. YOUR SKINNY-ASS FELLA HERE CAME LOOKING FOR TROUBLE WHEN HE WROTE DOWN OUR PLATE NUMBERS.
THEN DOUBLED DOWN WHEN HE POPPED ME IN THE *FUCKING JAW.*
AND YOUR WHOLE "JUST HERE ON VACATION" BIT. NAW, I'M NOT BUYING IT. YOU'RE *COPS* MAYBE, OR *NEWSPAPER HACKS.* I GUESS WE'LL KNOW SOON ENOUGH.
WOODY, CHECK THE TRUCK.
SURE THING.

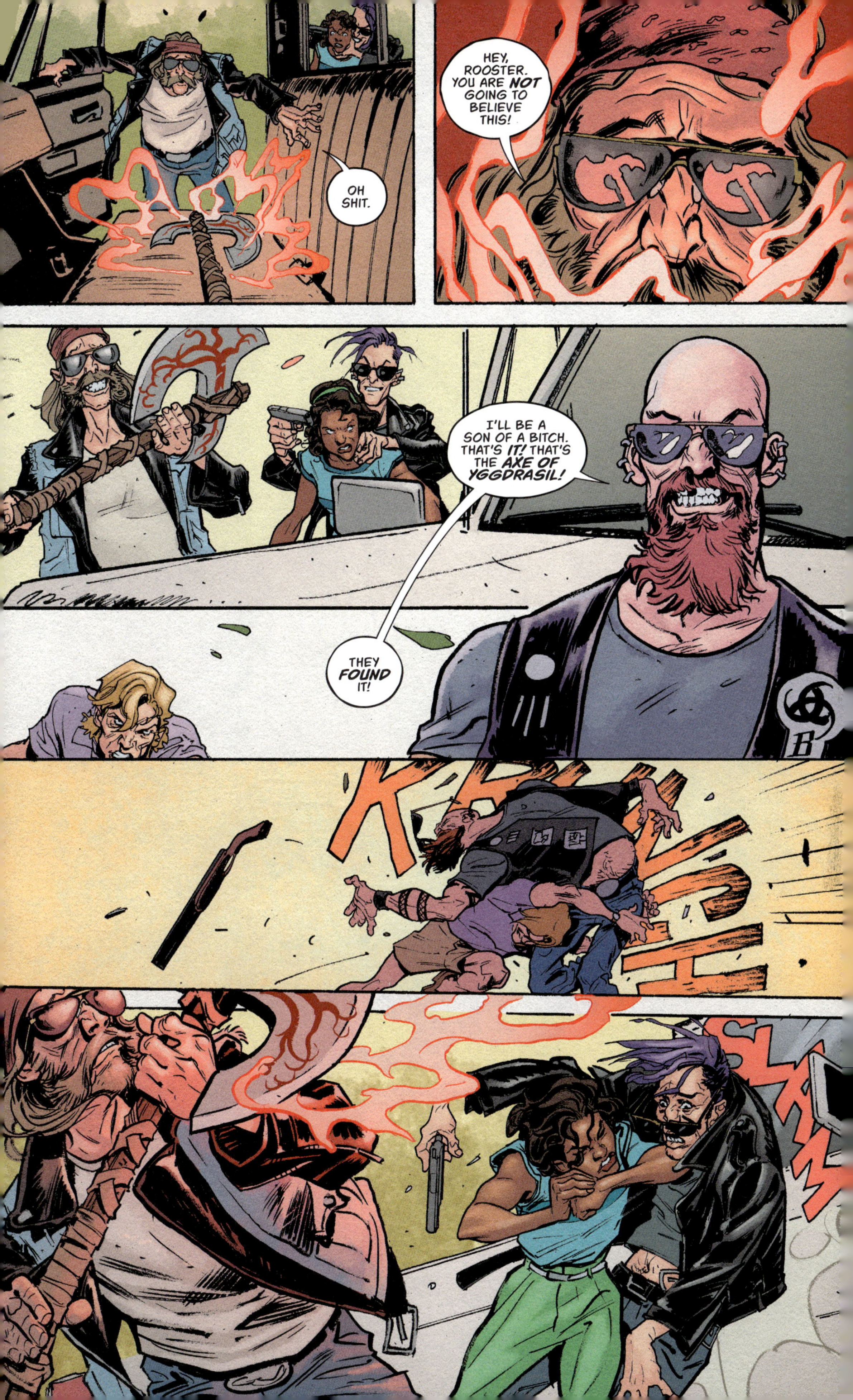
OH SHIT.
HEY, ROOSTER. YOU ARE NOT GOING TO BELIEVE THIS!
I'LL BE A SON OF A BITCH. THAT'S IT! THAT'S THE AXE OF YGGDRASIL!
THEY FOUND IT!

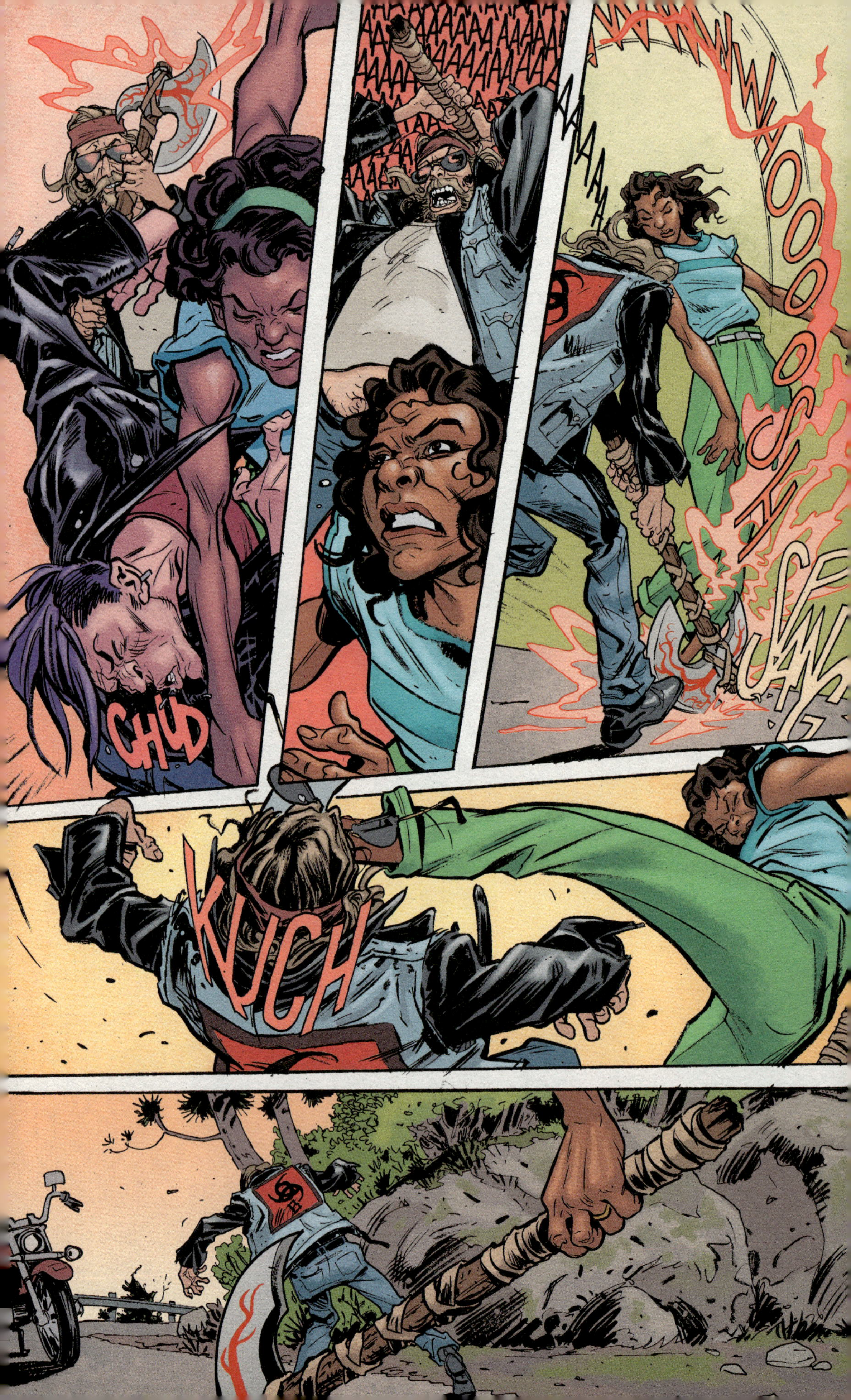
CHUD
AAAAAAAAAAAAAAAAAAAAAAAAAA
WWWWHOOOOOSH
CHANG
KUCH

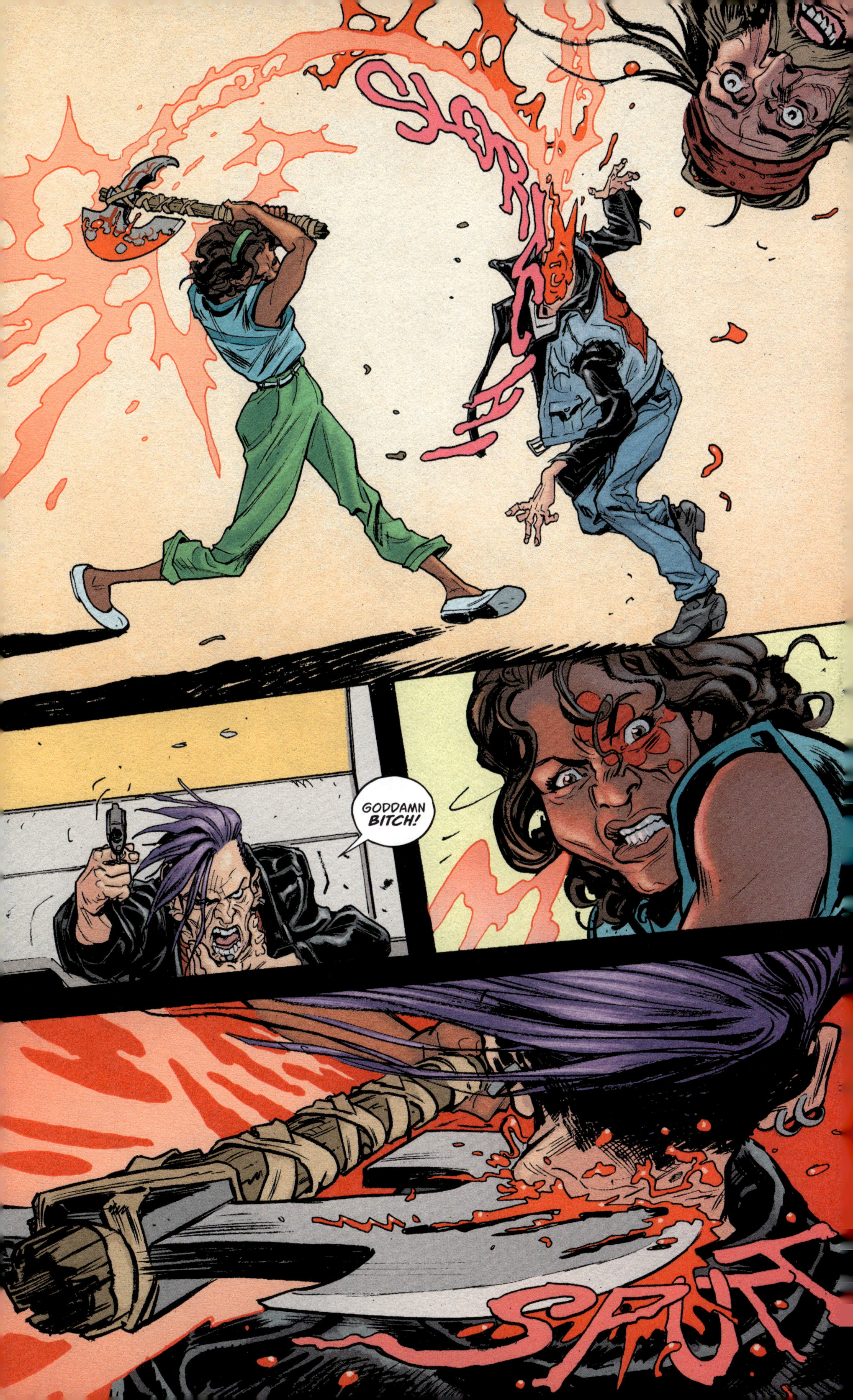
SPLORTCH
GODDAMN BITCH!
SPLUT

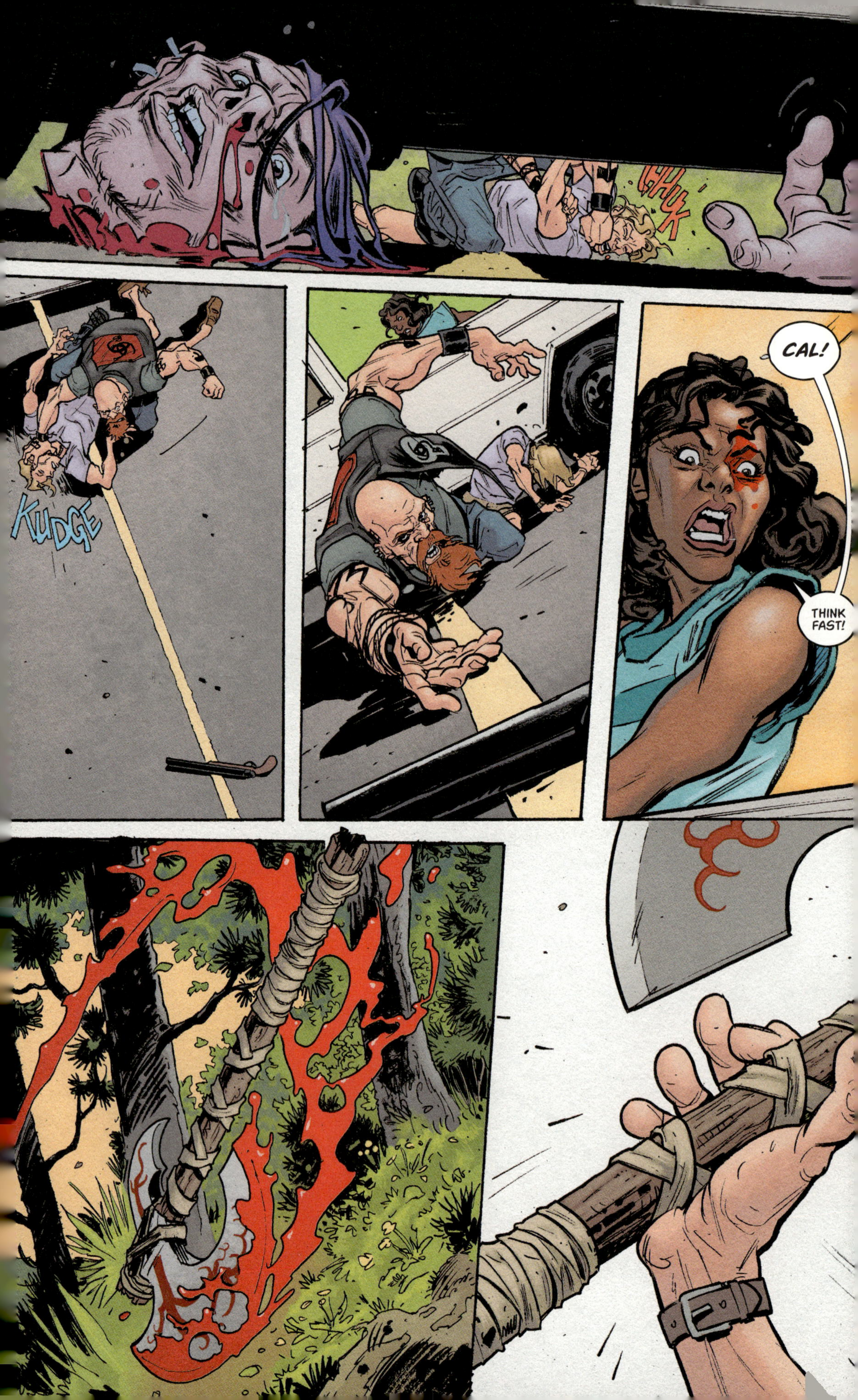

CHUK
KUDGE
CAL!
THINK FAST!

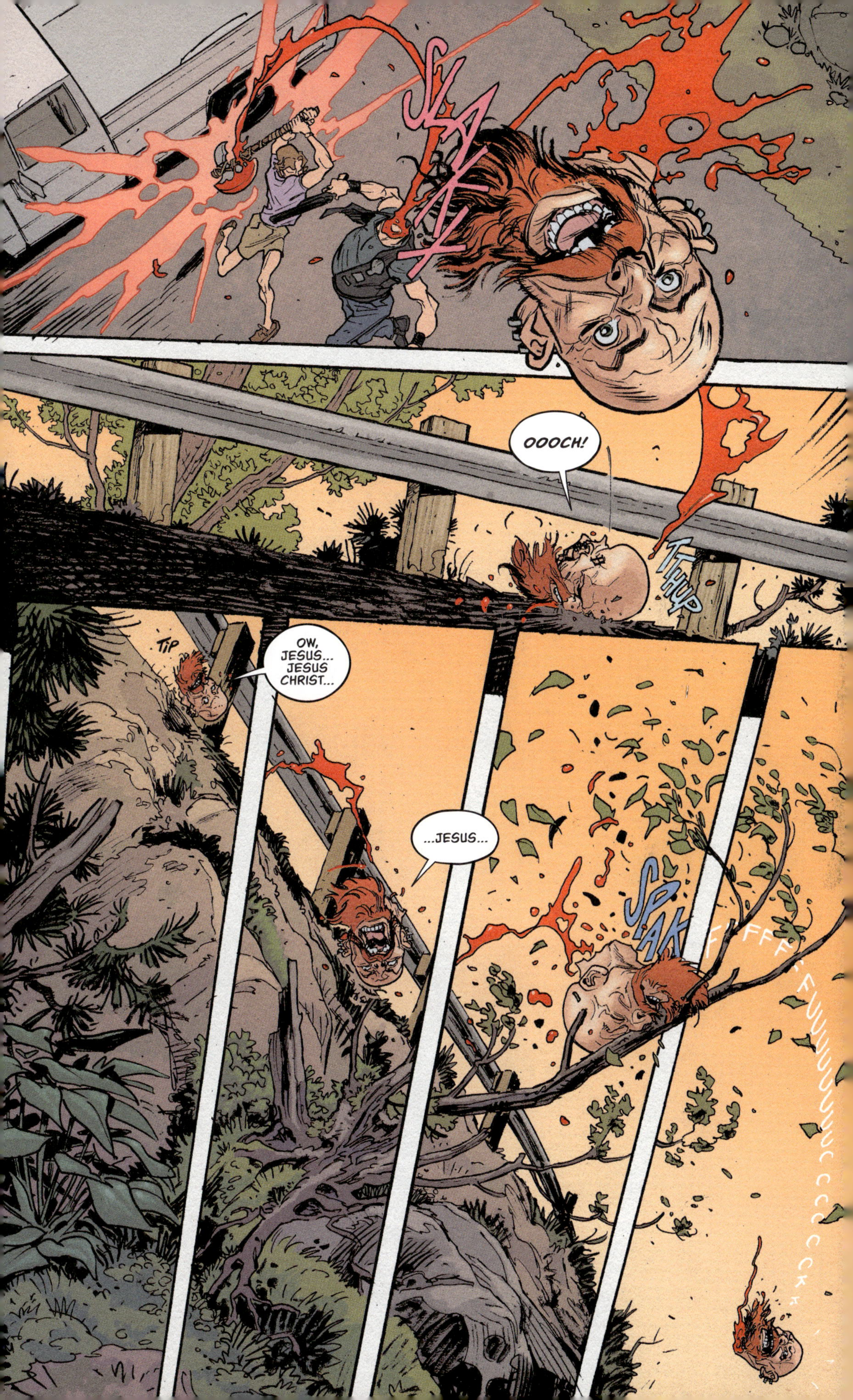
SLAKK
OOOCH!
THUP
TIP
OW, JESUS... JESUS CHRIST...
...JESUS...
SPAK
FFFFUUUUUUUCCCCCCKK

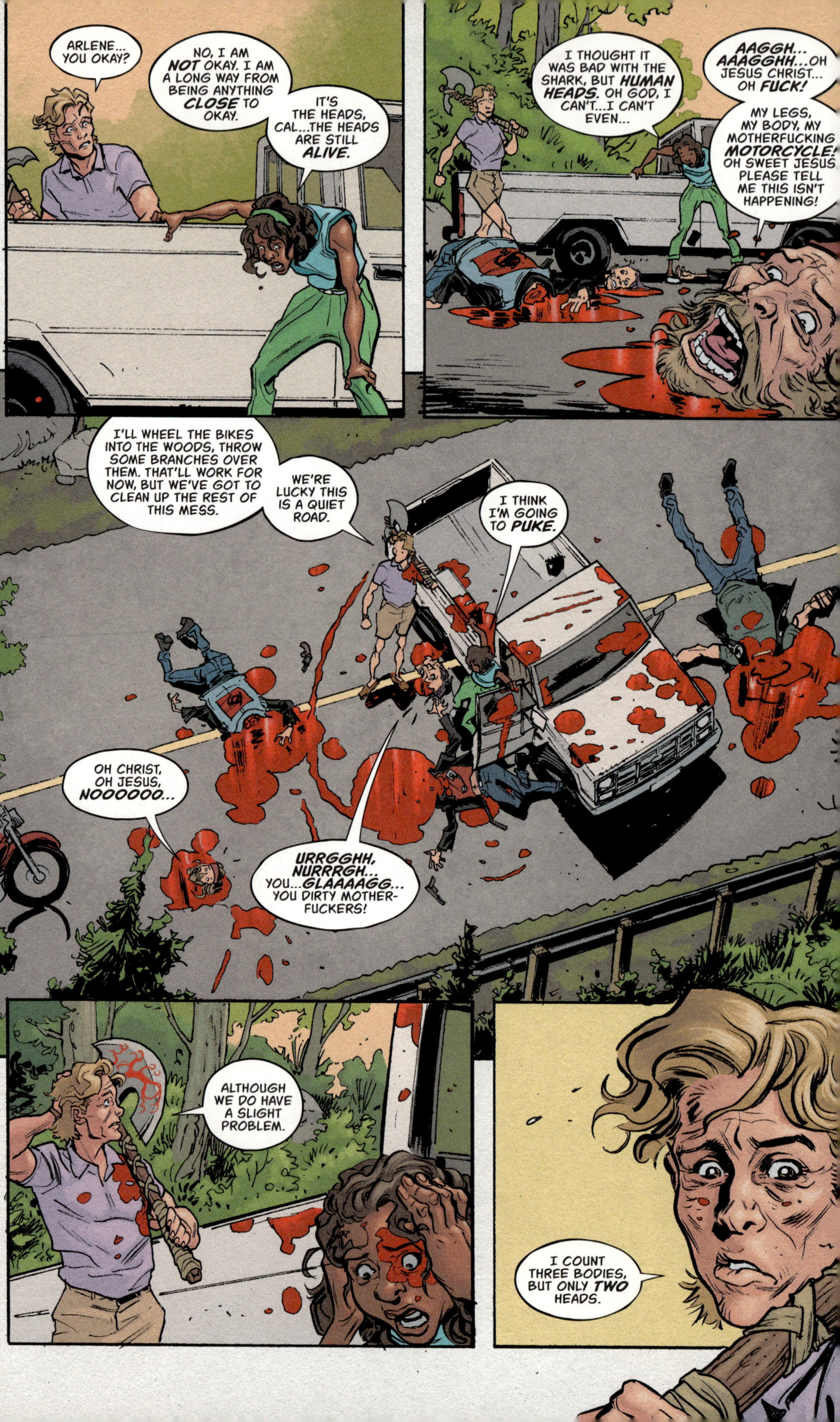
ARLENE... YOU OKAY?
NO, I AM **NOT** OKAY. I AM A LONG WAY FROM BEING ANYTHING **CLOSE** TO OKAY.
IT'S THE HEADS, CAL...THE HEADS ARE STILL **ALIVE**.
I THOUGHT IT WAS BAD WITH THE SHARK, BUT **HUMAN HEADS**. OH GOD, I CAN'T...I CAN'T EVEN...
AAGGH... AAAGGHH...OH JESUS CHRIST... OH **FUCK!**
MY LEGS, MY BODY, MY MOTHERFUCKING **MOTORCYCLE!** OH SWEET JESUS, PLEASE TELL ME THIS ISN'T HAPPENING!
I'LL WHEEL THE BIKES INTO THE WOODS, THROW SOME BRANCHES OVER THEM. THAT'LL WORK FOR NOW, BUT WE'VE GOT TO CLEAN UP THE REST OF THIS MESS.
WE'RE LUCKY THIS IS A QUIET ROAD.
I THINK I'M GOING TO **PUKE**.
OH CHRIST, OH JESUS, **NOOOOOO...**
URRGGHH, NURRRGH... YOU...**GLAAAAGG...** YOU DIRTY MOTHER-FUCKERS!
ALTHOUGH WE DO HAVE A SLIGHT PROBLEM.
I COUNT THREE BODIES, BUT ONLY **TWO** HEADS.

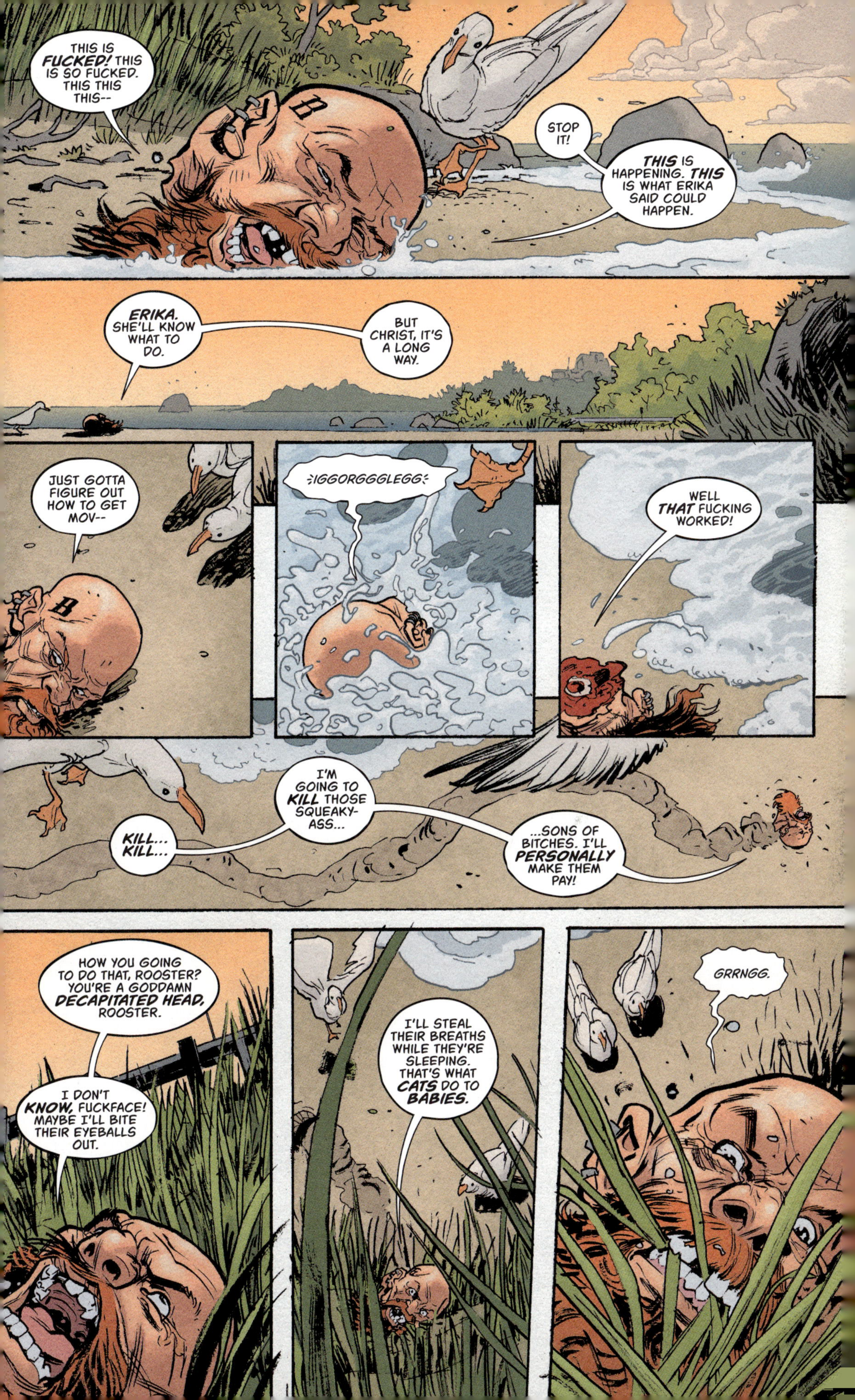
THIS IS FUCKED! THIS IS SO FUCKED. THIS THIS THIS--
STOP IT!
THIS IS HAPPENING. THIS IS WHAT ERIKA SAID COULD HAPPEN.
ERIKA. SHE'LL KNOW WHAT TO DO.
BUT CHRIST, IT'S A LONG WAY.
JUST GOTTA FIGURE OUT HOW TO GET MOV--
IGGORGGGLEGG
WELL THAT FUCKING WORKED!
KILL... KILL...
I'M GOING TO KILL THOSE SQUEAKY-ASS...
...SONS OF BITCHES. I'LL PERSONALLY MAKE THEM PAY!
HOW YOU GOING TO DO THAT, ROOSTER? YOU'RE A GODDAMN DECAPITATED HEAD, ROOSTER.
I DON'T KNOW, FUCKFACE! MAYBE I'LL BITE THEIR EYEBALLS OUT.
I'LL STEAL THEIR BREATHS WHILE THEY'RE SLEEPING. THAT'S WHAT CATS DO TO BABIES.
GRRNGG.

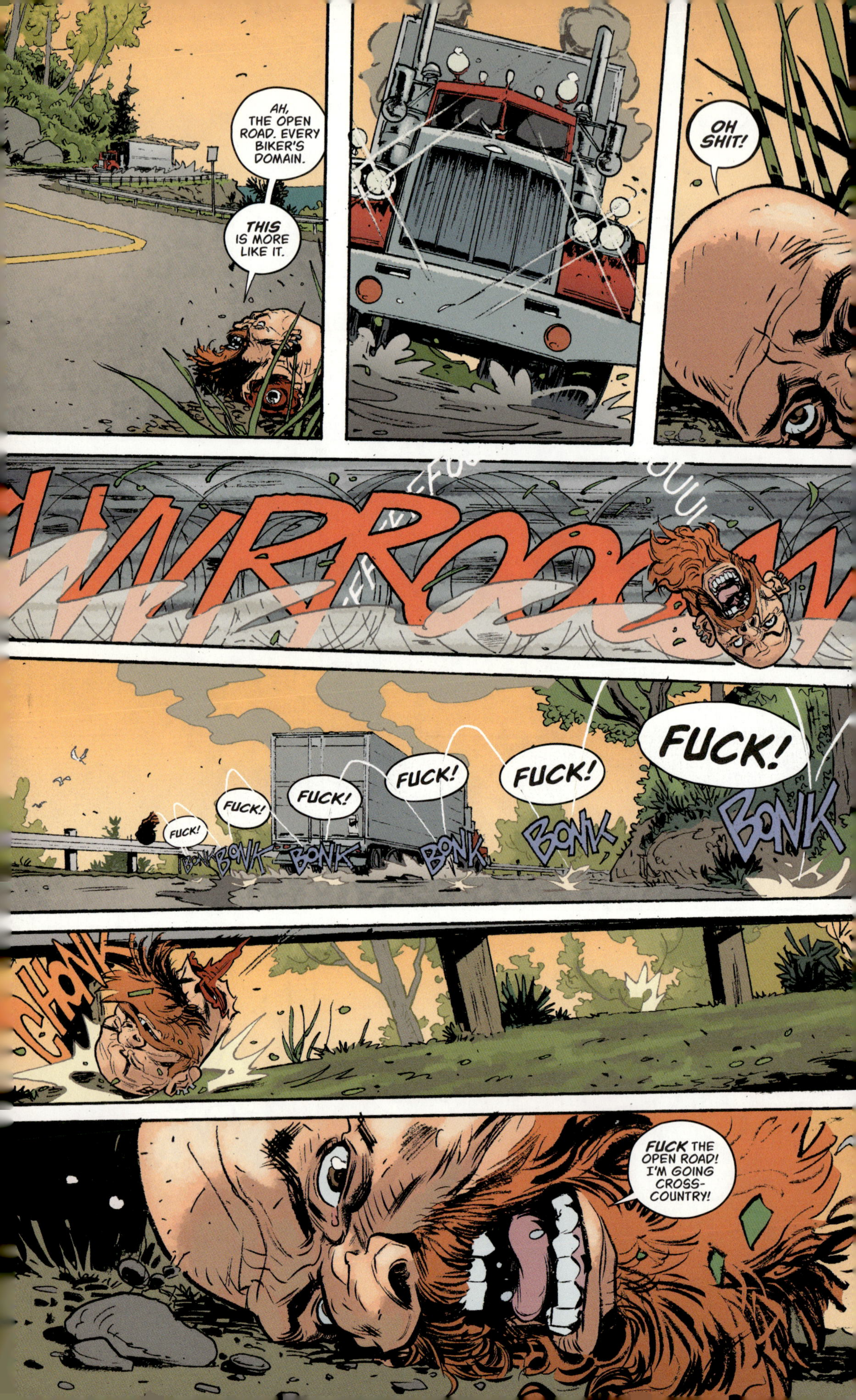
AH, THE OPEN ROAD. EVERY BIKER'S DOMAIN.
THIS IS MORE LIKE IT.
OH SHIT!
WHRROOOM
FUCK!
FUCK!
FUCK!
FUCK!
FUCK!
FUCK!
BONK
BONK
BONK
BONK
BONK
BONK
CHONK
FUCK THE OPEN ROAD! I'M GOING CROSS-COUNTRY!

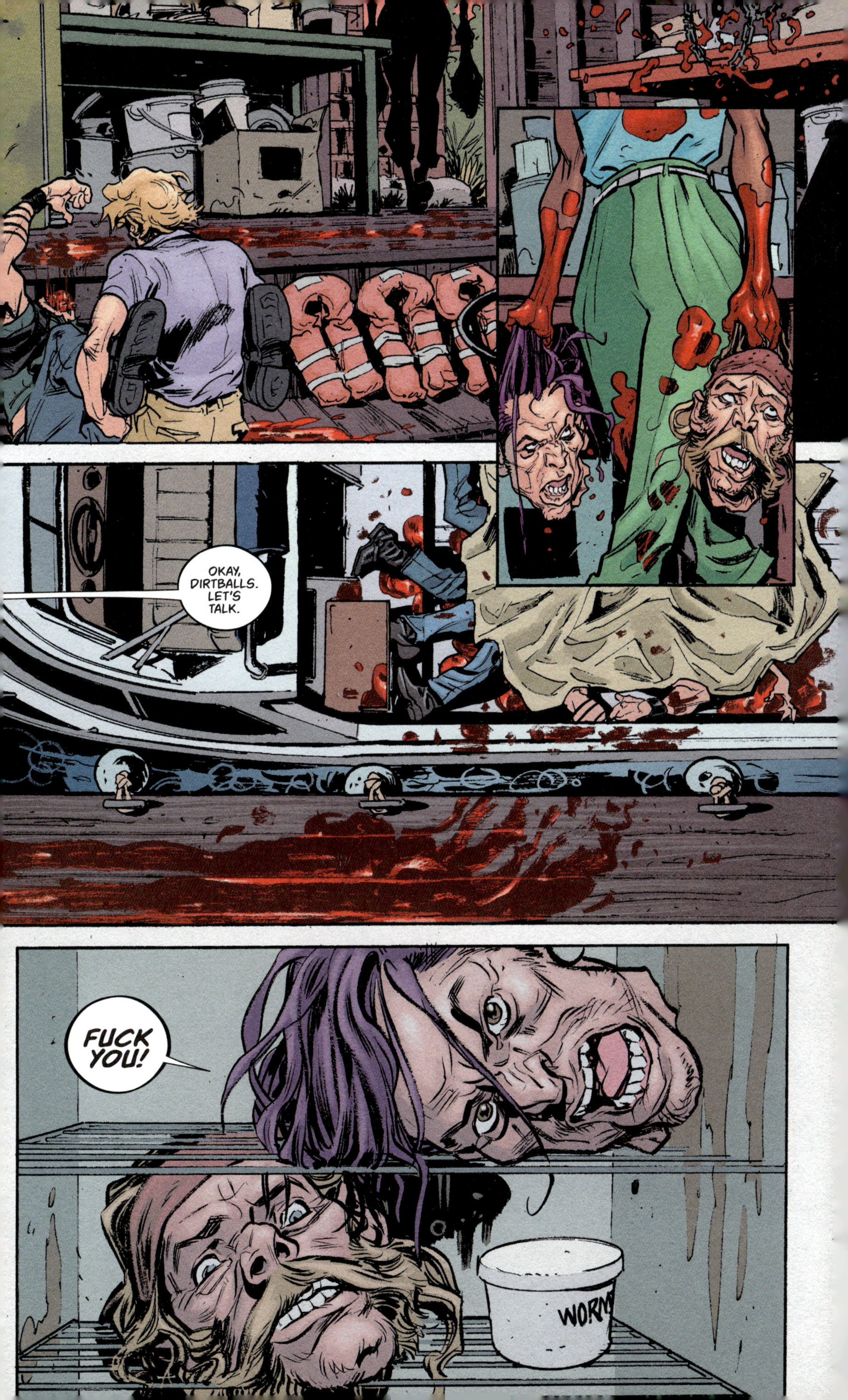
OKAY, DIRTBALLS. LET'S TALK.
FUCK YOU!
WORMS

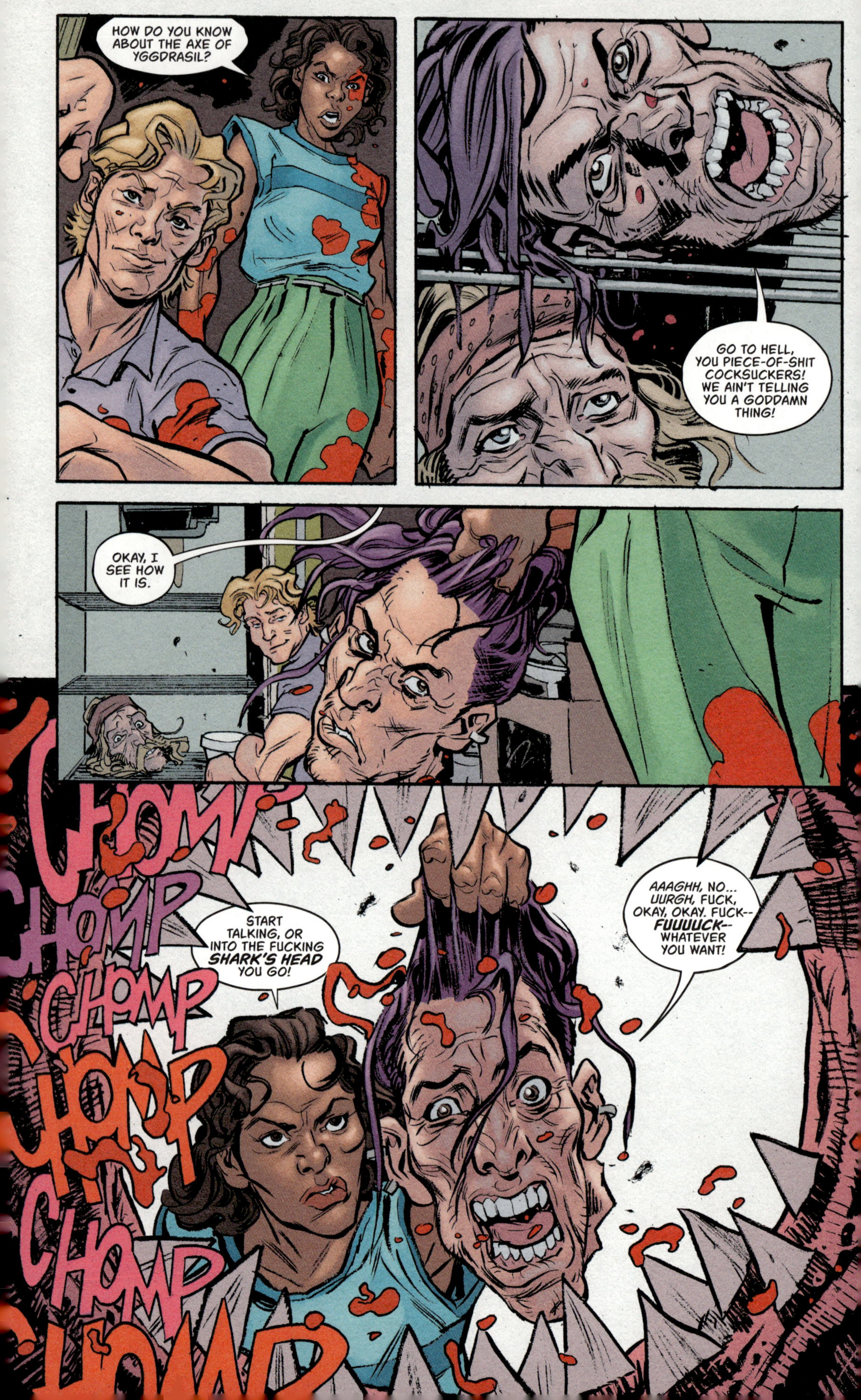
HOW DO YOU KNOW ABOUT THE AXE OF YGGDRASIL?
GO TO HELL, YOU PIECE-OF-SHIT COCKSUCKERS! WE AIN'T TELLING YOU A GODDAMN THING!
OKAY, I SEE HOW IT IS.
CHOMP CHOMP CHOMP CHOMP CHOMP CHOMP
START TALKING, OR INTO THE FUCKING **SHARK'S HEAD** YOU GO!
AAAGHH, NO... UURGH, FUCK, OKAY, OKAY. FUCK-- **FUUUUCK**-- WHATEVER YOU WANT!

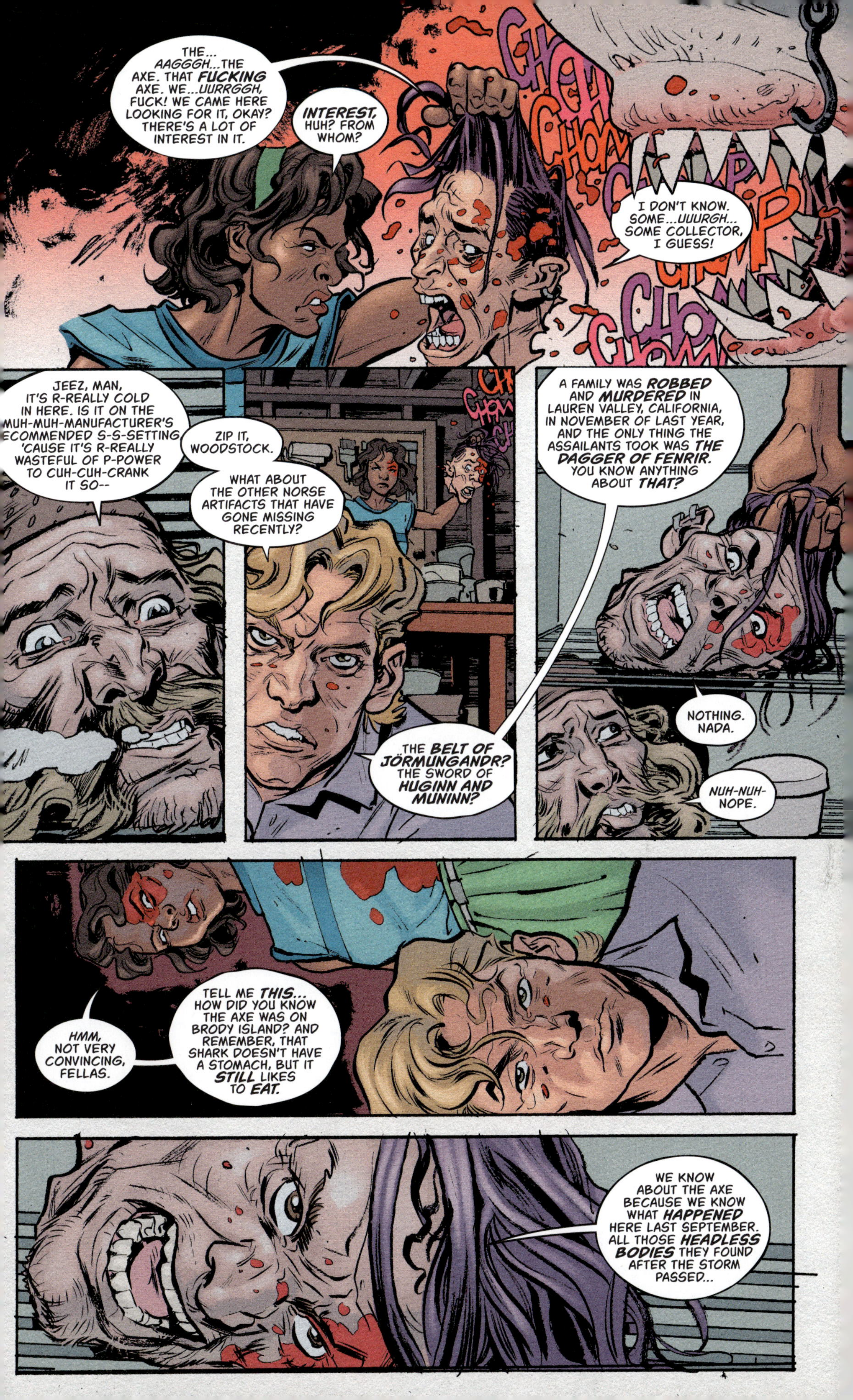
THE... AAGGGH...THE AXE. THAT FUCKING AXE. WE...UURRGGH, FUCK! WE CAME HERE LOOKING FOR IT, OKAY? THERE'S A LOT OF INTEREST IN IT.
INTEREST, HUH? FROM WHOM?
I DON'T KNOW. SOME...UUURGH... SOME COLLECTOR, I GUESS!
JEEZ, MAN, IT'S R-REALLY COLD IN HERE. IS IT ON THE MUH-MUH-MANUFACTURER'S ECOMMENDED S-S-SETTING 'CAUSE IT'S R-REALLY WASTEFUL OF P-POWER TO CUH-CUH-CRANK IT SO--
ZIP IT, WOODSTOCK.
WHAT ABOUT THE OTHER NORSE ARTIFACTS THAT HAVE GONE MISSING RECENTLY?
THE BELT OF JÖRMUNGANDR? THE SWORD OF HUGINN AND MUNINN?
A FAMILY WAS ROBBED AND MURDERED IN LAUREN VALLEY, CALIFORNIA, IN NOVEMBER OF LAST YEAR, AND THE ONLY THING THE ASSAILANTS TOOK WAS THE DAGGER OF FENRIR. YOU KNOW ANYTHING ABOUT THAT?
NOTHING. NADA.
NUH-NUH-NOPE.
HMM, NOT VERY CONVINCING, FELLAS.
TELL ME THIS... HOW DID YOU KNOW THE AXE WAS ON BRODY ISLAND? AND REMEMBER, THAT SHARK DOESN'T HAVE A STOMACH, BUT IT STILL LIKES TO EAT.
WE KNOW ABOUT THE AXE BECAUSE WE KNOW WHAT HAPPENED HERE LAST SEPTEMBER. ALL THOSE HEADLESS BODIES THEY FOUND AFTER THE STORM PASSED...

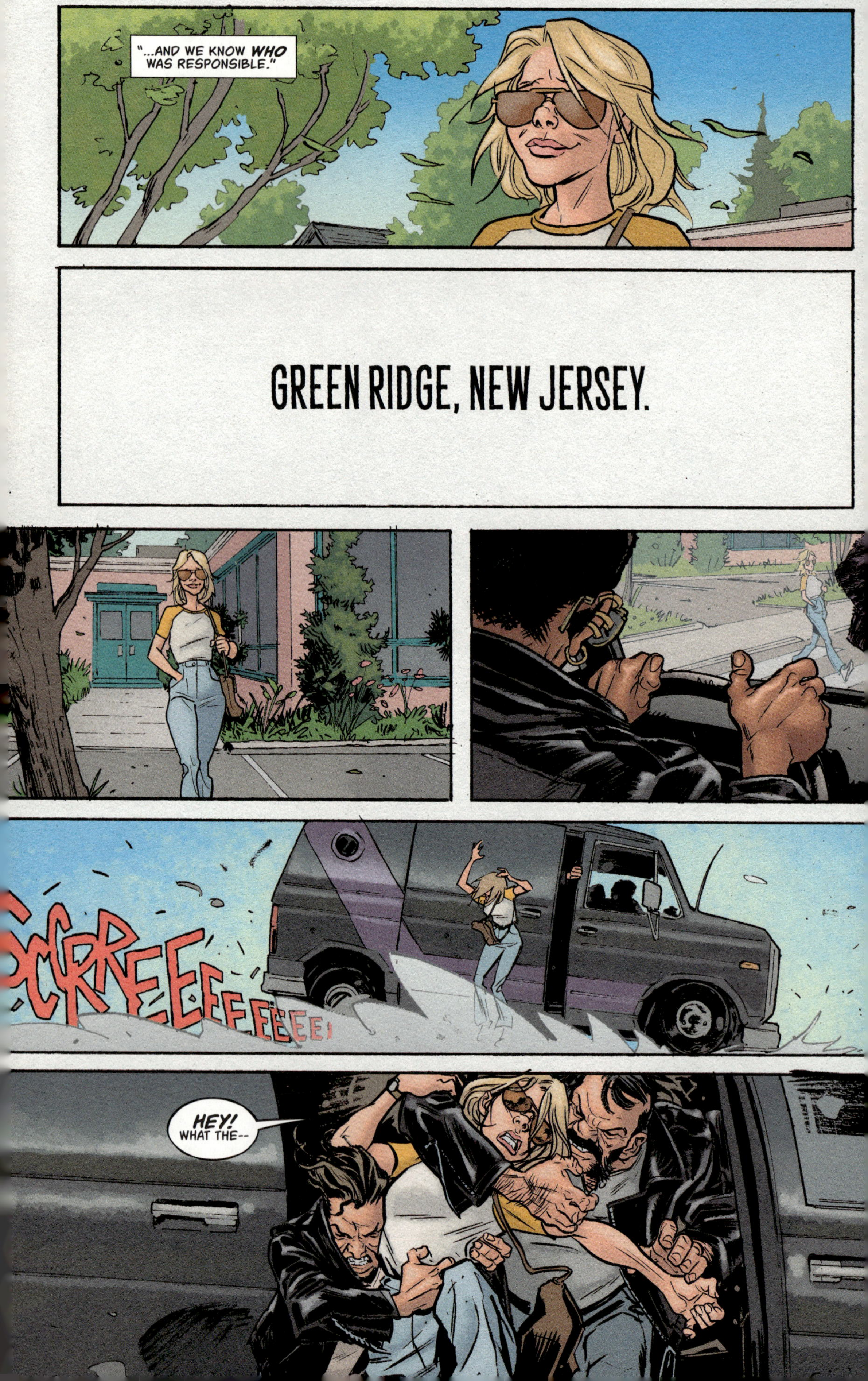

"...AND WE KNOW *WHO* WAS RESPONSIBLE."
GREEN RIDGE, NEW JERSEY.
SCREEEEEEEE
HEY! WHAT THE--

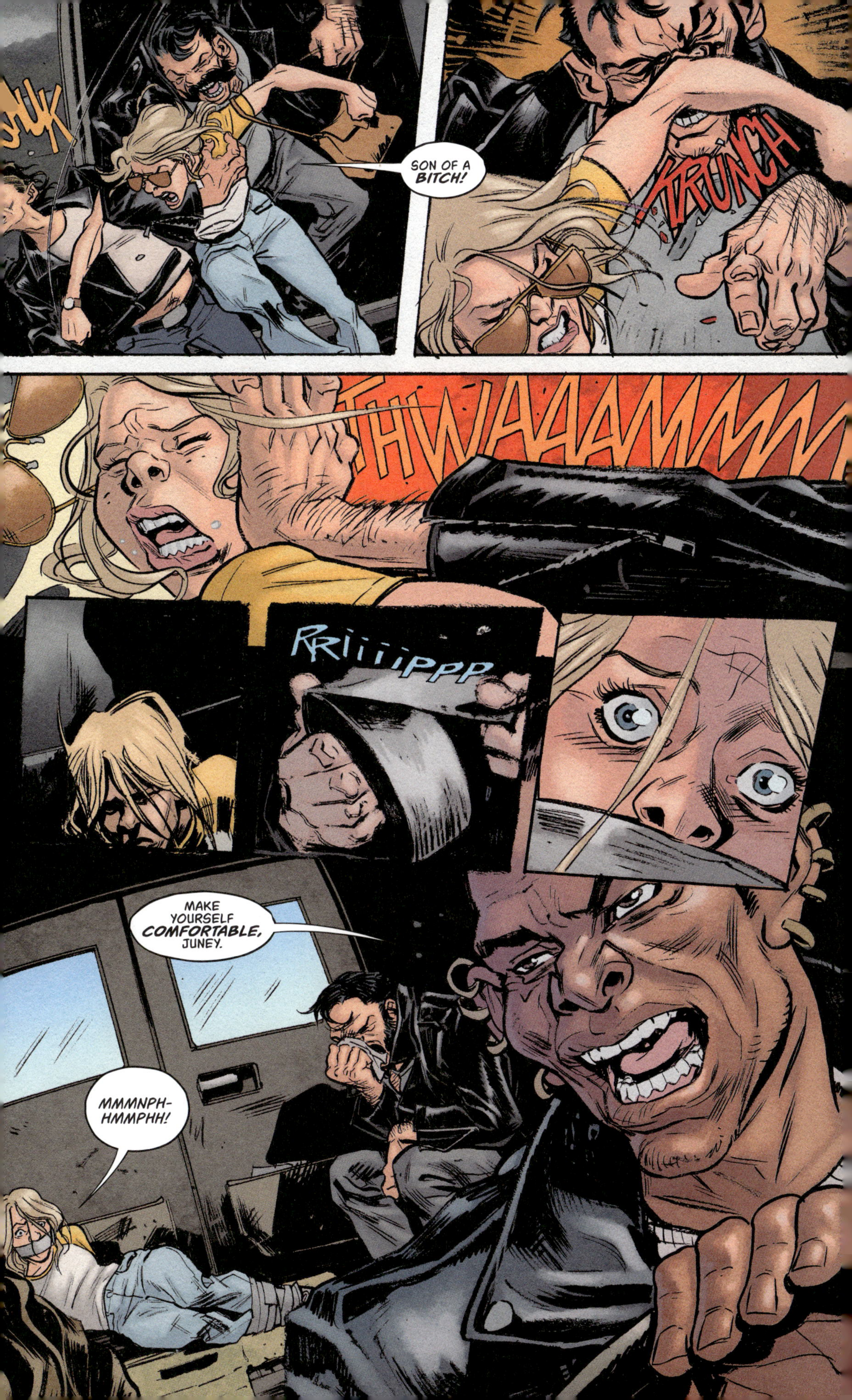

SON OF A BITCH!
KRUNCH
THWAAAMMM
RRiiiiPPP
MAKE YOURSELF COMFORTABLE, JUNEY.
MMMNPH-HMMPHH!

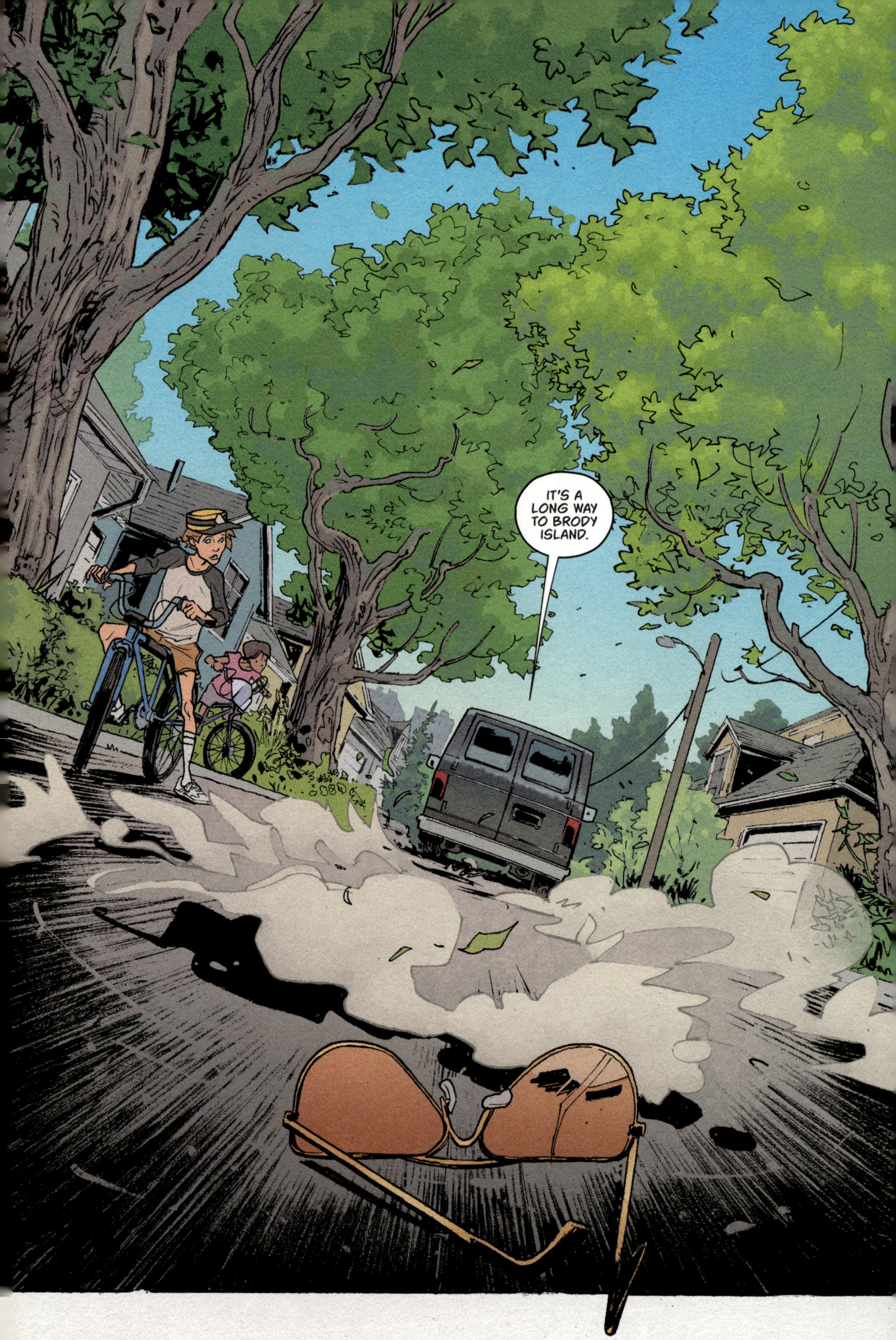
IT'S A LONG WAY TO BRODY ISLAND.

IN ONE MONTH...

NOTHING IS CERTAIN EXCEPT DEATH AND AXES.

REFRIGERATOR FULL OF HEADS

Written by RIO YOUERS Drawn by TOM FOWLER
Colored by BILL CRABTREE Lettered by ANDWORLD DESIGN
Cover by SAM WOLFE CONNELLY
Variant cover by TIFFANY TURRILL

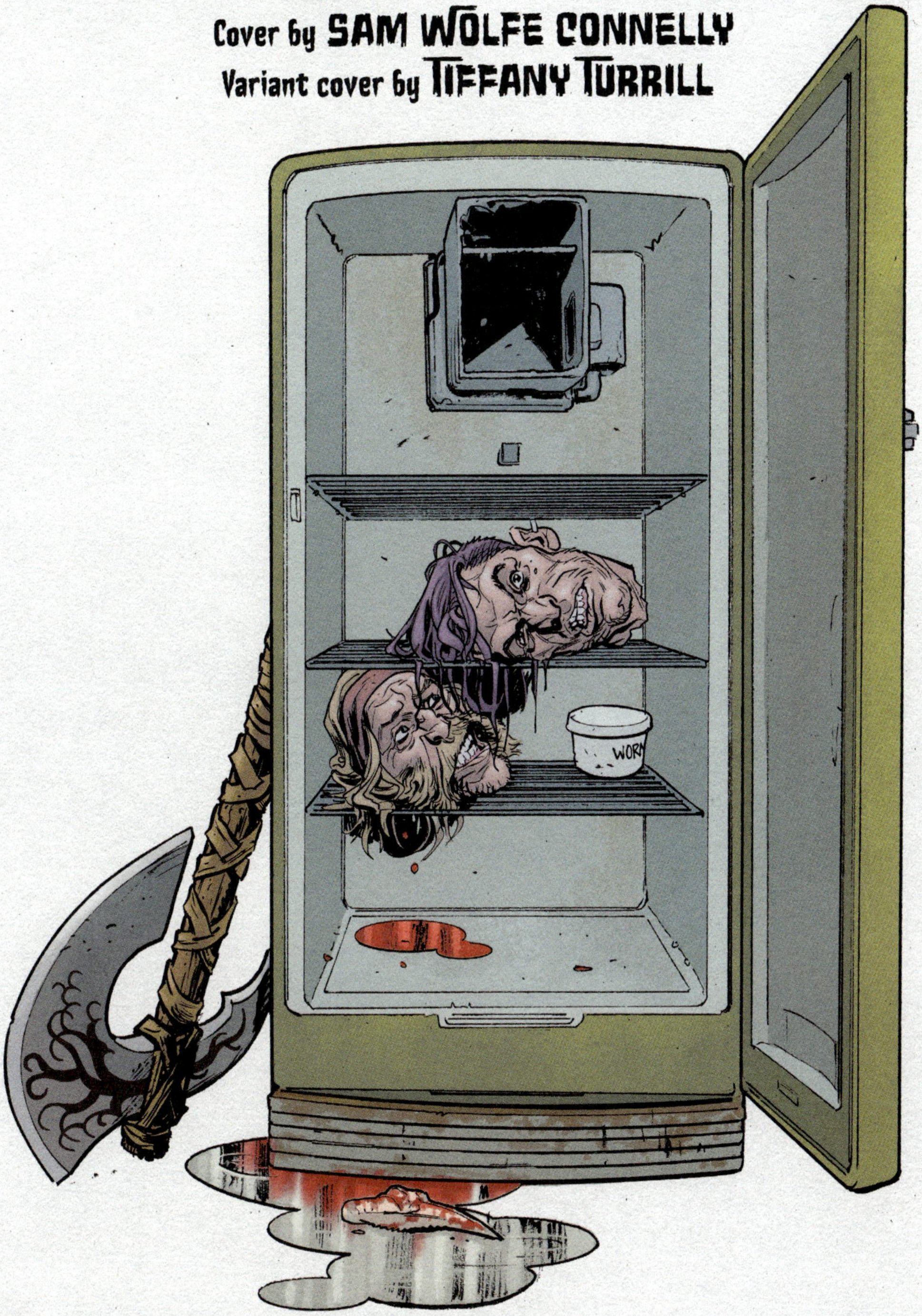

CHRIS CONROY Editor
ANDREA SHEA Associate Editor

BASKETFUL OF HEADS created by JOE HILL with art by LEOMACS
REFRIGERATOR FULL OF HEADS curated for HILL HOUSE COMICS by JOE HILL

"IT'S THE HEADS, CAL...
THE HEADS ARE
STILL ALIVE."

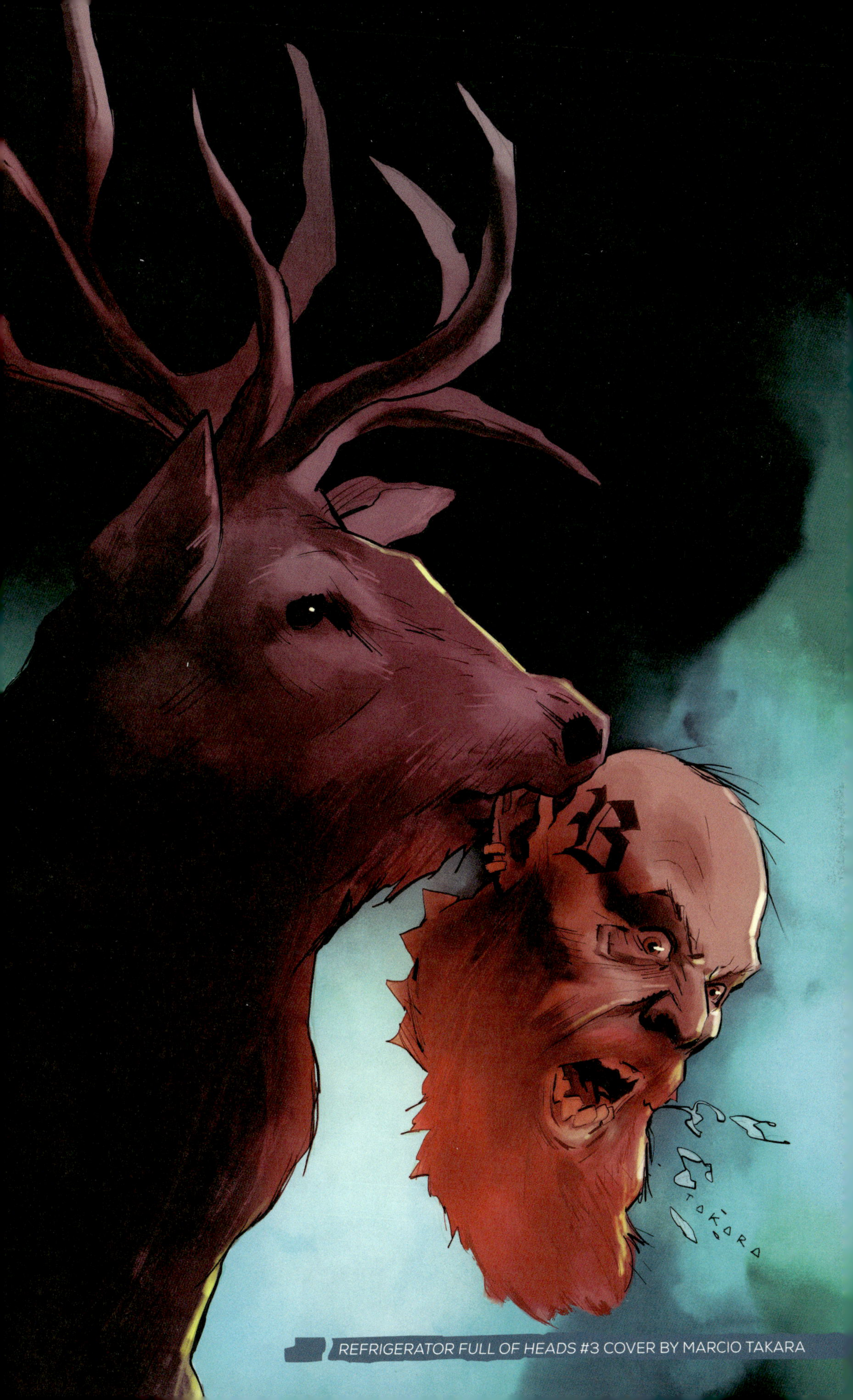

REFRIGERATOR FULL OF HEADS #3 COVER BY MARCIO TAKARA

REFRIGERATOR FULL OF HEADS #3 VARIANT COVER BY MARIA WOLF

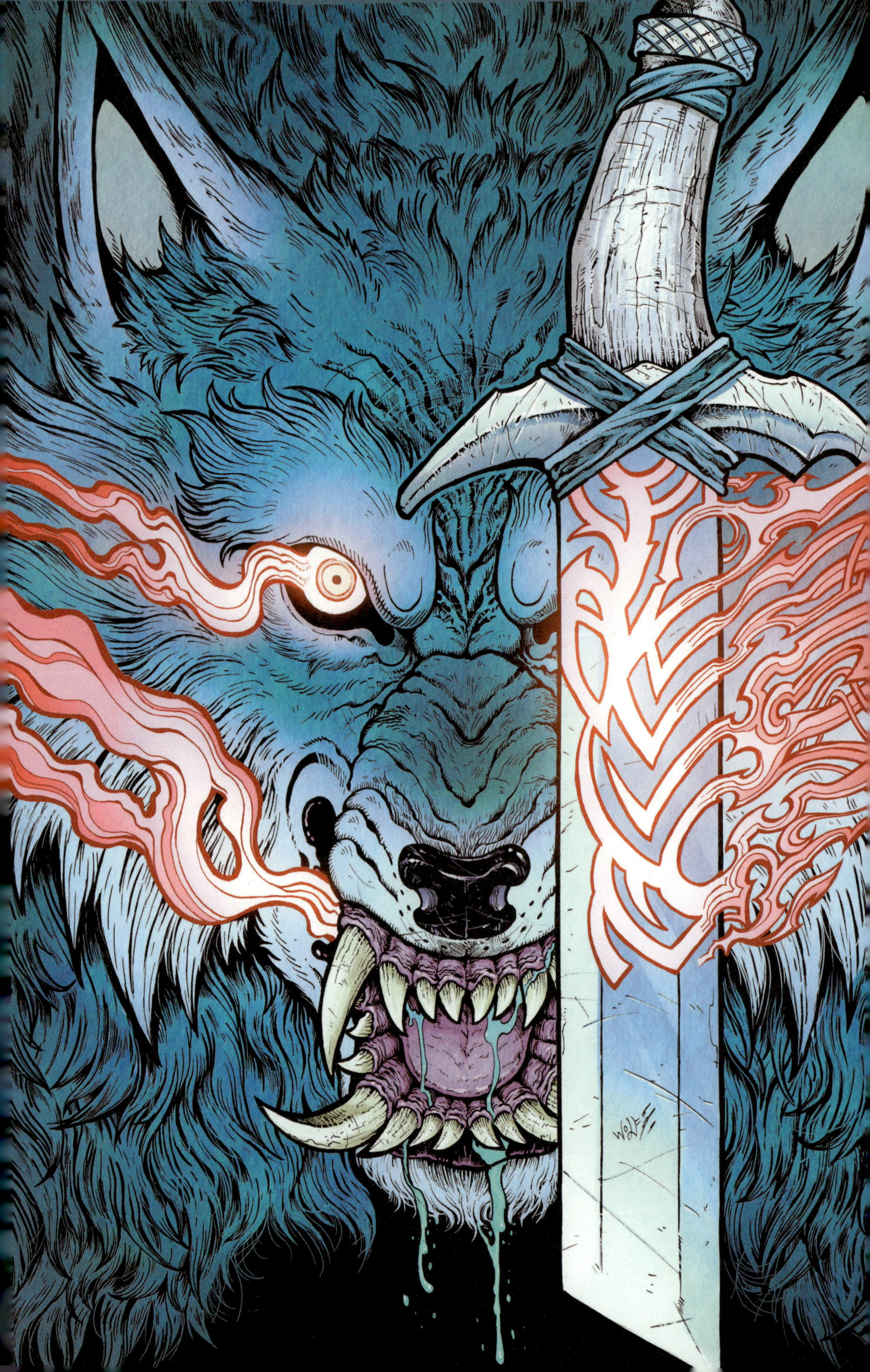

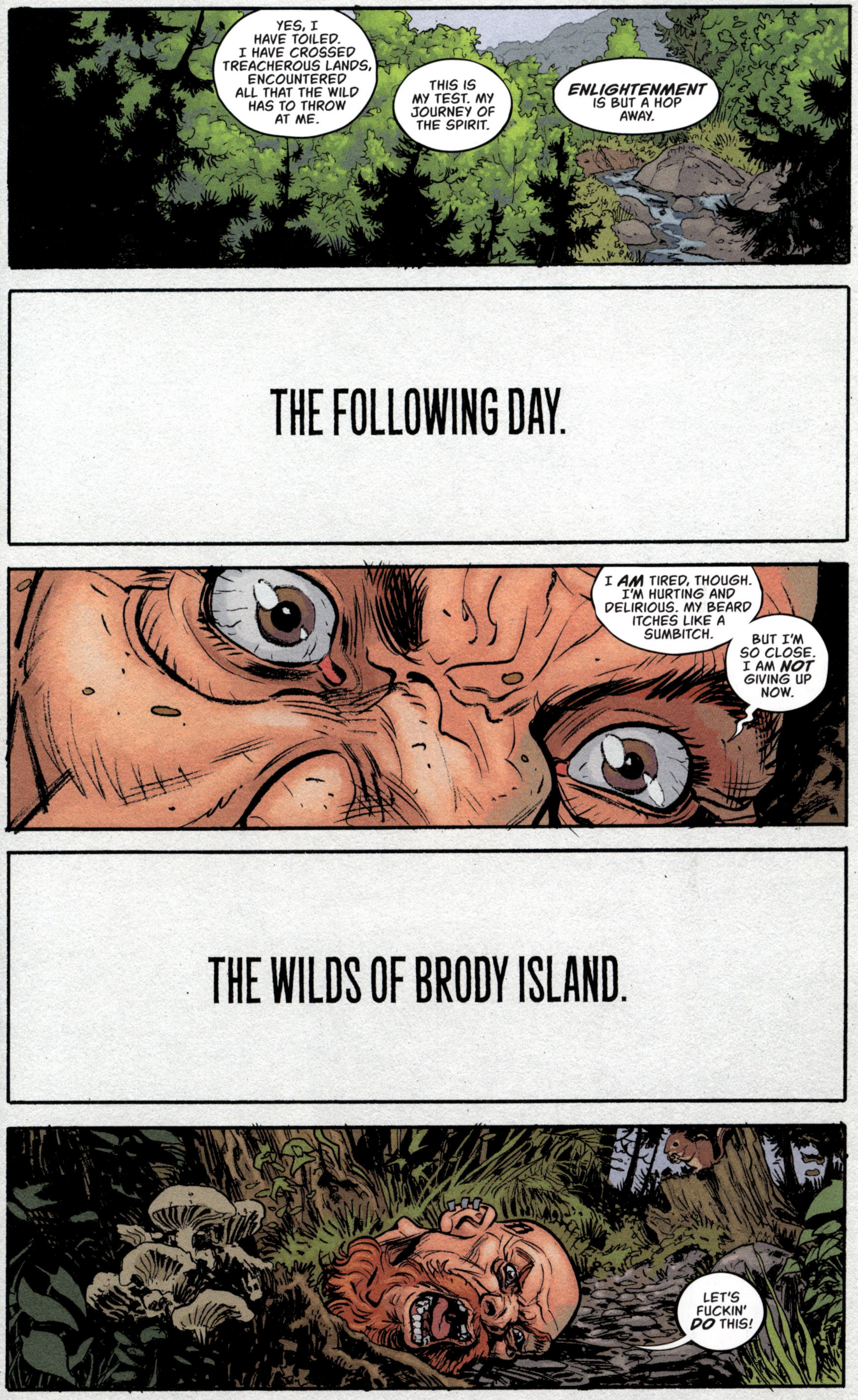
YES, I HAVE TOILED. I HAVE CROSSED TREACHEROUS LANDS, ENCOUNTERED ALL THAT THE WILD HAS TO THROW AT ME.
THIS IS MY TEST. MY JOURNEY OF THE SPIRIT.
ENLIGHTENMENT IS BUT A HOP AWAY.
THE FOLLOWING DAY.
I AM TIRED, THOUGH. I'M HURTING AND DELIRIOUS. MY BEARD ITCHES LIKE A SUMBITCH.
BUT I'M SO CLOSE. I AM NOT GIVING UP NOW.
THE WILDS OF BRODY ISLAND.
LET'S FUCKIN' DO THIS!

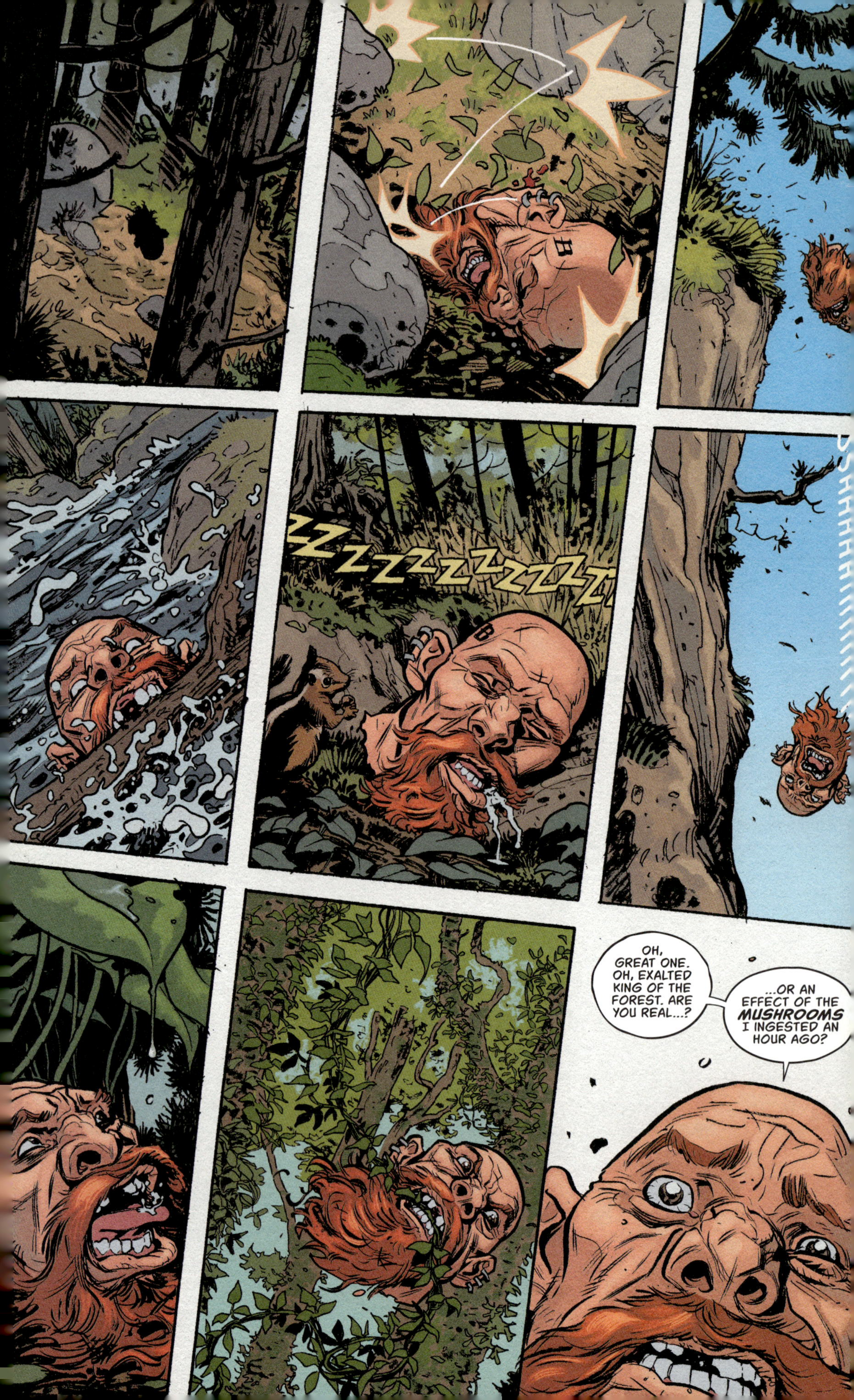
OH, GREAT ONE. OH, EXALTED KING OF THE FOREST. ARE YOU REAL...?
...OR AN EFFECT OF THE *MUSHROOMS* I INGESTED AN HOUR AGO?

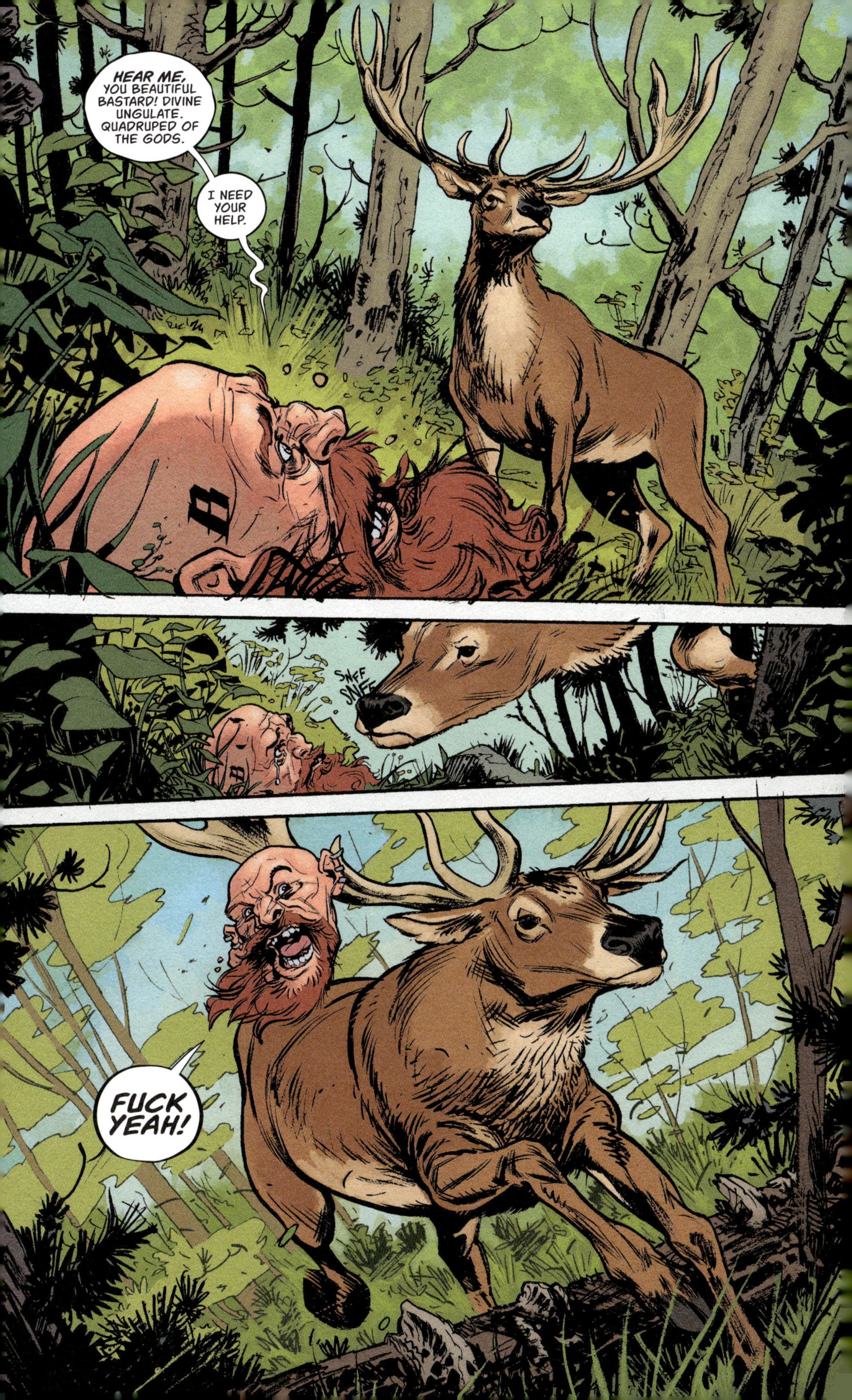
HEAR ME, YOU BEAUTIFUL BASTARD! DIVINE UNGULATE. QUADRUPED OF THE GODS.
I NEED YOUR HELP.
SNFF SNFF
FUCK YEAH!

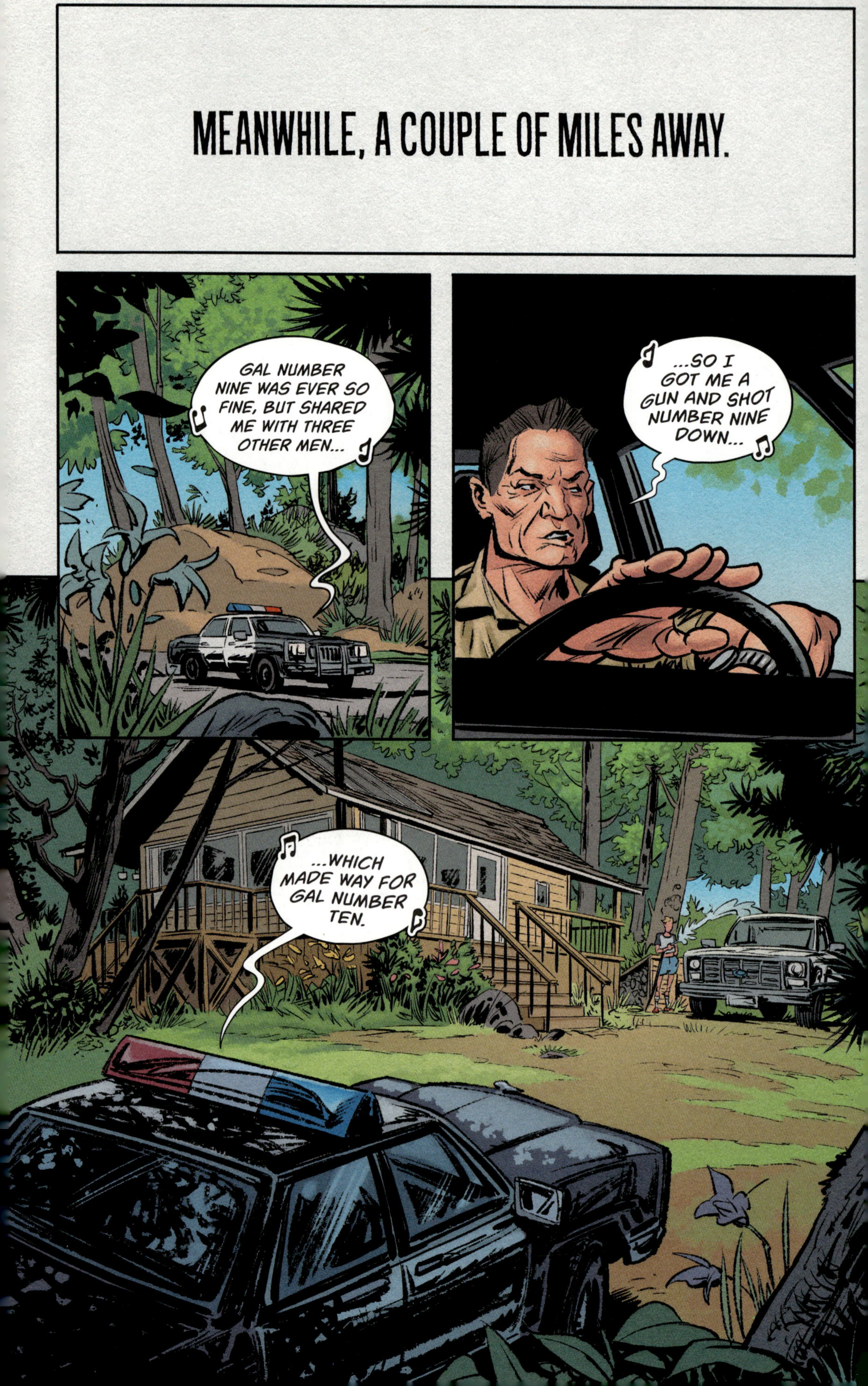
MEANWHILE, A COUPLE OF MILES AWAY.
GAL NUMBER NINE WAS EVER SO FINE, BUT SHARED ME WITH THREE OTHER MEN...
...SO I GOT ME A GUN AND SHOT NUMBER NINE DOWN...
...WHICH MADE WAY FOR GAL NUMBER TEN.

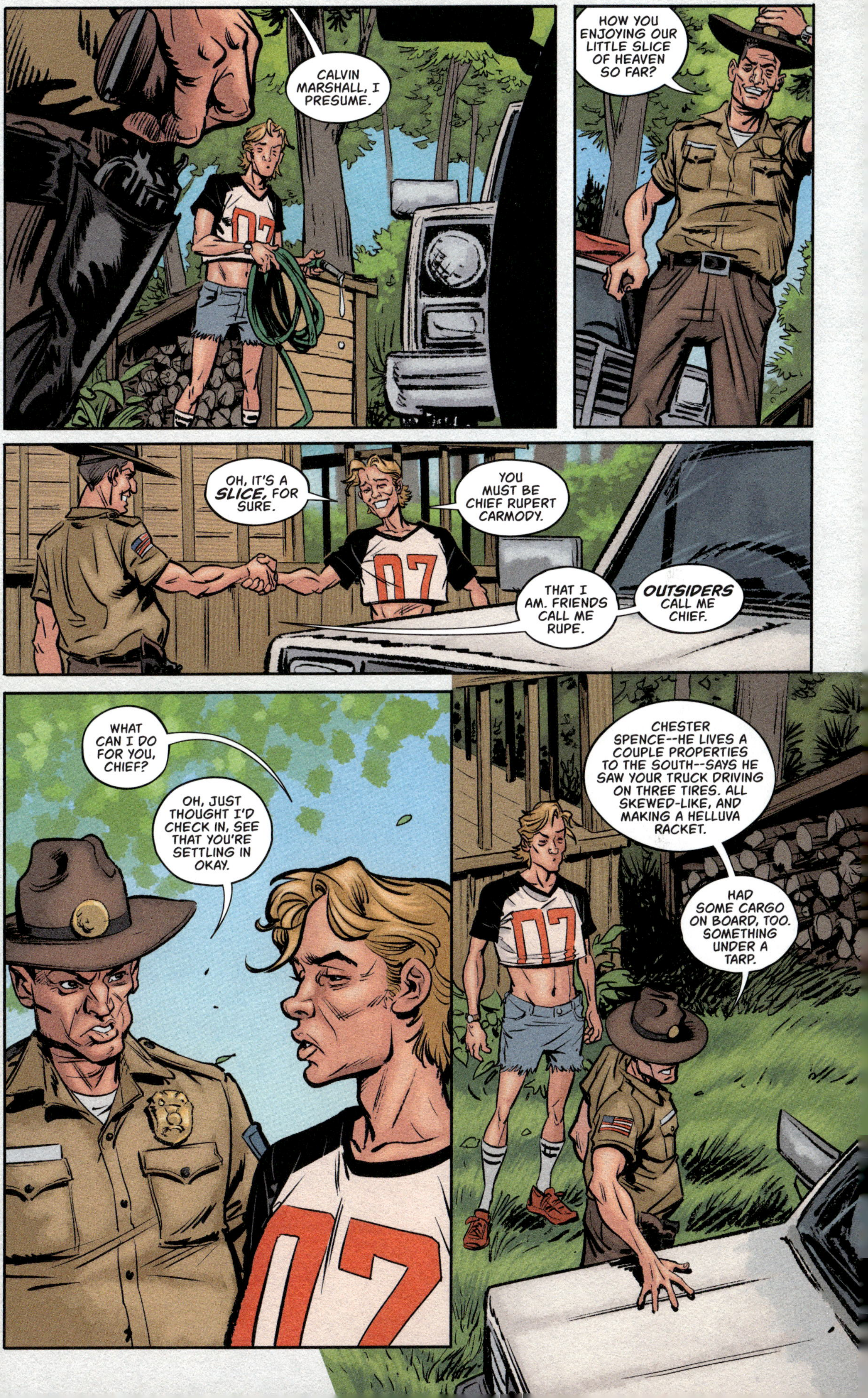
CALVIN MARSHALL, I PRESUME.
HOW YOU ENJOYING OUR LITTLE SLICE OF HEAVEN SO FAR?
OH, IT'S A SLICE, FOR SURE.
YOU MUST BE CHIEF RUPERT CARMODY.
THAT I AM. FRIENDS CALL ME RUPE.
OUTSIDERS CALL ME CHIEF.
WHAT CAN I DO FOR YOU, CHIEF?
OH, JUST THOUGHT I'D CHECK IN, SEE THAT YOU'RE SETTLING IN OKAY.
CHESTER SPENCE--HE LIVES A COUPLE PROPERTIES TO THE SOUTH--SAYS HE SAW YOUR TRUCK DRIVING ON THREE TIRES. ALL SKEWED-LIKE, AND MAKING A HELLUVA RACKET.
HAD SOME CARGO ON BOARD, TOO. SOMETHING UNDER A TARP.

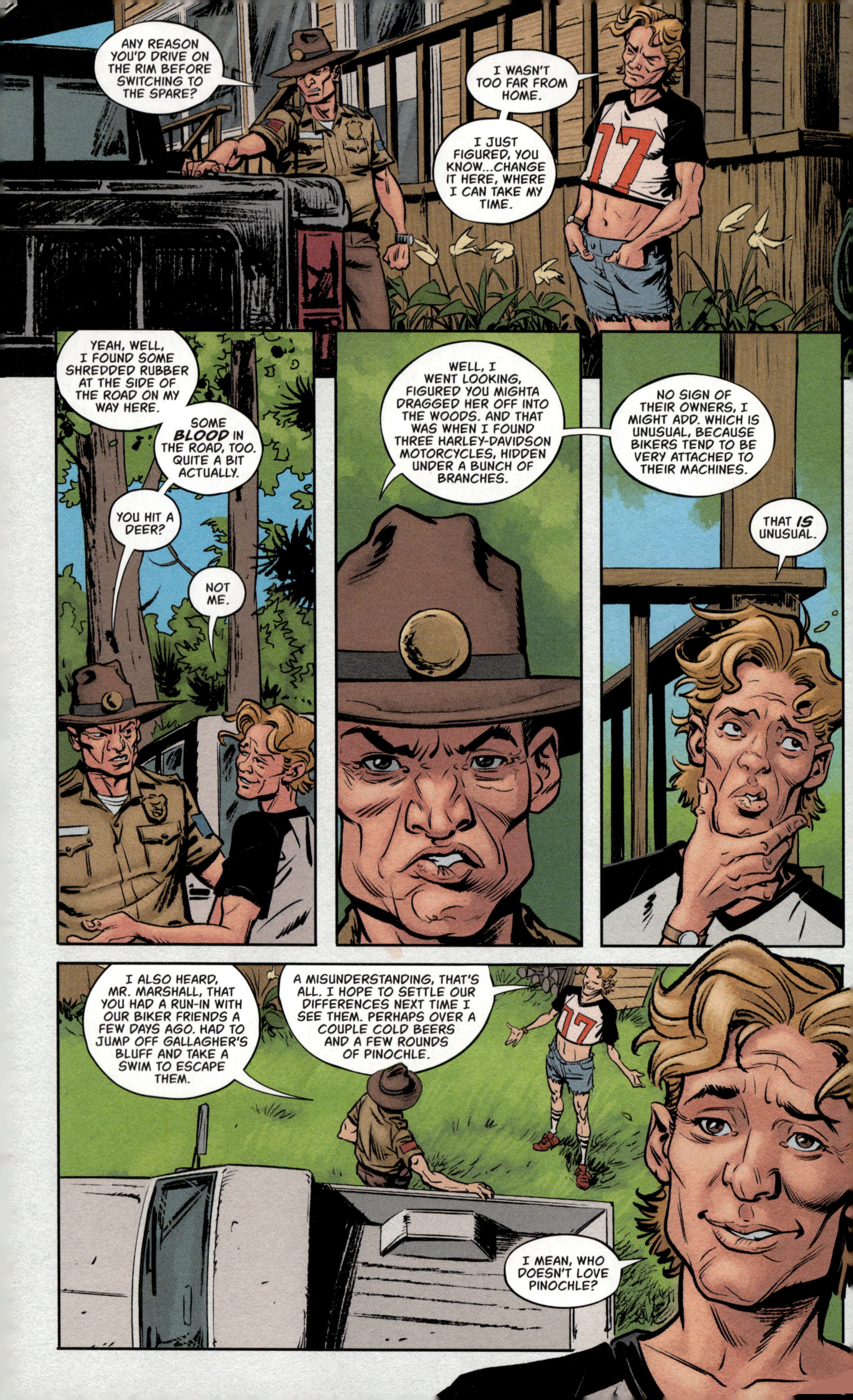

ANY REASON YOU'D DRIVE ON THE RIM BEFORE SWITCHING TO THE SPARE?
I WASN'T TOO FAR FROM HOME.
I JUST FIGURED, YOU KNOW...CHANGE IT HERE, WHERE I CAN TAKE MY TIME.
YEAH, WELL, I FOUND SOME SHREDDED RUBBER AT THE SIDE OF THE ROAD ON MY WAY HERE.
SOME **BLOOD** IN THE ROAD, TOO. QUITE A BIT ACTUALLY.
YOU HIT A DEER?
NOT ME.
WELL, I WENT LOOKING, FIGURED YOU MIGHTA DRAGGED HER OFF INTO THE WOODS. AND THAT WAS WHEN I FOUND THREE HARLEY-DAVIDSON MOTORCYCLES, HIDDEN UNDER A BUNCH OF BRANCHES.
NO SIGN OF THEIR OWNERS, I MIGHT ADD. WHICH IS UNUSUAL, BECAUSE BIKERS TEND TO BE VERY ATTACHED TO THEIR MACHINES.
THAT ***IS*** UNUSUAL.
I ALSO HEARD, MR. MARSHALL, THAT YOU HAD A RUN-IN WITH OUR BIKER FRIENDS A FEW DAYS AGO. HAD TO JUMP OFF GALLAGHER'S BLUFF AND TAKE A SWIM TO ESCAPE THEM.
A MISUNDERSTANDING, THAT'S ALL. I HOPE TO SETTLE OUR DIFFERENCES NEXT TIME I SEE THEM. PERHAPS OVER A COUPLE COLD BEERS AND A FEW ROUNDS OF PINOCHLE.
I MEAN, WHO DOESN'T LOVE PINOCHLE?

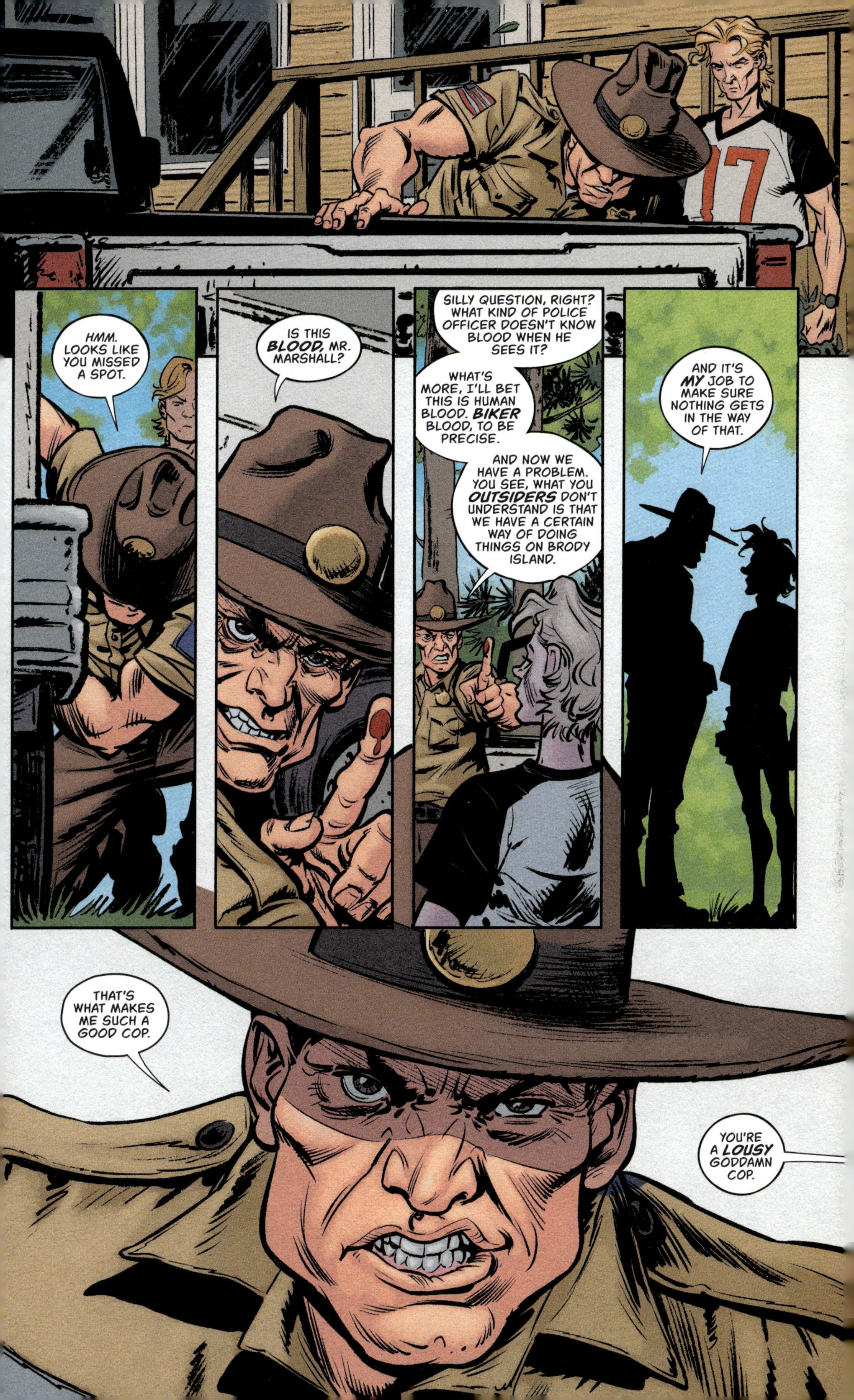
HMM. LOOKS LIKE YOU MISSED A SPOT.
IS THIS BLOOD, MR. MARSHALL?
SILLY QUESTION, RIGHT? WHAT KIND OF POLICE OFFICER DOESN'T KNOW BLOOD WHEN HE SEES IT?
WHAT'S MORE, I'LL BET THIS IS HUMAN BLOOD. BIKER BLOOD, TO BE PRECISE.
AND NOW WE HAVE A PROBLEM. YOU SEE, WHAT YOU OUTSIDERS DON'T UNDERSTAND IS THAT WE HAVE A CERTAIN WAY OF DOING THINGS ON BRODY ISLAND.
AND IT'S MY JOB TO MAKE SURE NOTHING GETS IN THE WAY OF THAT.
THAT'S WHAT MAKES ME SUCH A GOOD COP.
YOU'RE A LOUSY GODDAMN COP.

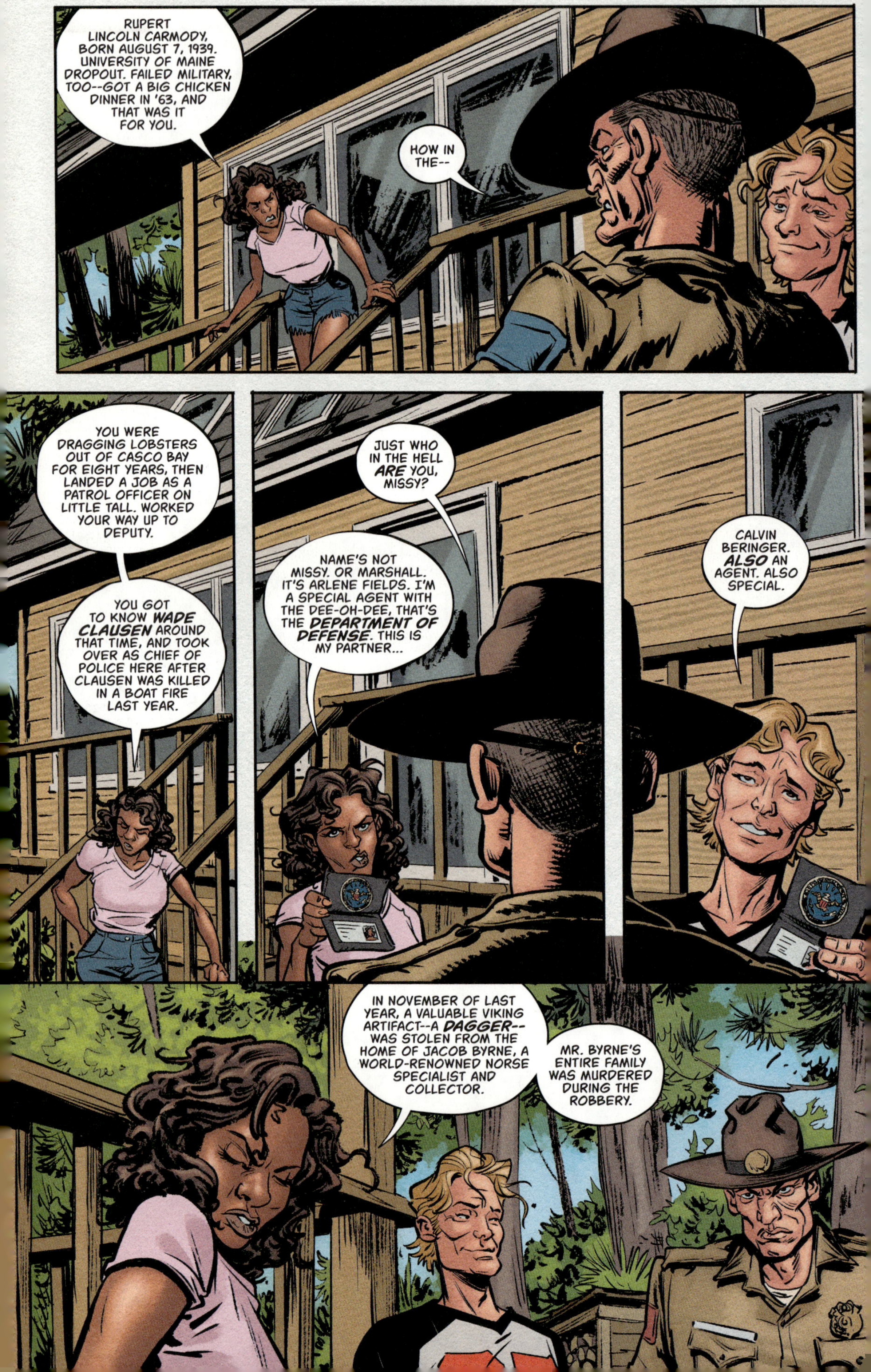

RUPERT LINCOLN CARMODY, BORN AUGUST 7, 1939. UNIVERSITY OF MAINE DROPOUT. FAILED MILITARY, TOO--GOT A BIG CHICKEN DINNER IN '63, AND THAT WAS IT FOR YOU.
HOW IN THE--
YOU WERE DRAGGING LOBSTERS OUT OF CASCO BAY FOR EIGHT YEARS, THEN LANDED A JOB AS A PATROL OFFICER ON LITTLE TALL. WORKED YOUR WAY UP TO DEPUTY.
YOU GOT TO KNOW *WADE CLAUSEN* AROUND THAT TIME, AND TOOK OVER AS CHIEF OF POLICE HERE AFTER CLAUSEN WAS KILLED IN A BOAT FIRE LAST YEAR.
JUST WHO IN THE HELL *ARE* YOU, MISSY?
NAME'S NOT MISSY. OR MARSHALL. IT'S ARLENE FIELDS. I'M A SPECIAL AGENT WITH THE DEE-OH-DEE, THAT'S THE *DEPARTMENT OF DEFENSE*. THIS IS MY PARTNER...
CALVIN BERINGER. *ALSO* AN AGENT. ALSO SPECIAL.
IN NOVEMBER OF LAST YEAR, A VALUABLE VIKING ARTIFACT--A *DAGGER*--WAS STOLEN FROM THE HOME OF JACOB BYRNE, A WORLD-RENOWNED NORSE SPECIALIST AND COLLECTOR.
MR. BYRNE'S ENTIRE FAMILY WAS MURDERED DURING THE ROBBERY.

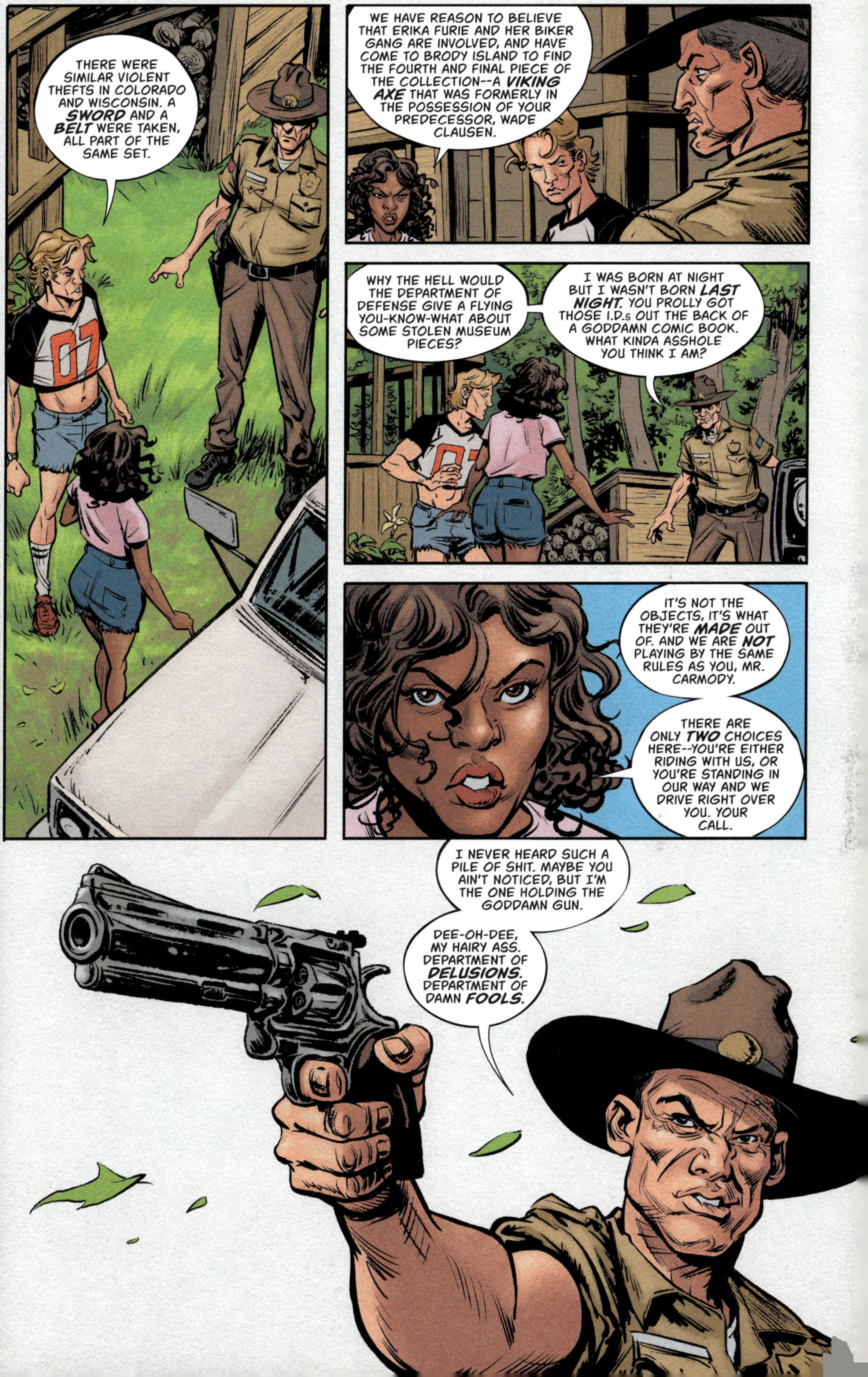
THERE WERE SIMILAR VIOLENT THEFTS IN COLORADO AND WISCONSIN. A SWORD AND A BELT WERE TAKEN, ALL PART OF THE SAME SET.
WE HAVE REASON TO BELIEVE THAT ERIKA FURIE AND HER BIKER GANG ARE INVOLVED, AND HAVE COME TO BRODY ISLAND TO FIND THE FOURTH AND FINAL PIECE OF THE COLLECTION--A VIKING AXE THAT WAS FORMERLY IN THE POSSESSION OF YOUR PREDECESSOR, WADE CLAUSEN.
WHY THE HELL WOULD THE DEPARTMENT OF DEFENSE GIVE A FLYING YOU-KNOW-WHAT ABOUT SOME STOLEN MUSEUM PIECES?
I WAS BORN AT NIGHT BUT I WASN'T BORN LAST NIGHT. YOU PROLLY GOT THOSE I.D.s OUT THE BACK OF A GODDAMN COMIC BOOK. WHAT KINDA ASSHOLE YOU THINK I AM?
IT'S NOT THE OBJECTS, IT'S WHAT THEY'RE MADE OUT OF. AND WE ARE NOT PLAYING BY THE SAME RULES AS YOU, MR. CARMODY.
THERE ARE ONLY TWO CHOICES HERE--YOU'RE EITHER RIDING WITH US, OR YOU'RE STANDING IN OUR WAY AND WE DRIVE RIGHT OVER YOU. YOUR CALL.
I NEVER HEARD SUCH A PILE OF SHIT. MAYBE YOU AIN'T NOTICED, BUT I'M THE ONE HOLDING THE GODDAMN GUN.
DEE-OH-DEE, MY HAIRY ASS. DEPARTMENT OF DELUSIONS. DEPARTMENT OF DAMN FOOLS.

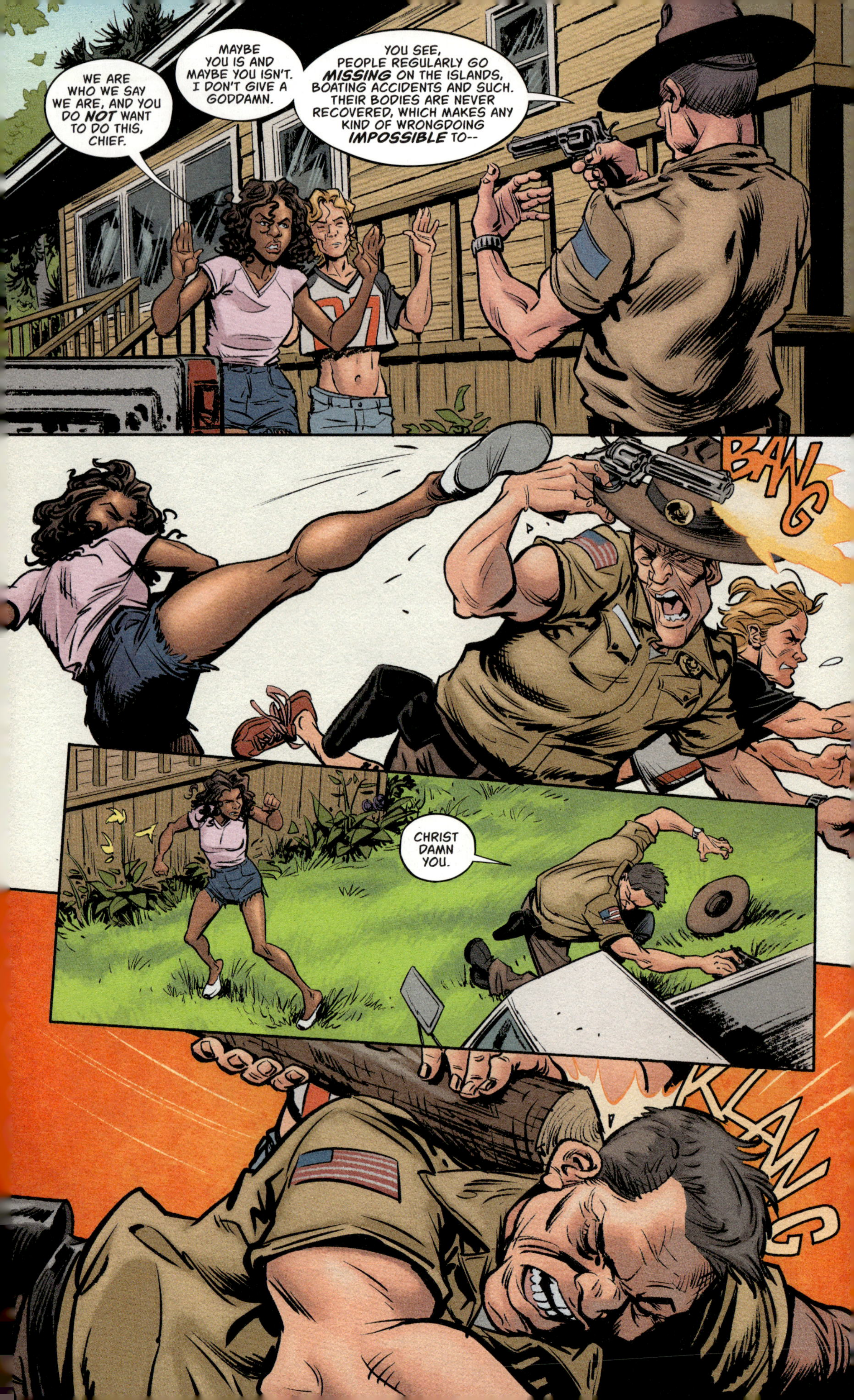
WE ARE WHO WE SAY WE ARE, AND YOU DO NOT WANT TO DO THIS, CHIEF.
MAYBE YOU IS AND MAYBE YOU ISN'T. I DON'T GIVE A GODDAMN.
YOU SEE, PEOPLE REGULARLY GO MISSING ON THE ISLANDS, BOATING ACCIDENTS AND SUCH. THEIR BODIES ARE NEVER RECOVERED, WHICH MAKES ANY KIND OF WRONGDOING IMPOSSIBLE TO--
BANG
CHRIST DAMN YOU.
KLANG

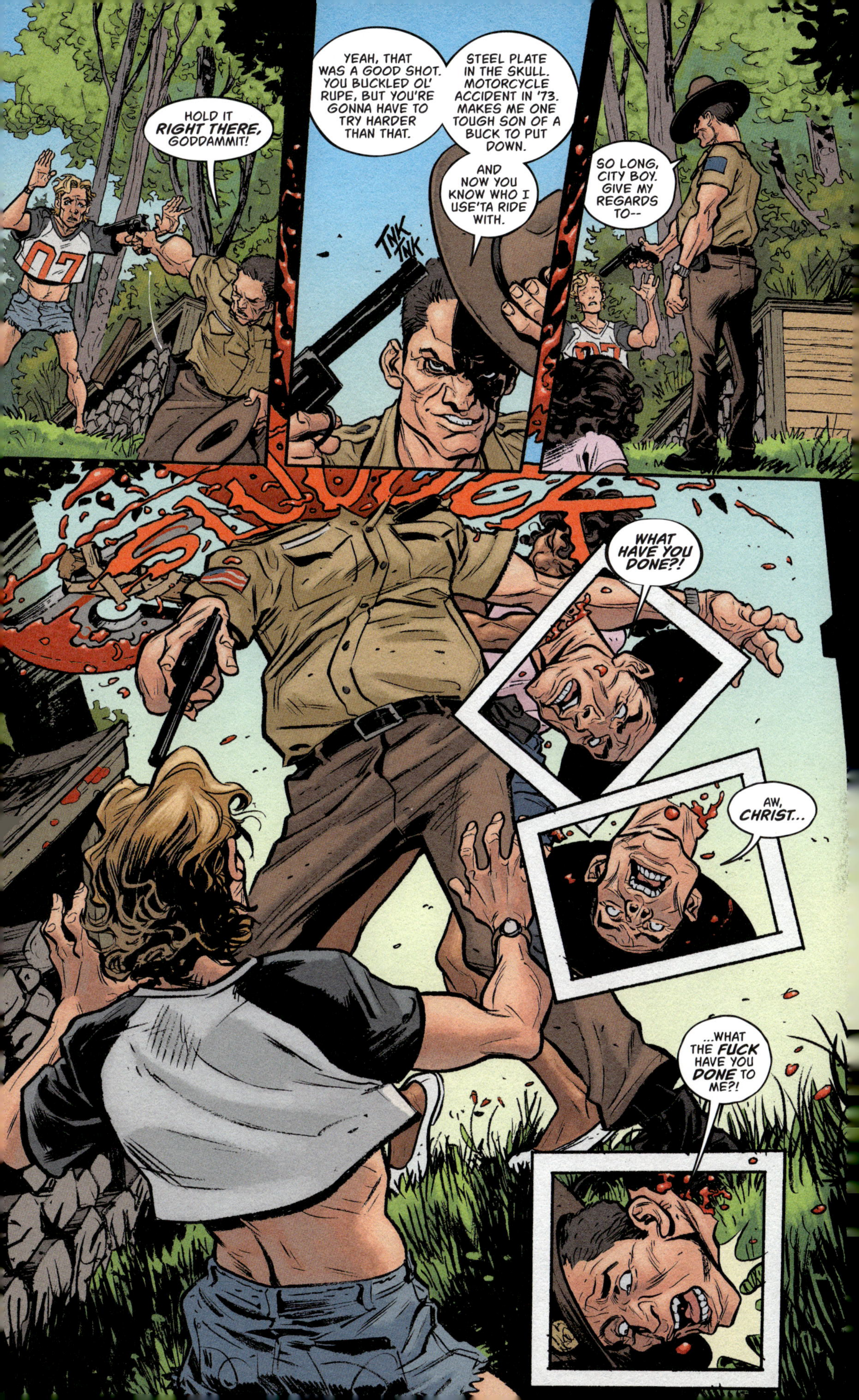

HOLD IT **RIGHT THERE,** GODDAMMIT!
YEAH, THAT WAS A *GOOD* SHOT. YOU BUCKLED OL' RUPE, BUT YOU'RE GONNA HAVE TO TRY HARDER THAN THAT.
STEEL PLATE IN THE SKULL. MOTORCYCLE ACCIDENT IN '73. MAKES ME ONE TOUGH SON OF A BUCK TO PUT DOWN.
AND NOW YOU KNOW WHO I USE'TA RIDE WITH.
TNK TNK
SO LONG, CITY BOY. GIVE MY REGARDS TO--
WHAT HAVE YOU DONE?!
AW, **CHRIST...**
...WHAT THE **FUCK** HAVE YOU **DONE** TO ME?!

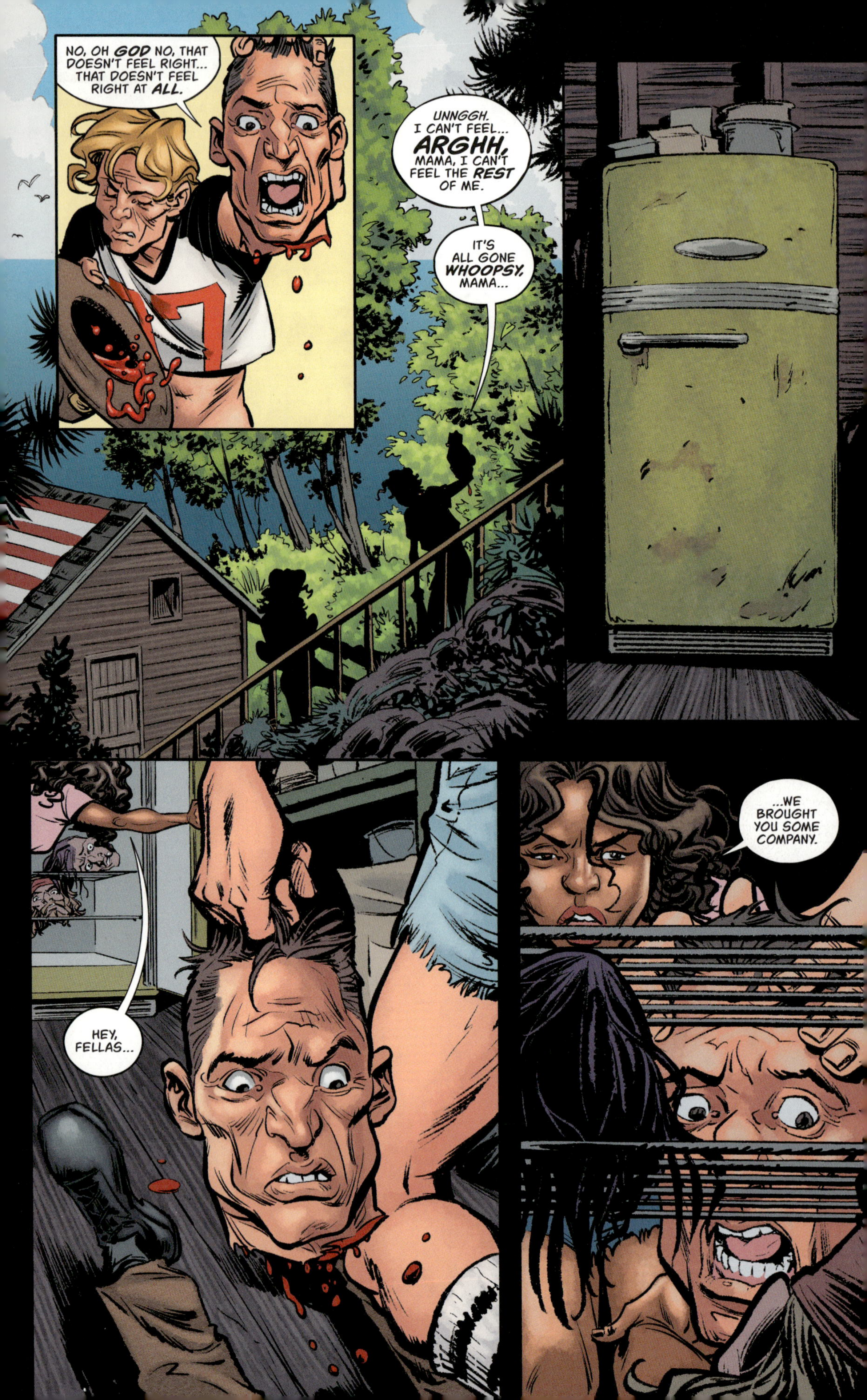
NO, OH GOD NO, THAT DOESN'T FEEL RIGHT... THAT DOESN'T FEEL RIGHT AT ALL.
UNNGGH. I CAN'T FEEL... ARGHH, MAMA, I CAN'T FEEL THE REST OF ME.
IT'S ALL GONE WHOOPSY, MAMA...
HEY, FELLAS...
...WE BROUGHT YOU SOME COMPANY.

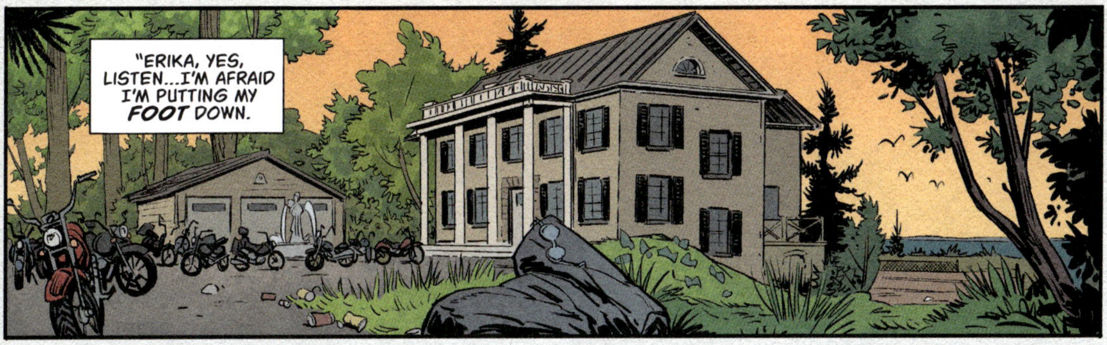
"ERIKA, YES, LISTEN...I'M AFRAID I'M PUTTING MY *FOOT* DOWN.

MAYOR WASHINGTON'S HOUSE. BRODY ISLAND.

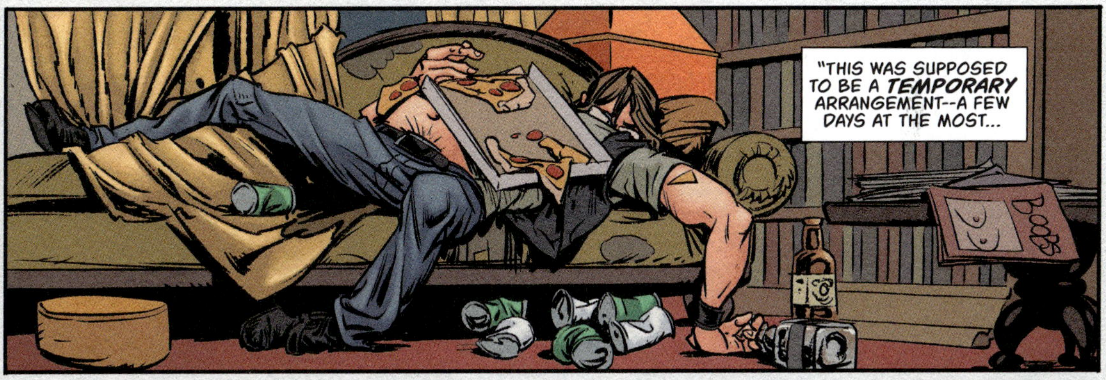
"THIS WAS SUPPOSED TO BE A *TEMPORARY* ARRANGEMENT--A FEW DAYS AT THE MOST...
BOOBS

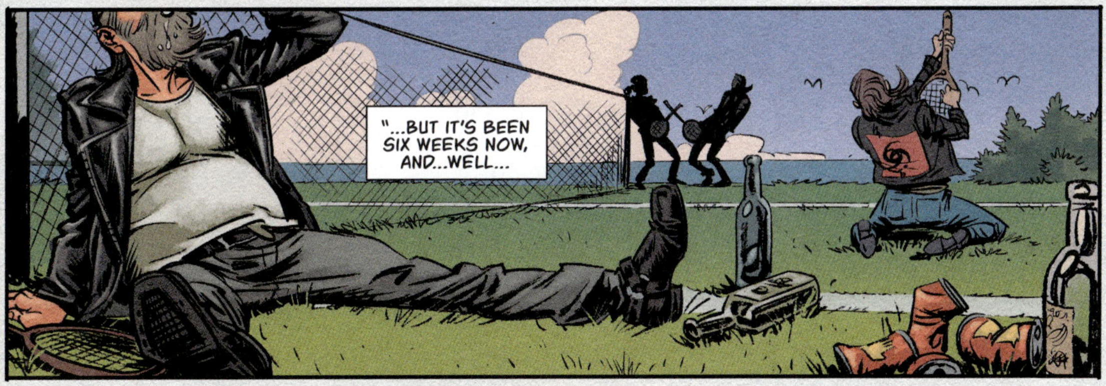
"...BUT IT'S BEEN SIX WEEKS NOW, AND...WELL...

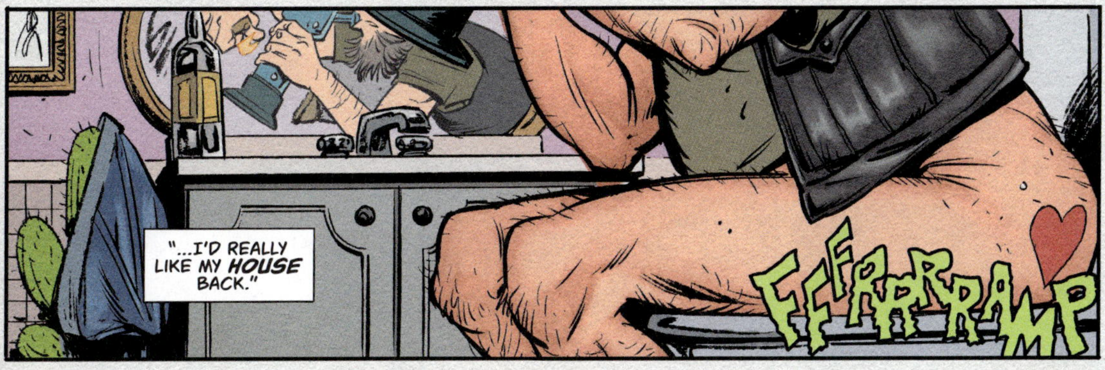
"...I'D REALLY LIKE MY *HOUSE* BACK."
FFFRRRRAMP

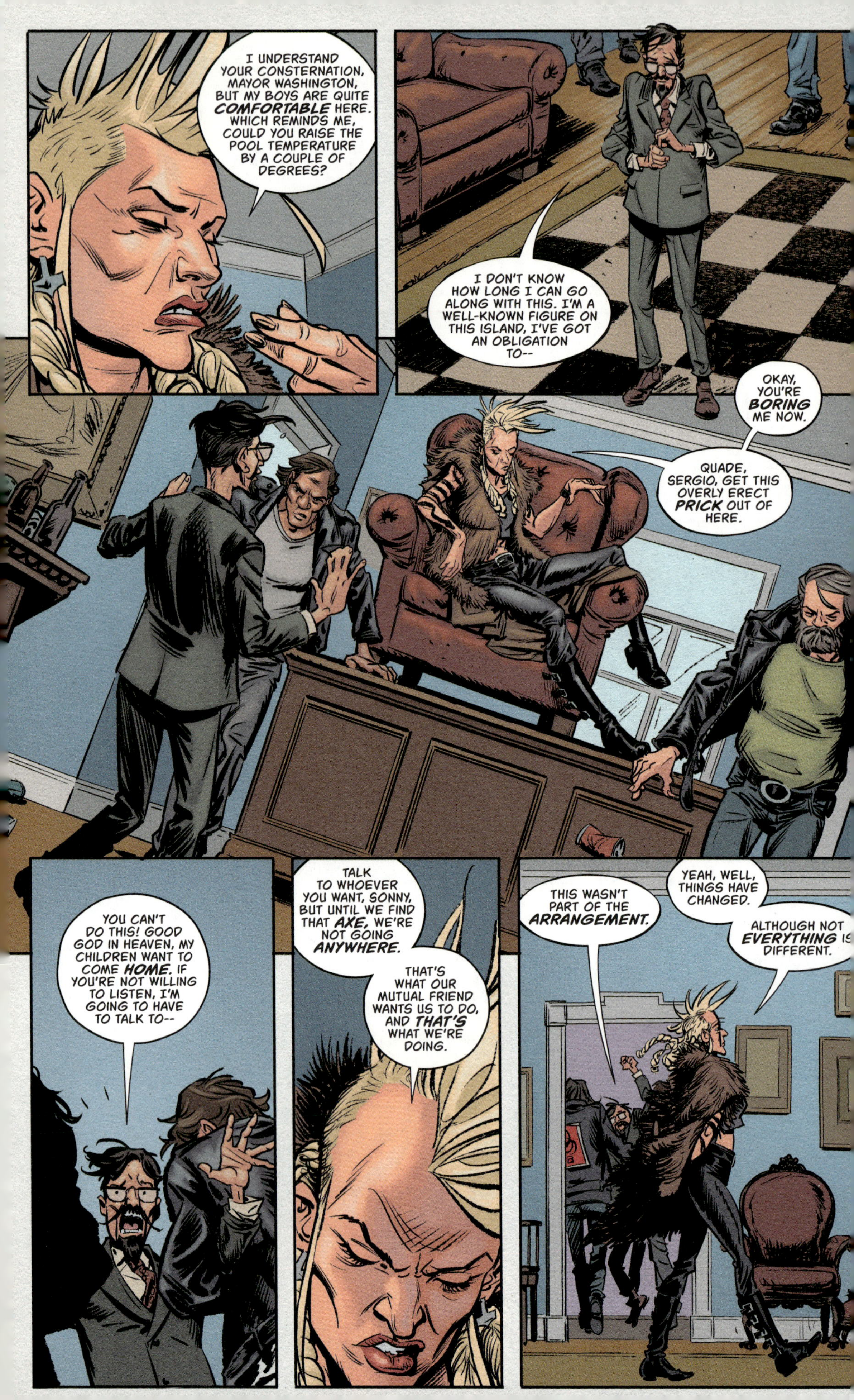
I UNDERSTAND YOUR CONSTERNATION, MAYOR WASHINGTON, BUT MY BOYS ARE QUITE COMFORTABLE HERE. WHICH REMINDS ME, COULD YOU RAISE THE POOL TEMPERATURE BY A COUPLE OF DEGREES?
I DON'T KNOW HOW LONG I CAN GO ALONG WITH THIS. I'M A WELL-KNOWN FIGURE ON THIS ISLAND, I'VE GOT AN OBLIGATION TO--
OKAY, YOU'RE BORING ME NOW.
QUADE, SERGIO, GET THIS OVERLY ERECT PRICK OUT OF HERE.
YOU CAN'T DO THIS! GOOD GOD IN HEAVEN, MY CHILDREN WANT TO COME HOME. IF YOU'RE NOT WILLING TO LISTEN, I'M GOING TO HAVE TO TALK TO--
TALK TO WHOEVER YOU WANT, SONNY, BUT UNTIL WE FIND THAT AXE, WE'RE NOT GOING ANYWHERE.
THAT'S WHAT OUR MUTUAL FRIEND WANTS US TO DO, AND THAT'S WHAT WE'RE DOING.
THIS WASN'T PART OF THE ARRANGEMENT.
YEAH, WELL, THINGS HAVE CHANGED.
ALTHOUGH NOT EVERYTHING IS DIFFERENT.

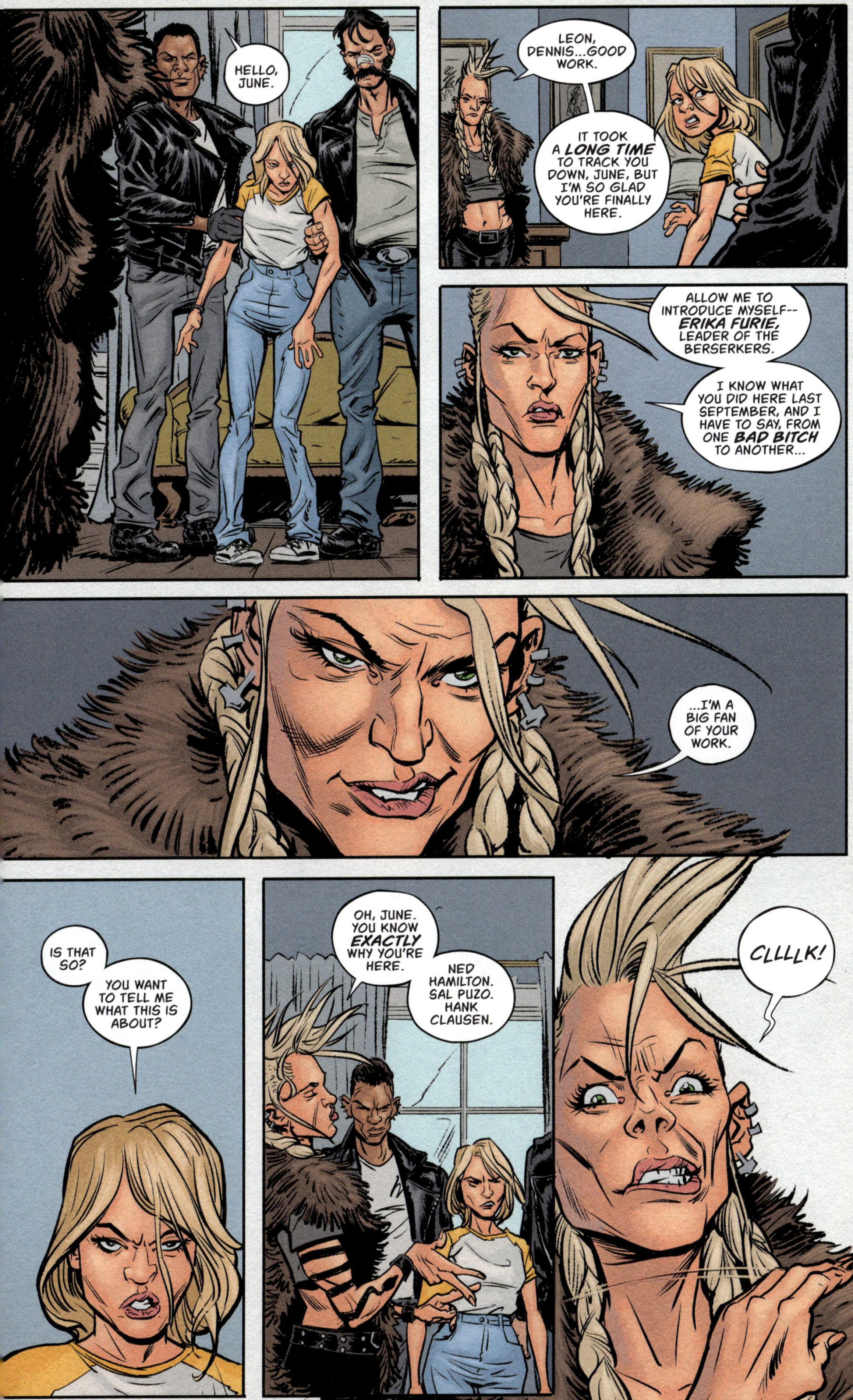
HELLO, JUNE.
LEON, DENNIS...GOOD WORK.
IT TOOK A **LONG TIME** TO TRACK YOU DOWN, JUNE, BUT I'M SO GLAD YOU'RE FINALLY HERE.
ALLOW ME TO INTRODUCE MYSELF-- **ERIKA FURIE,** LEADER OF THE BERSERKERS.
I KNOW WHAT YOU DID HERE LAST SEPTEMBER, AND I HAVE TO SAY, FROM ONE **BAD BITCH** TO ANOTHER...
...I'M A BIG FAN OF YOUR WORK.
IS THAT SO?
YOU WANT TO TELL ME WHAT THIS IS ABOUT?
OH, JUNE. YOU KNOW **EXACTLY** WHY YOU'RE HERE.
NED HAMILTON. SAL PUZO. HANK CLAUSEN.
CLLLLK!

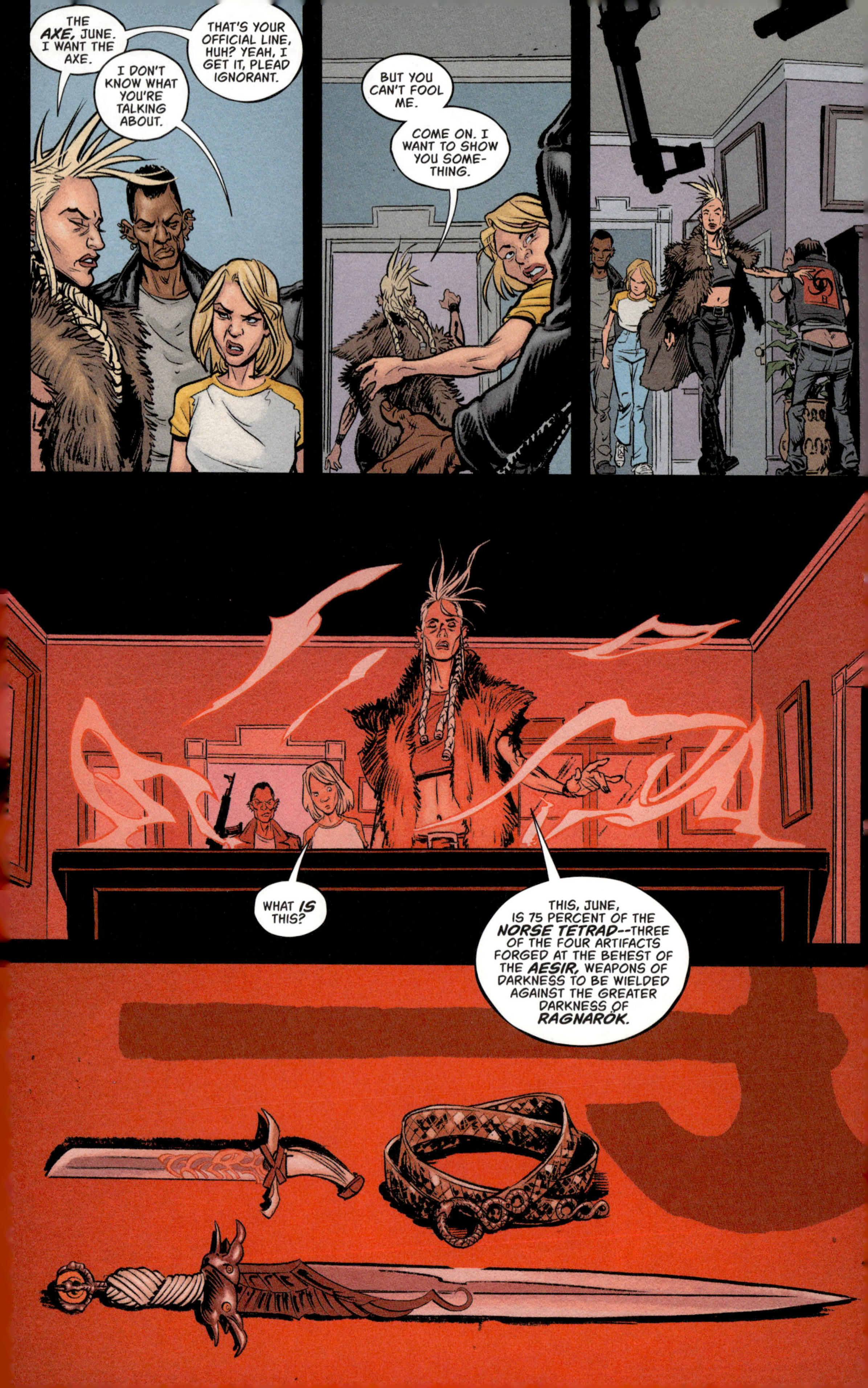
THE AXE, JUNE. I WANT THE AXE.
I DON'T KNOW WHAT YOU'RE TALKING ABOUT.
THAT'S YOUR OFFICIAL LINE, HUH? YEAH, I GET IT, PLEAD IGNORANT.
BUT YOU CAN'T FOOL ME.
COME ON. I WANT TO SHOW YOU SOME-THING.
WHAT IS THIS?
THIS, JUNE, IS 75 PERCENT OF THE NORSE TETRAD--THREE OF THE FOUR ARTIFACTS FORGED AT THE BEHEST OF THE AESIR, WEAPONS OF DARKNESS TO BE WIELDED AGAINST THE GREATER DARKNESS OF RAGNARÖK.

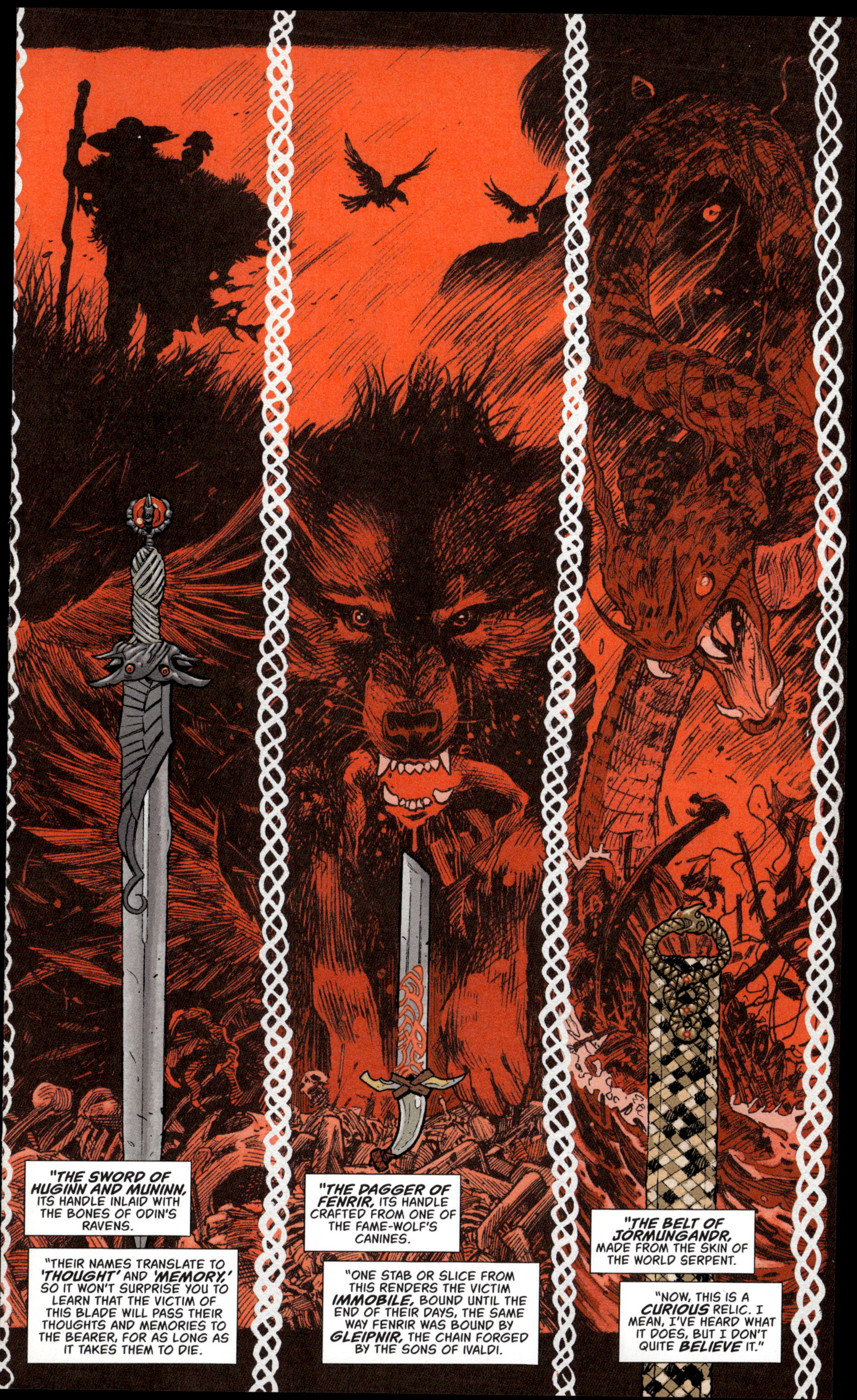
"THE SWORD OF HUGINN AND MUNINN, ITS HANDLE INLAID WITH THE BONES OF ODIN'S RAVENS.
"THEIR NAMES TRANSLATE TO 'THOUGHT' AND 'MEMORY,' SO IT WON'T SURPRISE YOU TO LEARN THAT THE VICTIM OF THIS BLADE WILL PASS THEIR THOUGHTS AND MEMORIES TO THE BEARER, FOR AS LONG AS IT TAKES THEM TO DIE.
"THE DAGGER OF FENRIR, ITS HANDLE CRAFTED FROM ONE OF THE FAME-WOLF'S CANINES.
"ONE STAB OR SLICE FROM THIS RENDERS THE VICTIM IMMOBILE, BOUND UNTIL THE END OF THEIR DAYS, THE SAME WAY FENRIR WAS BOUND BY GLEIPNIR, THE CHAIN FORGED BY THE SONS OF IVALDI.
"THE BELT OF JORMUNGANDR, MADE FROM THE SKIN OF THE WORLD SERPENT.
"NOW, THIS IS A CURIOUS RELIC. I MEAN, I'VE HEARD WHAT IT DOES, BUT I DON'T QUITE BELIEVE IT."

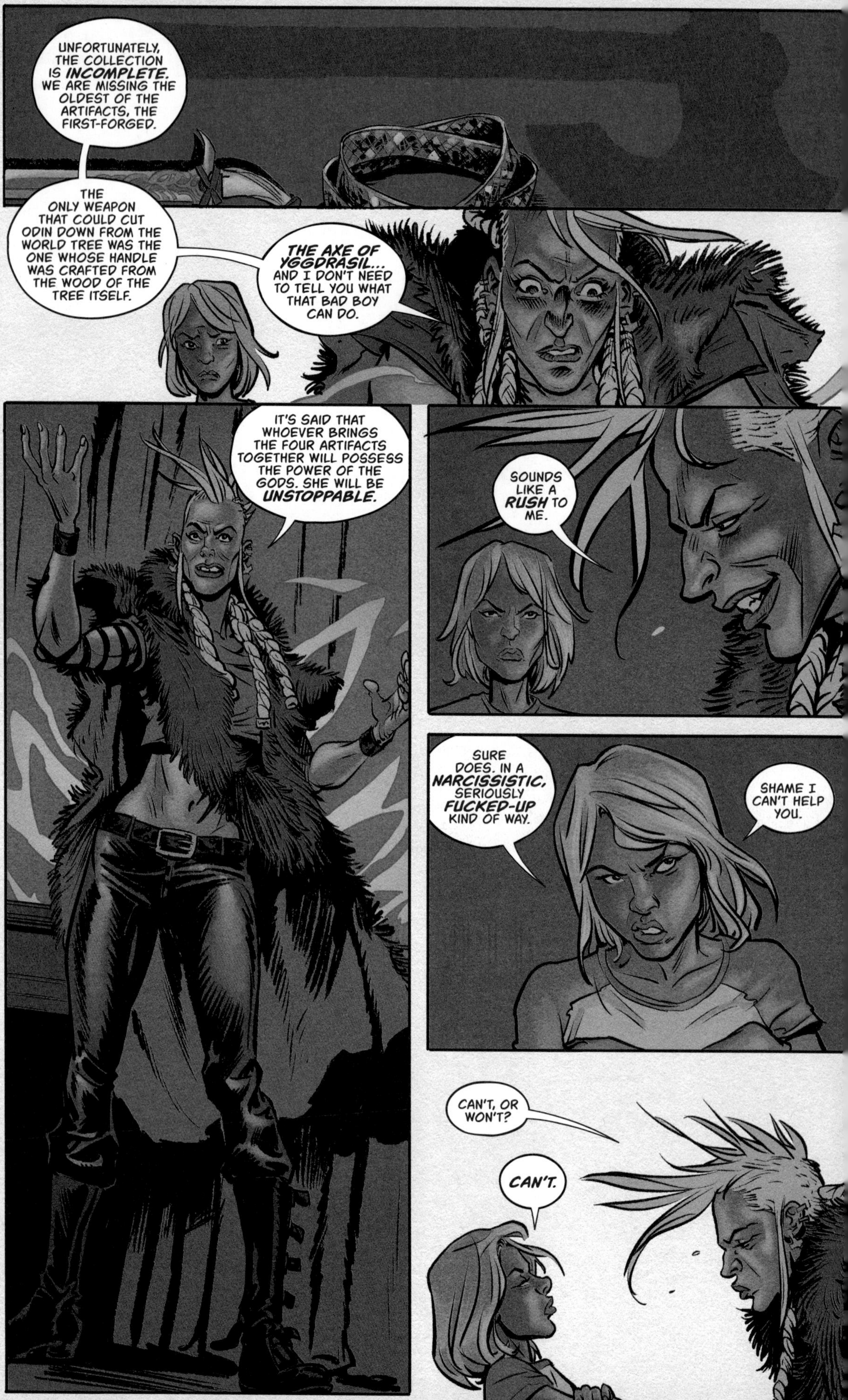
UNFORTUNATELY, THE COLLECTION IS INCOMPLETE. WE ARE MISSING THE OLDEST OF THE ARTIFACTS, THE FIRST-FORGED.
THE ONLY WEAPON THAT COULD CUT ODIN DOWN FROM THE WORLD TREE WAS THE ONE WHOSE HANDLE WAS CRAFTED FROM THE WOOD OF THE TREE ITSELF.
THE AXE OF YGGDRASIL... AND I DON'T NEED TO TELL YOU WHAT THAT BAD BOY CAN DO.
IT'S SAID THAT WHOEVER BRINGS THE FOUR ARTIFACTS TOGETHER WILL POSSESS THE POWER OF THE GODS. SHE WILL BE UNSTOPPABLE.
SOUNDS LIKE A RUSH TO ME.
SURE DOES. IN A NARCISSISTIC, SERIOUSLY FUCKED-UP KIND OF WAY.
SHAME I CAN'T HELP YOU.
CAN'T, OR WON'T?
CAN'T.

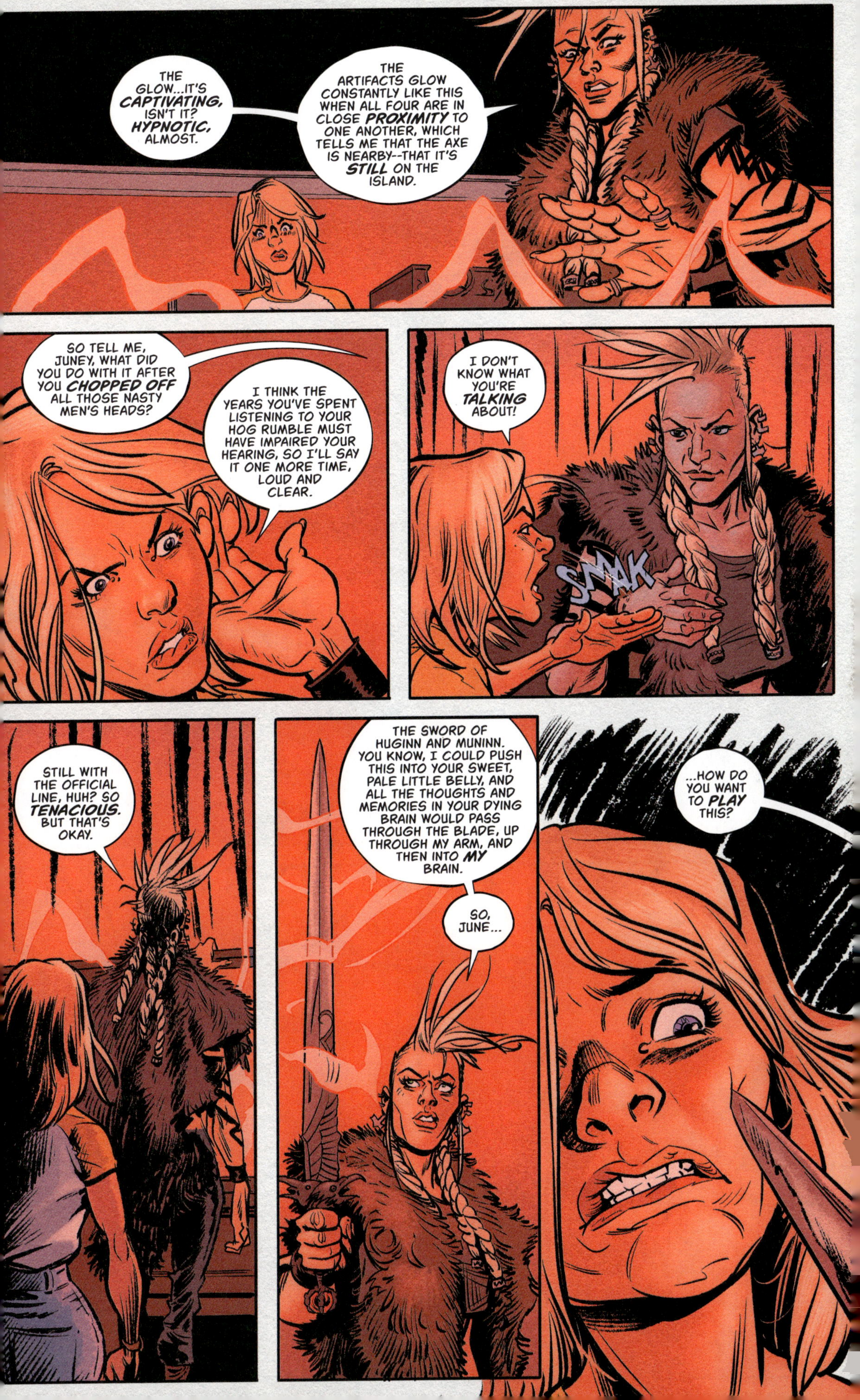
THE GLOW...IT'S CAPTIVATING, ISN'T IT? HYPNOTIC, ALMOST.
THE ARTIFACTS GLOW CONSTANTLY LIKE THIS WHEN ALL FOUR ARE IN CLOSE PROXIMITY TO ONE ANOTHER, WHICH TELLS ME THAT THE AXE IS NEARBY--THAT IT'S STILL ON THE ISLAND.
SO TELL ME, JUNEY, WHAT DID YOU DO WITH IT AFTER YOU CHOPPED OFF ALL THOSE NASTY MEN'S HEADS?
I THINK THE YEARS YOU'VE SPENT LISTENING TO YOUR HOG RUMBLE MUST HAVE IMPAIRED YOUR HEARING, SO I'LL SAY IT ONE MORE TIME, LOUD AND CLEAR.
I DON'T KNOW WHAT YOU'RE TALKING ABOUT!
SMAK
STILL WITH THE OFFICIAL LINE, HUH? SO TENACIOUS. BUT THAT'S OKAY.
THE SWORD OF HUGINN AND MUNINN. YOU KNOW, I COULD PUSH THIS INTO YOUR SWEET, PALE LITTLE BELLY, AND ALL THE THOUGHTS AND MEMORIES IN YOUR DYING BRAIN WOULD PASS THROUGH THE BLADE, UP THROUGH MY ARM, AND THEN INTO MY BRAIN.
SO, JUNE...
...HOW DO YOU WANT TO PLAY THIS?

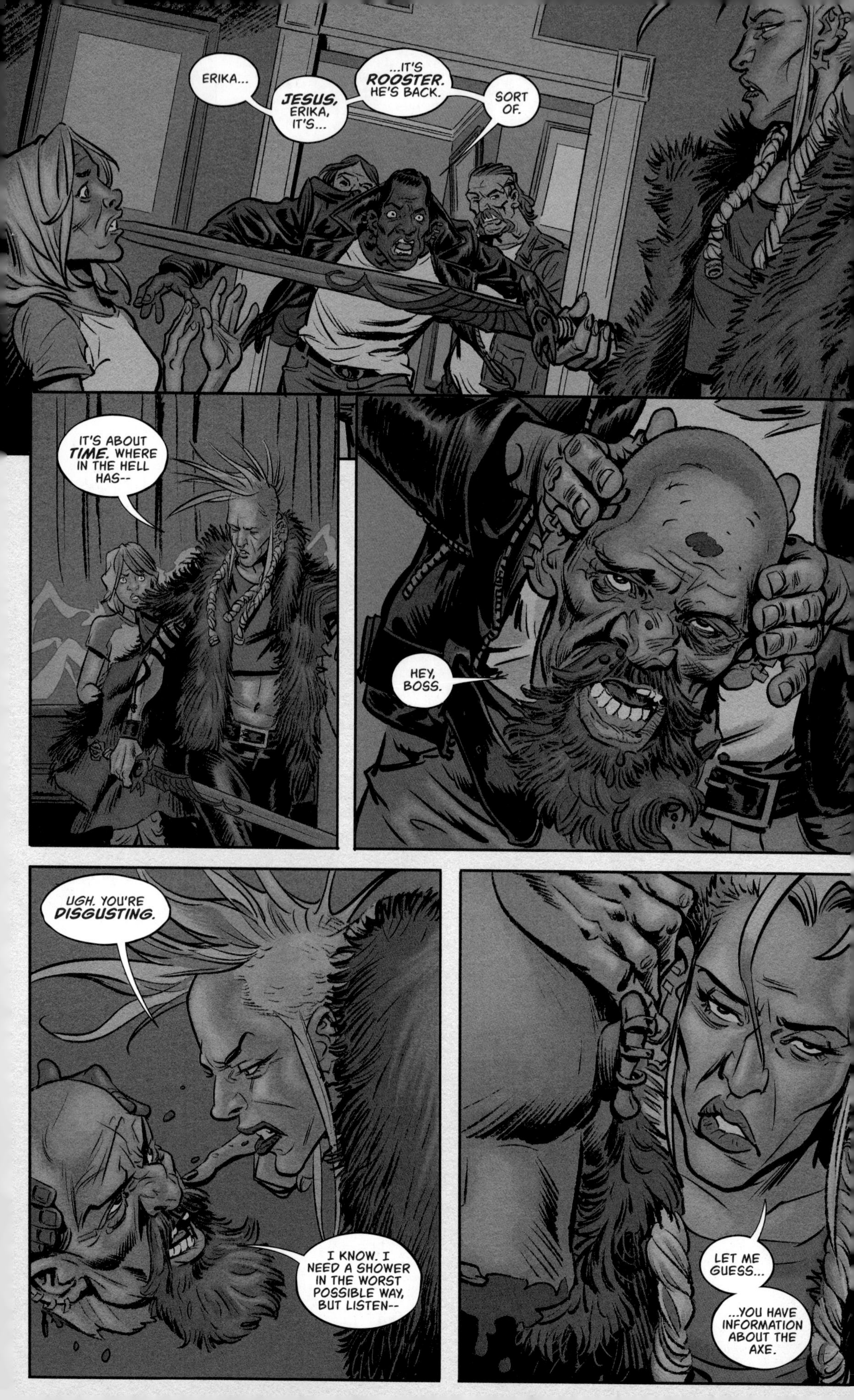

ERIKA...
JESUS, ERIKA, IT'S...
...IT'S ROOSTER. HE'S BACK.
SORT OF.
IT'S ABOUT TIME. WHERE IN THE HELL HAS--
HEY, BOSS.
UGH. YOU'RE DISGUSTING.
I KNOW. I NEED A SHOWER IN THE WORST POSSIBLE WAY, BUT LISTEN--
LET ME GUESS...
...YOU HAVE INFORMATION ABOUT THE AXE.

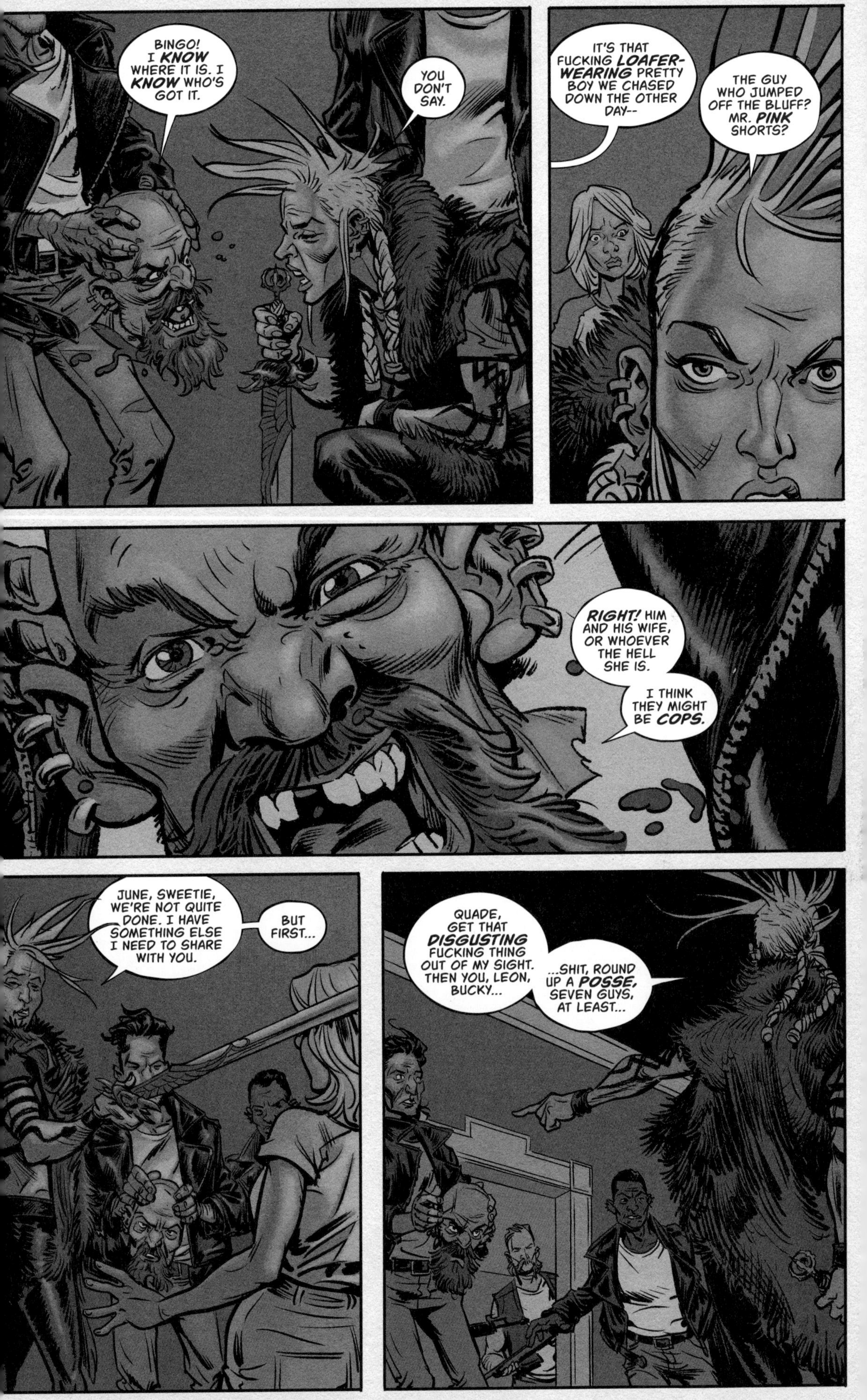
BINGO! I KNOW WHERE IT IS. I KNOW WHO'S GOT IT.
YOU DON'T SAY.
IT'S THAT FUCKING LOAFER-WEARING PRETTY BOY WE CHASED DOWN THE OTHER DAY--
THE GUY WHO JUMPED OFF THE BLUFF? MR. PINK SHORTS?
RIGHT! HIM AND HIS WIFE, OR WHOEVER THE HELL SHE IS.
I THINK THEY MIGHT BE COPS.
JUNE, SWEETIE, WE'RE NOT QUITE DONE. I HAVE SOMETHING ELSE I NEED TO SHARE WITH YOU.
BUT FIRST...
QUADE, GET THAT DISGUSTING FUCKING THING OUT OF MY SIGHT. THEN YOU, LEON, BUCKY...
...SHIT, ROUND UP A POSSE, SEVEN GUYS, AT LEAST...

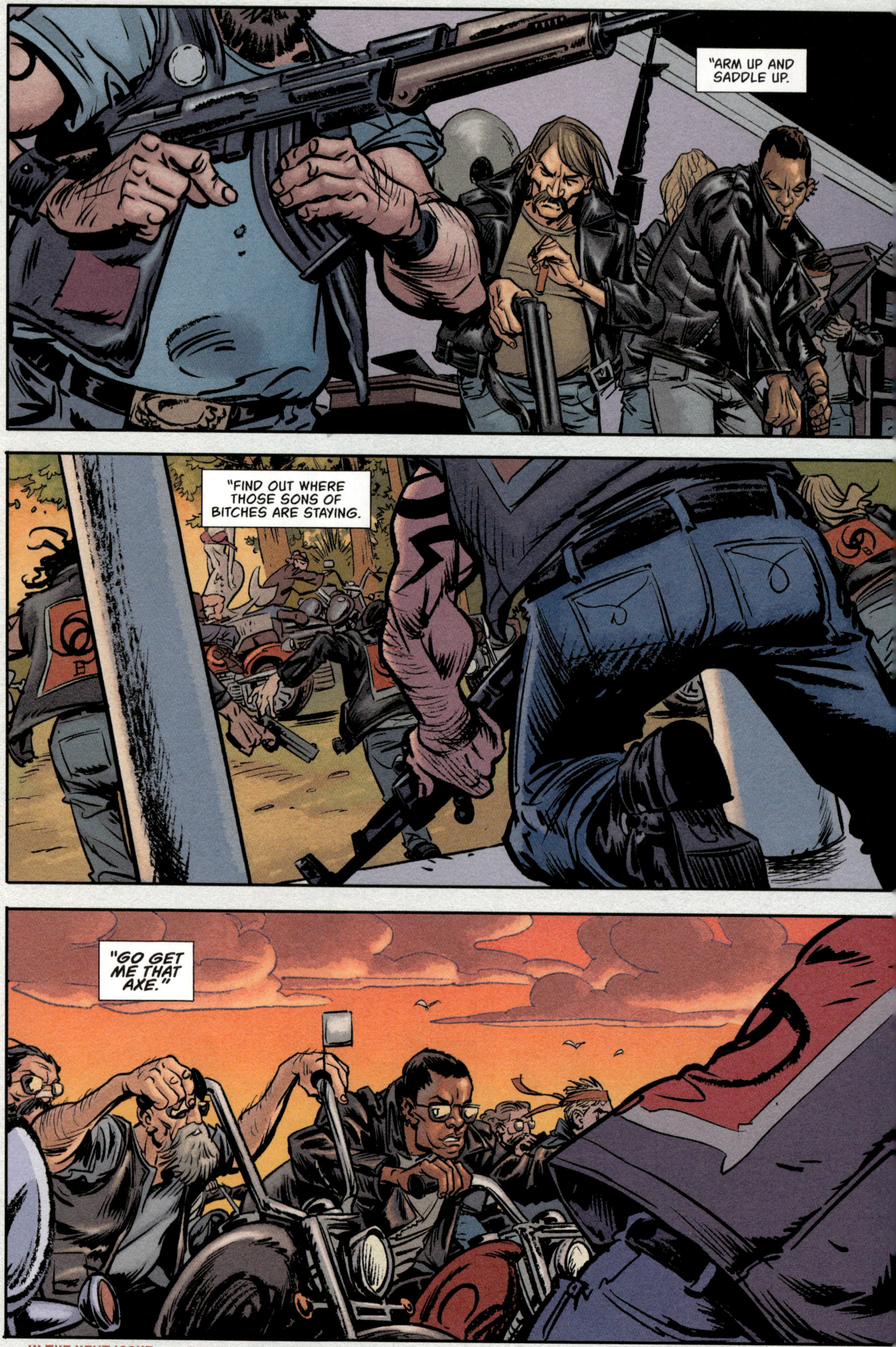
"ARM UP AND SADDLE UP.
"FIND OUT WHERE THOSE SONS OF BITCHES ARE STAYING.
"GO GET ME THAT AXE."

IN THE NEXT ISSUE...

WE'RE GONNA NEED A BIGGER REFRIGERATOR.

REFRIGERATOR FULL OF HEADS

Written by **RIO YOUERS** Pencils by **TOM FOWLER**

nks by **CRAIG TAILLEFER** and **TOM FOWLER** Colored by **BILL CRABTREE**

Lettered by **ANDWORLD DESIGN** Cover by **MARCIO TAKARA**

Variant cover by **MARIA WOLF** and **MIKE SPICER**

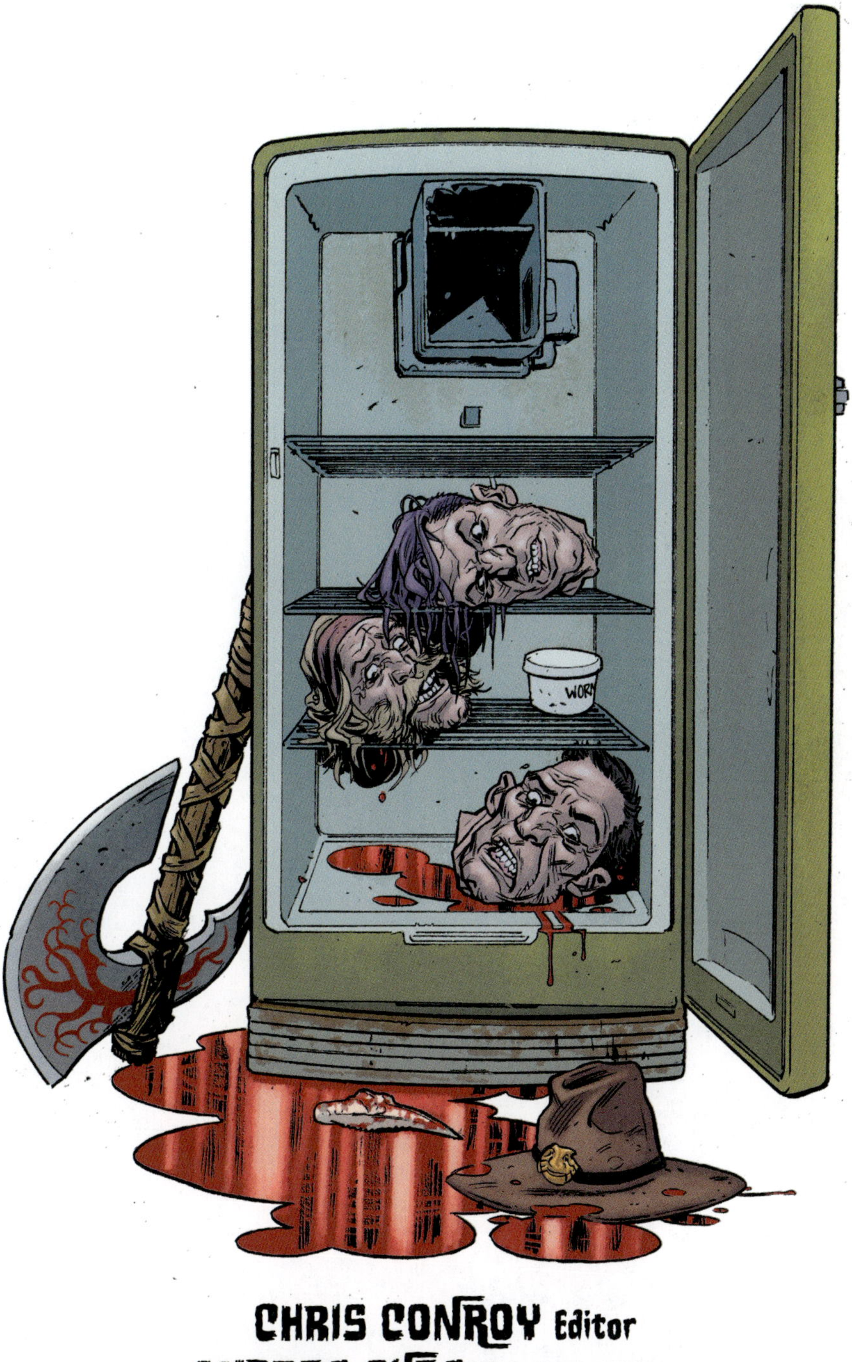

CHRIS CONROY Editor

ANDREA SHEA Associate Editor

BASKETFUL OF HEADS created by **JOE HILL** with art by **LEOMACS**

REFRIGERATOR FULL OF HEADS curated for **HILL HOUSE COMICS** by **JOE HILL**

"THE AXE OF YGGDRASIL... I DON'T NEED TO TELL YOU WHAT THAT BAD BOY CAN DO."

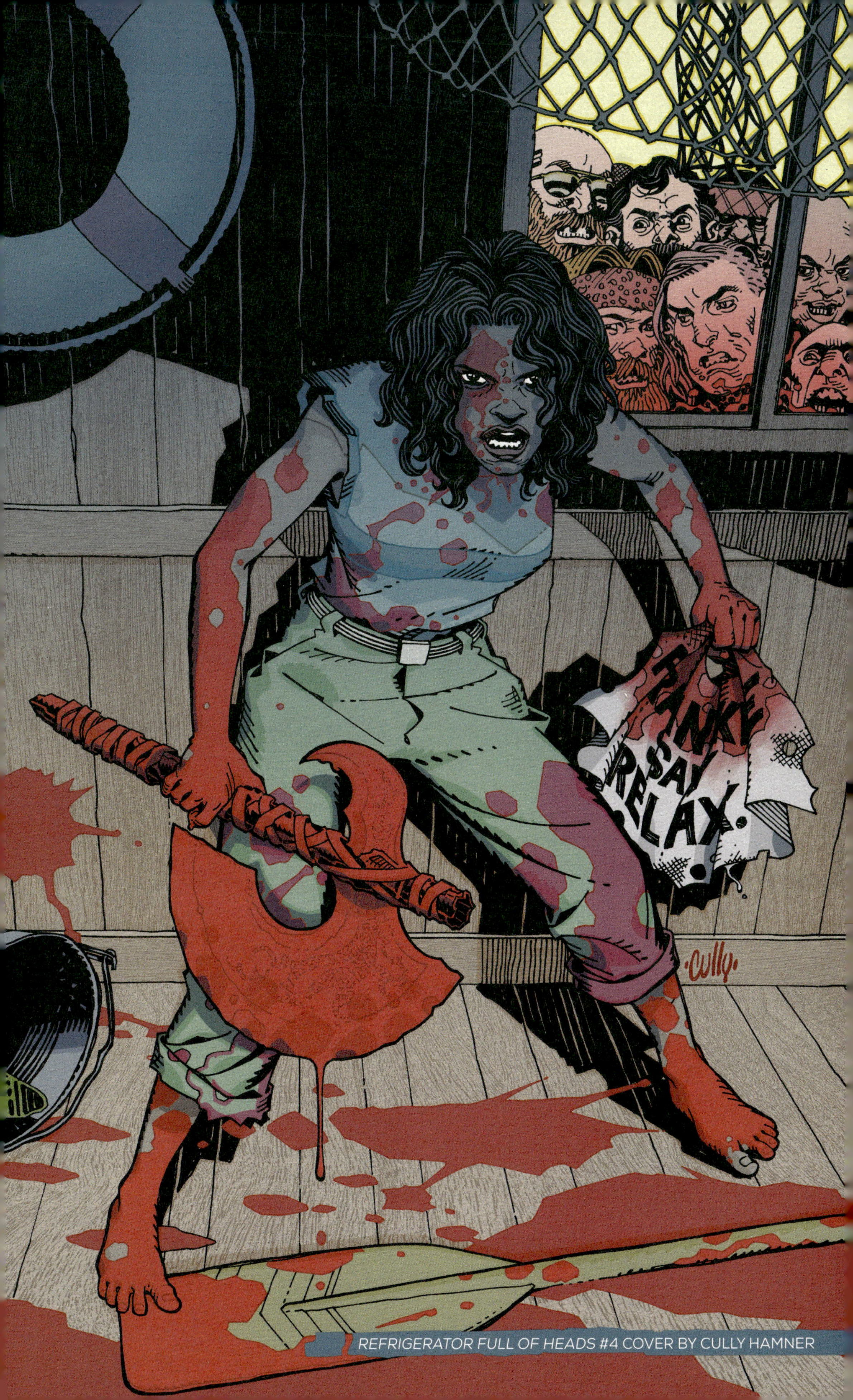
SAY
RELAX
Cully

REFRIGERATOR FULL OF HEADS #4 COVER BY CULLY HAMNER

REFRIGERATOR FULL OF HEADS #4 VARIANT COVER BY BRIAN LEVEL & LEE LOUGHRIDGE

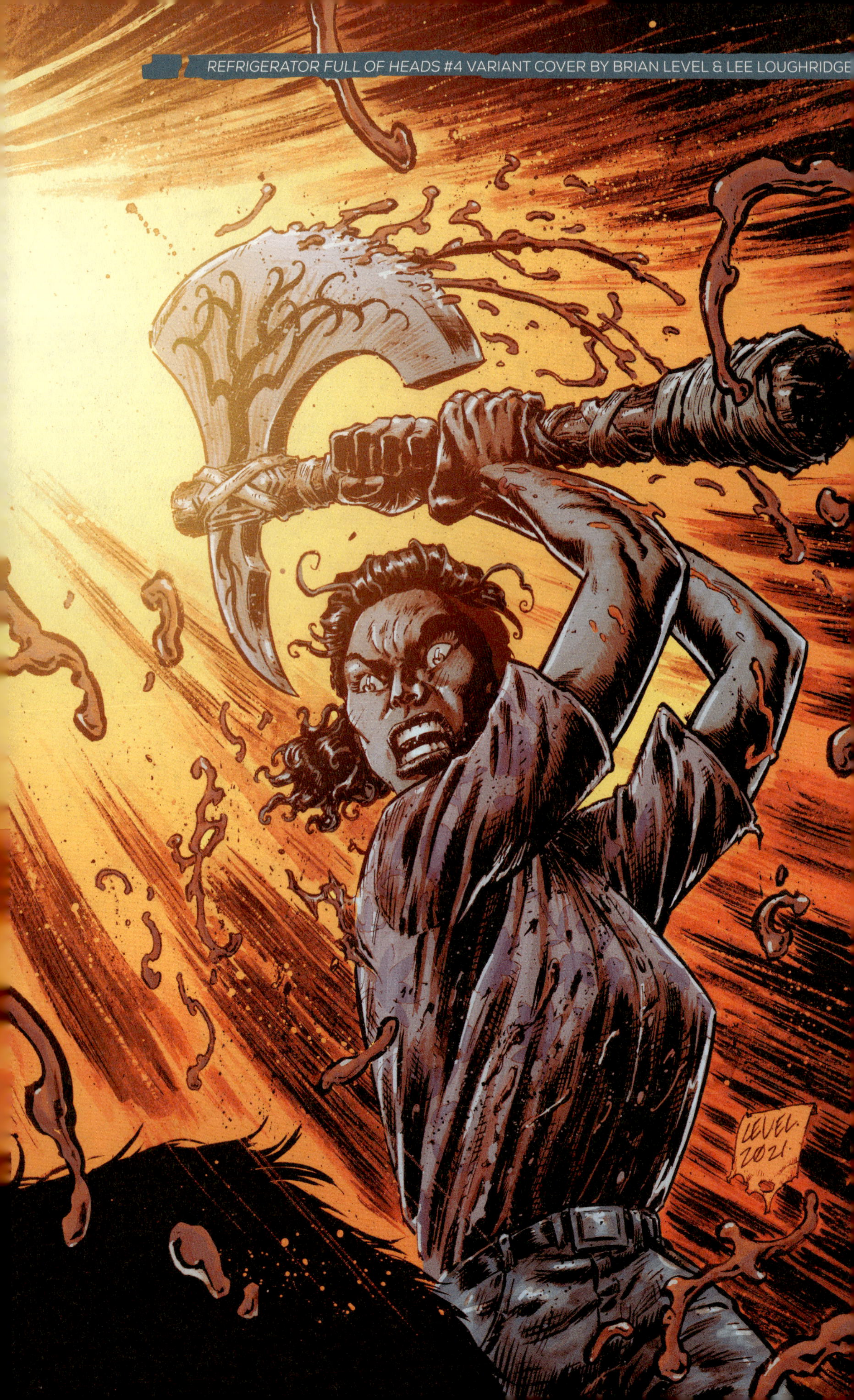
LEVEL
2021

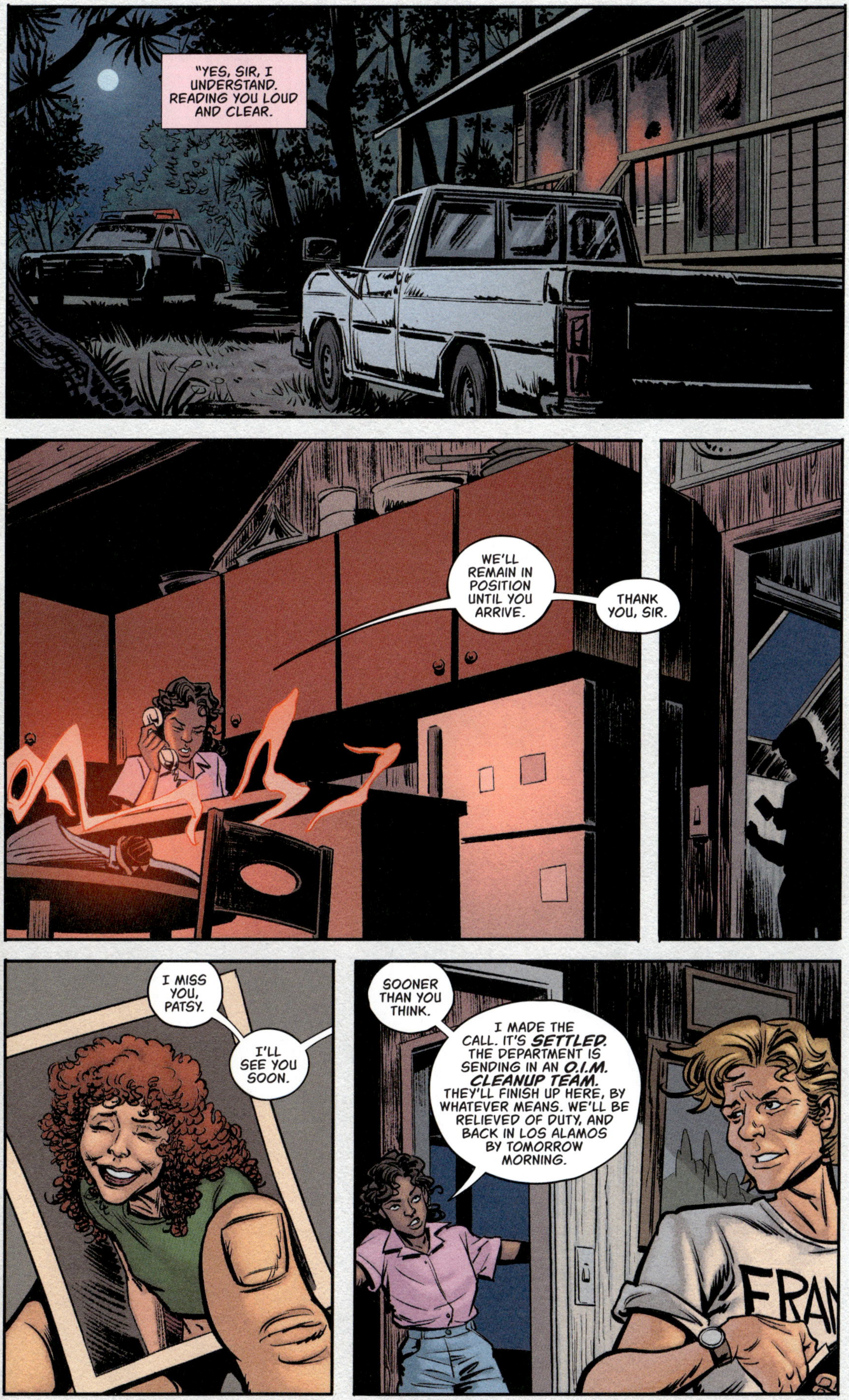
"YES, SIR, I UNDERSTAND. READING YOU LOUD AND CLEAR.
WE'LL REMAIN IN POSITION UNTIL YOU ARRIVE.
THANK YOU, SIR.
I MISS YOU, PATSY.
I'LL SEE YOU SOON.
SOONER THAN YOU THINK.
I MADE THE CALL. IT'S SETTLED. THE DEPARTMENT IS SENDING IN AN O.I.M. CLEANUP TEAM. THEY'LL FINISH UP HERE, BY WHATEVER MEANS. WE'LL BE RELIEVED OF DUTY, AND BACK IN LOS ALAMOS BY TOMORROW MORNING.

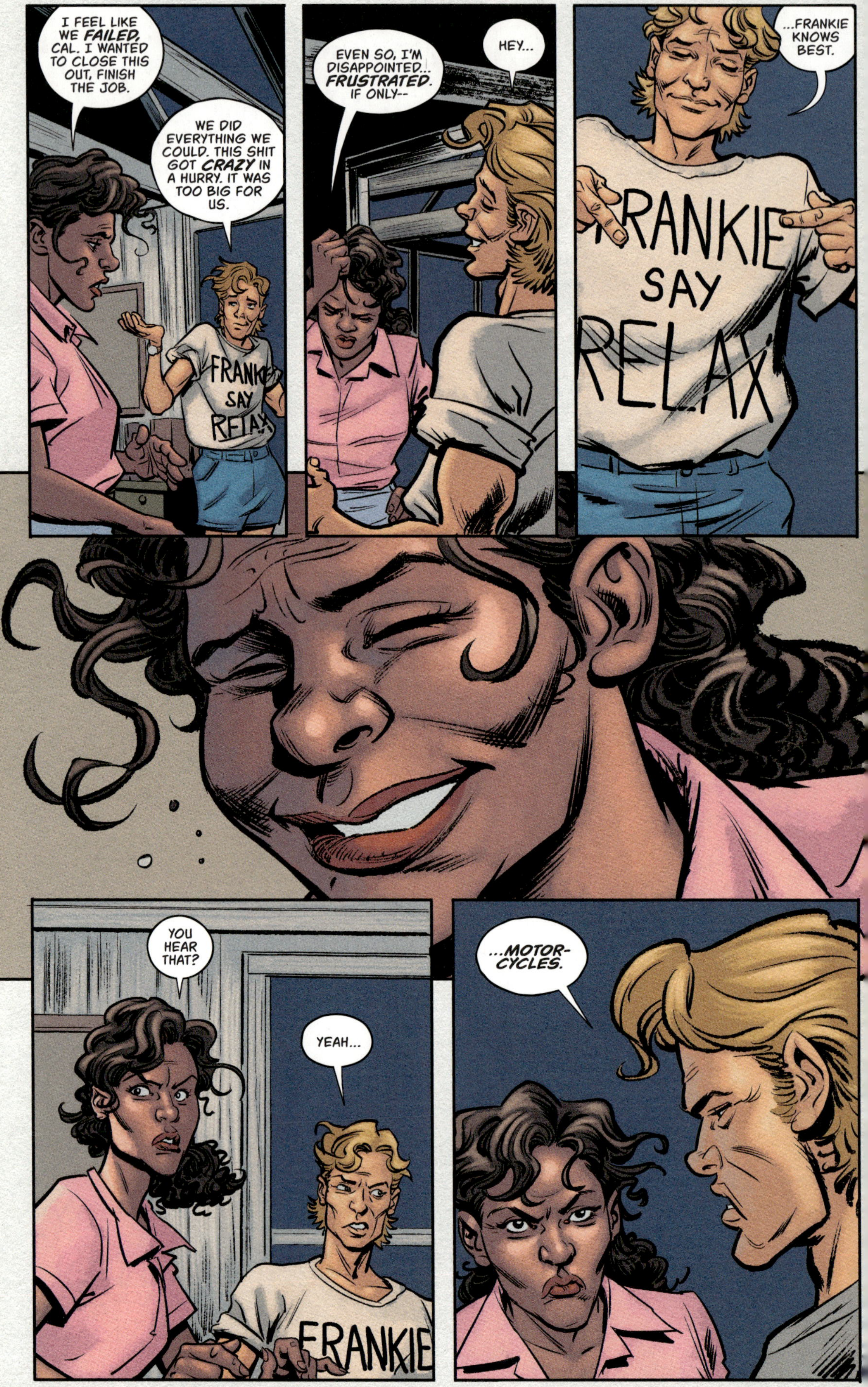
I FEEL LIKE WE ***FAILED***, CAL. I WANTED TO CLOSE THIS OUT, FINISH THE JOB.
WE DID EVERYTHING WE COULD. THIS SHIT GOT ***CRAZY*** IN A HURRY. IT WAS TOO BIG FOR US.
FRANKIE SAY RELAX
EVEN SO, I'M DISAPPOINTED... ***FRUSTRATED***. IF ONLY--
HEY...
...FRANKIE KNOWS BEST.
FRANKIE SAY RELAX
YOU HEAR THAT?
YEAH...
FRANKIE
...MOTOR-CYCLES.

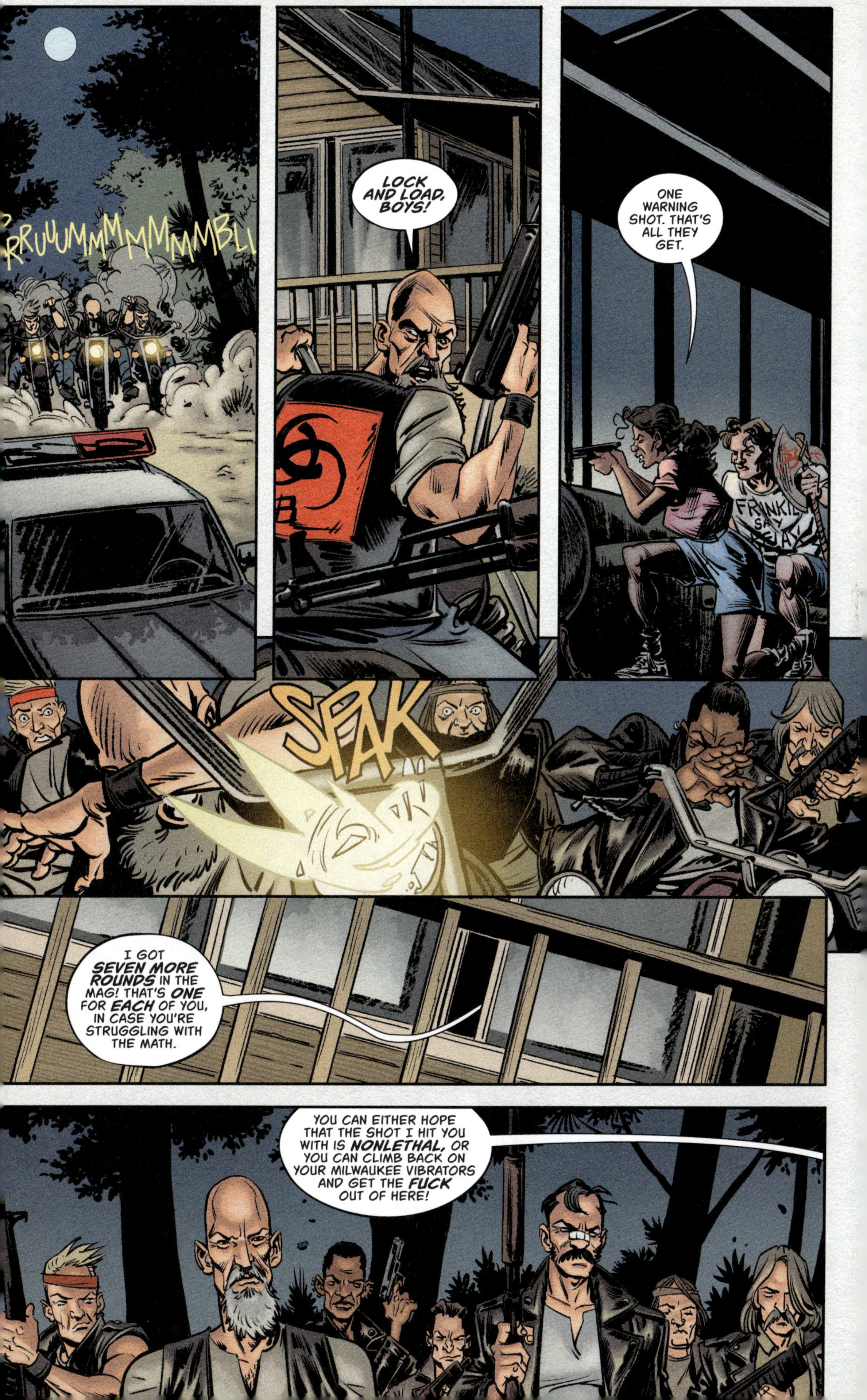
RRUUUMMMMMMMMBLI
LOCK AND LOAD, BOYS!
ONE WARNING SHOT. THAT'S ALL THEY GET.
SPAK
I GOT SEVEN MORE ROUNDS IN THE MAG! THAT'S ONE FOR EACH OF YOU, IN CASE YOU'RE STRUGGLING WITH THE MATH.
YOU CAN EITHER HOPE THAT THE SHOT I HIT YOU WITH IS NONLETHAL, OR YOU CAN CLIMB BACK ON YOUR MILWAUKEE VIBRATORS AND GET THE FUCK OUT OF HERE!

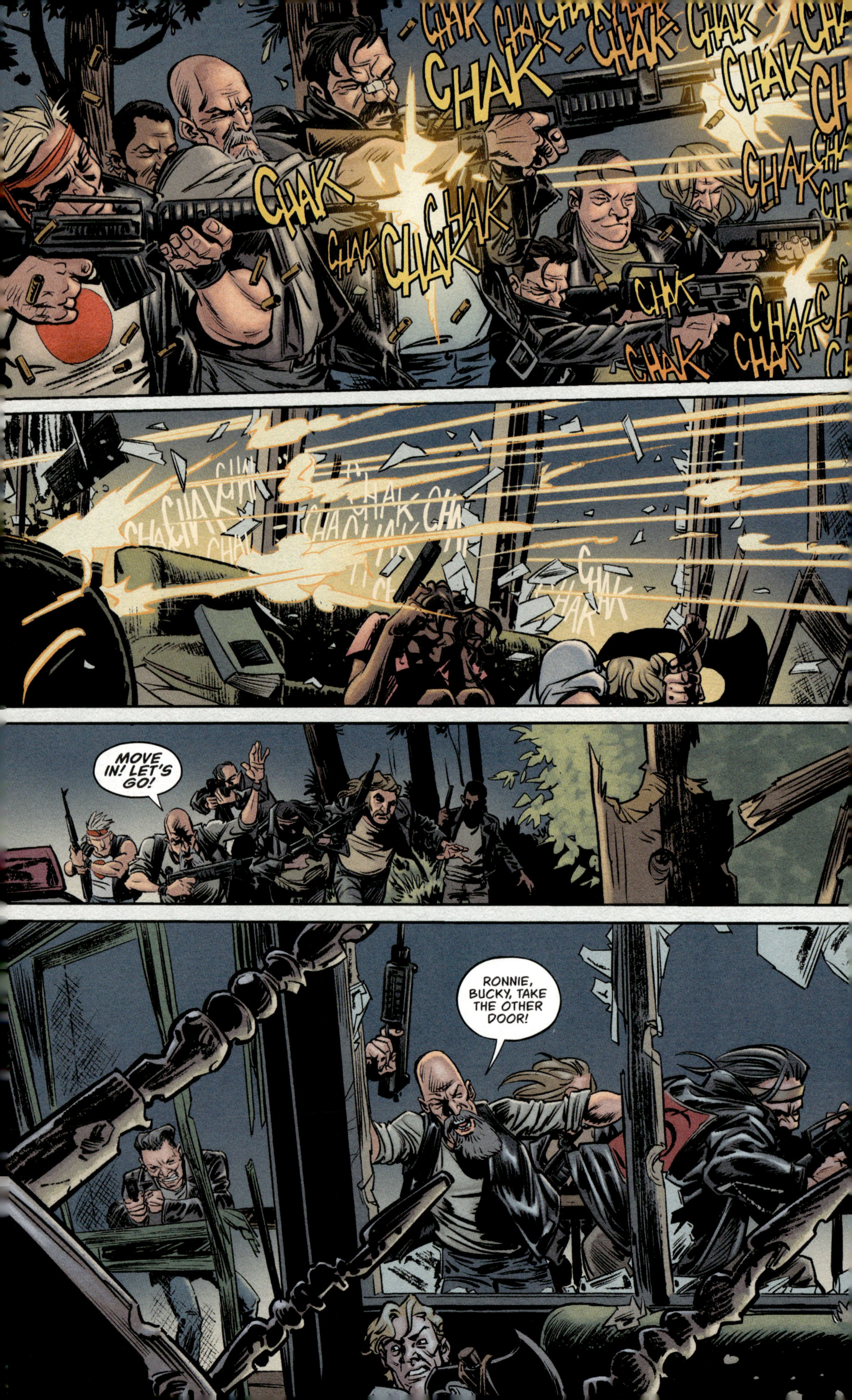
CHAK CHAK CHAK
CHAK
CHAK
CHAK
CHAK CHAK CHAK
CHAK
CHAK
CHAK CHAK
MOVE IN! LET'S GO!
RONNIE, BUCKY, TAKE THE OTHER DOOR!

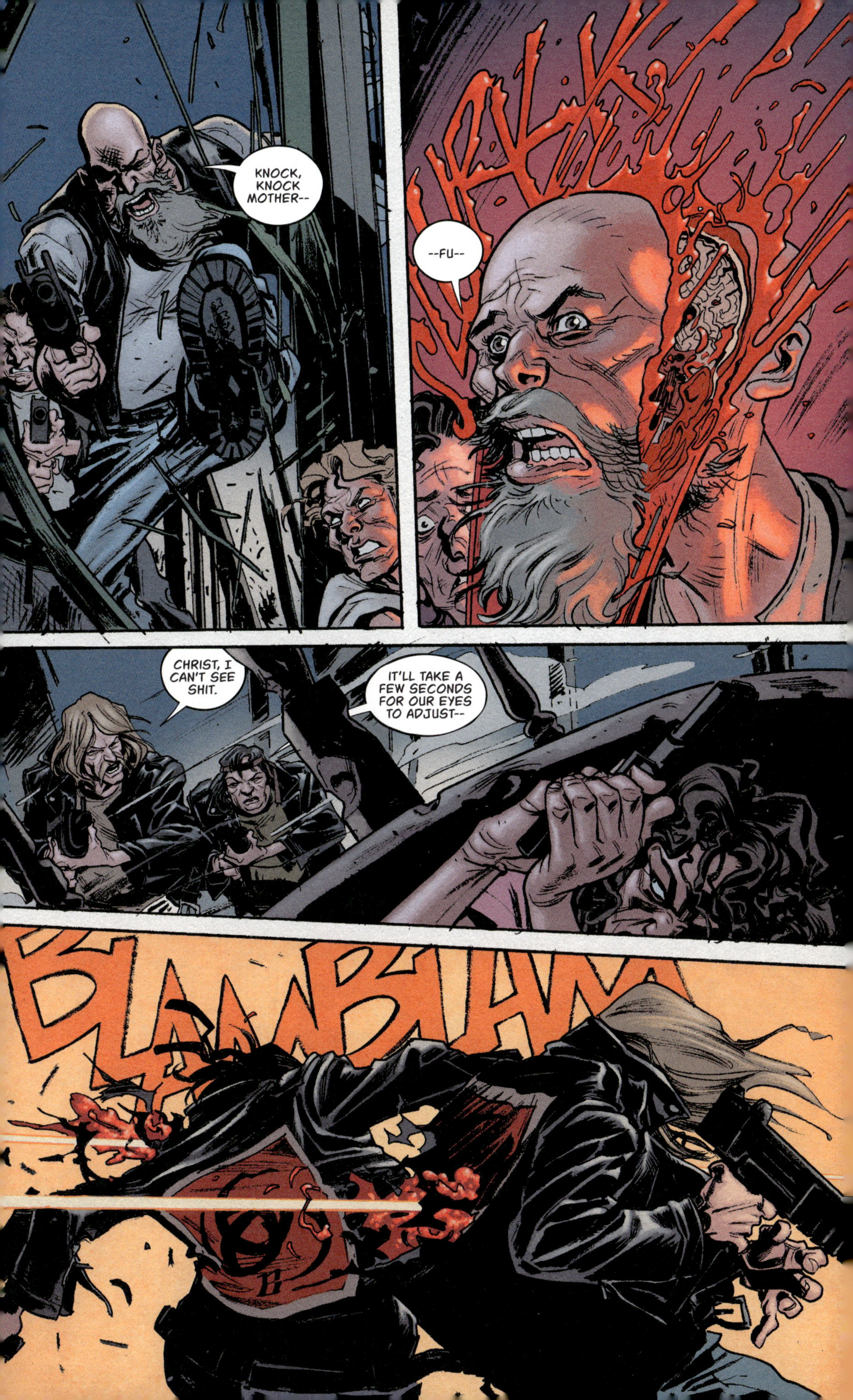
KNOCK, KNOCK MOTHER--
--FU--
CHRIST, I CAN'T SEE SHIT.
IT'LL TAKE A FEW SECONDS FOR OUR EYES TO ADJUST--

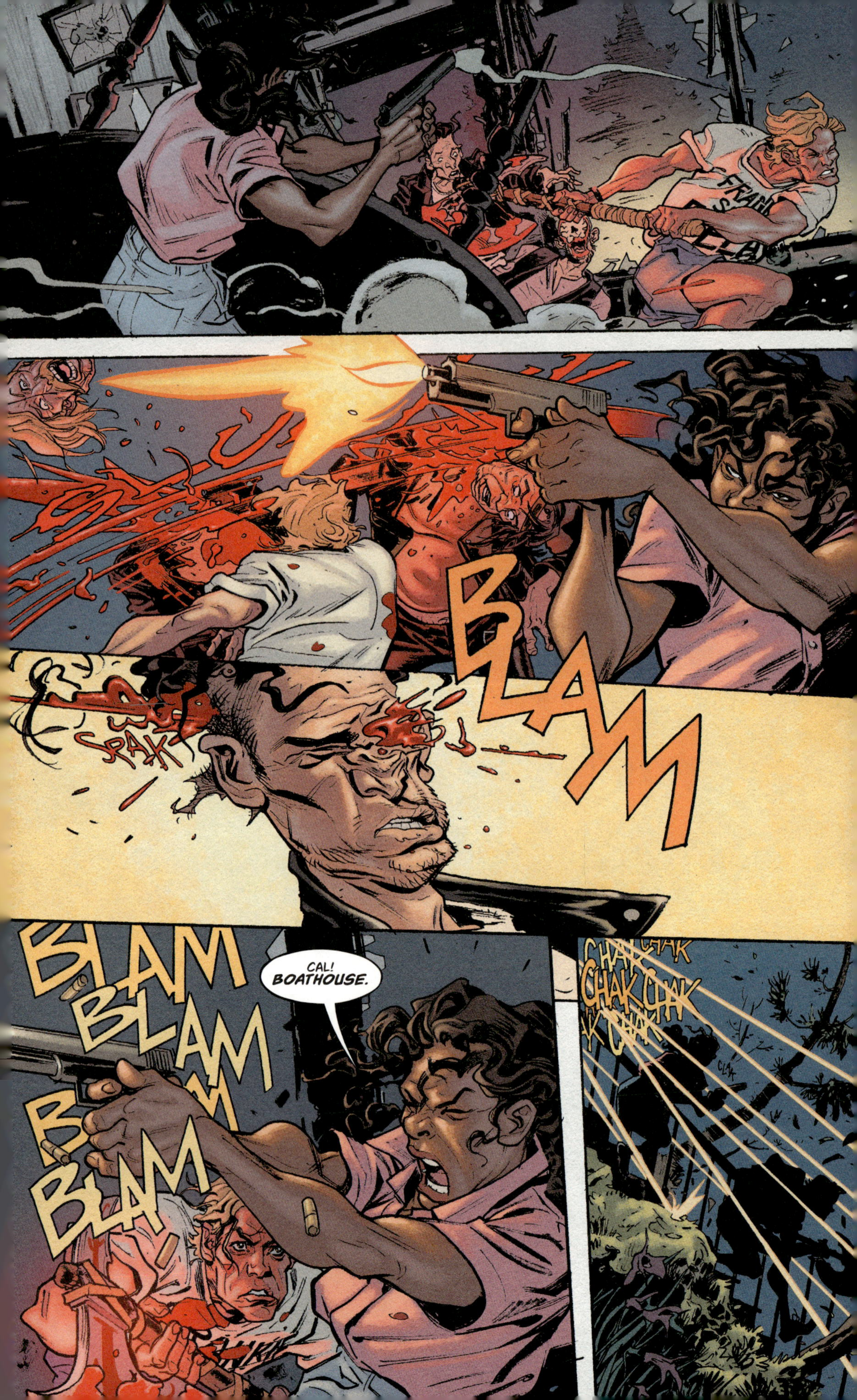

BLAM
SPAK
BLAM BLAM BLAM BLAM
CAL! BOATHOUSE.
CHAK CHAK CHAK CHAK

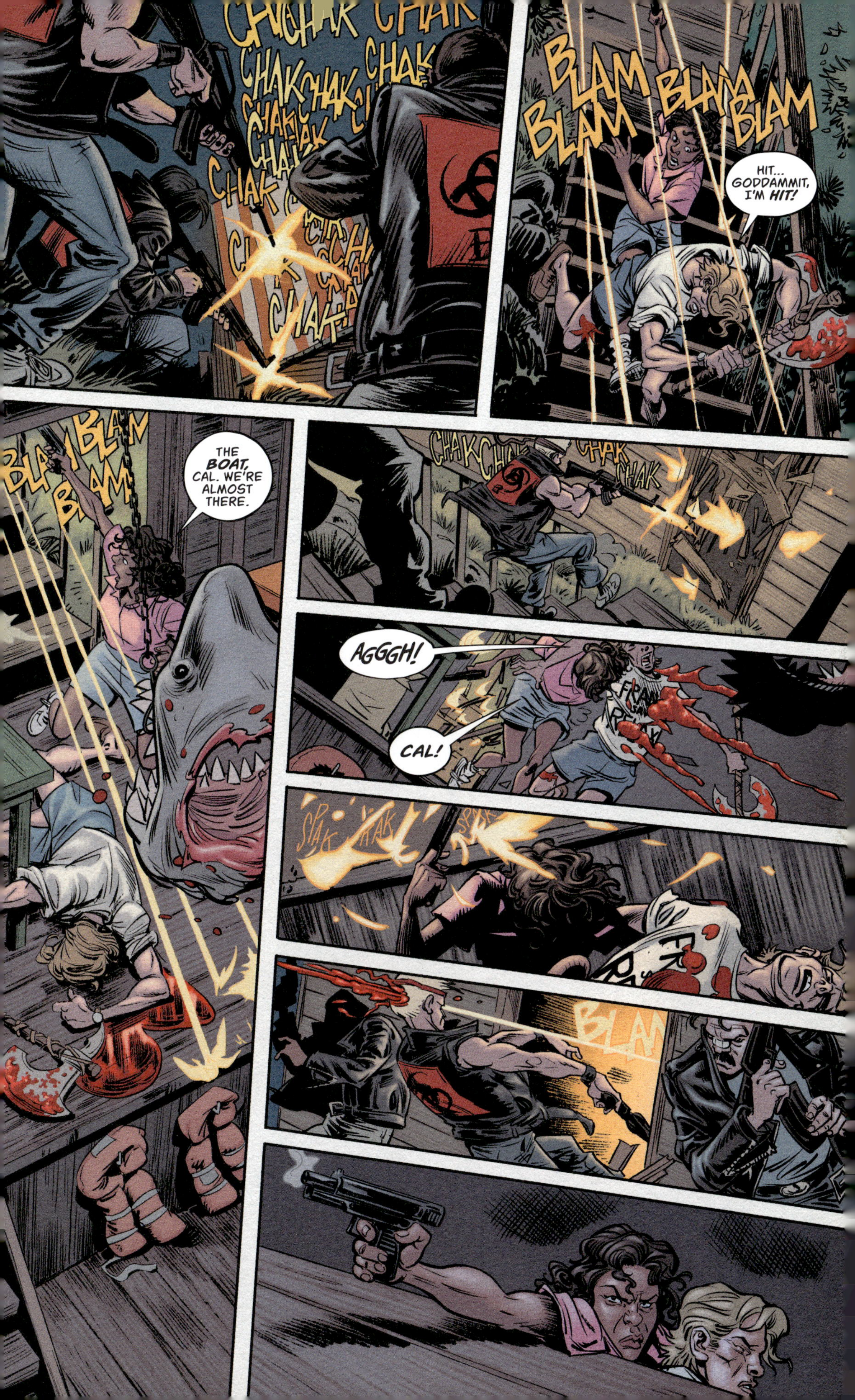
CHAK CHAK CHAK CHAK CHAK CHAK CHAK CHAK CHAK
BLAM BLAM BLAM BLAM
HIT... GODDAMMIT, I'M *HIT!*
BLAM BLAM BLAM
THE *BOAT,* CAL. WE'RE ALMOST THERE.
CHAK CHAK CHAK CHAK
AGGGH!
CAL!
BLAM

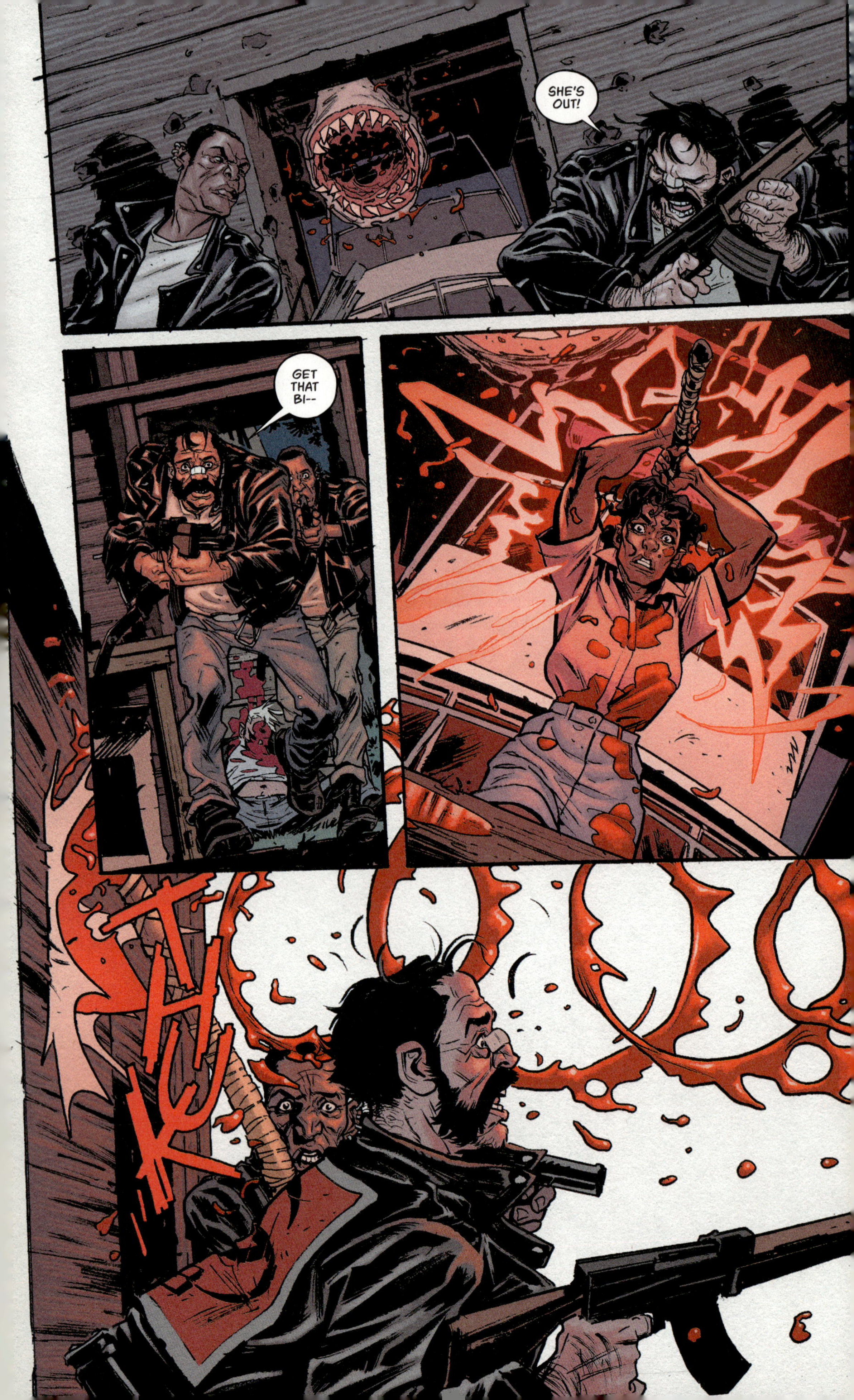
SHE'S OUT!
GET THAT BI--
THUK

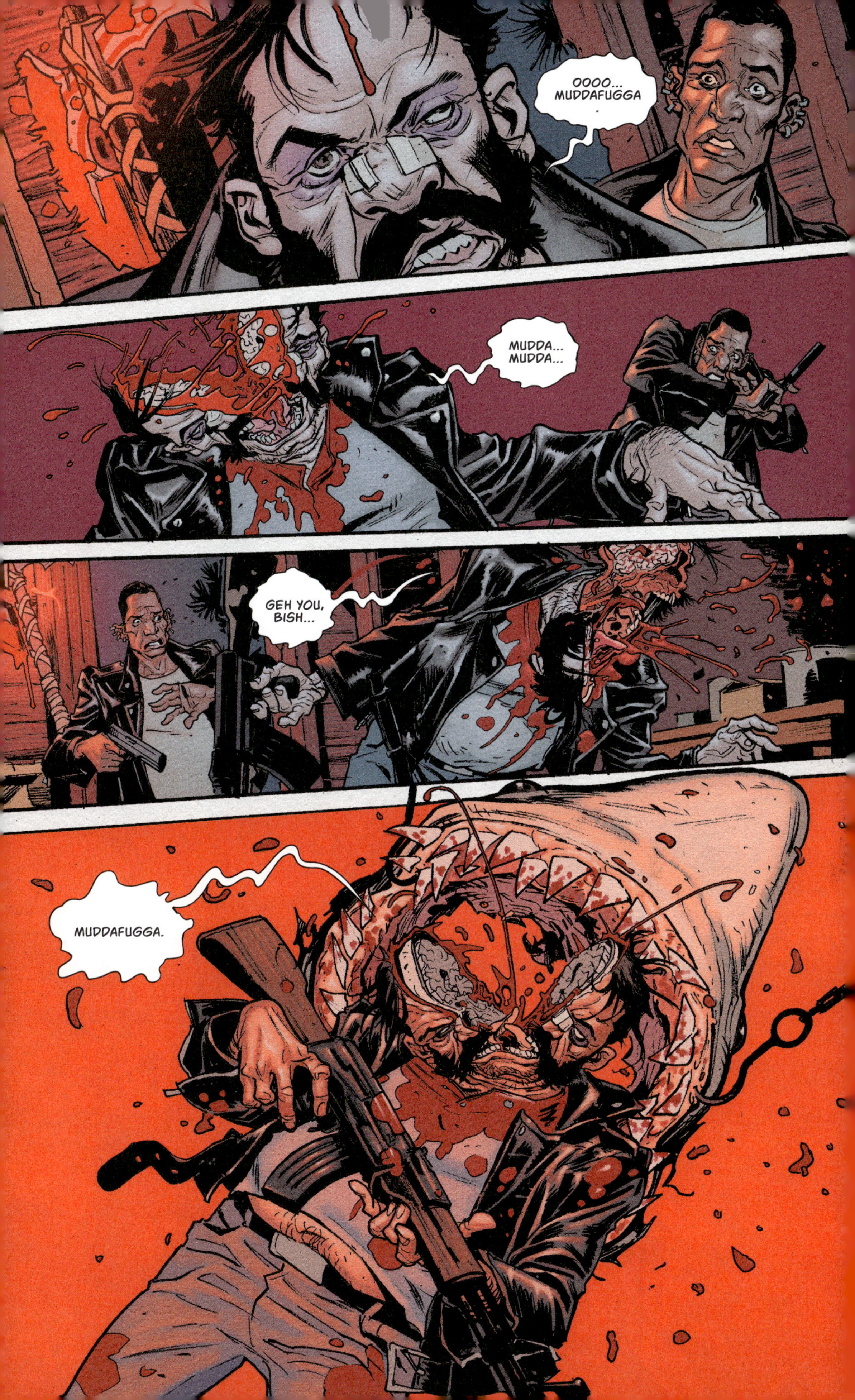
OOOO... MUDDAFUGGA
MUDDA... MUDDA...
GEH YOU, BISH...
MUDDAFUGGA.

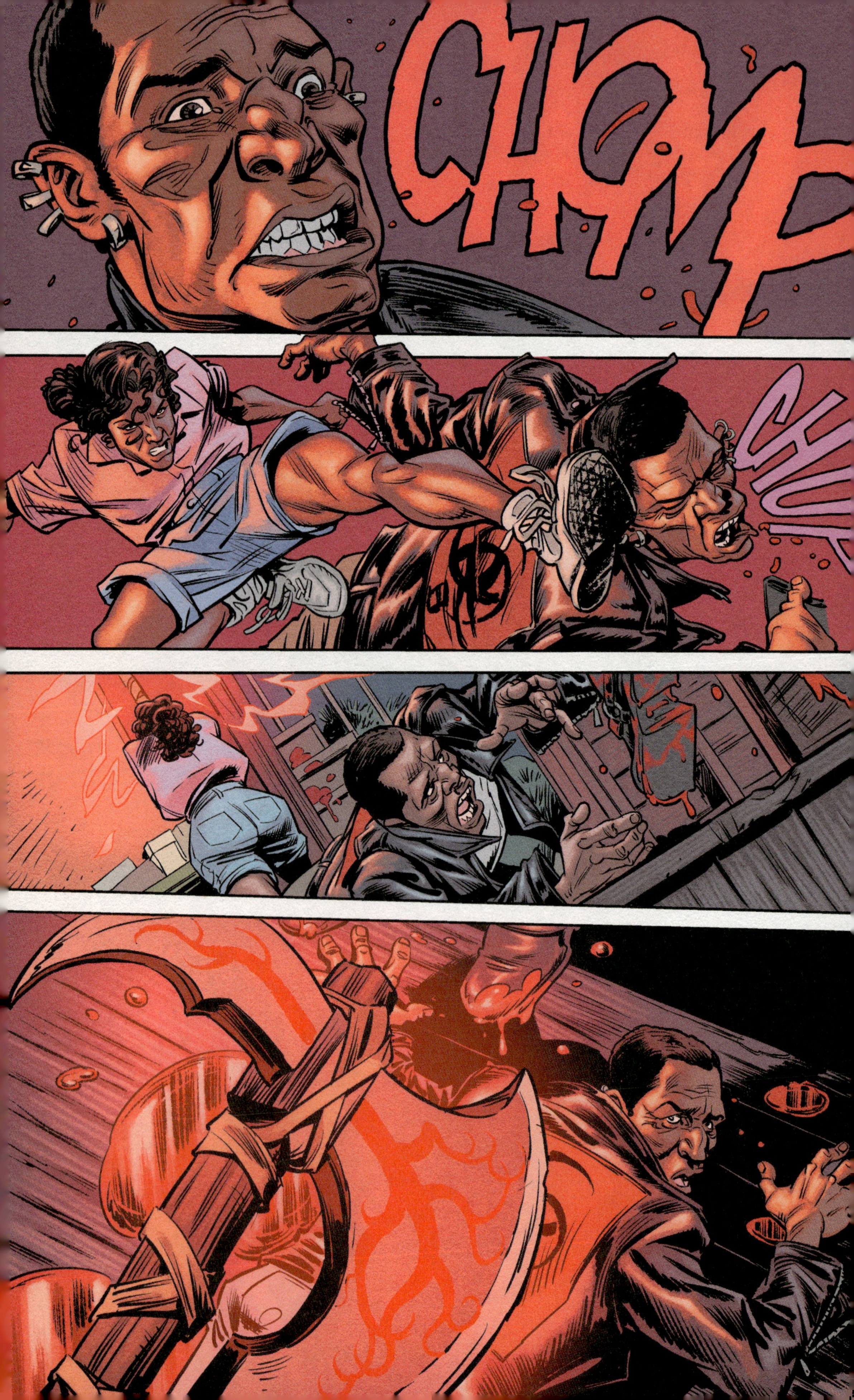
CHOMP
CHU

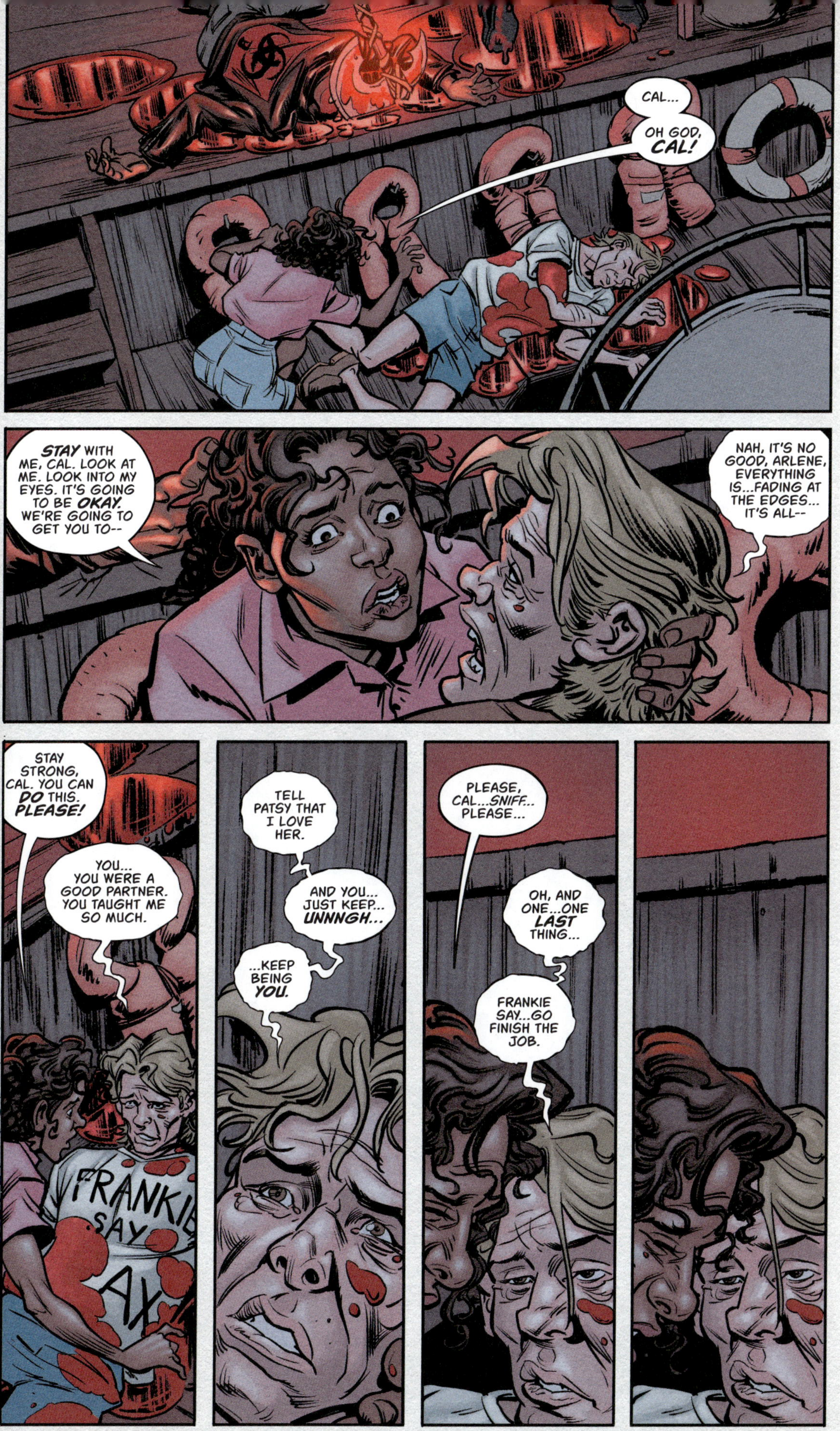
CAL...
OH GOD, CAL!
STAY WITH ME, CAL. LOOK AT ME. LOOK INTO MY EYES. IT'S GOING TO BE OKAY. WE'RE GOING TO GET YOU TO--
NAH, IT'S NO GOOD, ARLENE, EVERYTHING IS...FADING AT THE EDGES... IT'S ALL--
STAY STRONG, CAL. YOU CAN DO THIS. PLEASE!
YOU... YOU WERE A GOOD PARTNER. YOU TAUGHT ME SO MUCH.
FRANKIE SAY AX
TELL PATSY THAT I LOVE HER.
AND YOU... JUST KEEP... UNNNGH...
...KEEP BEING YOU.
PLEASE, CAL...SNIFF... PLEASE...
OH, AND ONE...ONE LAST THING...
FRANKIE SAY...GO FINISH THE JOB.

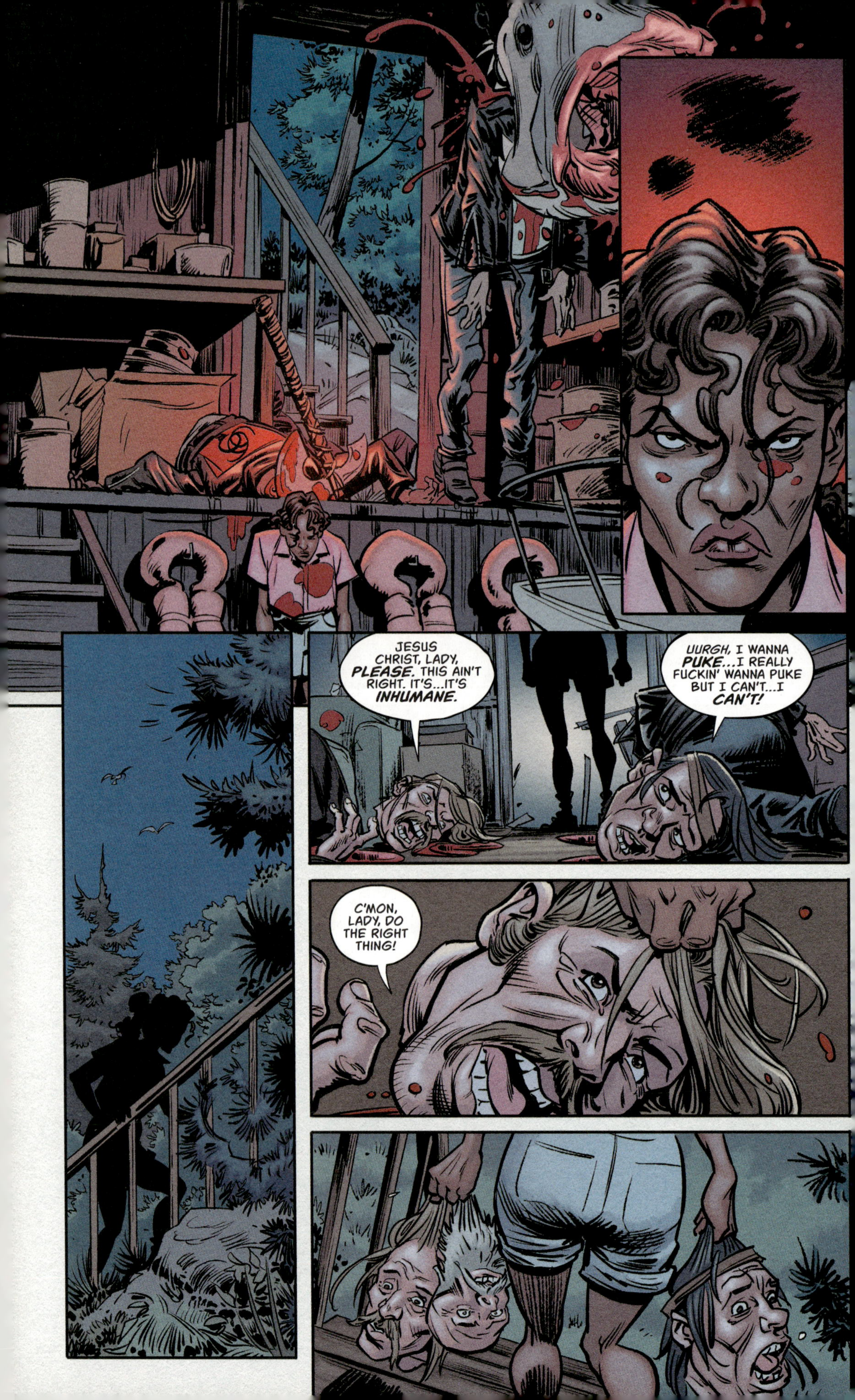
JESUS CHRIST, LADY, PLEASE. THIS AIN'T RIGHT. IT'S...IT'S INHUMANE.
UURGH, I WANNA PUKE...I REALLY FUCKIN' WANNA PUKE BUT I CAN'T...I CAN'T!
C'MON, LADY, DO THE RIGHT THING!

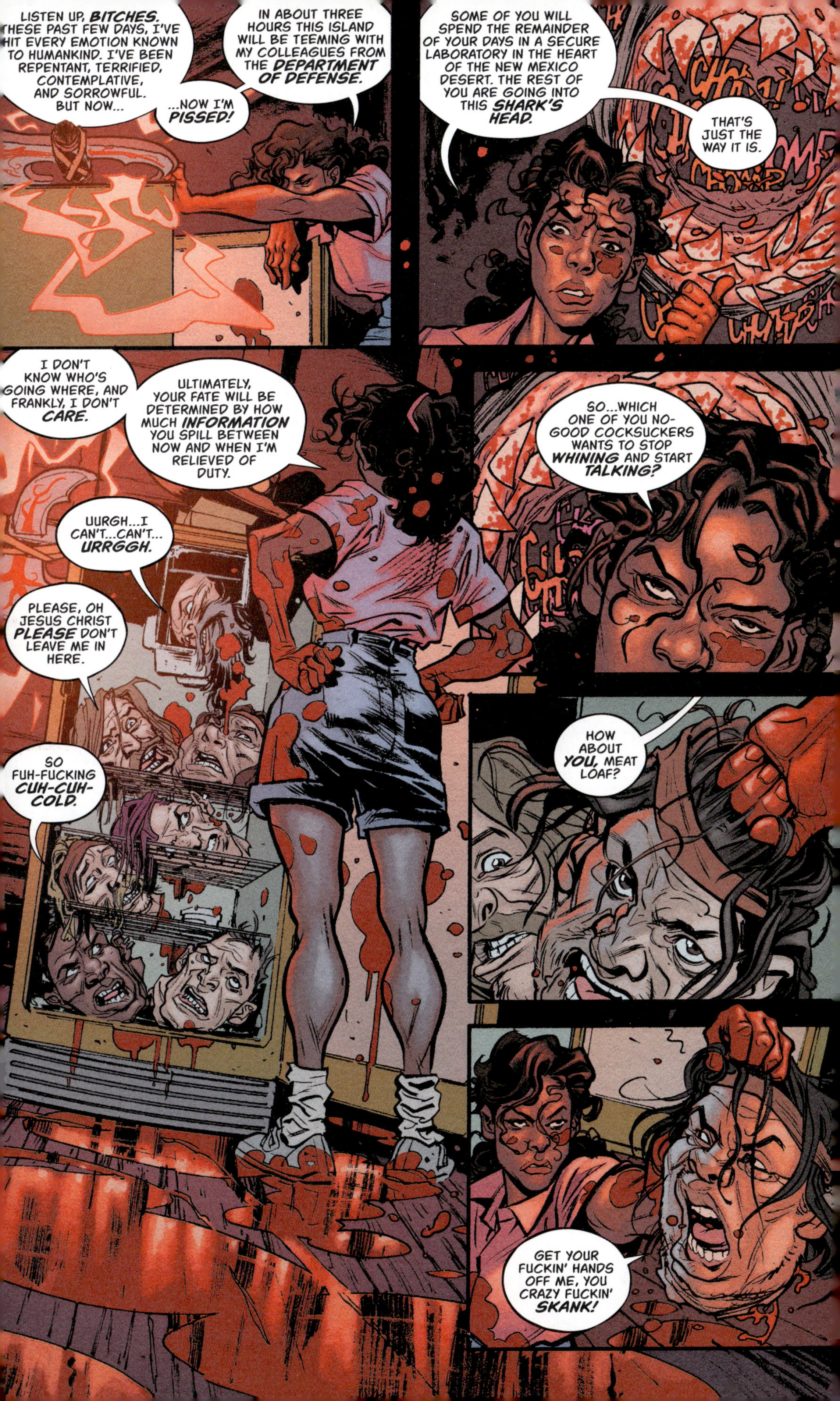
LISTEN UP, BITCHES. THESE PAST FEW DAYS, I'VE HIT EVERY EMOTION KNOWN TO HUMANKIND. I'VE BEEN REPENTANT, TERRIFIED, CONTEMPLATIVE, AND SORROWFUL. BUT NOW...
...NOW I'M PISSED!
IN ABOUT THREE HOURS THIS ISLAND WILL BE TEEMING WITH MY COLLEAGUES FROM THE DEPARTMENT OF DEFENSE.
SOME OF YOU WILL SPEND THE REMAINDER OF YOUR DAYS IN A SECURE LABORATORY IN THE HEART OF THE NEW MEXICO DESERT. THE REST OF YOU ARE GOING INTO THIS SHARK'S HEAD.
THAT'S JUST THE WAY IT IS.
I DON'T KNOW WHO'S GOING WHERE, AND FRANKLY, I DON'T CARE.
ULTIMATELY, YOUR FATE WILL BE DETERMINED BY HOW MUCH INFORMATION YOU SPILL BETWEEN NOW AND WHEN I'M RELIEVED OF DUTY.
UURGH...I CAN'T...CAN'T... URRGGH.
PLEASE, OH JESUS CHRIST PLEASE DON'T LEAVE ME IN HERE.
SO FUH-FUCKING CUH-CUH-COLD.
SO...WHICH ONE OF YOU NO-GOOD COCKSUCKERS WANTS TO STOP WHINING AND START TALKING?
HOW ABOUT YOU, MEAT LOAF?
GET YOUR FUCKIN' HANDS OFF ME, YOU CRAZY FUCKIN' SKANK!

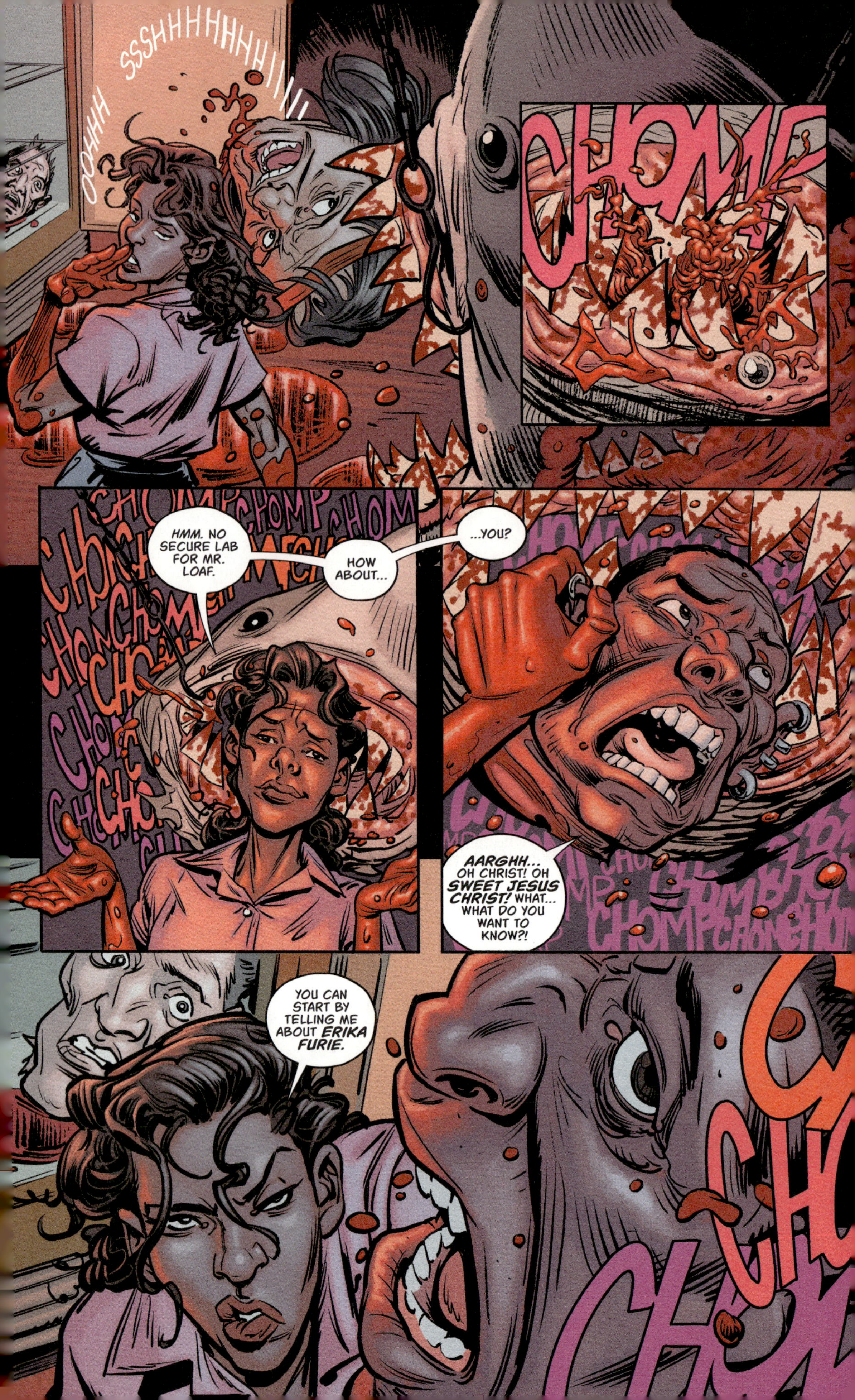

SSSHHHHHHHH!!!!
OOHHH
CHOMP
HMM. NO SECURE LAB FOR MR. LOAF.
HOW ABOUT...
...YOU?
AARGHH... OH CHRIST! OH SWEET JESUS CHRIST! WHAT... WHAT DO YOU WANT TO KNOW?!
YOU CAN START BY TELLING ME ABOUT ERIKA FURIE.

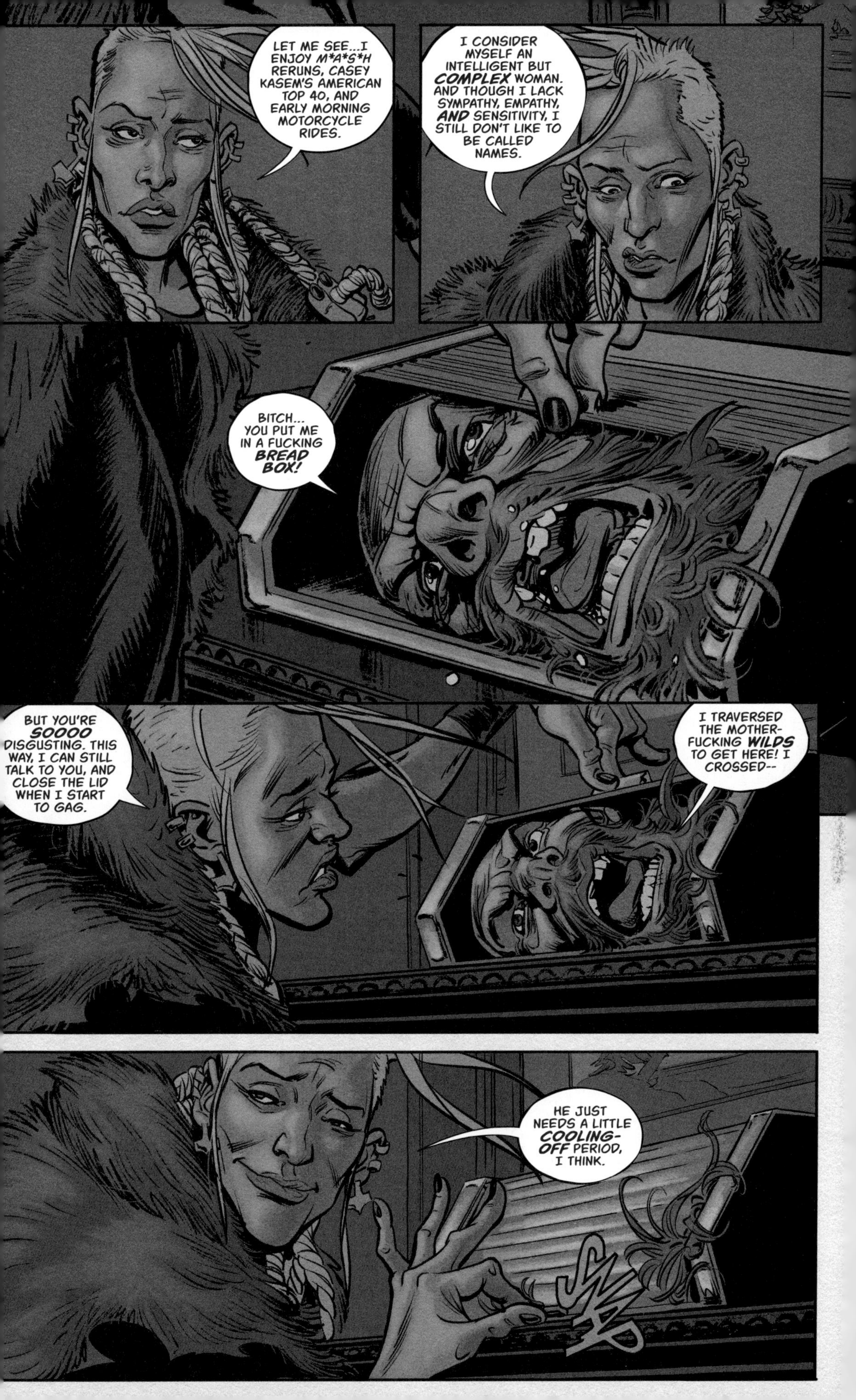

LET ME SEE...I ENJOY M*A*S*H RERUNS, CASEY KASEM'S AMERICAN TOP 40, AND EARLY MORNING MOTORCYCLE RIDES.
I CONSIDER MYSELF AN INTELLIGENT BUT COMPLEX WOMAN. AND THOUGH I LACK SYMPATHY, EMPATHY, AND SENSITIVITY, I STILL DON'T LIKE TO BE CALLED NAMES.
BITCH... YOU PUT ME IN A FUCKING BREAD BOX!
BUT YOU'RE SOOOO DISGUSTING. THIS WAY, I CAN STILL TALK TO YOU, AND CLOSE THE LID WHEN I START TO GAG.
I TRAVERSED THE MOTHER-FUCKING WILDS TO GET HERE! I CROSSED--
HE JUST NEEDS A LITTLE COOLING-OFF PERIOD, I THINK.
SNAP

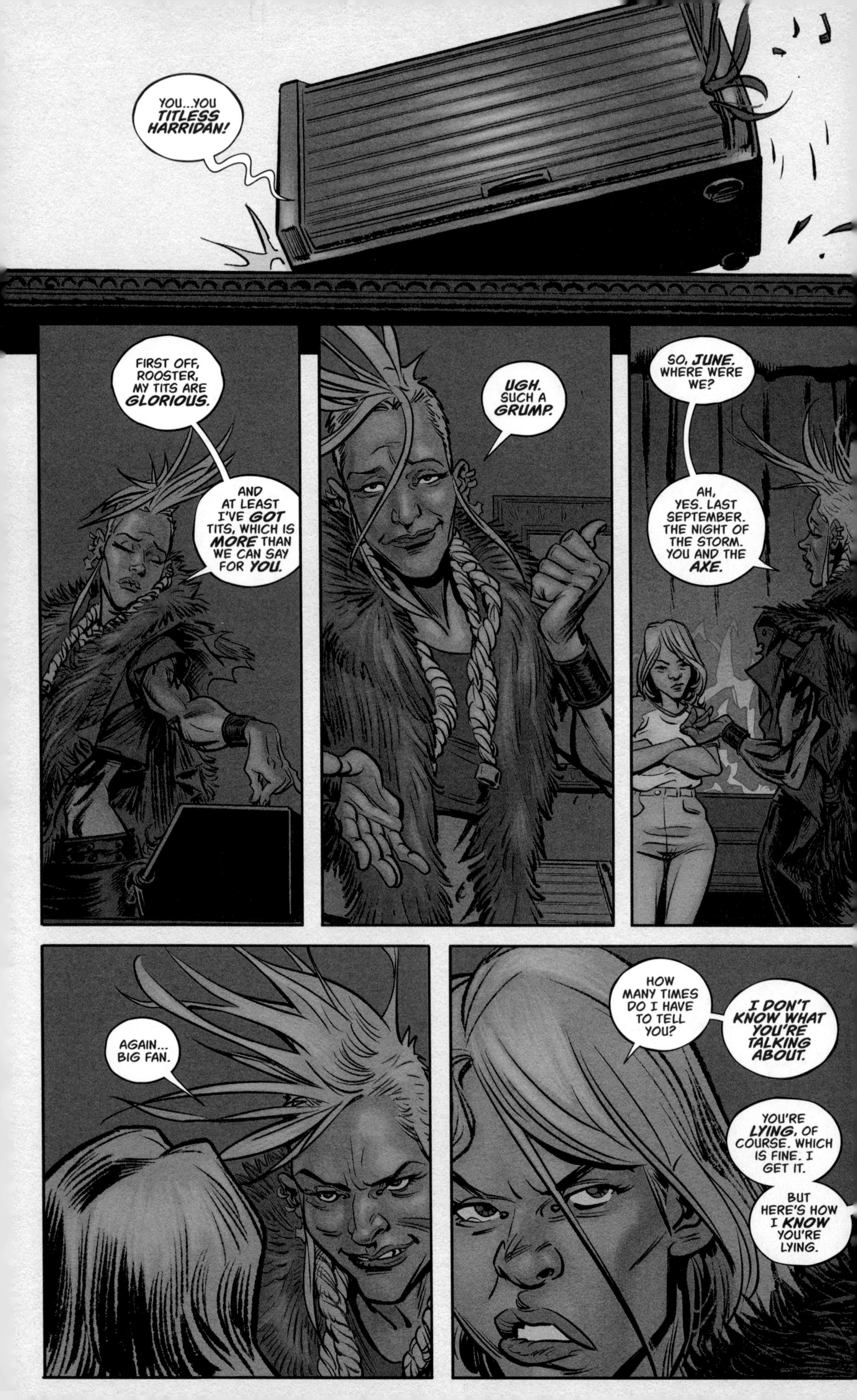
YOU...YOU TITLESS HARRIDAN!
FIRST OFF, ROOSTER, MY TITS ARE GLORIOUS.
AND AT LEAST I'VE GOT TITS, WHICH IS MORE THAN WE CAN SAY FOR YOU.
UGH. SUCH A GRUMP.
SO, JUNE. WHERE WERE WE?
AH, YES. LAST SEPTEMBER. THE NIGHT OF THE STORM. YOU AND THE AXE.
AGAIN... BIG FAN.
HOW MANY TIMES DO I HAVE TO TELL YOU?
I DON'T KNOW WHAT YOU'RE TALKING ABOUT.
YOU'RE LYING, OF COURSE. WHICH IS FINE. I GET IT.
BUT HERE'S HOW I KNOW YOU'RE LYING.

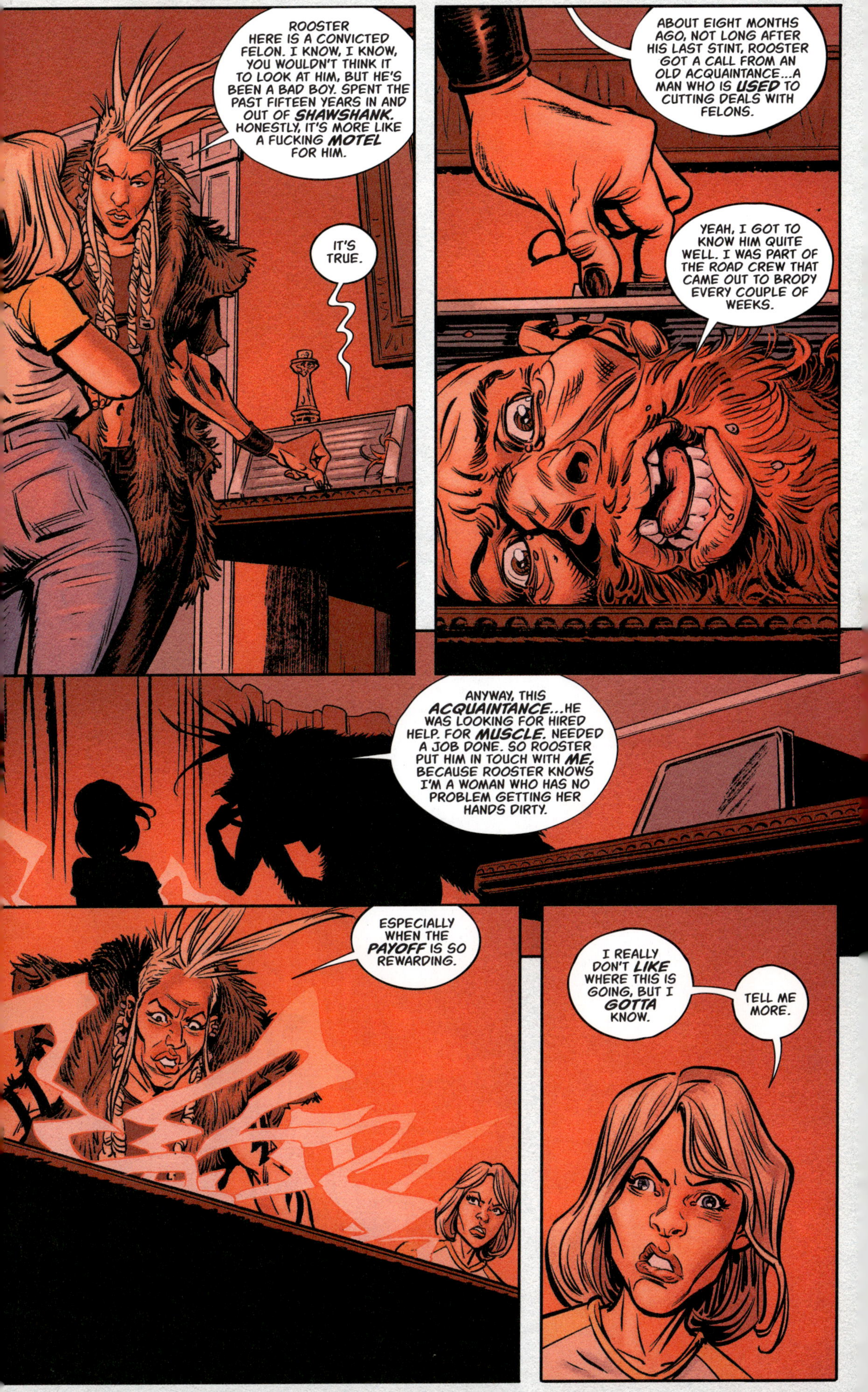
ROOSTER HERE IS A CONVICTED FELON. I KNOW, I KNOW, YOU WOULDN'T THINK IT TO LOOK AT HIM, BUT HE'S BEEN A BAD BOY. SPENT THE PAST FIFTEEN YEARS IN AND OUT OF SHAWSHANK. HONESTLY, IT'S MORE LIKE A FUCKING MOTEL FOR HIM.
IT'S TRUE.
ABOUT EIGHT MONTHS AGO, NOT LONG AFTER HIS LAST STINT, ROOSTER GOT A CALL FROM AN OLD ACQUAINTANCE...A MAN WHO IS USED TO CUTTING DEALS WITH FELONS.
YEAH, I GOT TO KNOW HIM QUITE WELL. I WAS PART OF THE ROAD CREW THAT CAME OUT TO BRODY EVERY COUPLE OF WEEKS.
ANYWAY, THIS ACQUAINTANCE...HE WAS LOOKING FOR HIRED HELP. FOR MUSCLE. NEEDED A JOB DONE. SO ROOSTER PUT HIM IN TOUCH WITH ME, BECAUSE ROOSTER KNOWS I'M A WOMAN WHO HAS NO PROBLEM GETTING HER HANDS DIRTY.
ESPECIALLY WHEN THE PAYOFF IS SO REWARDING.
I REALLY DON'T LIKE WHERE THIS IS GOING, BUT I GOTTA KNOW.
TELL ME MORE.

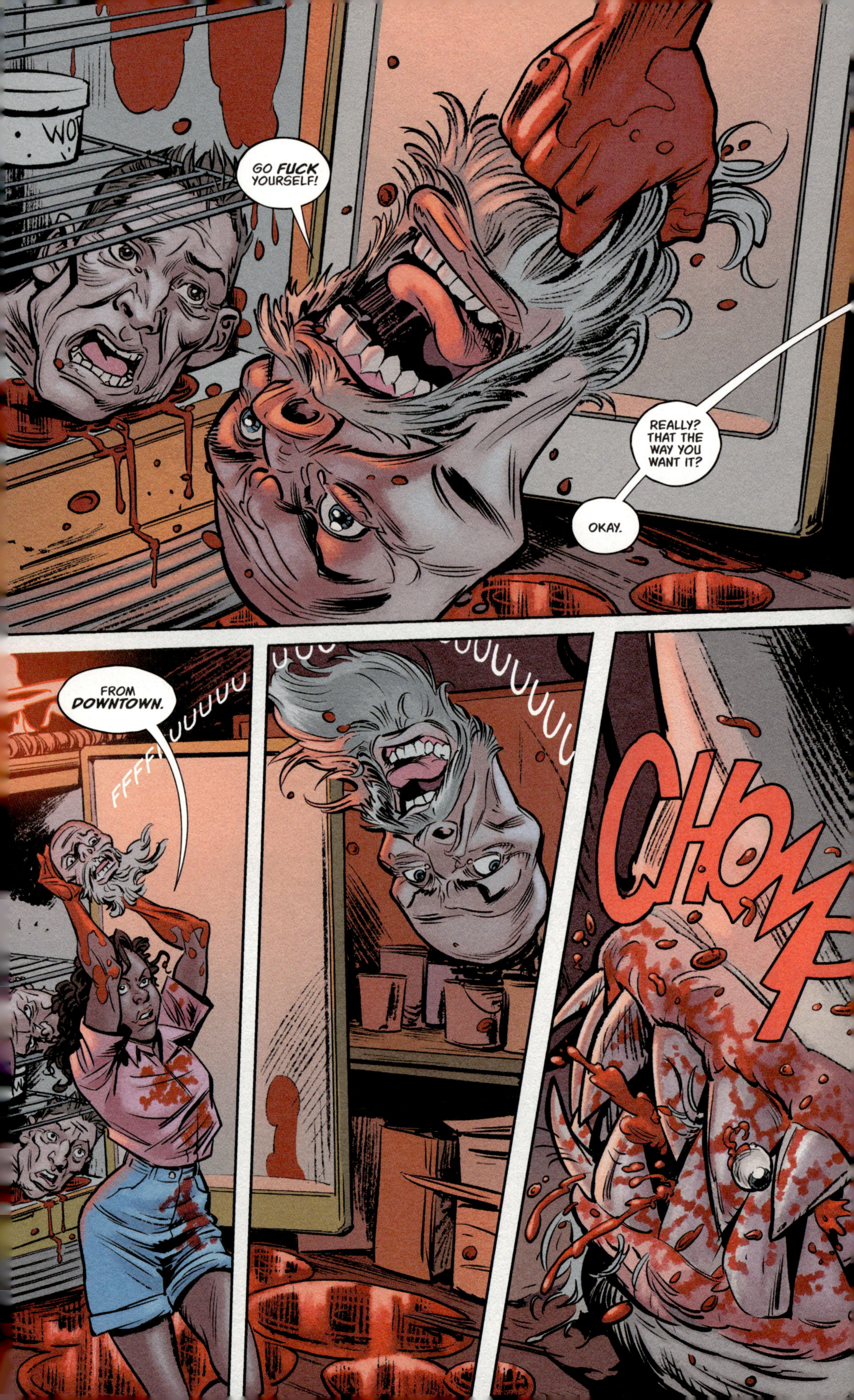

GO FUCK YOURSELF!
REALLY? THAT THE WAY YOU WANT IT?
OKAY.
FROM DOWNTOWN.
FFFFUUUUUUUUUUUUUUUUUUUU
CHOMP

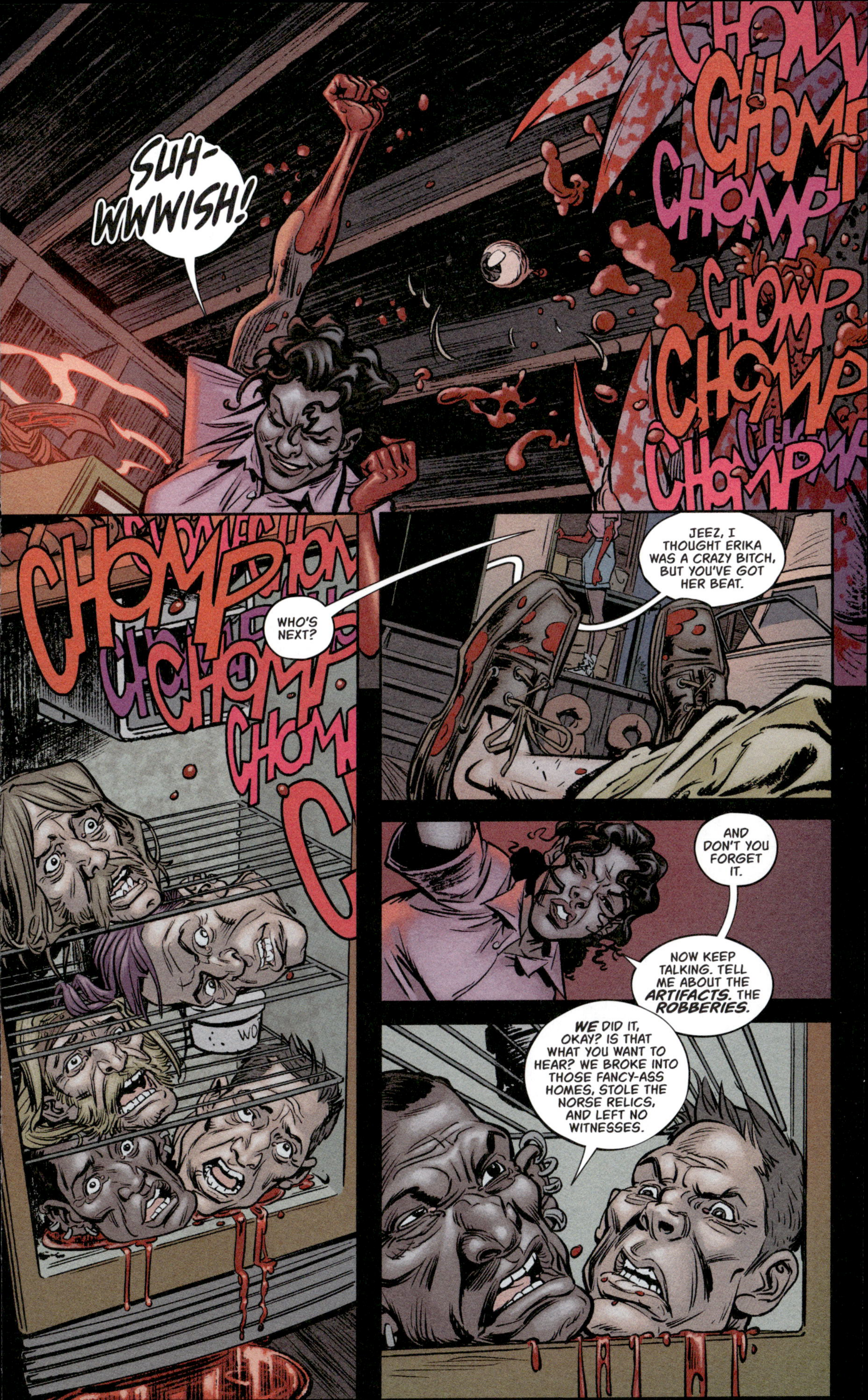
SUH-WWWISH!
CHOMP
CHOMP
CHOMP
CHOMP
CHOMP
CHOMP
CHOMP
WHO'S NEXT?
CHOMP
CHOMP
JEEZ, I THOUGHT ERIKA WAS A CRAZY BITCH, BUT YOU'VE GOT HER BEAT.
AND DON'T YOU FORGET IT.
NOW KEEP TALKING. TELL ME ABOUT THE ARTIFACTS. THE ROBBERIES.
WE DID IT, OKAY? IS THAT WHAT YOU WANT TO HEAR? WE BROKE INTO THOSE FANCY-ASS HOMES, STOLE THE NORSE RELICS, AND LEFT NO WITNESSES.

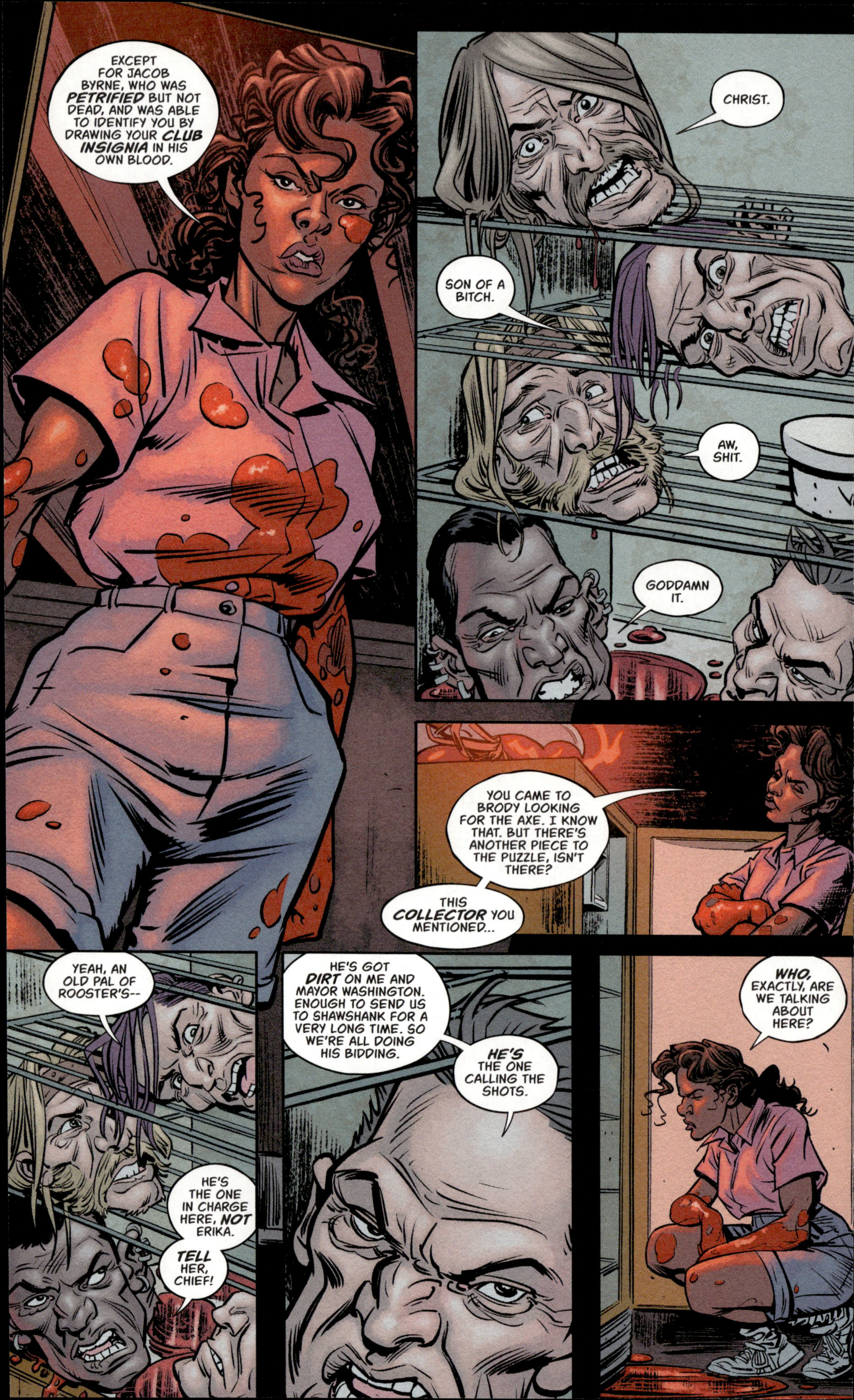
EXCEPT FOR JACOB BYRNE, WHO WAS PETRIFIED BUT NOT DEAD, AND WAS ABLE TO IDENTIFY YOU BY DRAWING YOUR CLUB INSIGNIA IN HIS OWN BLOOD.
CHRIST.
SON OF A BITCH.
AW, SHIT.
GODDAMN IT.
YOU CAME TO BRODY LOOKING FOR THE AXE. I KNOW THAT. BUT THERE'S ANOTHER PIECE TO THE PUZZLE, ISN'T THERE?
THIS COLLECTOR YOU MENTIONED...
YEAH, AN OLD PAL OF ROOSTER'S--
HE'S THE ONE IN CHARGE HERE, NOT ERIKA.
TELL HER, CHIEF!
HE'S GOT DIRT ON ME AND MAYOR WASHINGTON. ENOUGH TO SEND US TO SHAWSHANK FOR A VERY LONG TIME. SO WE'RE ALL DOING HIS BIDDING.
HE'S THE ONE CALLING THE SHOTS.
WHO, EXACTLY, ARE WE TALKING ABOUT HERE?

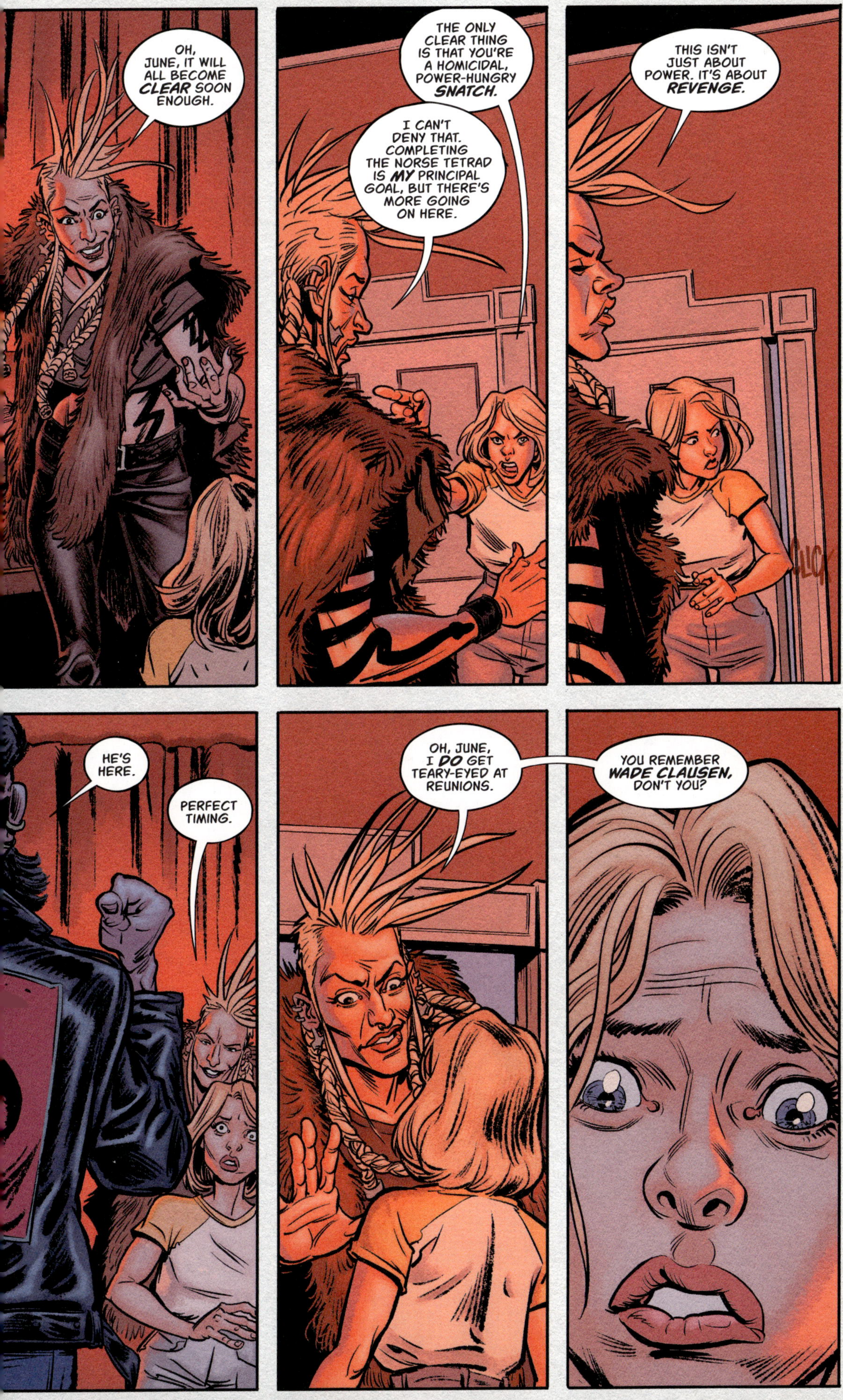
OH, JUNE, IT WILL ALL BECOME CLEAR SOON ENOUGH.
THE ONLY CLEAR THING IS THAT YOU'RE A HOMICIDAL, POWER-HUNGRY SNATCH.
I CAN'T DENY THAT. COMPLETING THE NORSE TETRAD IS MY PRINCIPAL GOAL, BUT THERE'S MORE GOING ON HERE.
THIS ISN'T JUST ABOUT POWER. IT'S ABOUT REVENGE.
HE'S HERE.
PERFECT TIMING.
OH, JUNE, I DO GET TEARY-EYED AT REUNIONS.
YOU REMEMBER WADE CLAUSEN, DON'T YOU?

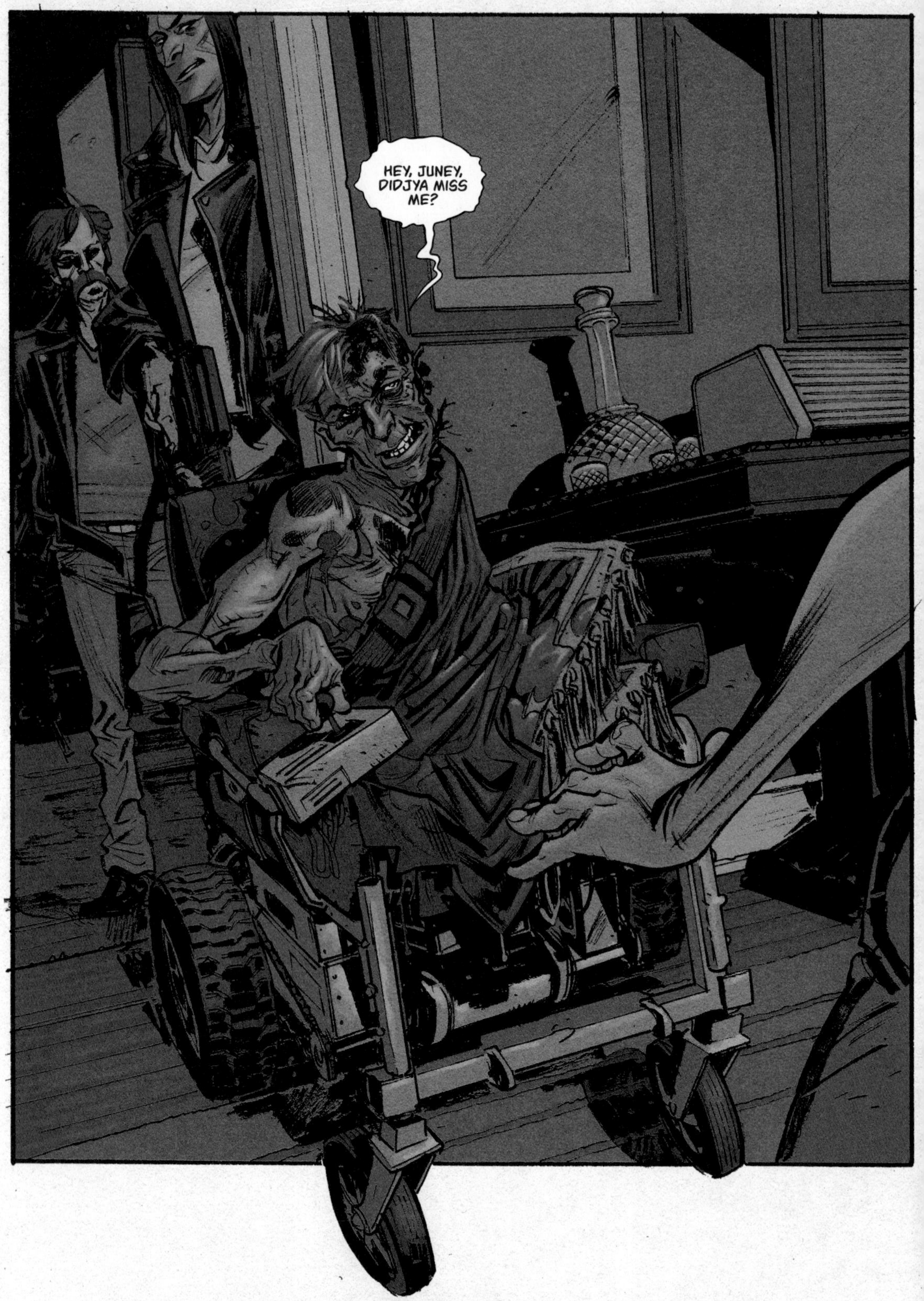
HEY, JUNEY, DIDJYA MISS ME?

IS IT TIME TO BURY THE HATCHET?

FIND OUT NEXT MONTH!

REFRIGERATOR FULL OF HEADS

Written by RIO YOUERS Pencils by TOM FOWLER
Inks by CRAIG TAILLEFER and TOM FOWLER Colored by BILL CRABTREE
Lettered by ANDWORLD DESIGN Cover by CULLY HAMNER
Variant cover by BRIAN LEVEL & LEE LOUGHRIDGE

ANDREA SHEA & CHRIS CONROY Editors

BASKETFUL OF HEADS created by JOE HILL with art by LEOMACS
REFRIGERATOR FULL OF HEADS curated for HILL HOUSE COMICS by JOE HILL

"THIS ISN'T JUST ABOUT POWER, JUNE. IT'S ABOUT REVENGE."

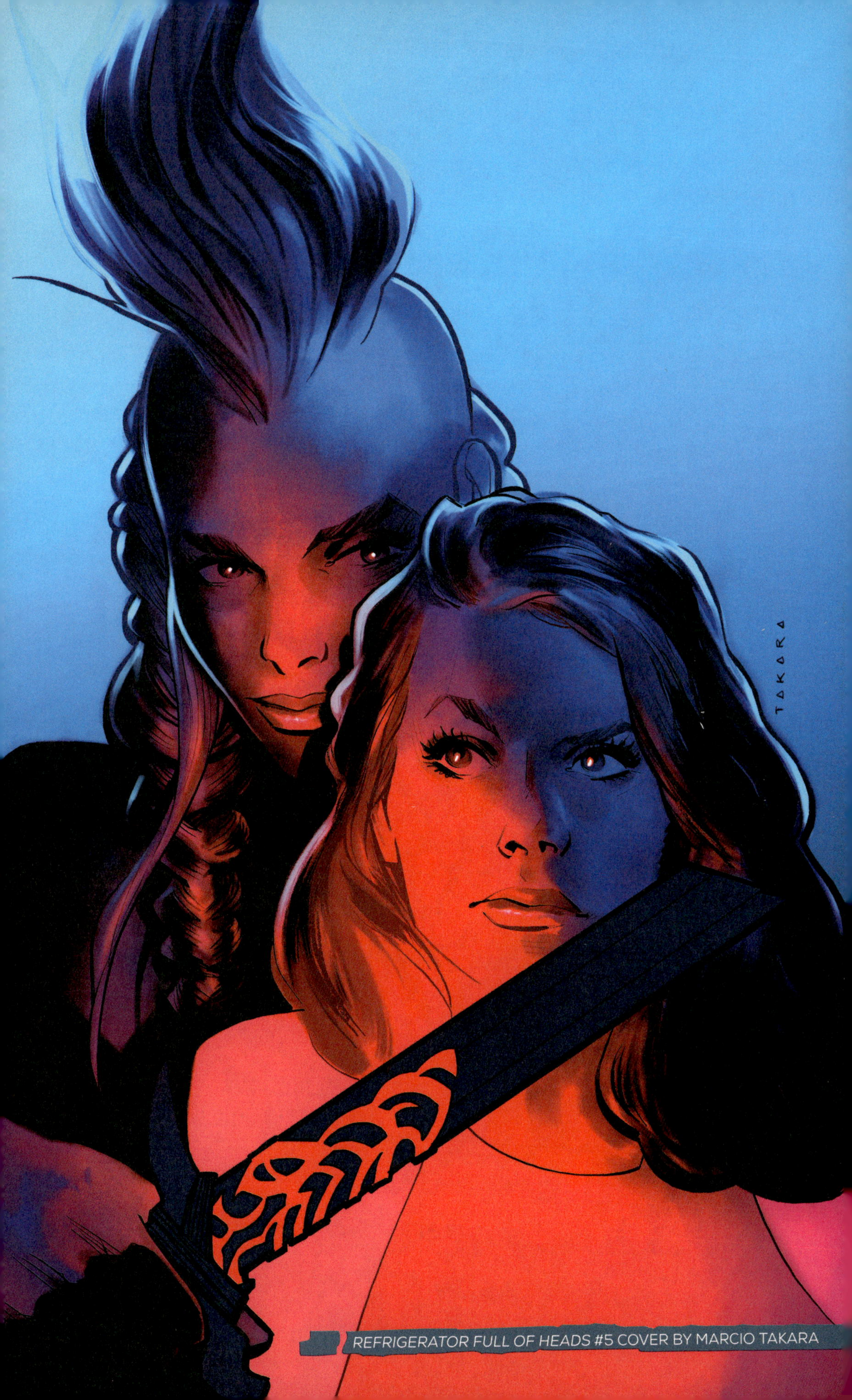
TAKARA

REFRIGERATOR FULL OF HEADS #5 COVER BY MARCIO TAKARA

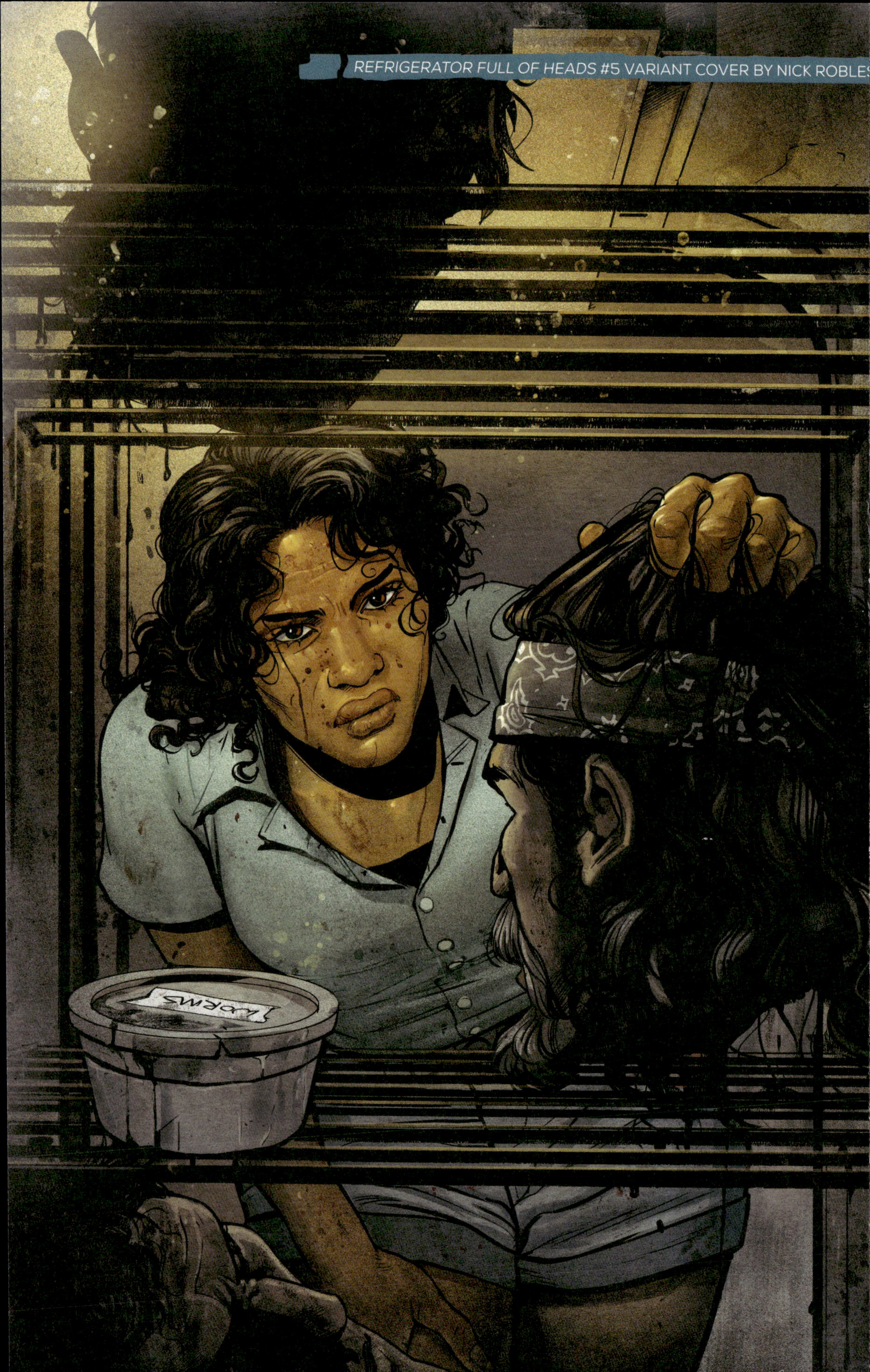

REFRIGERATOR FULL OF HEADS #5 VARIANT COVER BY NICK ROBLES

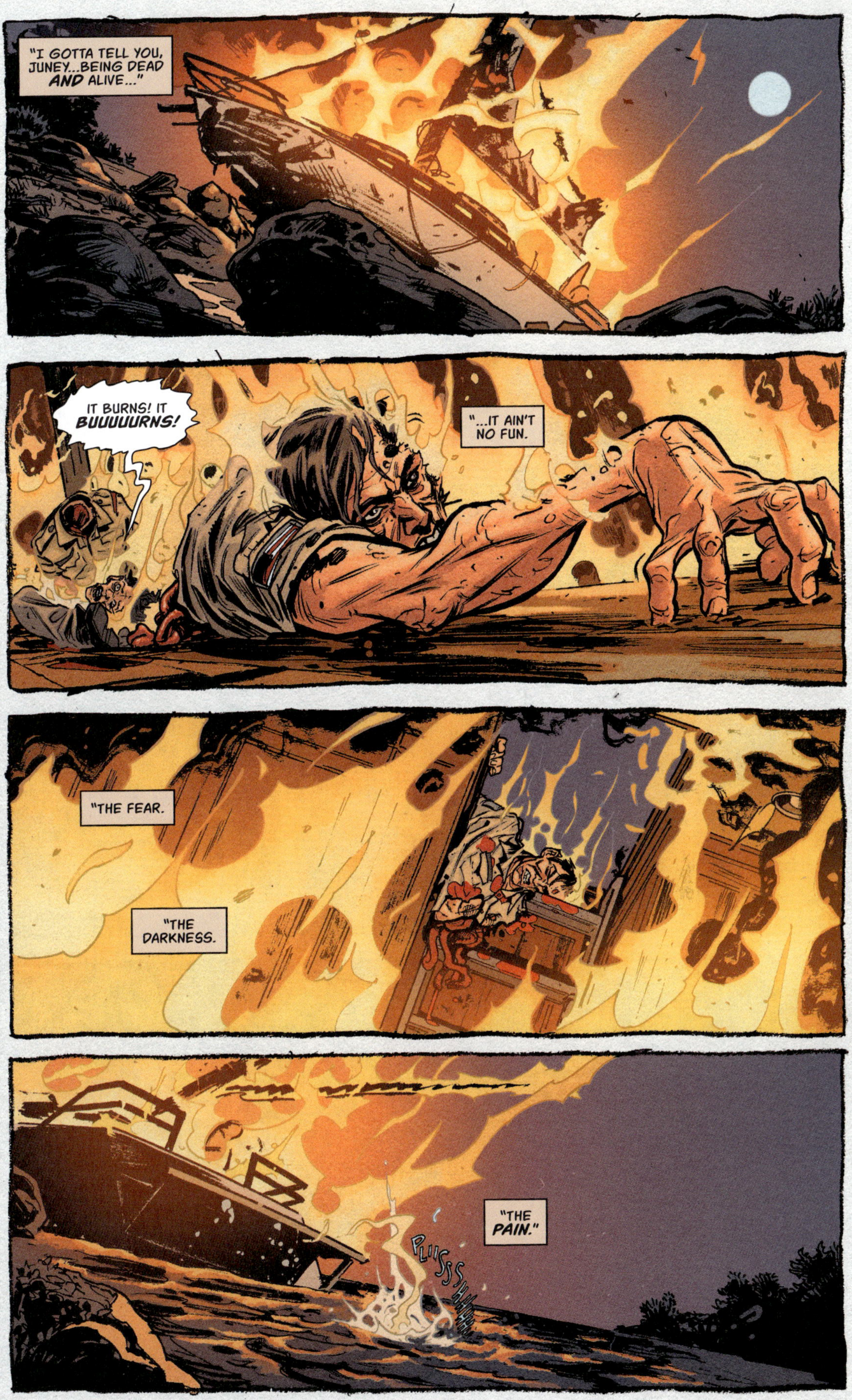
"I GOTTA TELL YOU, JUNEY...BEING DEAD AND ALIVE..."
IT BURNS! IT BUUUUURNS!
"...IT AIN'T NO FUN.
"THE FEAR.
"THE DARKNESS.
"THE PAIN."
PLISSSHHHH

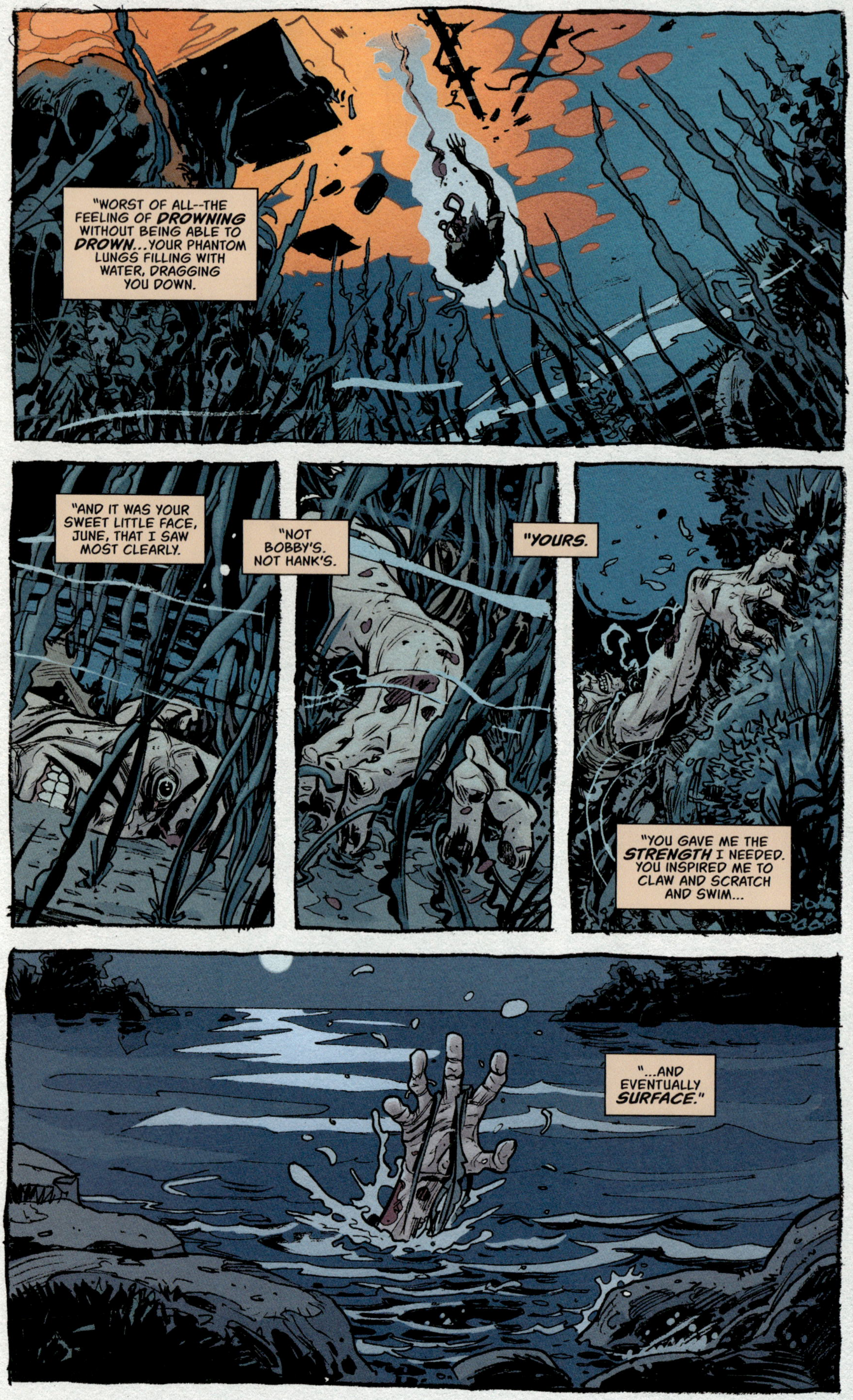
"WORST OF ALL--THE FEELING OF DROWNING WITHOUT BEING ABLE TO DROWN...YOUR PHANTOM LUNGS FILLING WITH WATER, DRAGGING YOU DOWN.
"AND IT WAS YOUR SWEET LITTLE FACE, JUNE, THAT I SAW MOST CLEARLY.
"NOT BOBBY'S. NOT HANK'S.
"YOURS.
"YOU GAVE ME THE STRENGTH I NEEDED. YOU INSPIRED ME TO CLAW AND SCRATCH AND SWIM...
"...AND EVENTUALLY SURFACE."

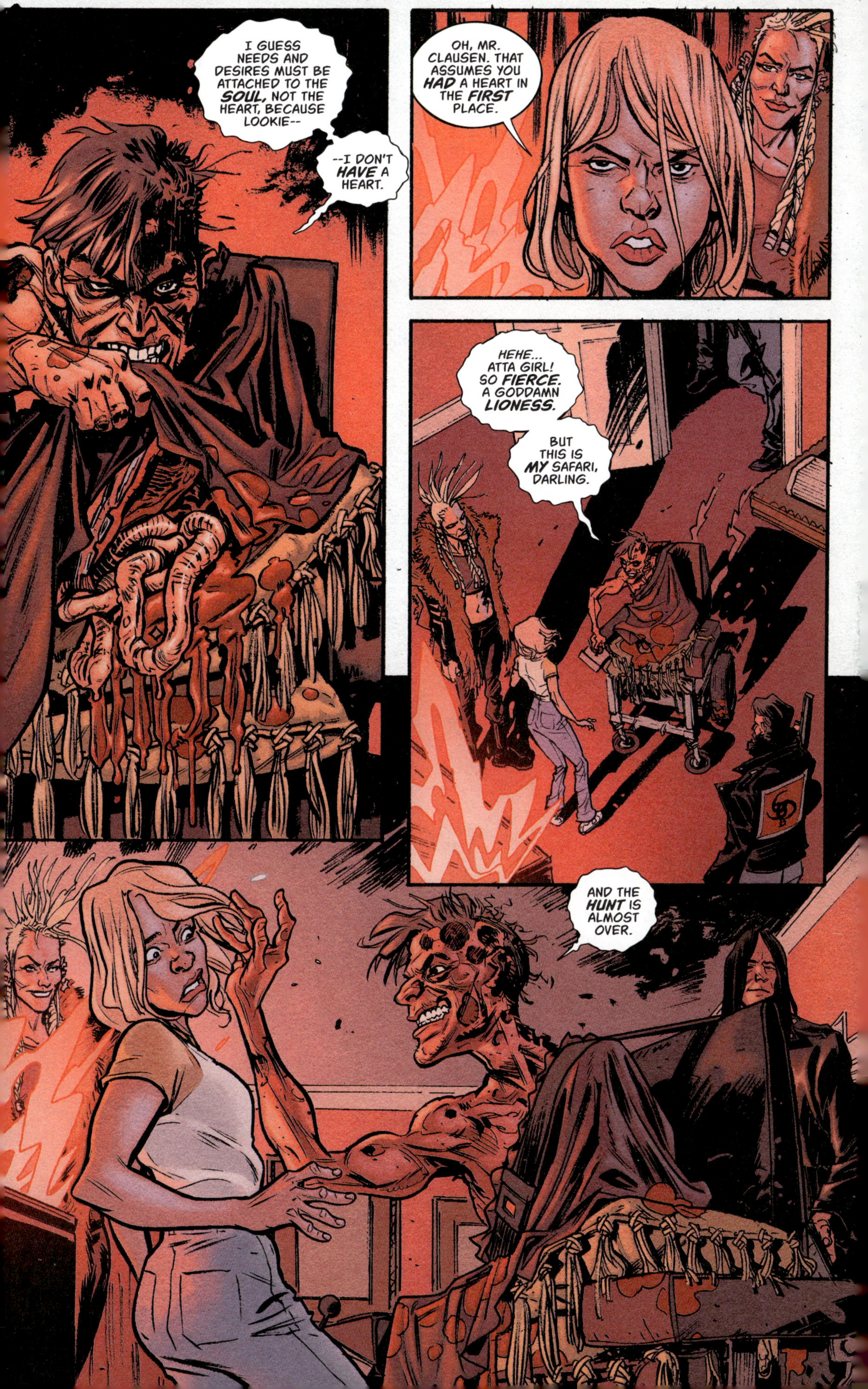
I GUESS NEEDS AND DESIRES MUST BE ATTACHED TO THE *SOUL*, NOT THE HEART, BECAUSE LOOKIE--
--I DON'T *HAVE* A HEART.
OH, MR. CLAUSEN. THAT ASSUMES YOU *HAD* A HEART IN THE *FIRST* PLACE.
HEHE... ATTA GIRL! SO *FIERCE*. A GODDAMN *LIONESS*.
BUT THIS IS *MY* SAFARI, DARLING.
AND THE *HUNT* IS ALMOST OVER.

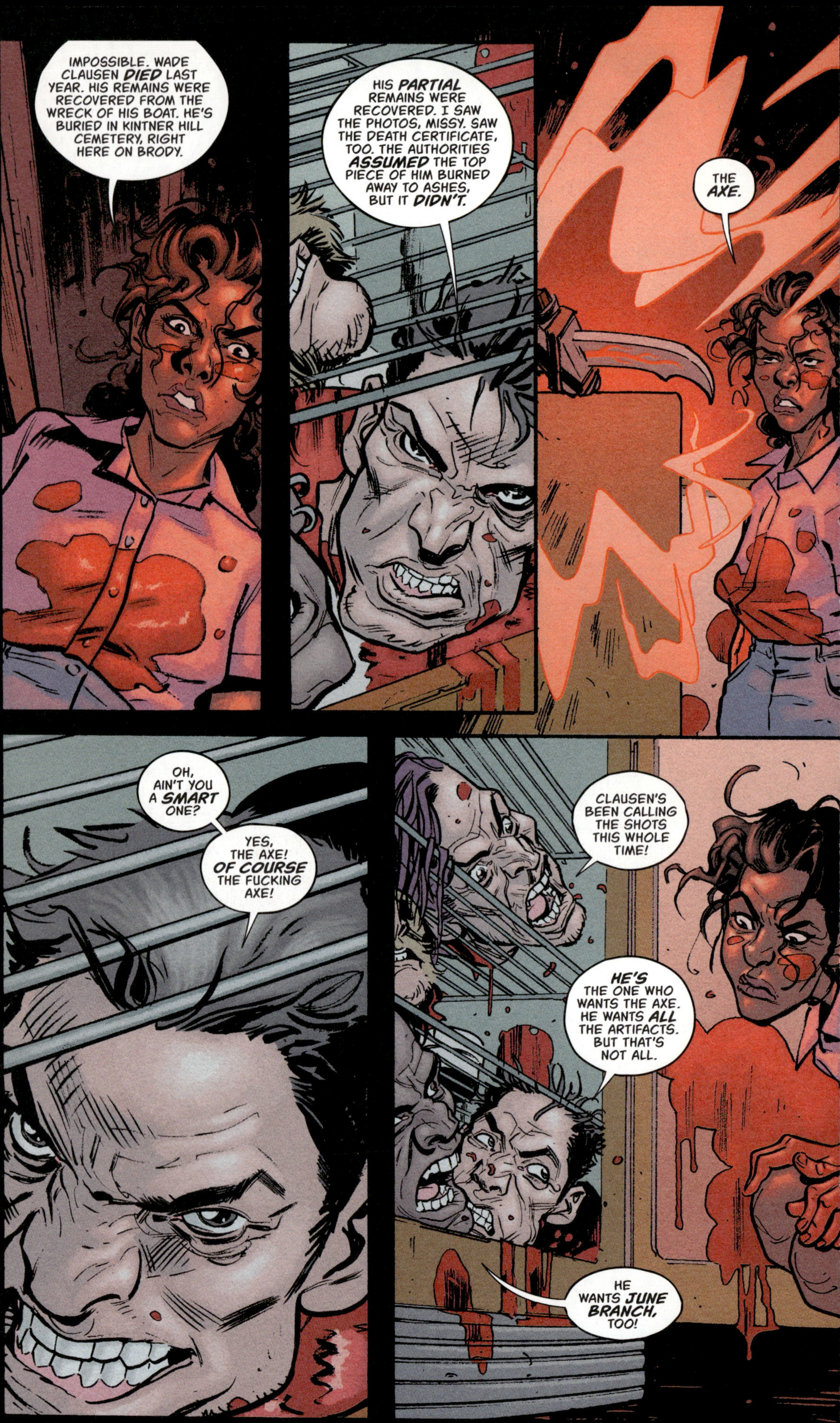
IMPOSSIBLE. WADE CLAUSEN **DIED** LAST YEAR. HIS REMAINS WERE RECOVERED FROM THE WRECK OF HIS BOAT. HE'S BURIED IN KINTNER HILL CEMETERY, RIGHT HERE ON BRODY.
HIS **PARTIAL** REMAINS WERE RECOVERED. I SAW THE PHOTOS, MISSY. SAW THE DEATH CERTIFICATE, TOO. THE AUTHORITIES **ASSUMED** THE TOP PIECE OF HIM BURNED AWAY TO ASHES, BUT IT **DIDN'T**.
THE **AXE**.
OH, AIN'T YOU A **SMART** ONE?
YES, THE AXE! **OF COURSE** THE FUCKING AXE!
CLAUSEN'S BEEN CALLING THE SHOTS THIS WHOLE TIME!
HE'S THE ONE WHO WANTS THE AXE. HE WANTS **ALL** THE ARTIFACTS. BUT THAT'S NOT ALL.
HE WANTS **JUNE BRANCH**, TOO!

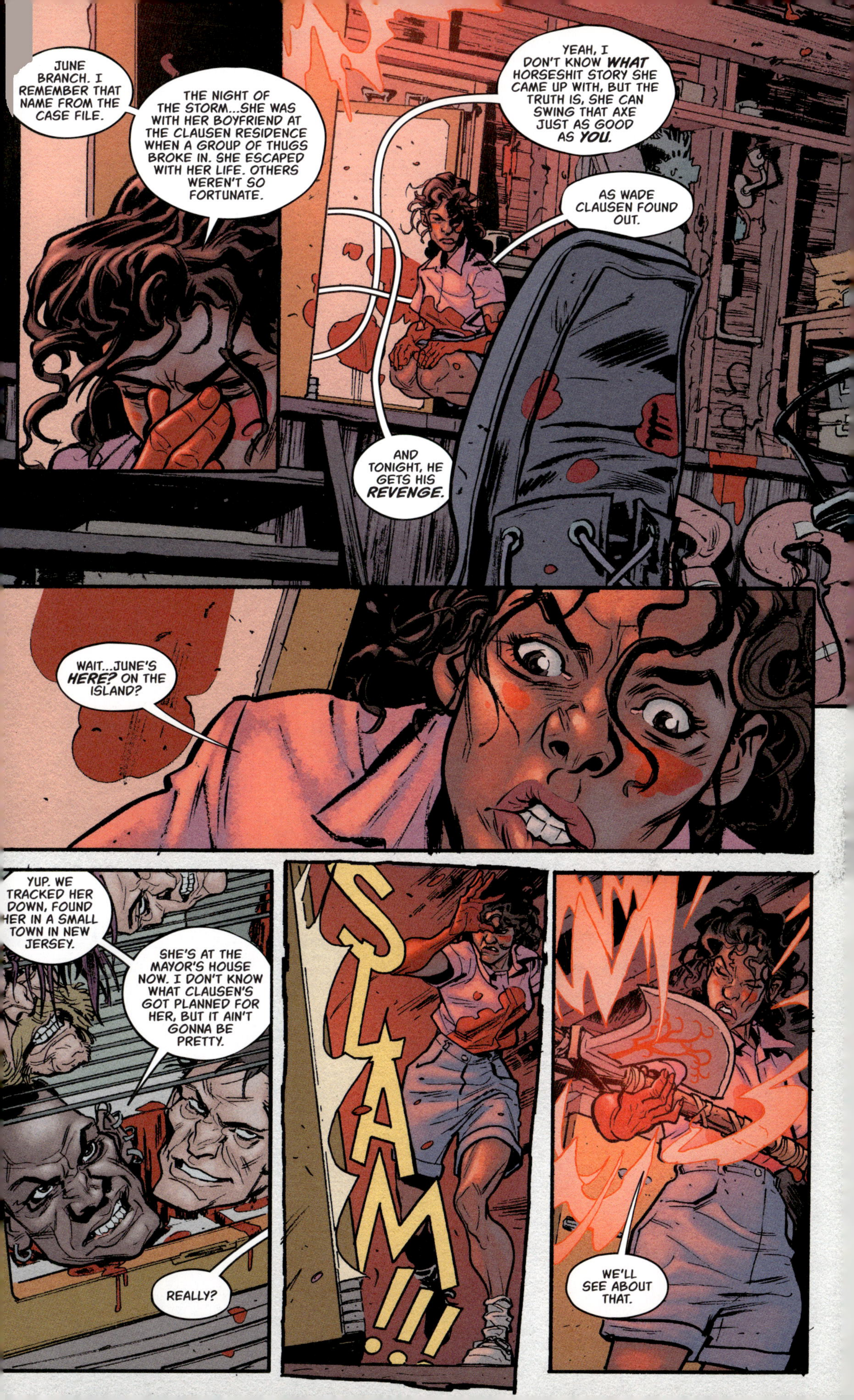
JUNE BRANCH. I REMEMBER THAT NAME FROM THE CASE FILE.
THE NIGHT OF THE STORM...SHE WAS WITH HER BOYFRIEND AT THE CLAUSEN RESIDENCE WHEN A GROUP OF THUGS BROKE IN. SHE ESCAPED WITH HER LIFE. OTHERS WEREN'T SO FORTUNATE.
YEAH, I DON'T KNOW **WHAT** HORSESHIT STORY SHE CAME UP WITH, BUT THE TRUTH IS, SHE CAN SWING THAT AXE JUST AS GOOD AS **YOU.**
AS WADE CLAUSEN FOUND OUT.
AND TONIGHT, HE GETS HIS **REVENGE.**
WAIT...JUNE'S **HERE?** ON THE ISLAND?
YUP. WE TRACKED HER DOWN, FOUND HER IN A SMALL TOWN IN NEW JERSEY.
SHE'S AT THE MAYOR'S HOUSE NOW. I DON'T KNOW WHAT CLAUSEN'S GOT PLANNED FOR HER, BUT IT AIN'T GONNA BE PRETTY.
REALLY?
SLAM!!!
WE'LL SEE ABOUT THAT.

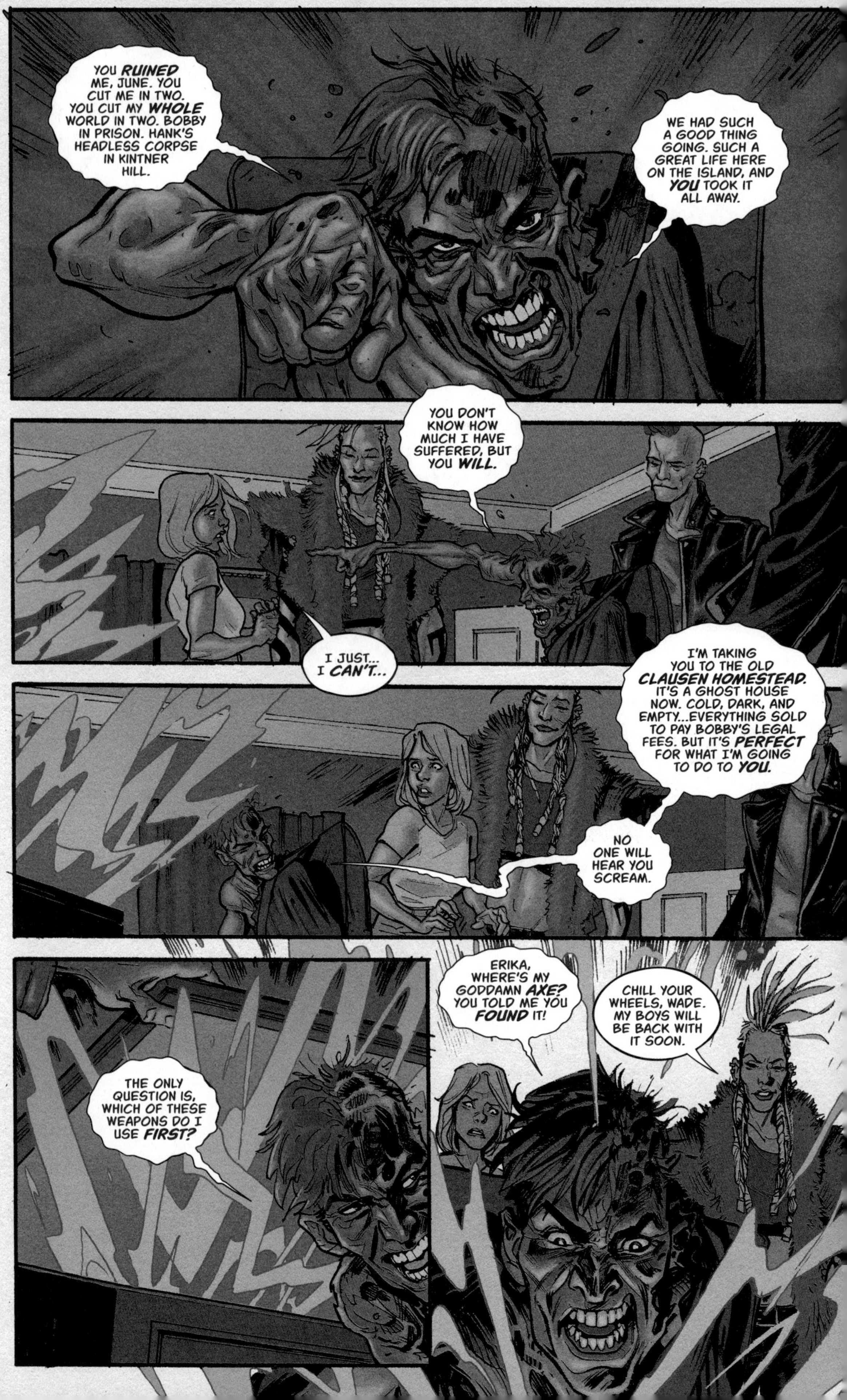
YOU **RUINED** ME, JUNE. YOU CUT ME IN TWO. YOU CUT MY **WHOLE** WORLD IN TWO. BOBBY IN PRISON. HANK'S HEADLESS CORPSE IN KINTNER HILL.
WE HAD SUCH A GOOD THING GOING. SUCH A GREAT LIFE HERE ON THE ISLAND, AND **YOU** TOOK IT ALL AWAY.
YOU DON'T KNOW HOW MUCH I HAVE SUFFERED, BUT YOU **WILL.**
I JUST... I **CAN'T...**
I'M TAKING YOU TO THE OLD **CLAUSEN HOMESTEAD.** IT'S A GHOST HOUSE NOW. COLD, DARK, AND EMPTY...EVERYTHING SOLD TO PAY BOBBY'S LEGAL FEES. BUT IT'S **PERFECT** FOR WHAT I'M GOING TO DO TO **YOU.**
NO ONE WILL HEAR YOU SCREAM.
THE ONLY QUESTION IS, WHICH OF THESE WEAPONS DO I USE **FIRST?**
ERIKA, WHERE'S MY GODDAMN **AXE?** YOU TOLD ME YOU **FOUND** IT!
CHILL YOUR WHEELS, WADE. MY BOYS WILL BE BACK WITH IT SOON.

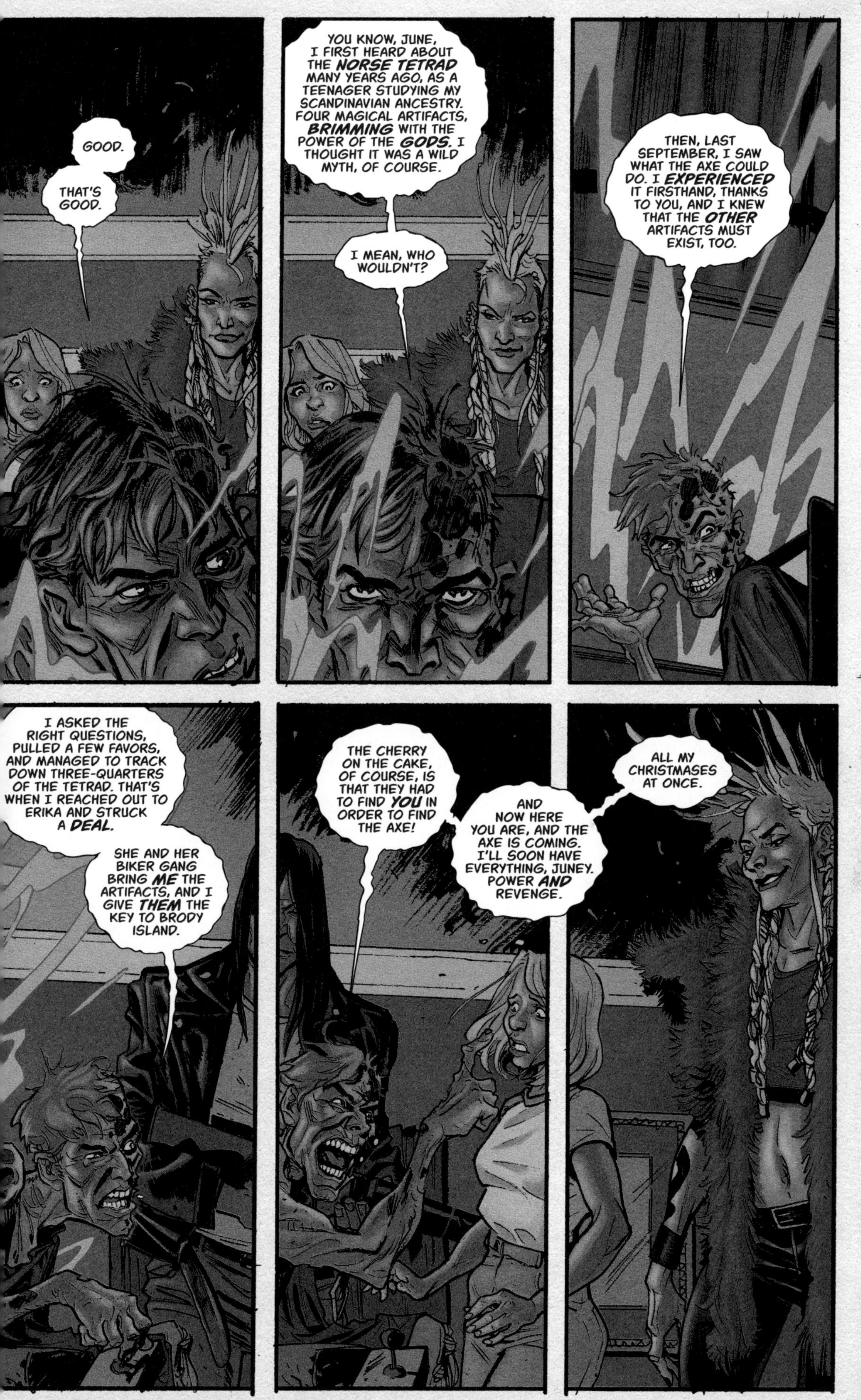
GOOD.
THAT'S GOOD.
YOU KNOW, JUNE, I FIRST HEARD ABOUT THE NORSE TETRAD MANY YEARS AGO, AS A TEENAGER STUDYING MY SCANDINAVIAN ANCESTRY. FOUR MAGICAL ARTIFACTS, BRIMMING WITH THE POWER OF THE GODS. I THOUGHT IT WAS A WILD MYTH, OF COURSE.
I MEAN, WHO WOULDN'T?
THEN, LAST SEPTEMBER, I SAW WHAT THE AXE COULD DO. I EXPERIENCED IT FIRSTHAND, THANKS TO YOU, AND I KNEW THAT THE OTHER ARTIFACTS MUST EXIST, TOO.
I ASKED THE RIGHT QUESTIONS, PULLED A FEW FAVORS, AND MANAGED TO TRACK DOWN THREE-QUARTERS OF THE TETRAD. THAT'S WHEN I REACHED OUT TO ERIKA AND STRUCK A DEAL.
SHE AND HER BIKER GANG BRING ME THE ARTIFACTS, AND I GIVE THEM THE KEY TO BRODY ISLAND.
THE CHERRY ON THE CAKE, OF COURSE, IS THAT THEY HAD TO FIND YOU IN ORDER TO FIND THE AXE!
AND NOW HERE YOU ARE, AND THE AXE IS COMING. I'LL SOON HAVE EVERYTHING, JUNEY. POWER AND REVENGE.
ALL MY CHRISTMASES AT ONCE.

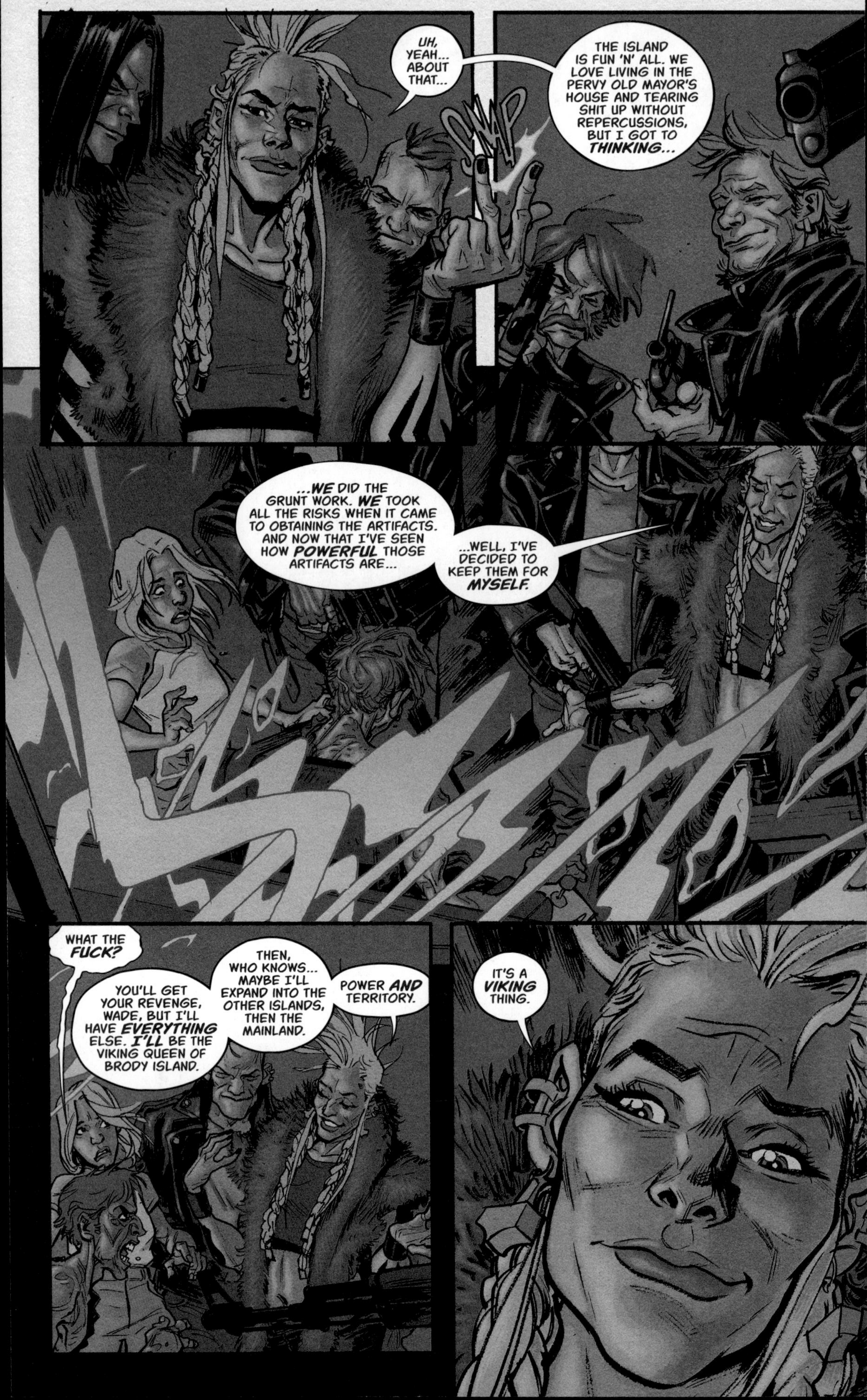
UH, YEAH... ABOUT THAT...
SNAP
THE ISLAND IS FUN 'N' ALL. WE LOVE LIVING IN THE PERVY OLD MAYOR'S HOUSE AND TEARING SHIT UP WITHOUT REPERCUSSIONS, BUT I GOT TO *THINKING*...
...*WE* DID THE GRUNT WORK. *WE* TOOK ALL THE RISKS WHEN IT CAME TO OBTAINING THE ARTIFACTS. AND NOW THAT I'VE SEEN HOW *POWERFUL* THOSE ARTIFACTS ARE...
...WELL, I'VE DECIDED TO KEEP THEM FOR *MYSELF*.
WHAT THE *FUCK?*
YOU'LL GET YOUR REVENGE, WADE, BUT I'LL HAVE *EVERYTHING* ELSE. *I'LL* BE THE VIKING QUEEN OF BRODY ISLAND.
THEN, WHO KNOWS... MAYBE I'LL EXPAND INTO THE OTHER ISLANDS, THEN THE MAINLAND.
POWER *AND* TERRITORY.
IT'S A *VIKING* THING.

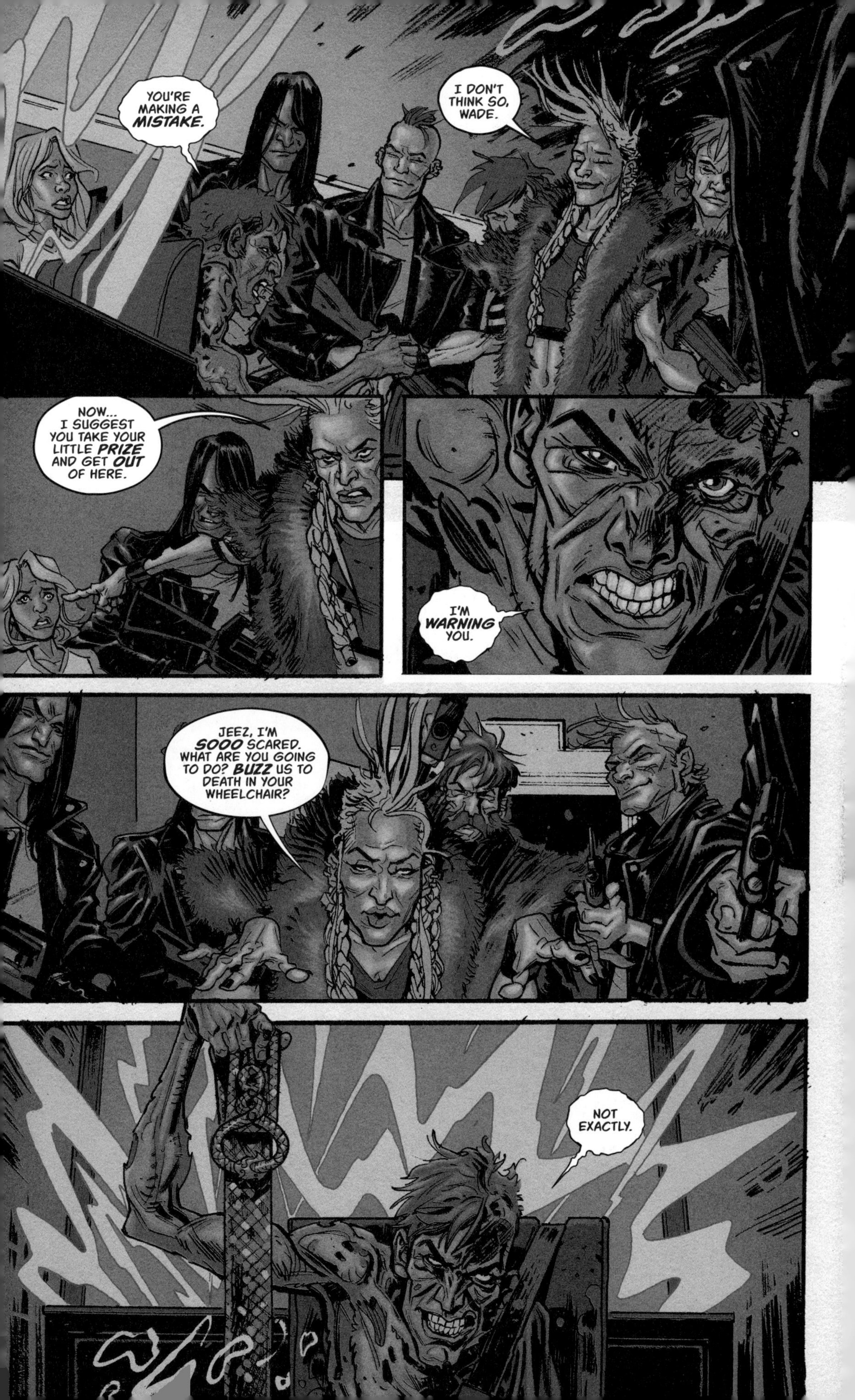
YOU'RE MAKING A MISTAKE.
I DON'T THINK SO, WADE.
NOW... I SUGGEST YOU TAKE YOUR LITTLE PRIZE AND GET OUT OF HERE.
I'M WARNING YOU.
JEEZ, I'M SOOO SCARED. WHAT ARE YOU GOING TO DO? BUZZ US TO DEATH IN YOUR WHEELCHAIR?
NOT EXACTLY.

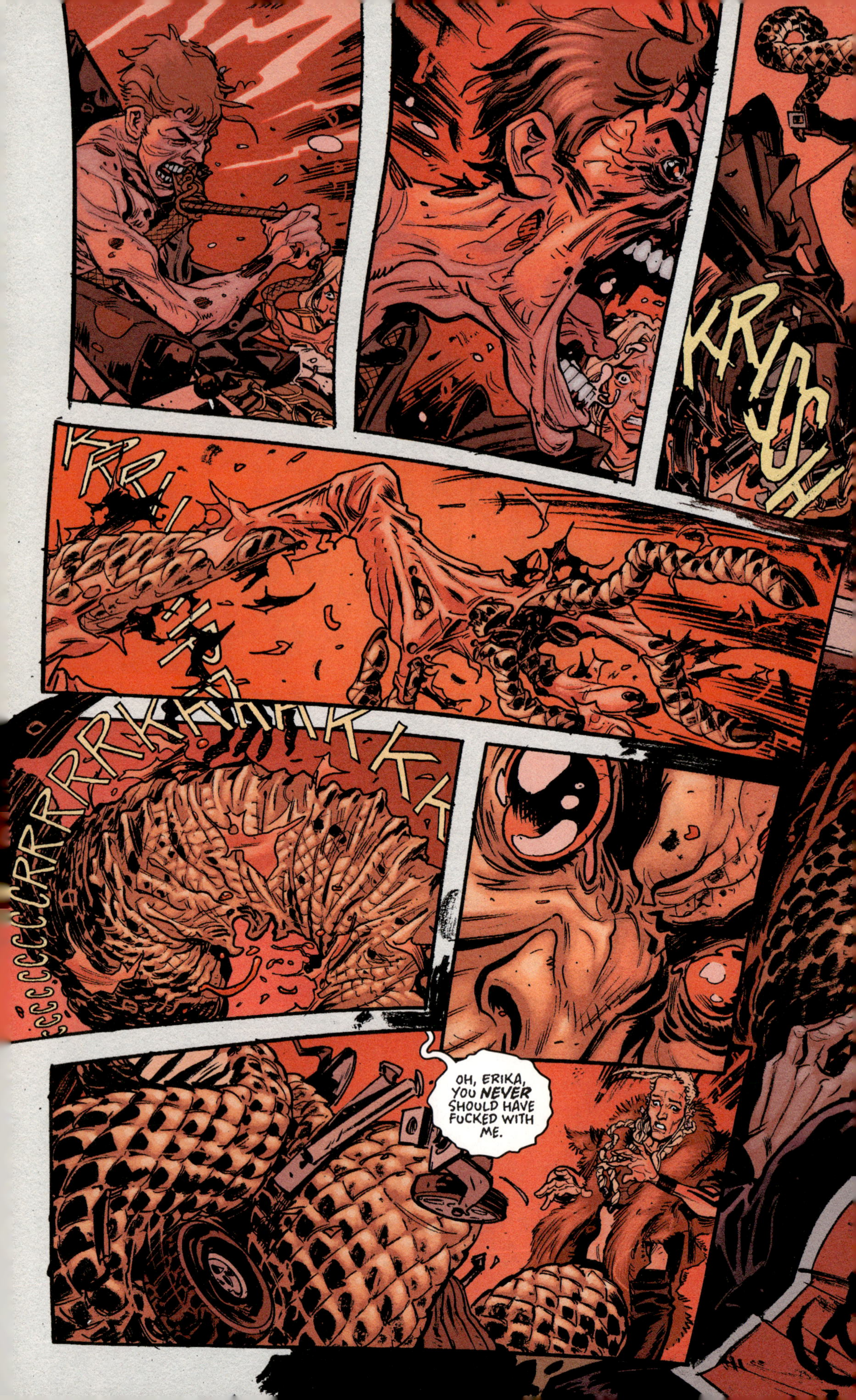
KRUSH
KRRII
KRRRRRRRKHHHHKKK
CCCCCCCCCCRRRRRRRRKKHHHHKKK
OH, ERIKA, YOU NEVER SHOULD HAVE FUCKED WITH ME.

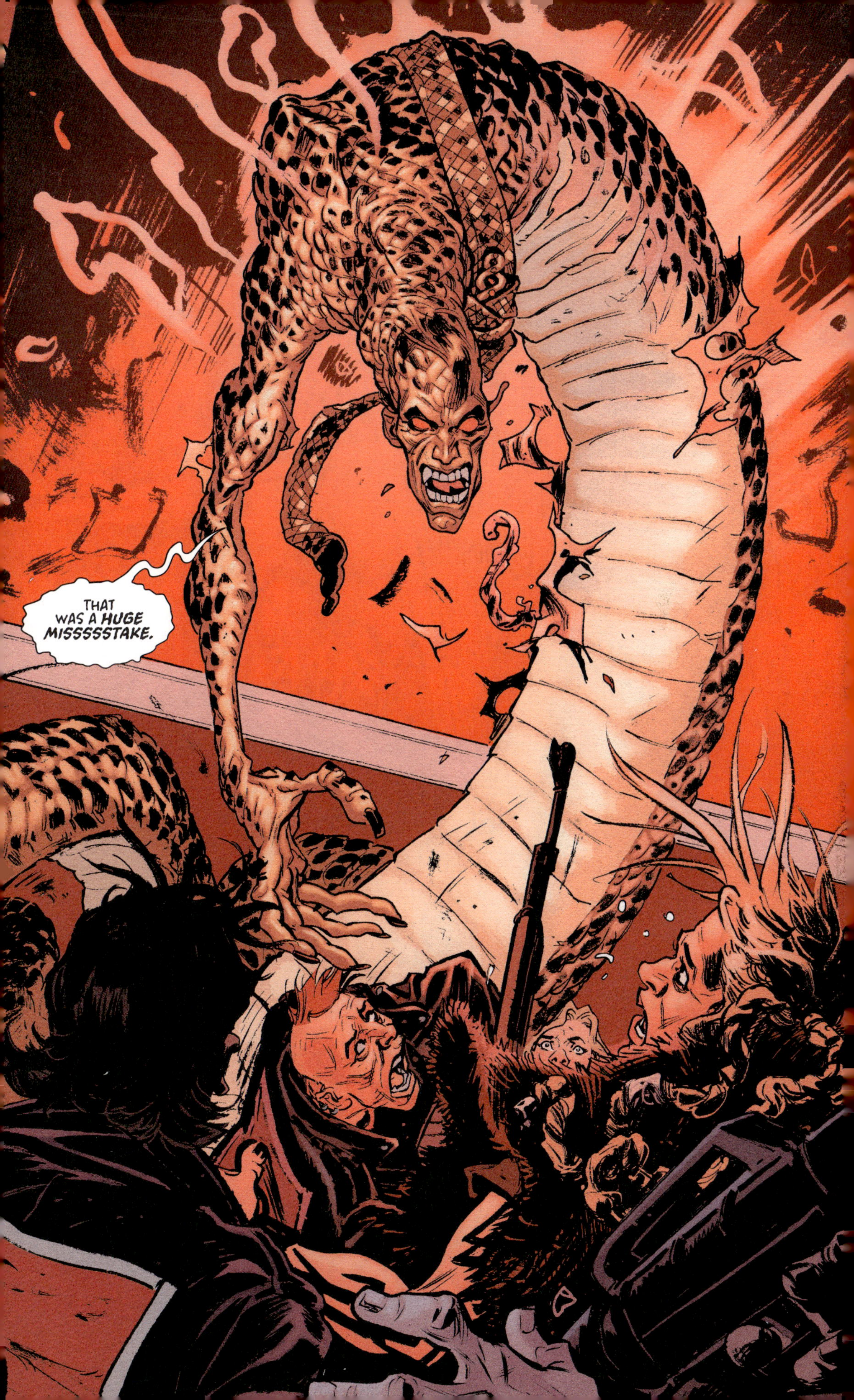
THAT WAS A HUGE MISSSSSTAKE.

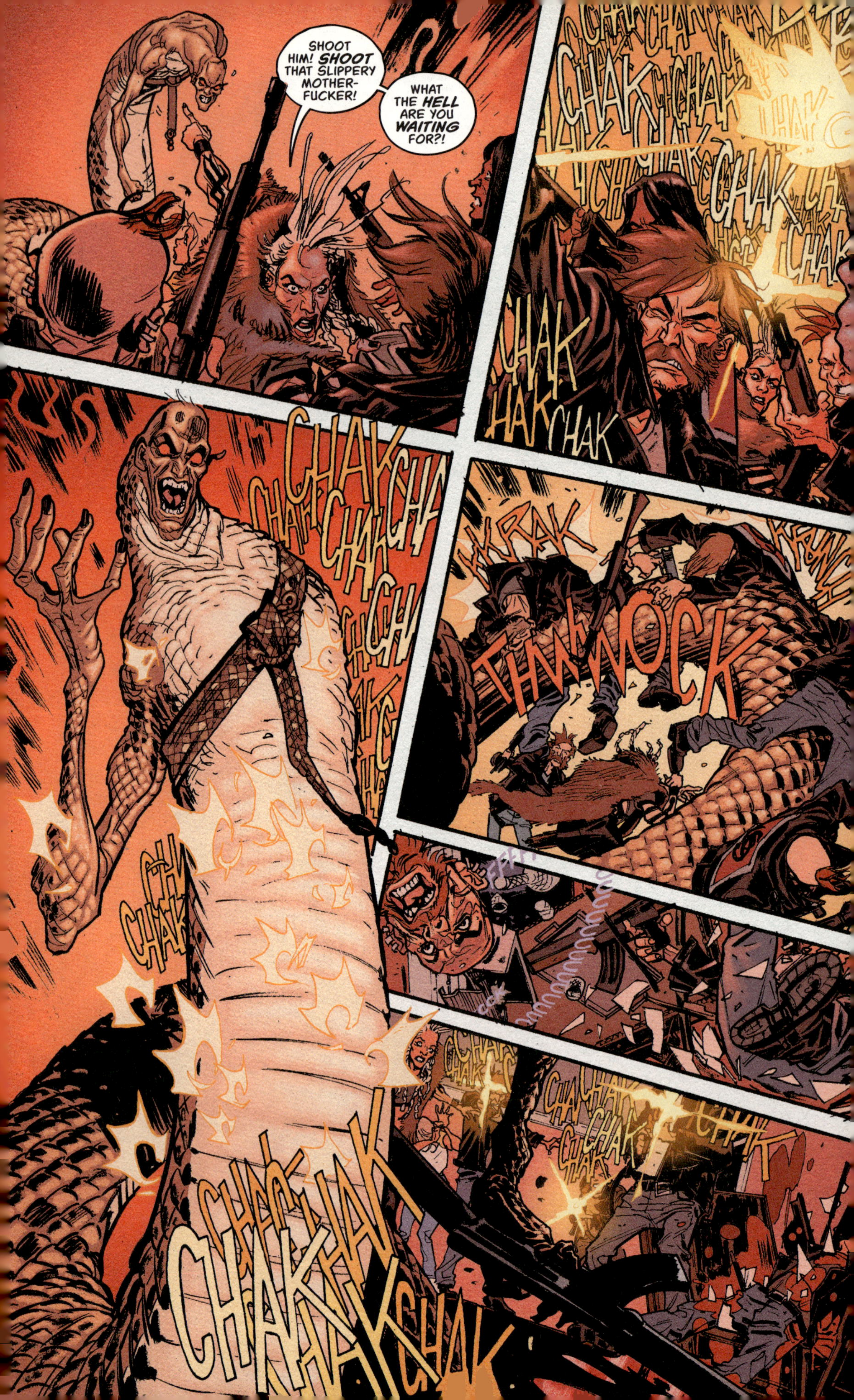

SHOOT HIM! SHOOT THAT SLIPPERY MOTHER-FUCKER!
WHAT THE HELL ARE YOU WAITING FOR?!
CHAK CHAK CHAK CHAK CHAK
CHAK CHAK CHAK CHAK
CHAK CHAK CHAK CHAK
KRAK
THWOCK
CHAK CHAK CHAK
CHAK CHAK CHAK CHAK

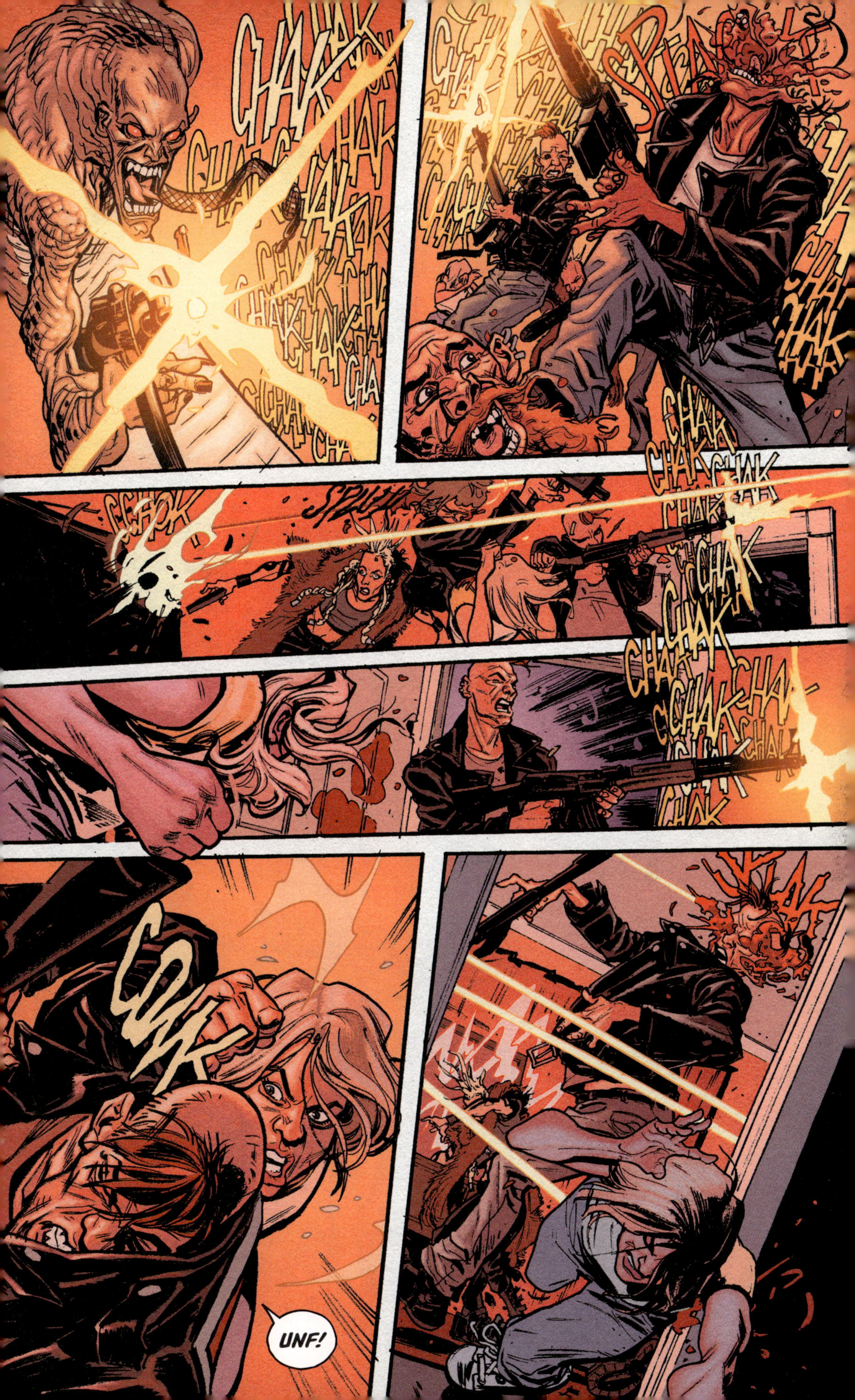

CHAK
CHAK
SPLAT
CHAK
SPLUT
CHAK
CHAK
COK
SPLAK
UNF!

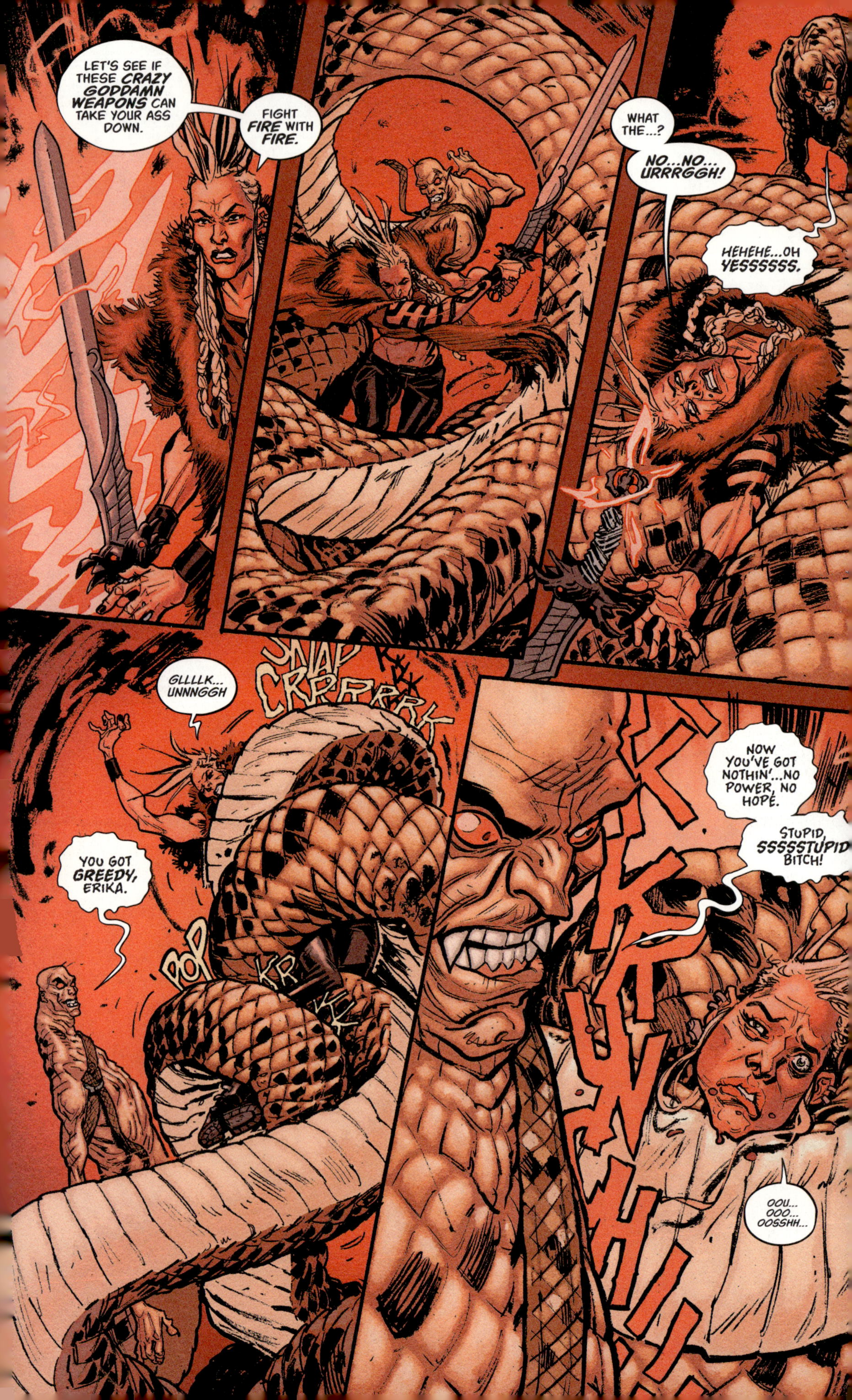
LET'S SEE IF THESE ***CRAZY GODDAMN WEAPONS*** CAN TAKE YOUR ASS DOWN.
FIGHT ***FIRE*** WITH ***FIRE.***
WHAT THE...?
NO...NO... URRRGGH!
HEHEHE...OH ***YESSSSSS.***
GLLLLK... UNNNGGH
SNAP
CRRRRRK
YOU GOT ***GREEDY,*** ERIKA.
POP
KR
NOW YOU'VE GOT NOTHIN'...NO POWER, NO HOPE.
STUPID, ***SSSSSTUPID*** BITCH!
OOU... OOO... OOSSHH...

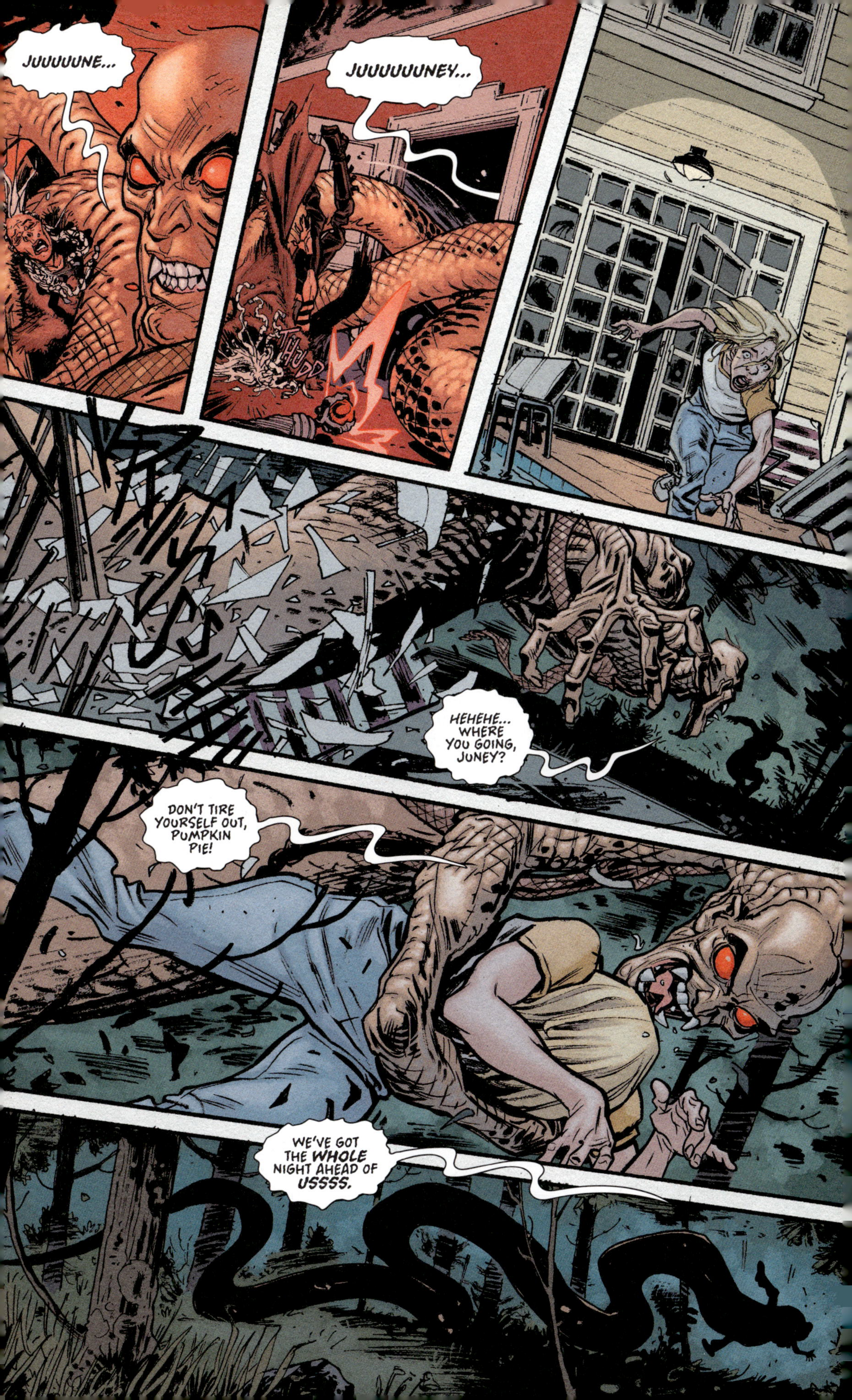
JUUUUUNE...
JUUUUUUNEY...
HEHEHE... WHERE YOU GOING, JUNEY?
DON'T TIRE YOURSELF OUT, PUMPKIN PIE!
WE'VE GOT THE WHOLE NIGHT AHEAD OF USSSS.

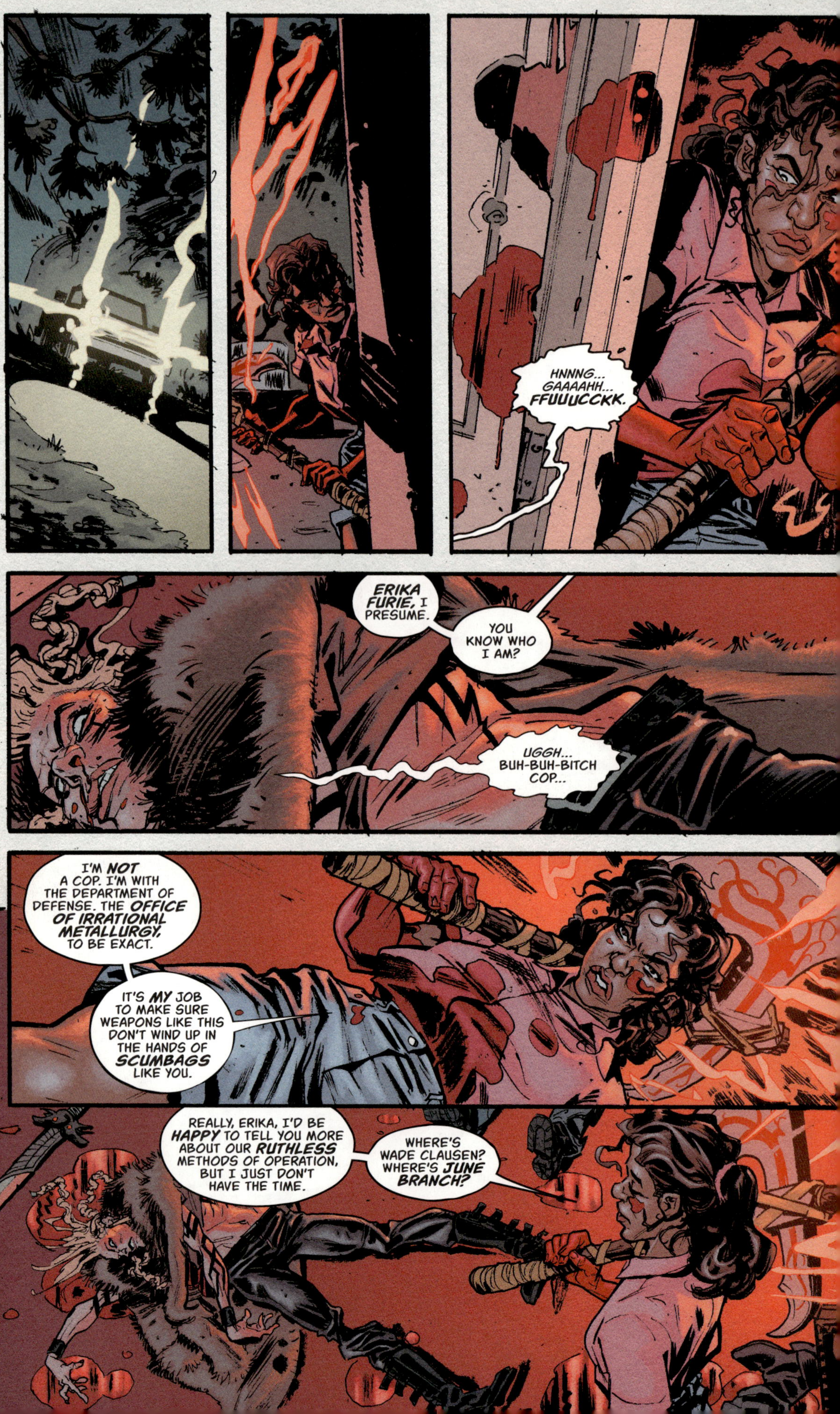
HNNNG... GAAAAHH... FFUUUCCKK.
ERIKA FURIE, I PRESUME.
YOU KNOW WHO I AM?
UGGH... BUH-BUH-BITCH COP...
I'M NOT A COP. I'M WITH THE DEPARTMENT OF DEFENSE. THE OFFICE OF IRRATIONAL METALLURGY, TO BE EXACT.
IT'S MY JOB TO MAKE SURE WEAPONS LIKE THIS DON'T WIND UP IN THE HANDS OF SCUMBAGS LIKE YOU.
REALLY, ERIKA, I'D BE HAPPY TO TELL YOU MORE ABOUT OUR RUTHLESS METHODS OF OPERATION, BUT I JUST DON'T HAVE THE TIME.
WHERE'S WADE CLAUSEN? WHERE'S JUNE BRANCH?

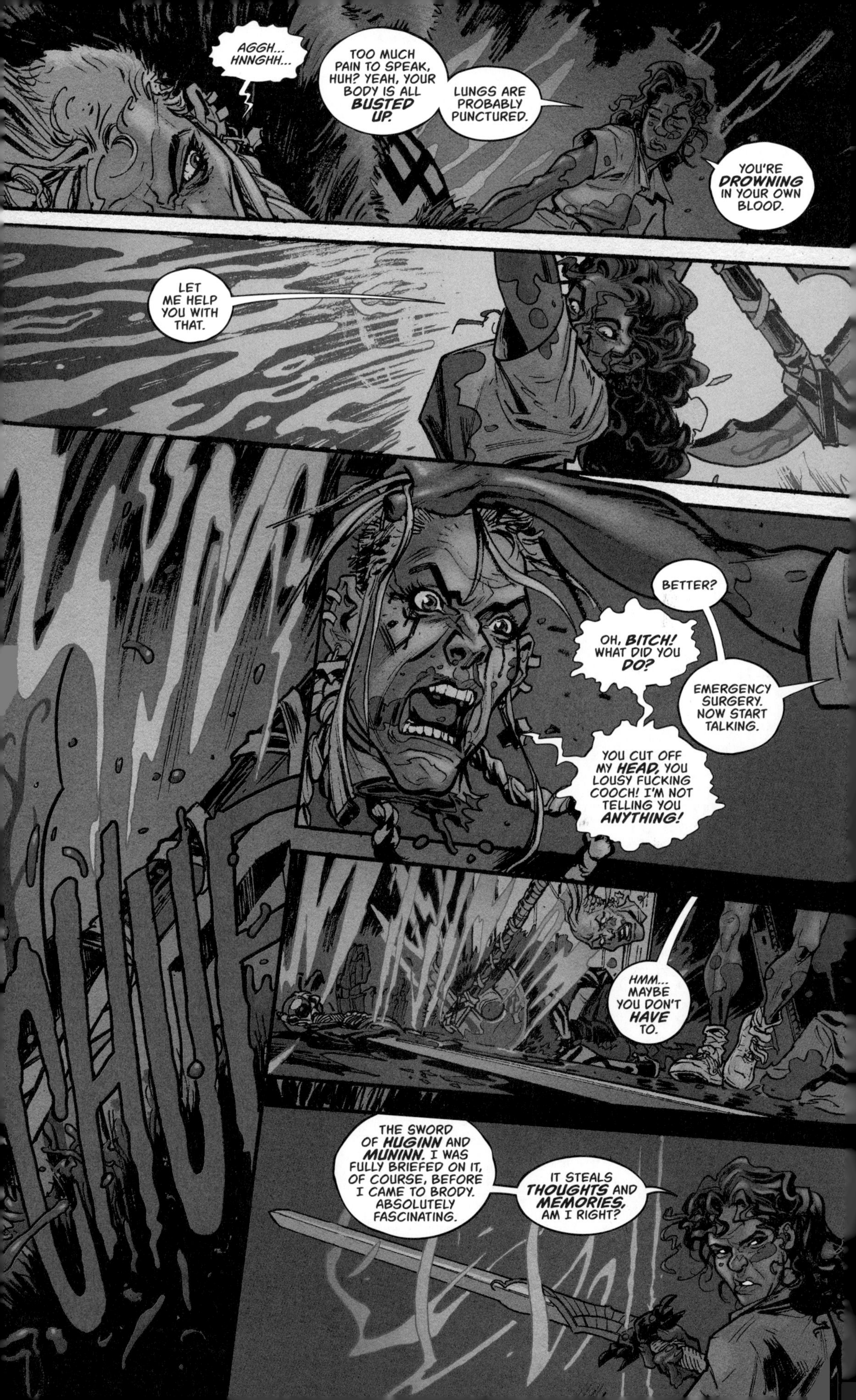
AGGH... HNNGHH...
TOO MUCH PAIN TO SPEAK, HUH? YEAH, YOUR BODY IS ALL BUSTED UP.
LUNGS ARE PROBABLY PUNCTURED.
YOU'RE DROWNING IN YOUR OWN BLOOD.
LET ME HELP YOU WITH THAT.
BETTER?
OH, BITCH! WHAT DID YOU DO?
EMERGENCY SURGERY. NOW START TALKING.
YOU CUT OFF MY HEAD, YOU LOUSY FUCKING COOCH! I'M NOT TELLING YOU ANYTHING!
HMM... MAYBE YOU DON'T HAVE TO.
THE SWORD OF HUGINN AND MUNINN. I WAS FULLY BRIEFED ON IT, OF COURSE, BEFORE I CAME TO BRODY. ABSOLUTELY FASCINATING.
IT STEALS THOUGHTS AND MEMORIES, AM I RIGHT?

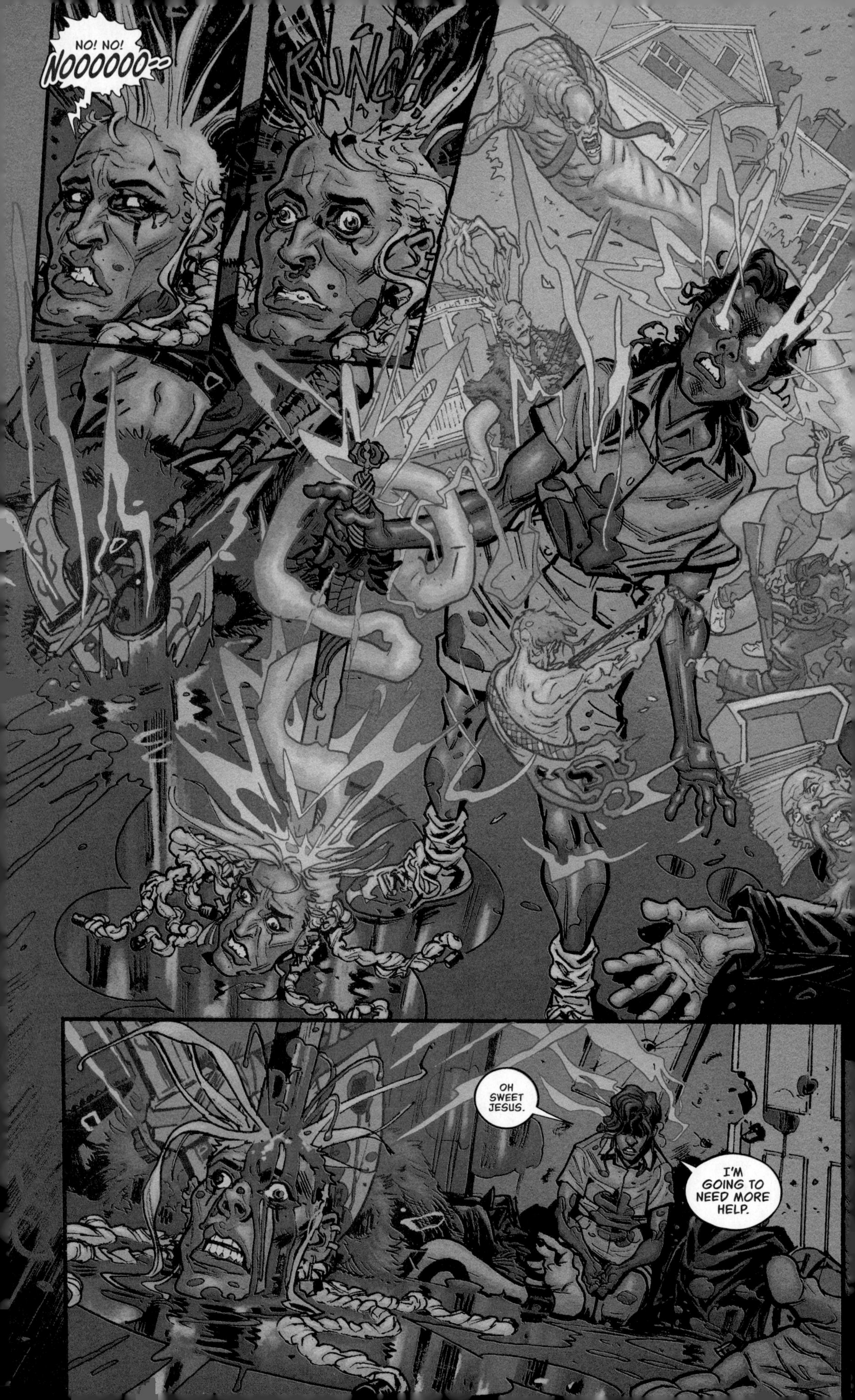
NO! NO! NOOOOOO--
KRUNCH!
OH SWEET JESUS.
I'M GOING TO NEED MORE HELP.

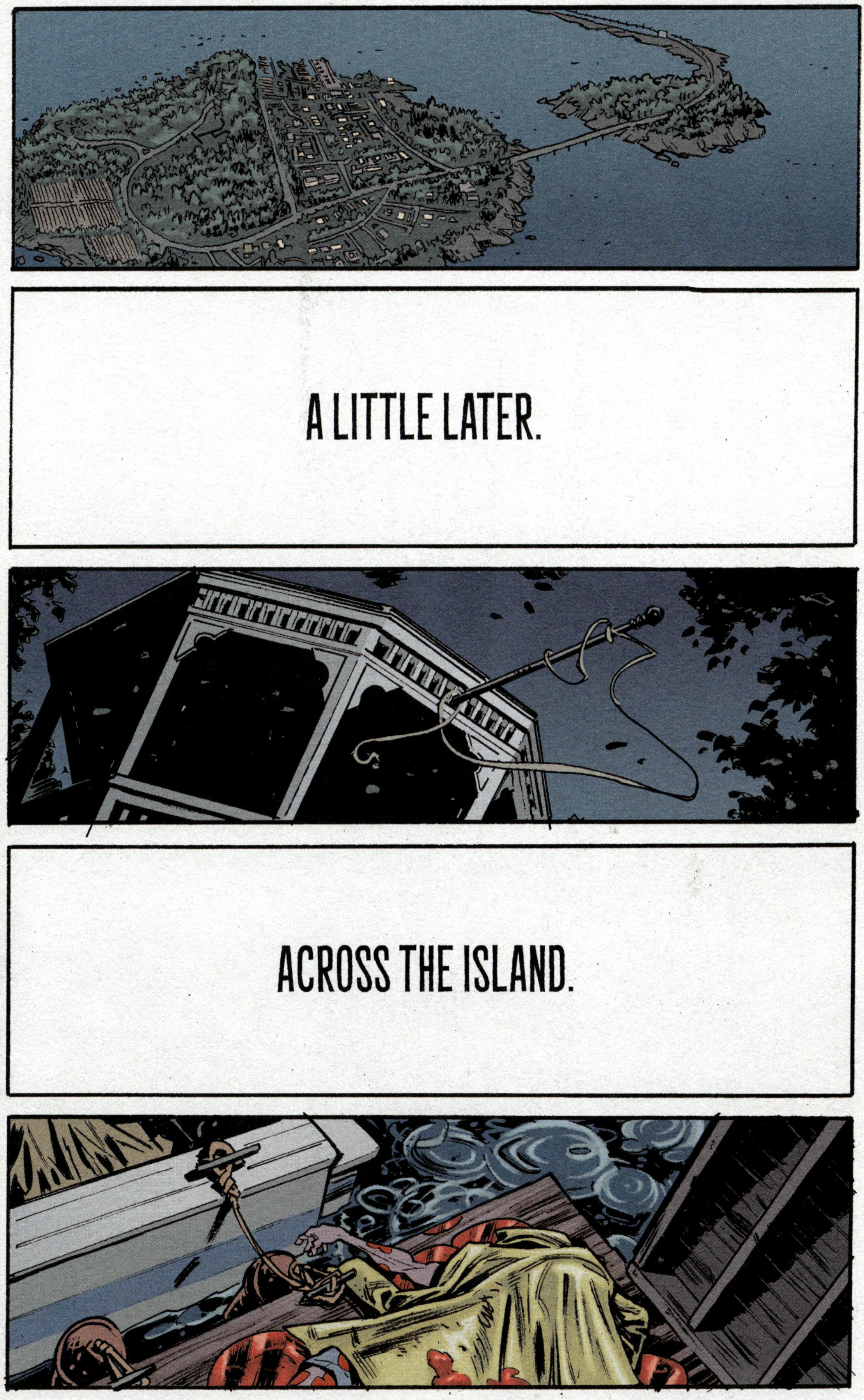
A LITTLE LATER.
ACROSS THE ISLAND.

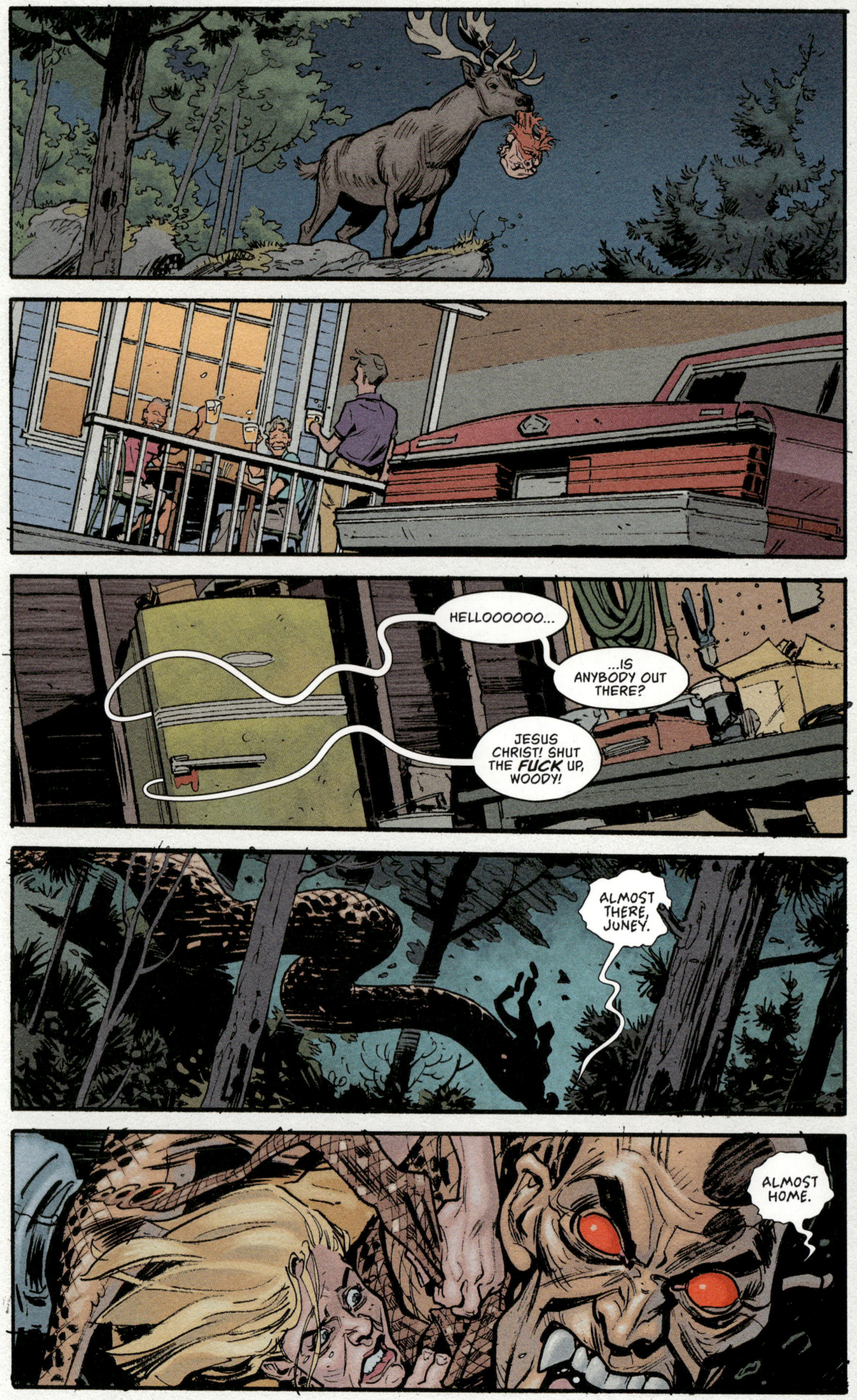
HELLOOOOOO...
...IS ANYBODY OUT THERE?
JESUS CHRIST! SHUT THE FUCK UP, WOODY!
ALMOST THERE, JUNEY.
ALMOST HOME.

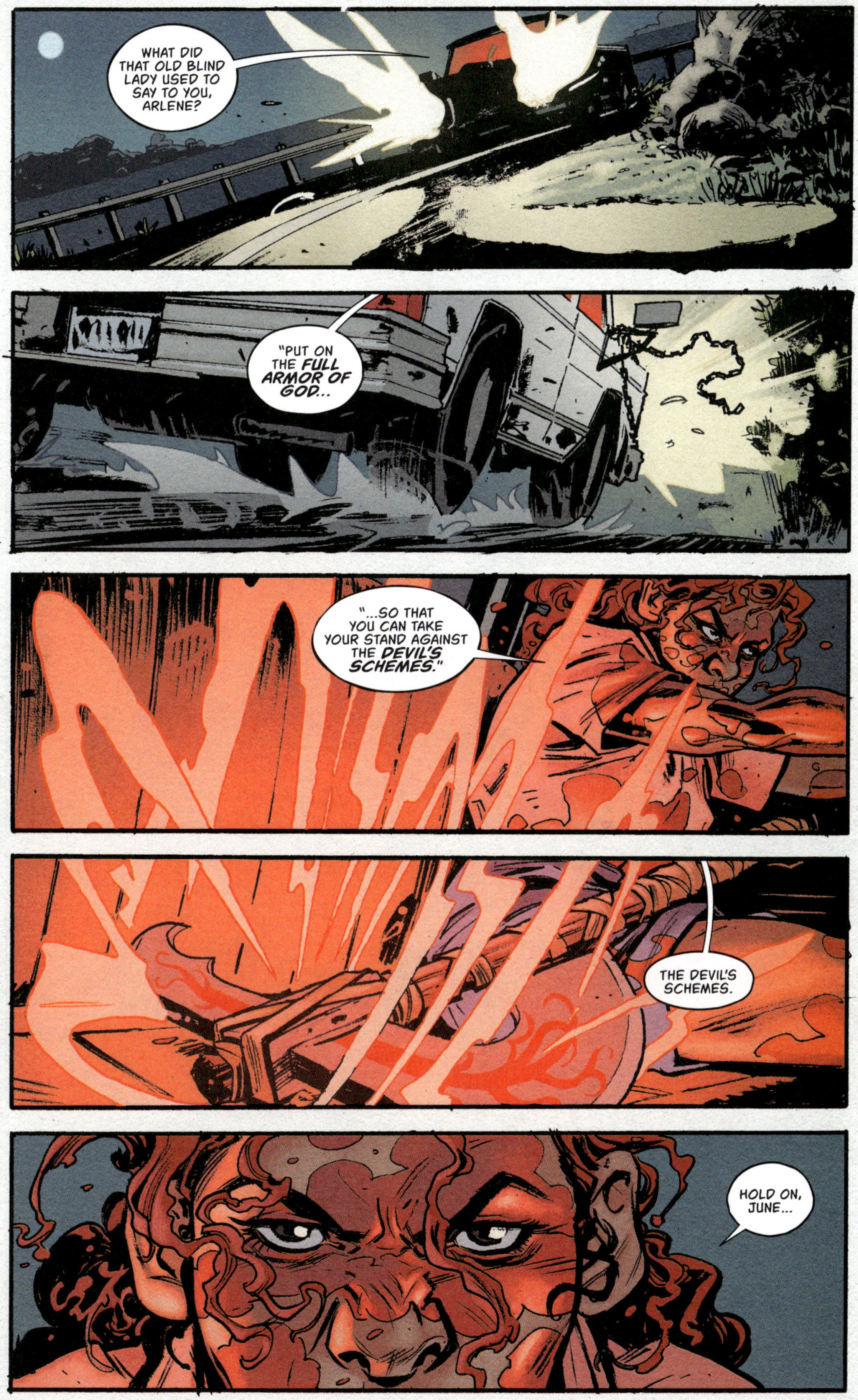
WHAT DID THAT OLD BLIND LADY USED TO SAY TO YOU, ARLENE?
"PUT ON THE FULL ARMOR OF GOD...
"...SO THAT YOU CAN TAKE YOUR STAND AGAINST THE DEVIL'S SCHEMES."
THE DEVIL'S SCHEMES.
HOLD ON, JUNE...

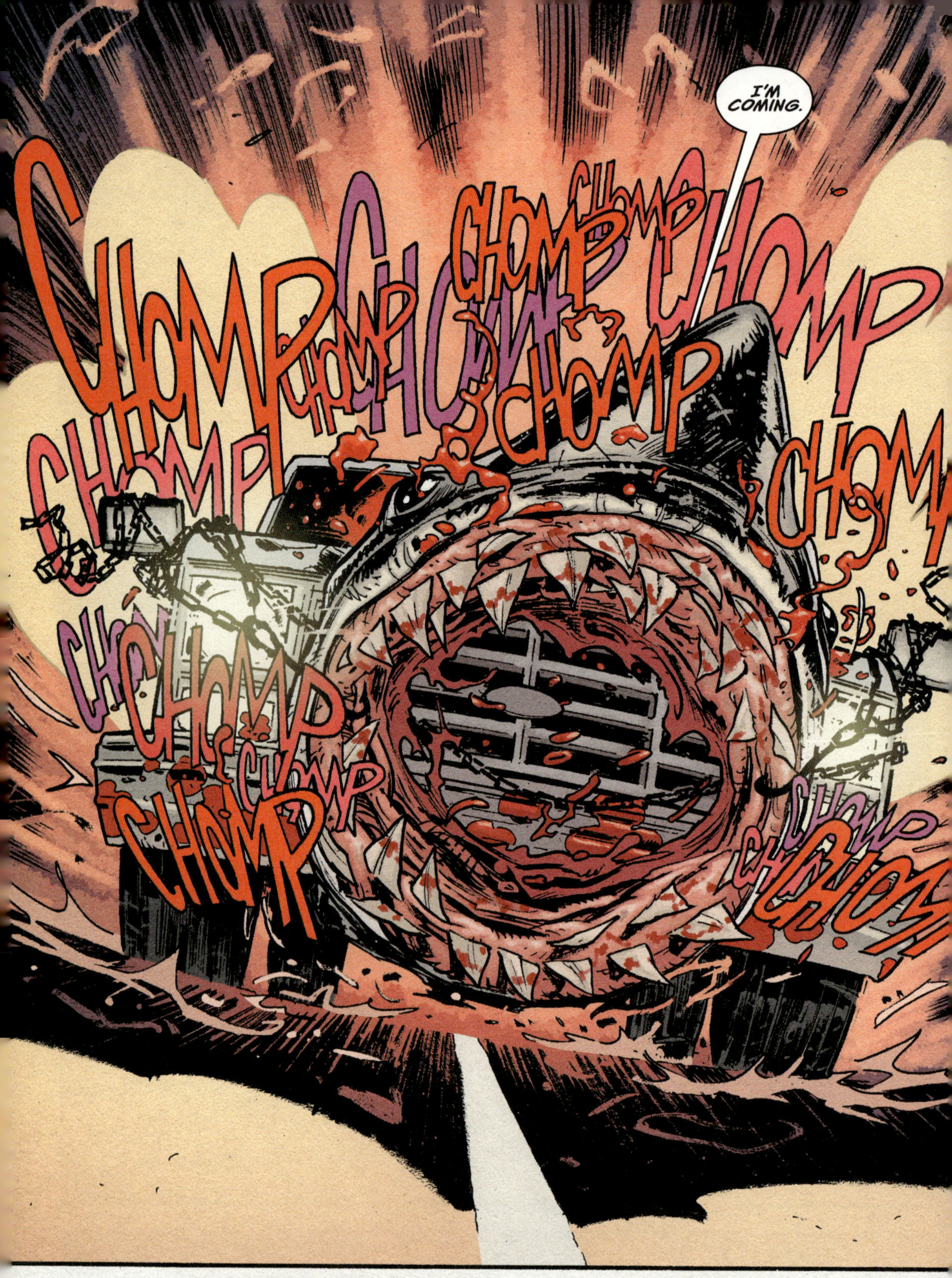
I'M COMING.
CHOMP
CHOMP
CHOMP
CHOMP
CHOMP
CHOMP
CHOMP
CHOMP
CHOMP

TO BE CONCLUDED. . .

REFRIGERATOR FULL OF HEADS

Written by RIO YOUERS Drawn by TOM FOWLER
Colored by BILL CRABTREE Lettered by ANDWORLD DESIGN
Cover by MARCIO TAKARA Variant cover by NICK ROBLES

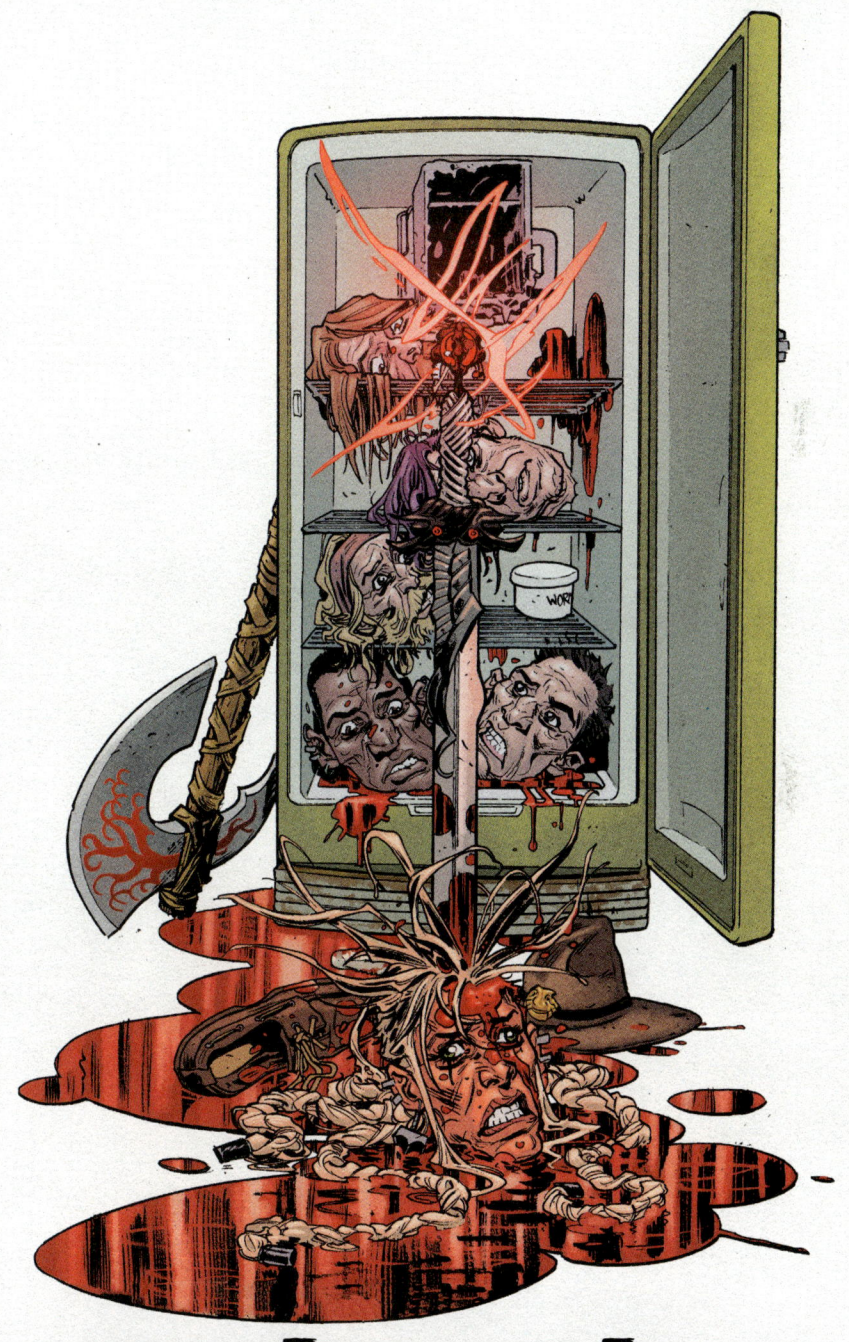

ANDREA SHEA & CHRIS CONROY Editors

BASKETFUL OF HEADS created by JOE HILL with art by LEOMACS
REFRIGERATOR FULL OF HEADS curated for HILL HOUSE COMICS by JOE HILL

"YOU DON'T KNOW HOW MUCH I HAVE SUFFERED, BUT YOU WILL."

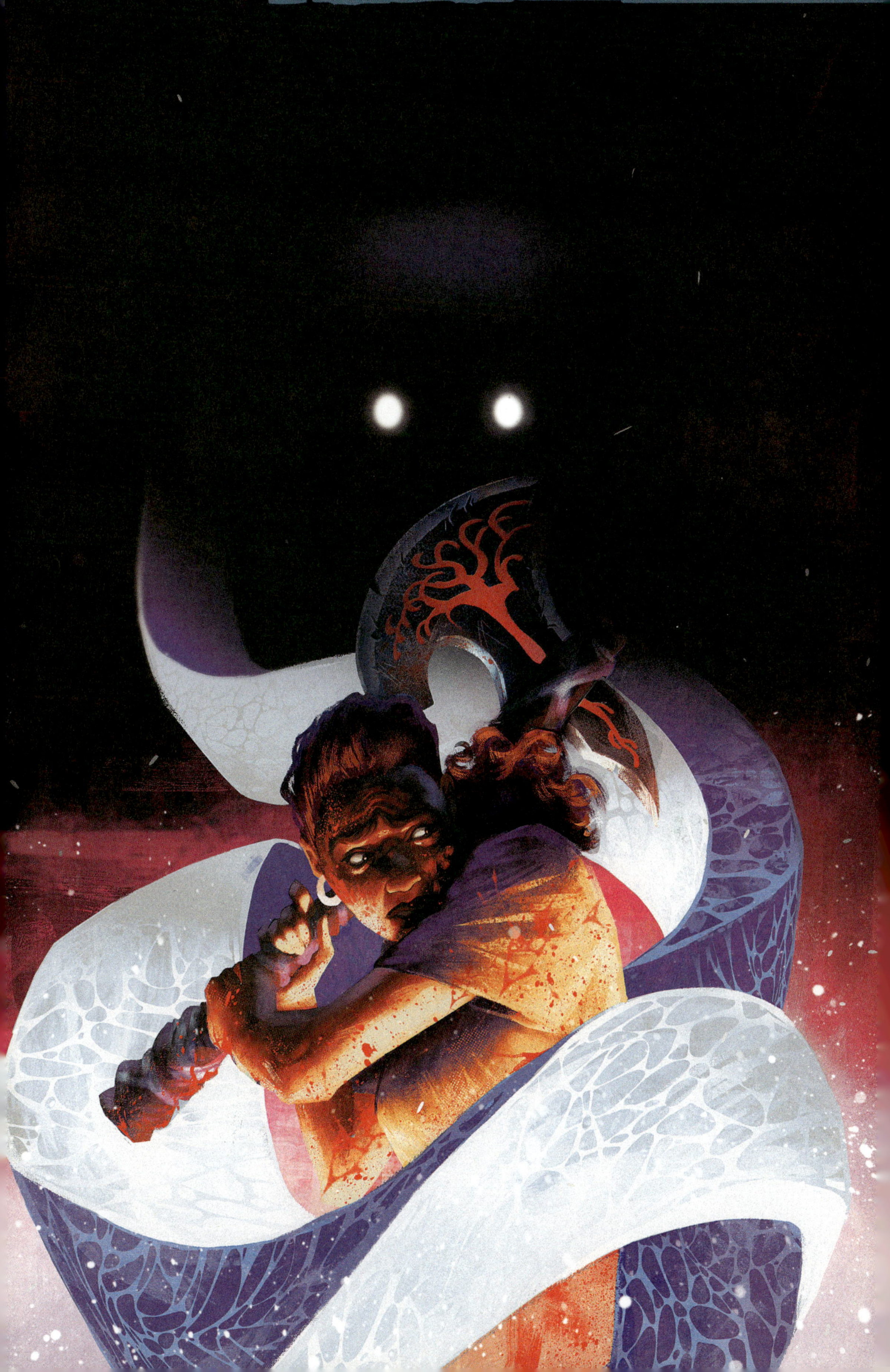

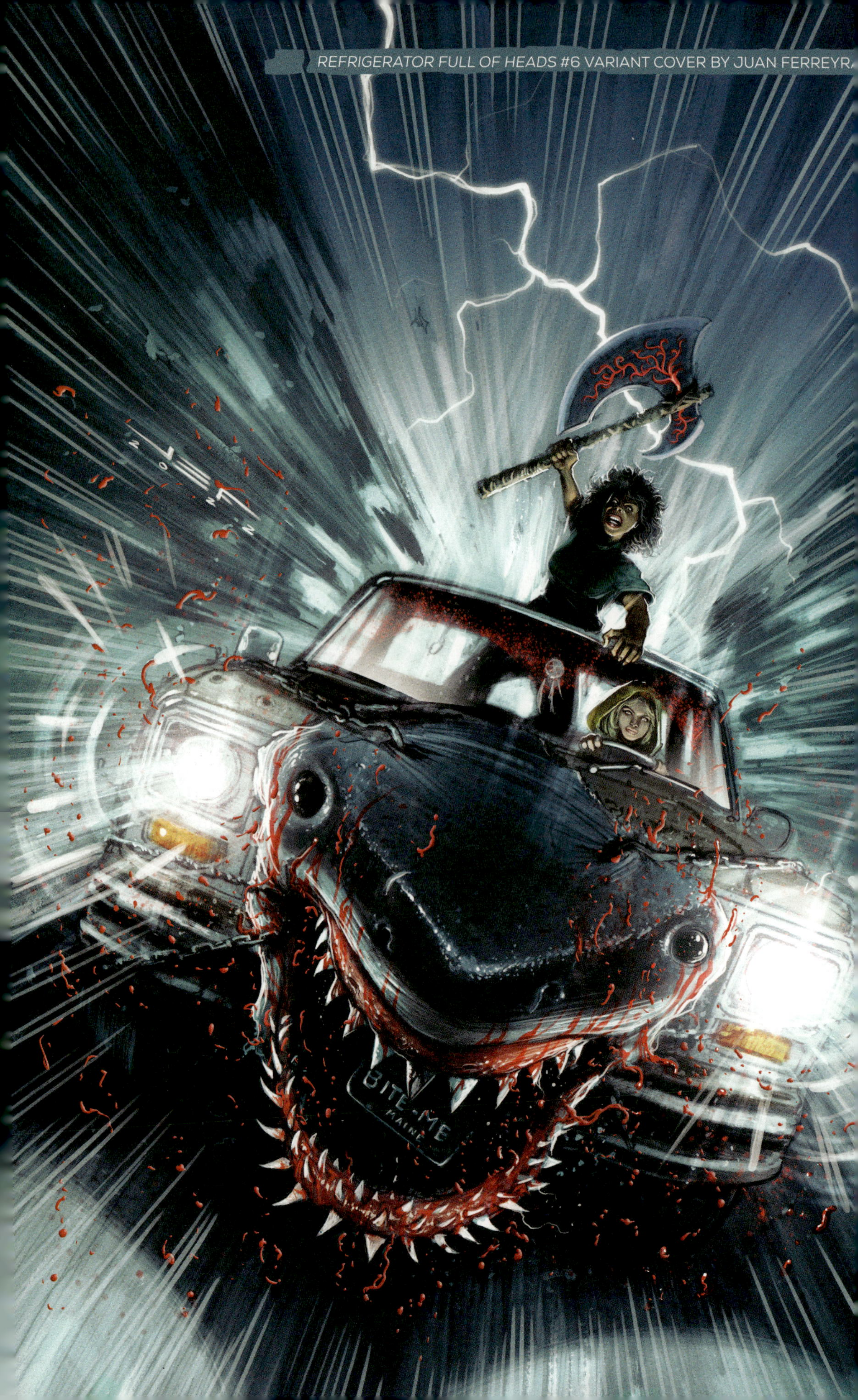
BITE-ME
MAINE
REFRIGERATOR FULL OF HEADS #6 VARIANT COVER BY JUAN FERREYR

BEFORE.

"NOTHING TO IT, RIGHT? WE BLEND IN, CHAT WITH THE LOCALS, AND GATHER INTEL. AND IF WE SHOULD HAPPEN TO ENJOY A FEW LOBSTER DINNERS ALONG THE WAY, THEN SO BE IT."

"LOBSTER..."

U.S. DEPARTMENT OF DEFENSE.
THE OFFICE OF IRRATIONAL METALLURGY.

A. FIELDS
C. BERINGER

OH, AND THE HOUSE COMES WITH A BOAT. I MEAN...WE'LL *HAVE* TO TAKE IT OUT, TO MAINTAIN OUR COVER. IT'S WHAT ANY *NORMAL* COUPLE WOULD DO.

YEAH, I... I GUESS.

LOS ALAMOS, NEW MEXICO.

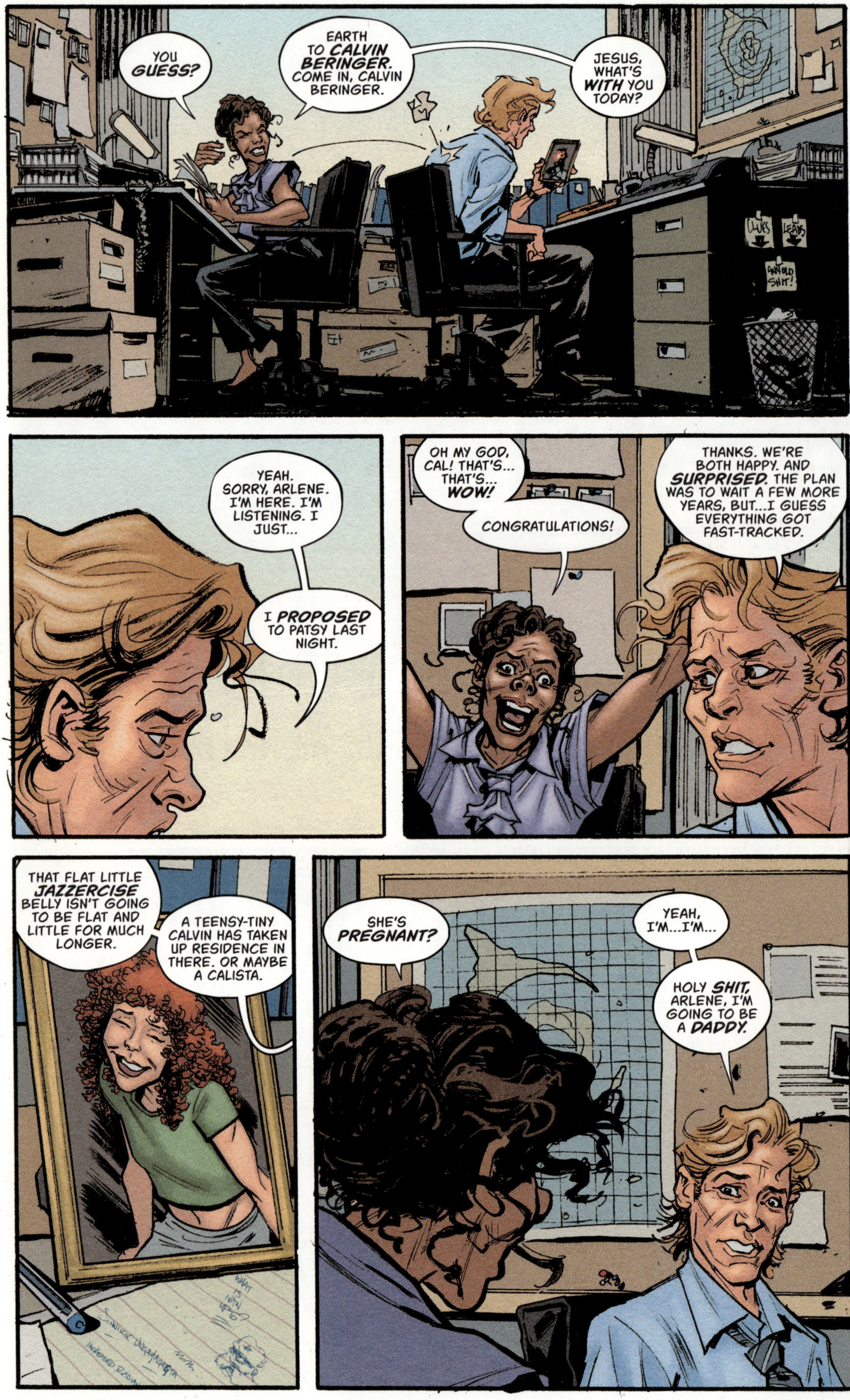
YOU GUESS?
EARTH TO CALVIN BERINGER. COME IN, CALVIN BERINGER.
JESUS, WHAT'S WITH YOU TODAY?
YEAH. SORRY, ARLENE. I'M HERE. I'M LISTENING. I JUST...
I PROPOSED TO PATSY LAST NIGHT.
OH MY GOD, CAL! THAT'S... THAT'S... WOW!
CONGRATULATIONS!
THANKS. WE'RE BOTH HAPPY. AND SURPRISED. THE PLAN WAS TO WAIT A FEW MORE YEARS, BUT...I GUESS EVERYTHING GOT FAST-TRACKED.
THAT FLAT LITTLE JAZZERCISE BELLY ISN'T GOING TO BE FLAT AND LITTLE FOR MUCH LONGER.
A TEENSY-TINY CALVIN HAS TAKEN UP RESIDENCE IN THERE. OR MAYBE A CALISTA.
SHE'S PREGNANT?
YEAH, I'M...I'M...
HOLY SHIT, ARLENE, I'M GOING TO BE A DADDY.

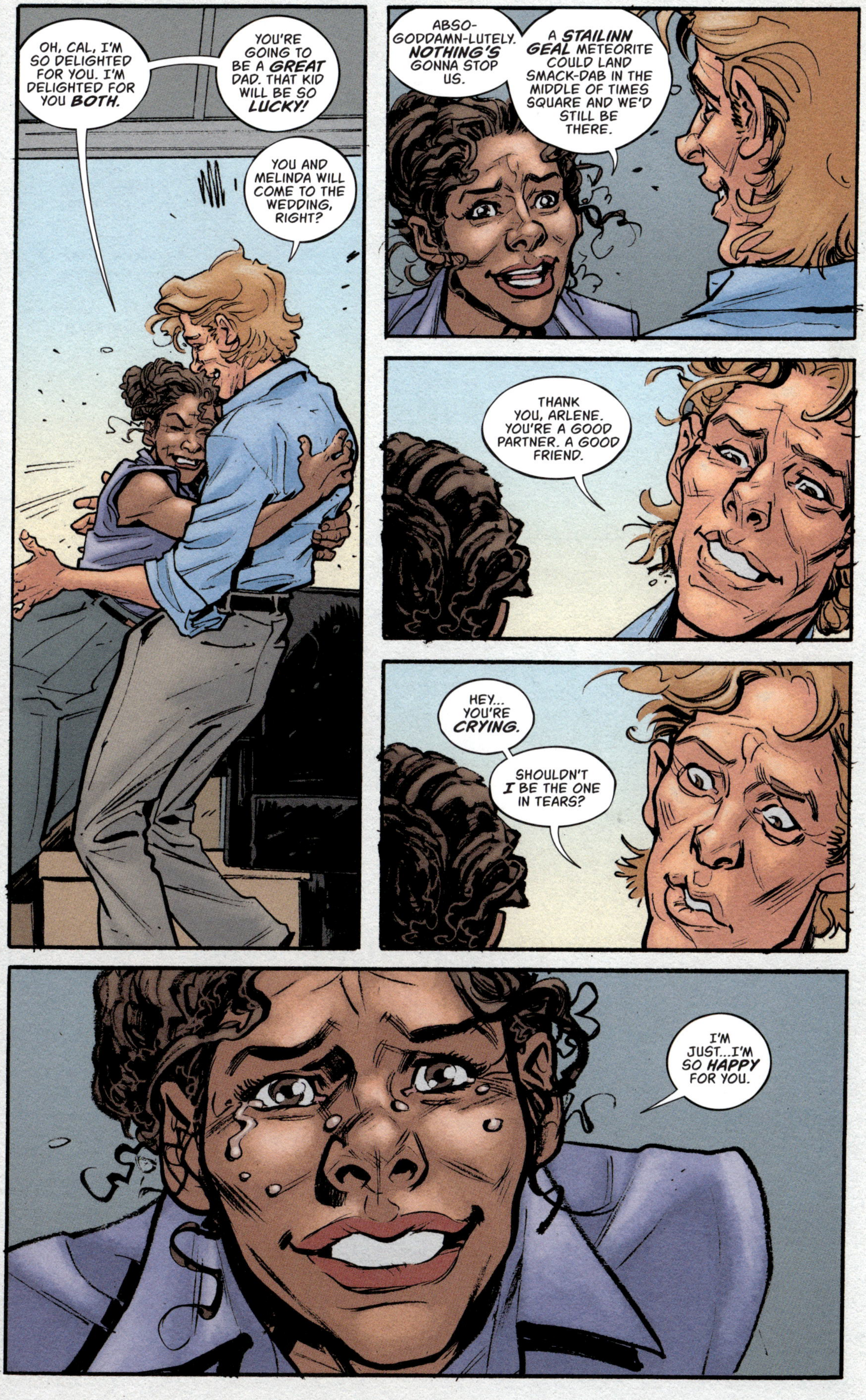
OH, CAL, I'M SO DELIGHTED FOR YOU. I'M DELIGHTED FOR YOU **BOTH.**
YOU'RE GOING TO BE A **GREAT** DAD. THAT KID WILL BE SO **LUCKY!**
YOU AND MELINDA WILL COME TO THE WEDDING, RIGHT?
ABSO-GODDAMN-LUTELY. **NOTHING'S** GONNA STOP US.
A **STAILINN GEAL** METEORITE COULD LAND SMACK-DAB IN THE MIDDLE OF TIMES SQUARE AND WE'D STILL BE THERE.
THANK YOU, ARLENE. YOU'RE A GOOD PARTNER. A GOOD FRIEND.
HEY... YOU'RE **CRYING.**
SHOULDN'T **I** BE THE ONE IN TEARS?
I'M JUST...I'M SO **HAPPY** FOR YOU.

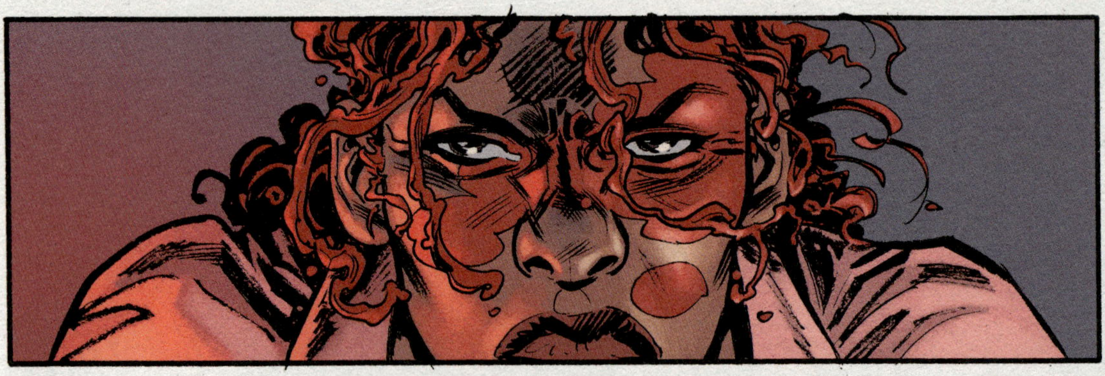

NOW.

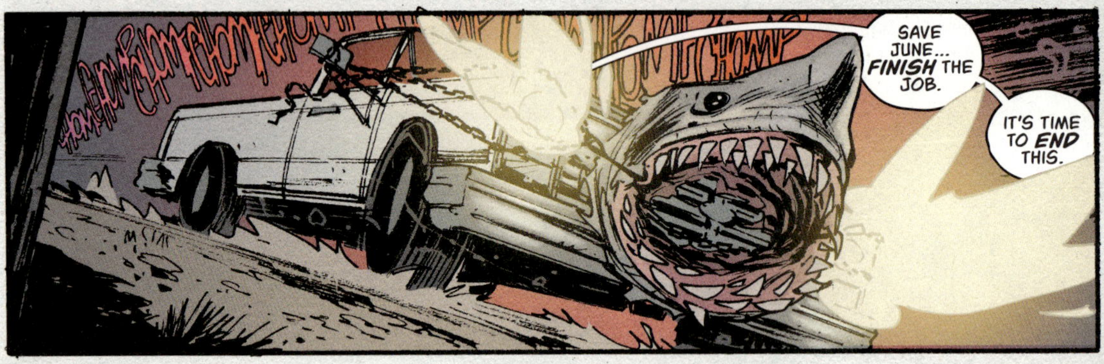
SAVE JUNE... **FINISH** THE JOB.
IT'S TIME TO **END** THIS.

BRODY ISLAND.

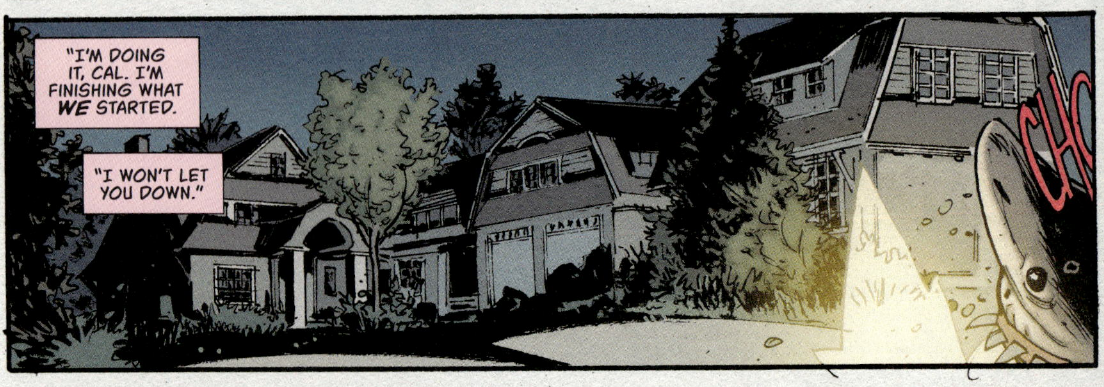
"I'M DOING IT, CAL. I'M FINISHING WHAT **WE** STARTED.
"I WON'T LET YOU DOWN."

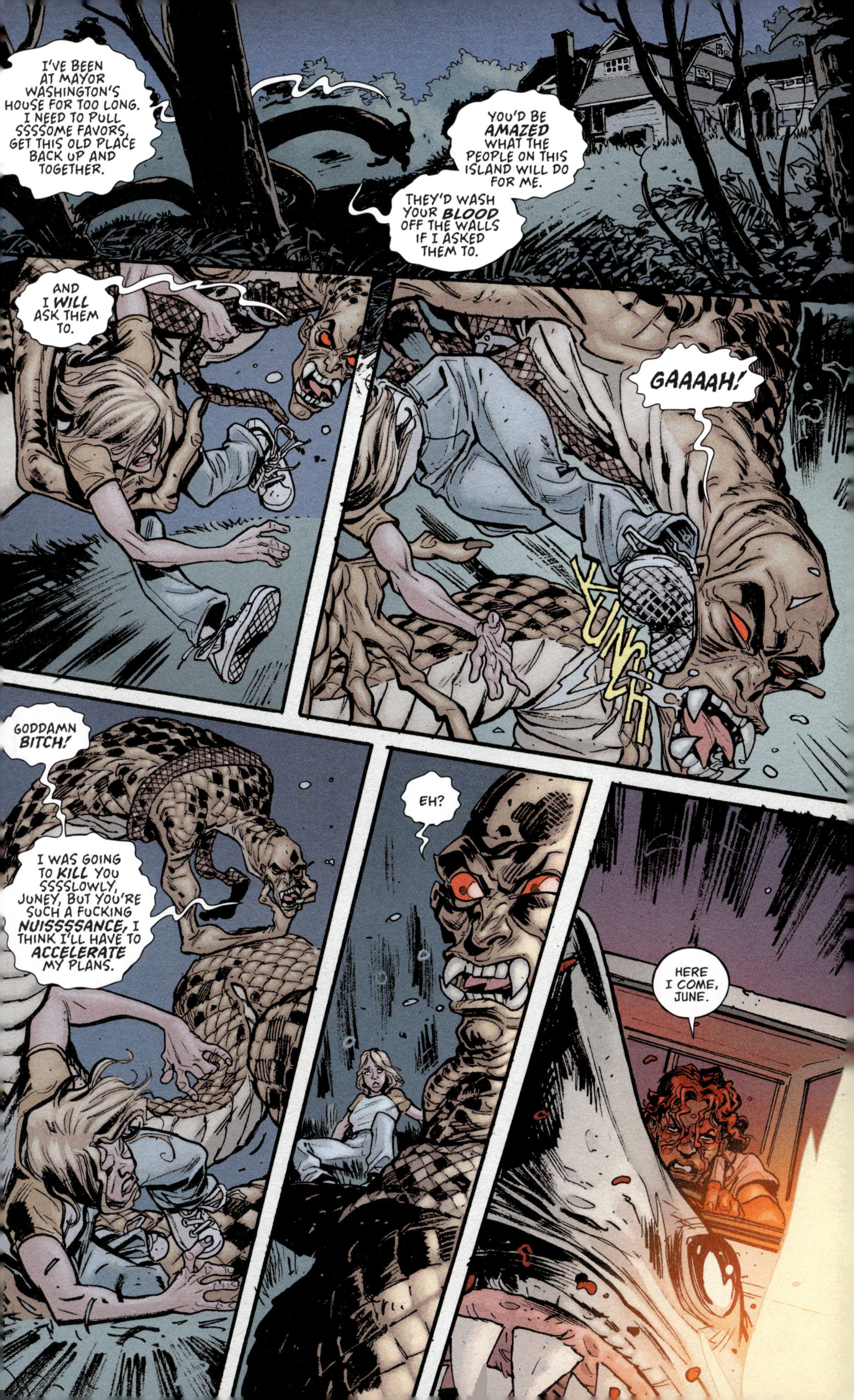
I'VE BEEN AT MAYOR WASHINGTON'S HOUSE FOR TOO LONG. I NEED TO PULL SSSSOME FAVORS, GET THIS OLD PLACE BACK UP AND TOGETHER.
YOU'D BE AMAZED WHAT THE PEOPLE ON THIS ISLAND WILL DO FOR ME.
THEY'D WASH YOUR BLOOD OFF THE WALLS IF I ASKED THEM TO.
AND I WILL ASK THEM TO.
GAAAAH!
KLUNCH
GODDAMN BITCH!
I WAS GOING TO KILL YOU SSSSLOWLY, JUNEY, BUT YOU'RE SUCH A FUCKING NUISSSSANCE, I THINK I'LL HAVE TO ACCELERATE MY PLANS.
EH?
HERE I COME, JUNE.

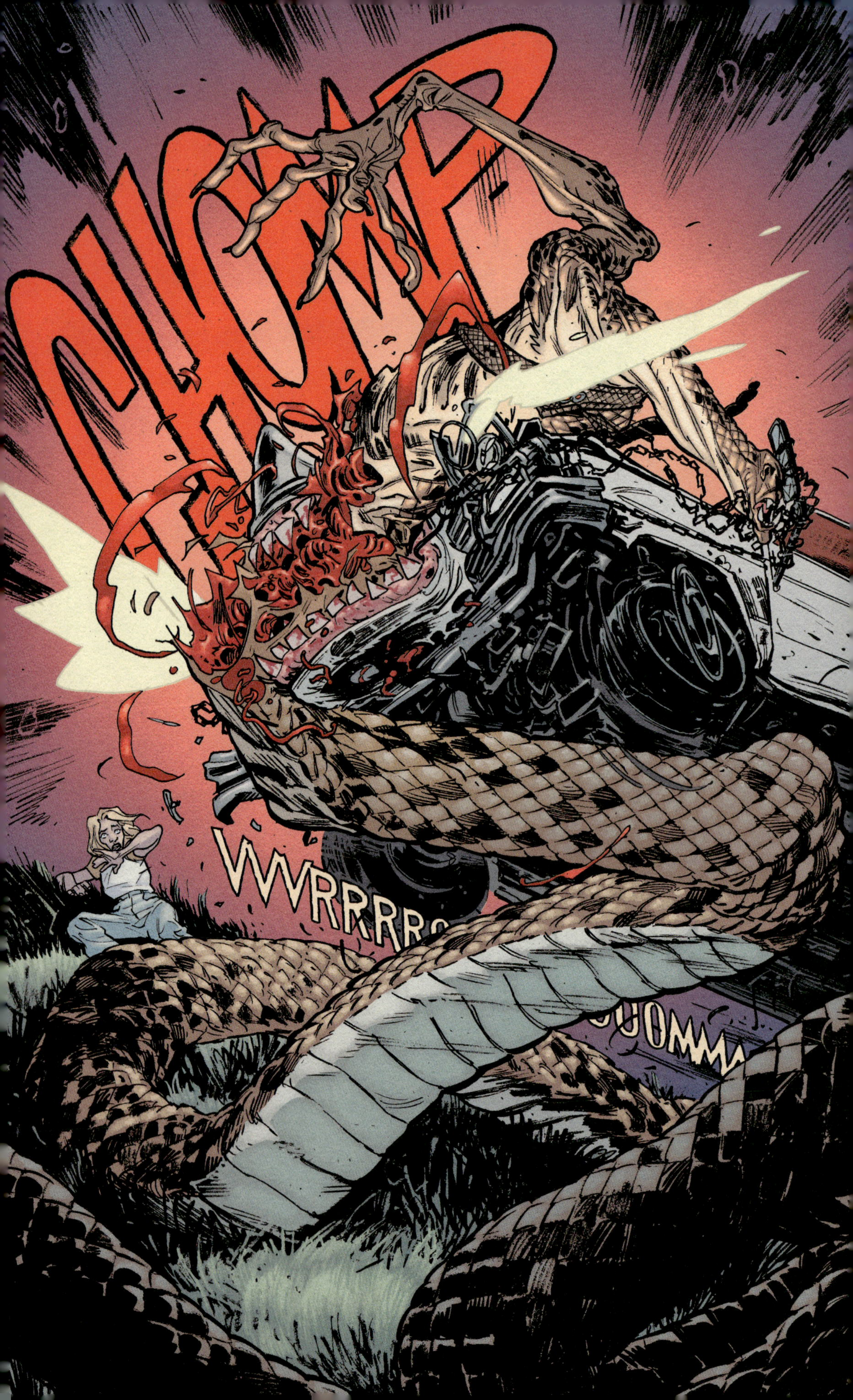
CHOMP
VVVRRRRO
OOOMMM

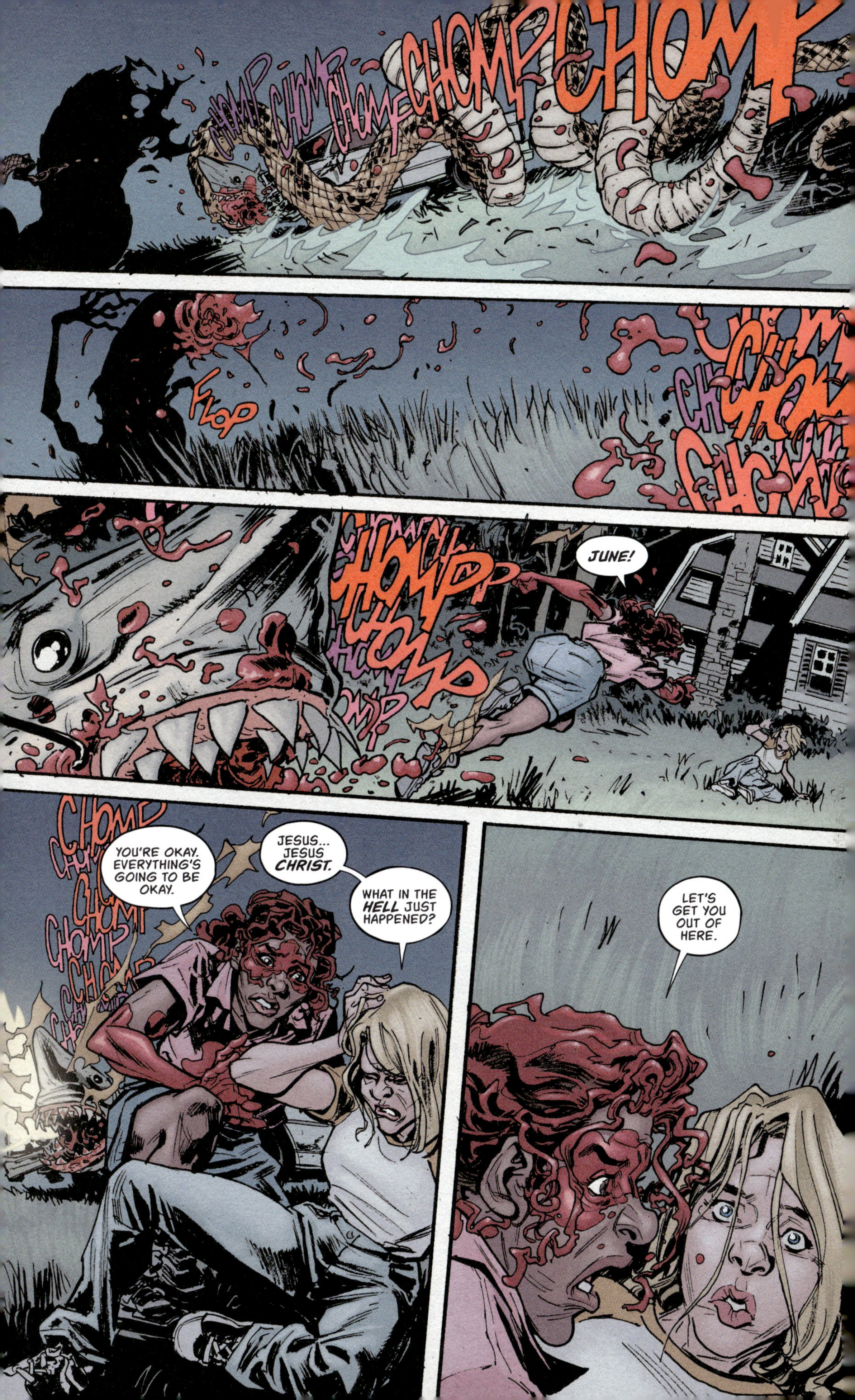

CHOMP CHOMP CHOMP CHOMP CHOMP CHOMP
FLOP
CHOMP CHOMP CHOMP
CHOMP CHOMP CHOMP
JUNE!
CHOMP CHOMP CHOMP
YOU'RE OKAY. EVERYTHING'S GOING TO BE OKAY.
JESUS... JESUS CHRIST.
WHAT IN THE HELL JUST HAPPENED?
LET'S GET YOU OUT OF HERE.

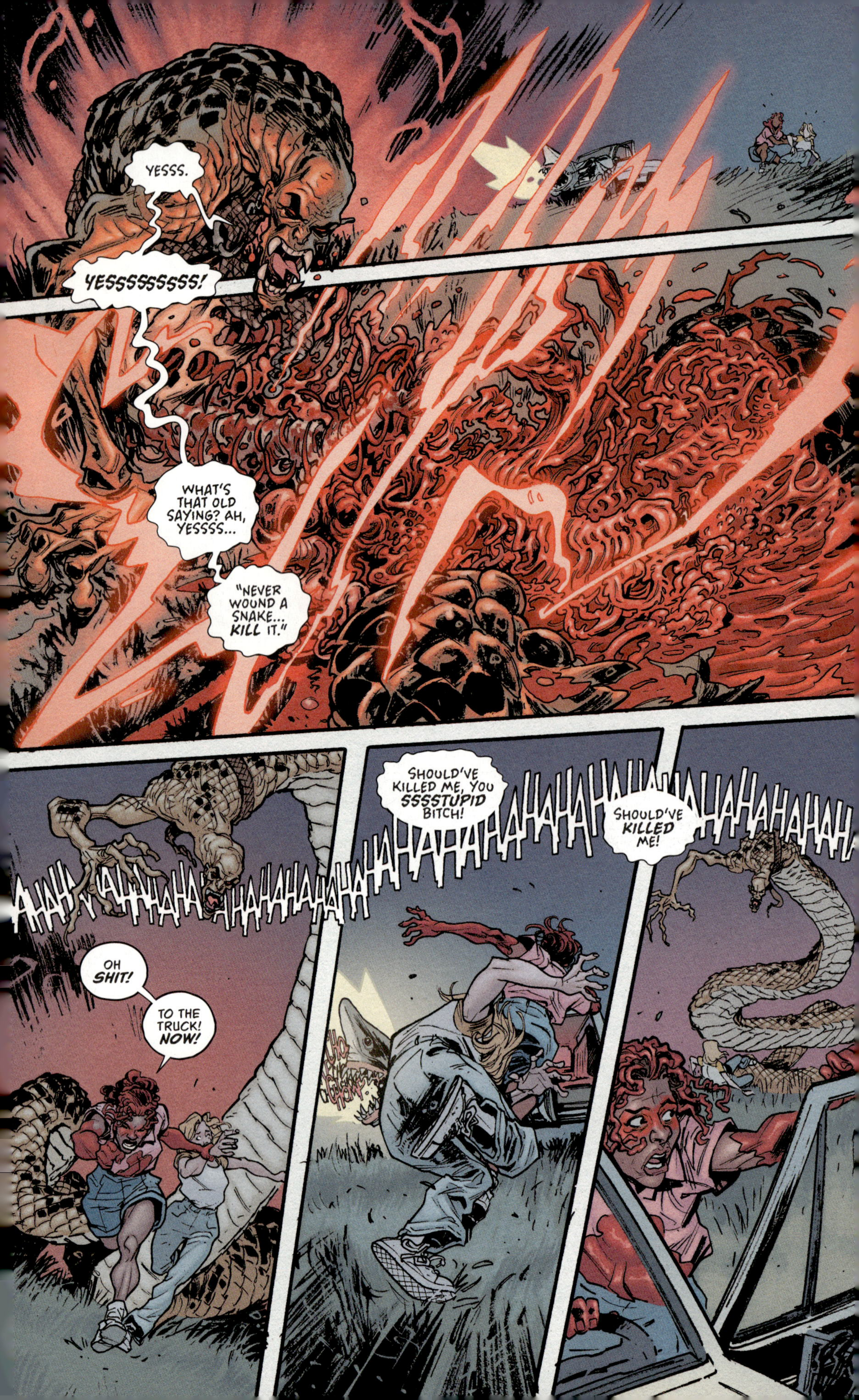
YESSS.
YESSSSSSSSS!
WHAT'S THAT OLD SAYING? AH, YESSSS...
"NEVER WOUND A SNAKE... KILL IT."
SHOULD'VE KILLED ME, YOU SSSSTUPID BITCH!
SHOULD'VE KILLED ME!
OH SHIT!
TO THE TRUCK! NOW!

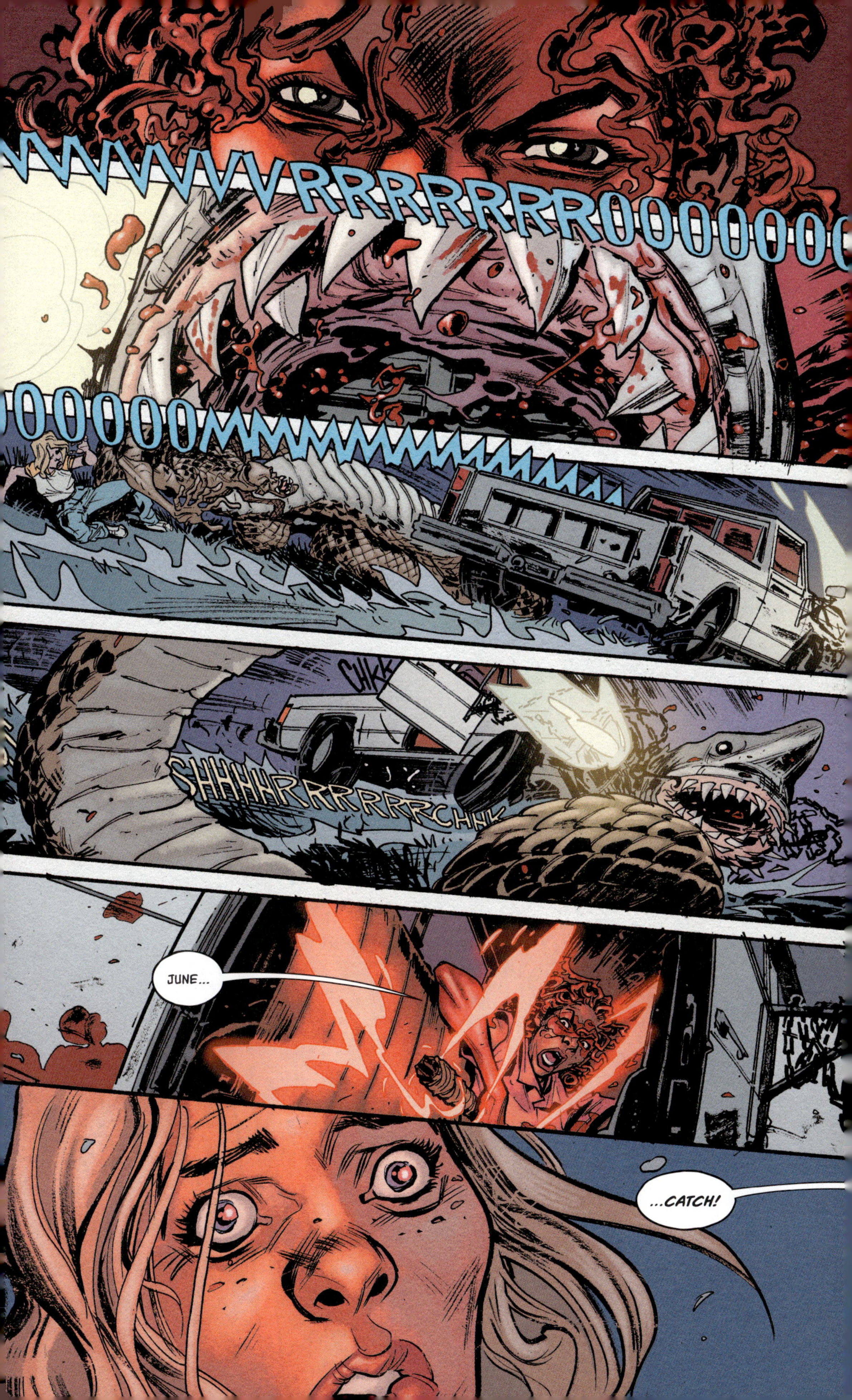
WWVVVVVVRRRRRRRRROOOOOOOOOOOOOOOMMMMMMMMMM
CHKK
SHHHHRRRRRRRCHHK
JUNE...
...CATCH!

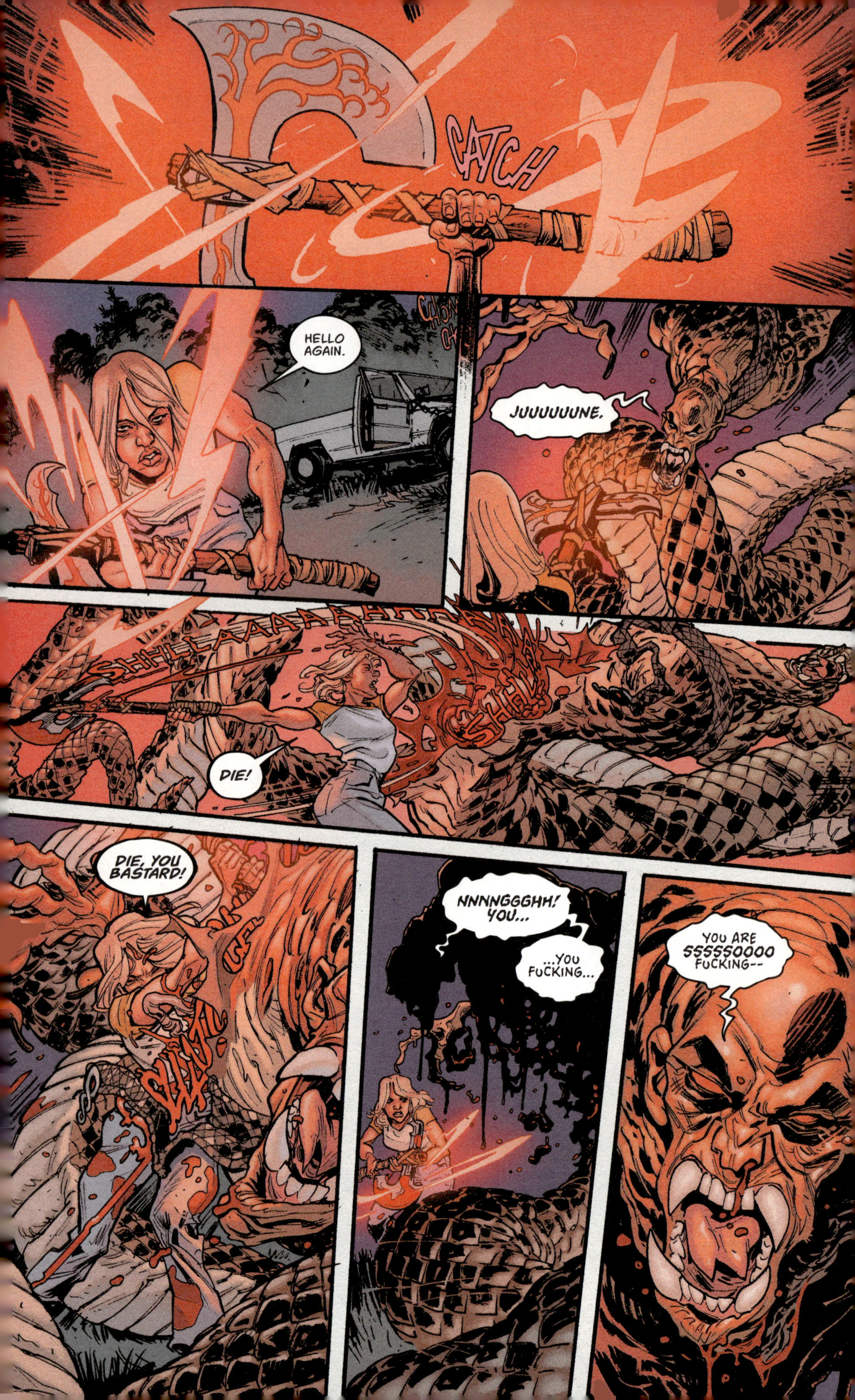
CATCH
HELLO AGAIN.
JUUUUUUNE.
SHHLLAAAAAHHH
DIE!
DIE, YOU BASTARD!
NNNNGGGHH! YOU...
...YOU FUCKING...
YOU ARE SSSSSOOOO FUCKING--

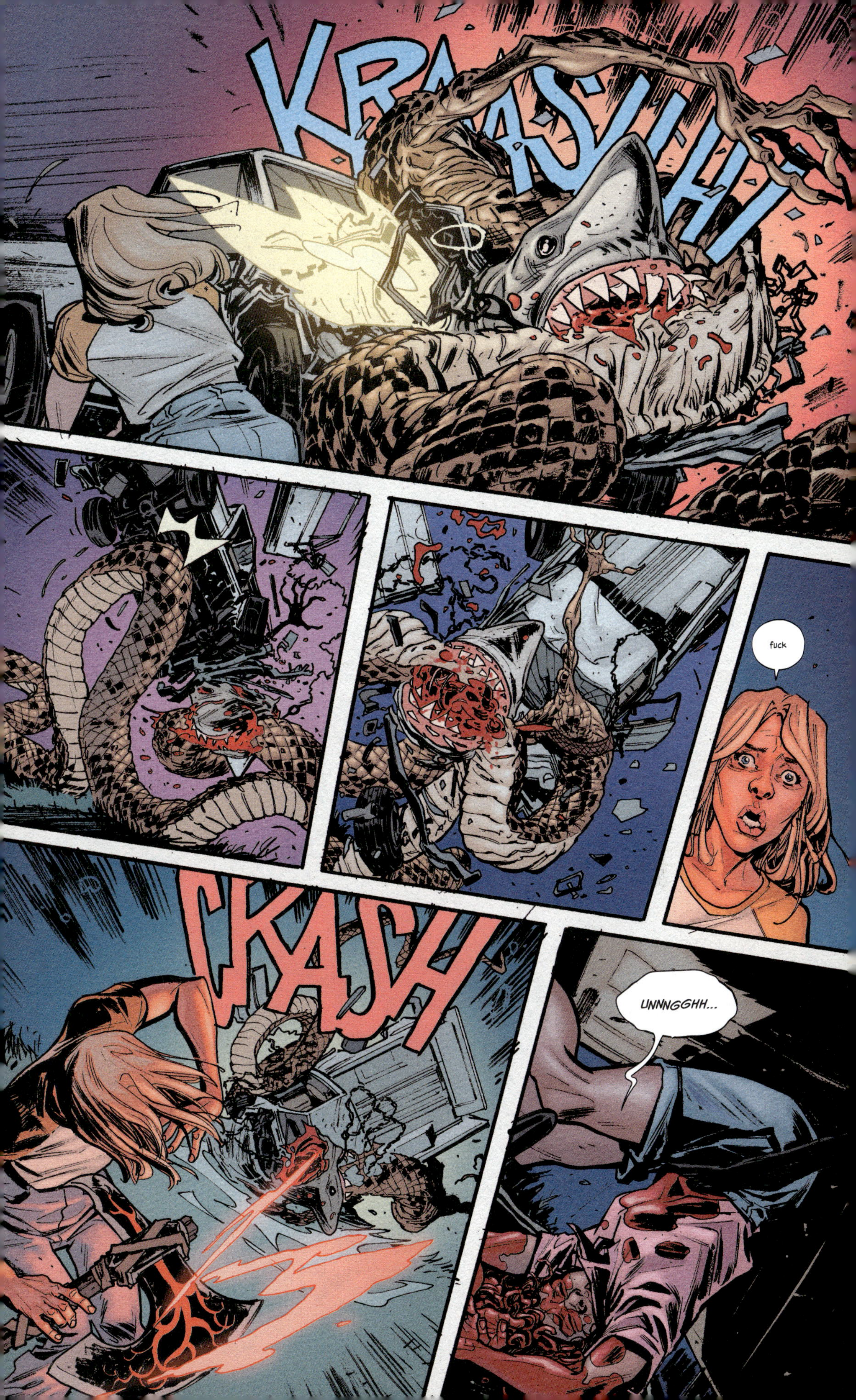
KRAASHH
fuck
CRASH
UNNNGGHH...

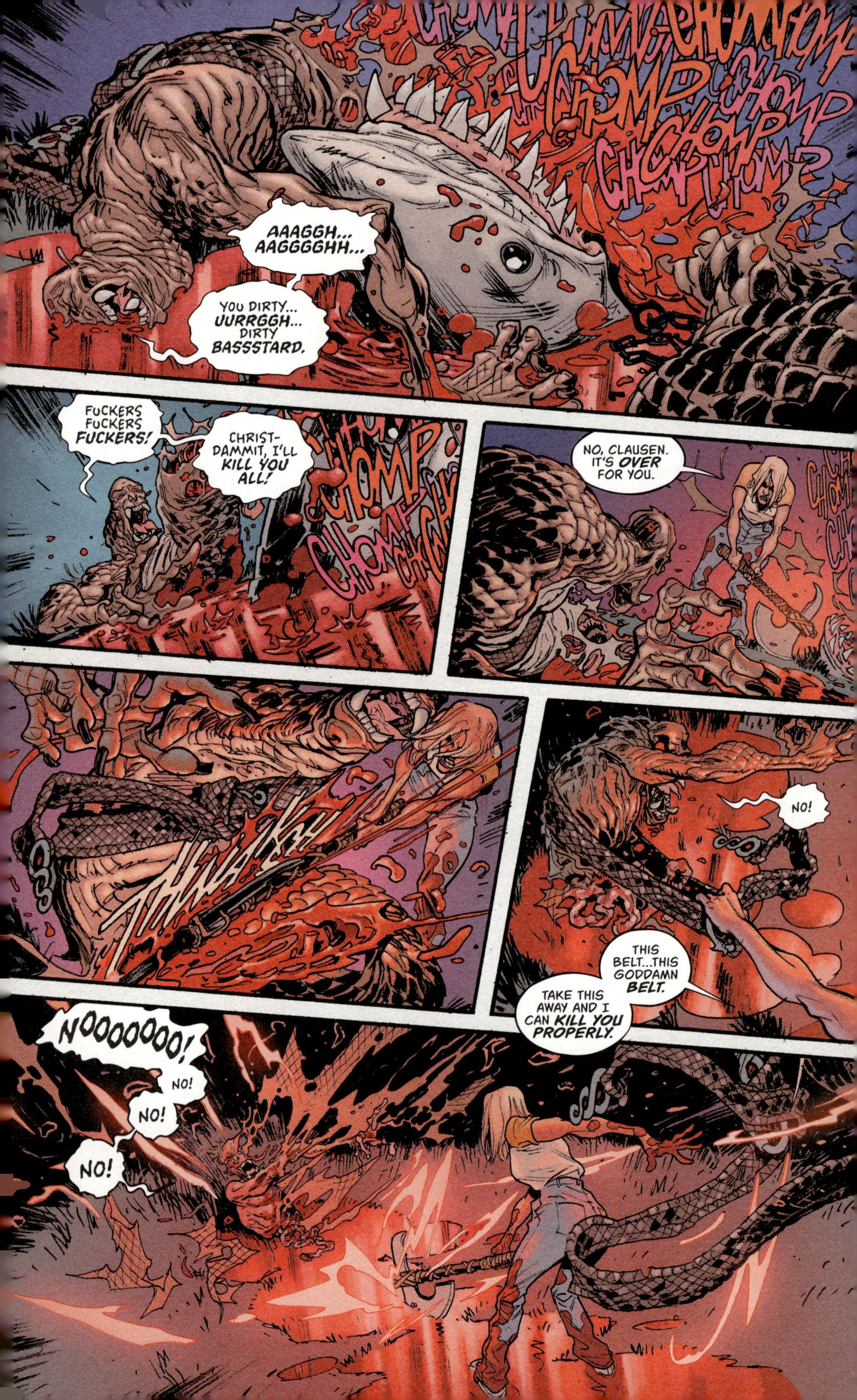
CHOMP CHOMP CHOMP
CHOMP CHOMP
CHOMP CHOMP CHOMP
AAAGGH... AAGGGGHH...
YOU DIRTY... UURRGGH... DIRTY BASSSTARD.
FUCKERS FUCKERS FUCKERS!
CHRIST-DAMMIT, I'LL KILL YOU ALL!
CHOMP CHOMP CHOMP
NO, CLAUSEN. IT'S OVER FOR YOU.
NO!
THIS BELT...THIS GODDAMN BELT.
TAKE THIS AWAY AND I CAN KILL YOU PROPERLY.
NOOOOOOO!
NO!
NO!
NO!

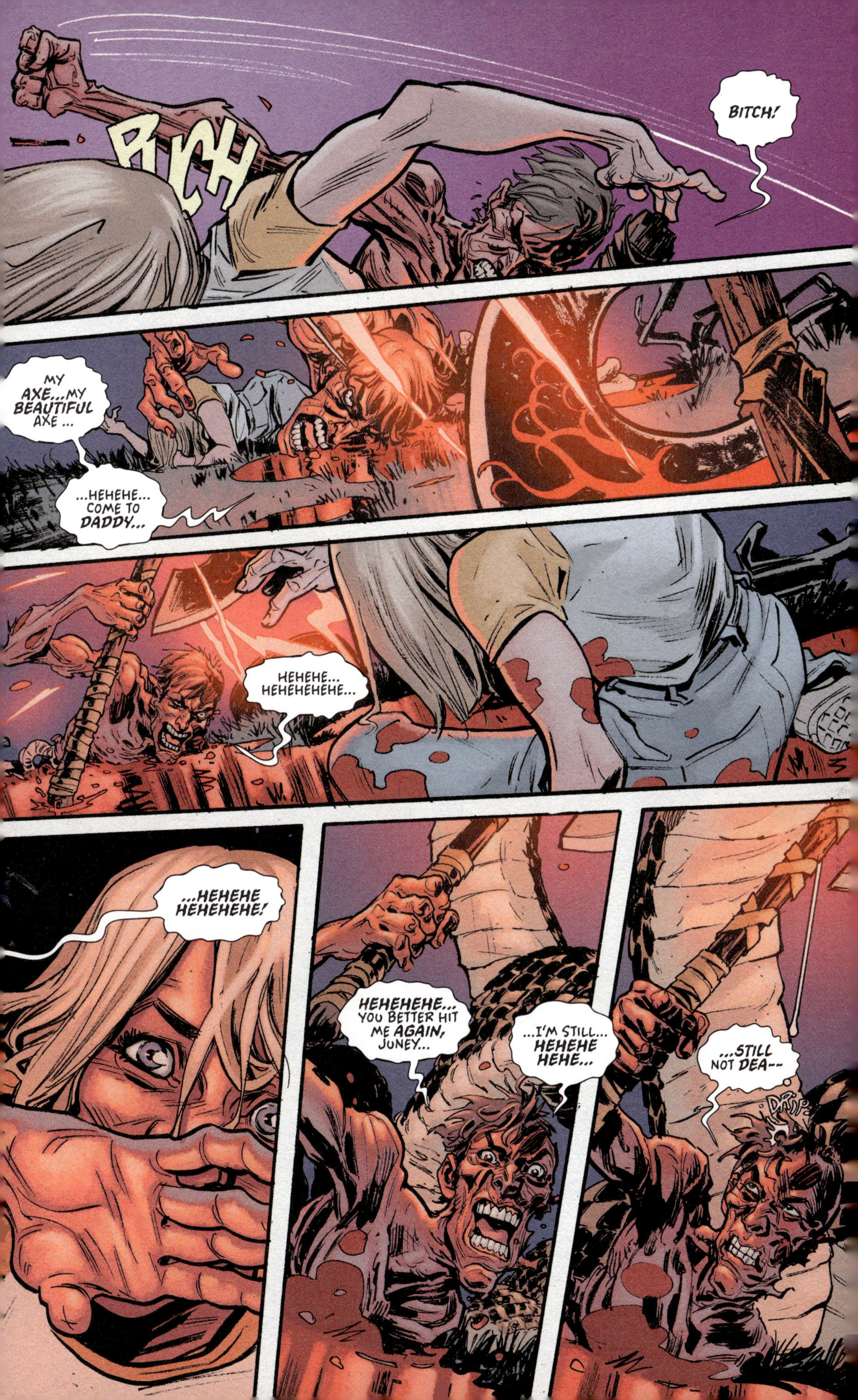
BITCH!
MY AXE...MY BEAUTIFUL AXE ...
...HEHEHE... COME TO DADDY...
HEHEHE... HEHEHEHEHE...
...HEHEHE HEHEHEHE!
HEHEHEHE... YOU BETTER HIT ME AGAIN, JUNEY...
...I'M STILL... HEHEHE HEHE...
...STILL NOT DEA--

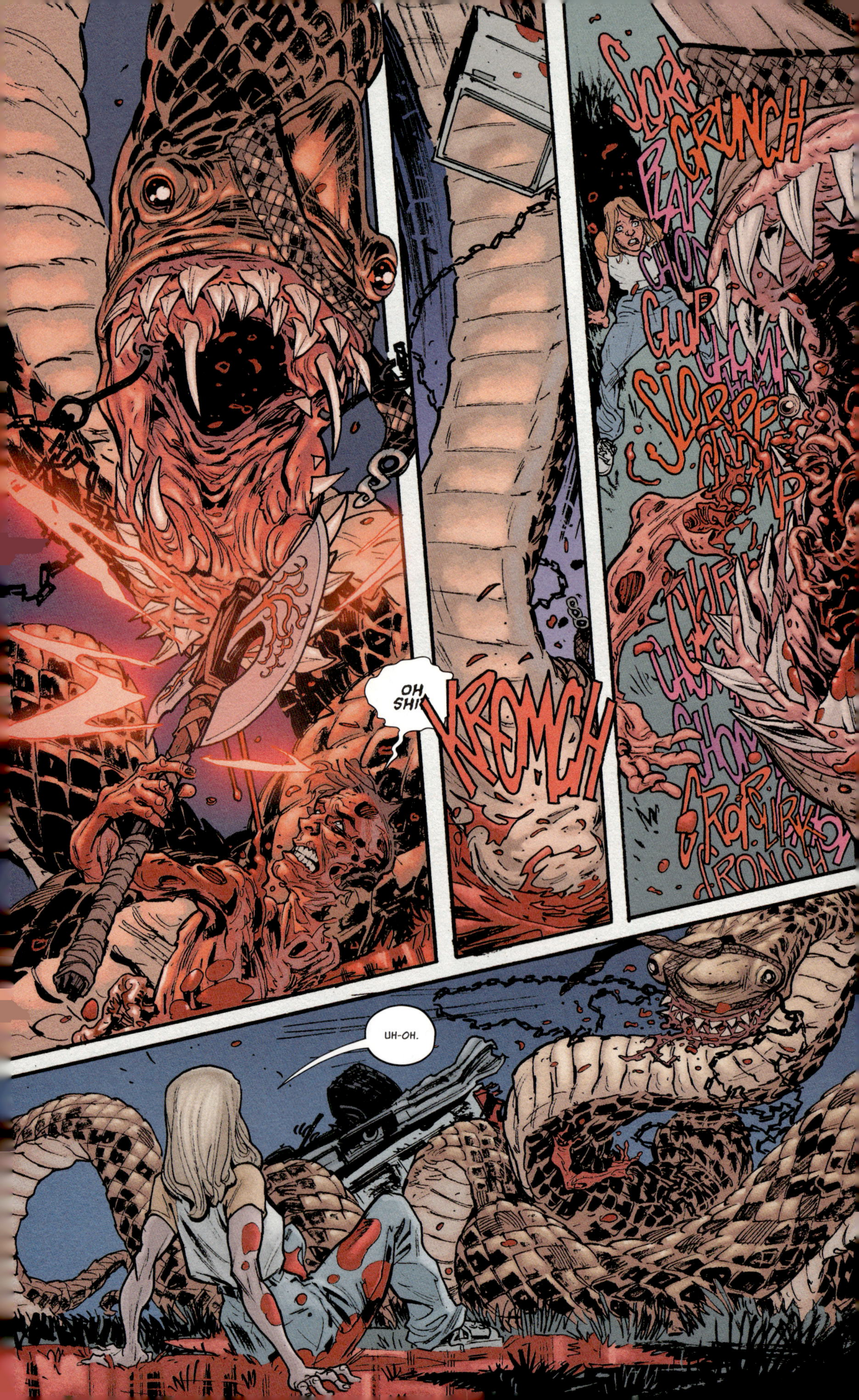
OH SHI
KROMCH
GRUNCH
BLAK
GULP
SLORP
CHOMP
GRONCH
UH-OH.

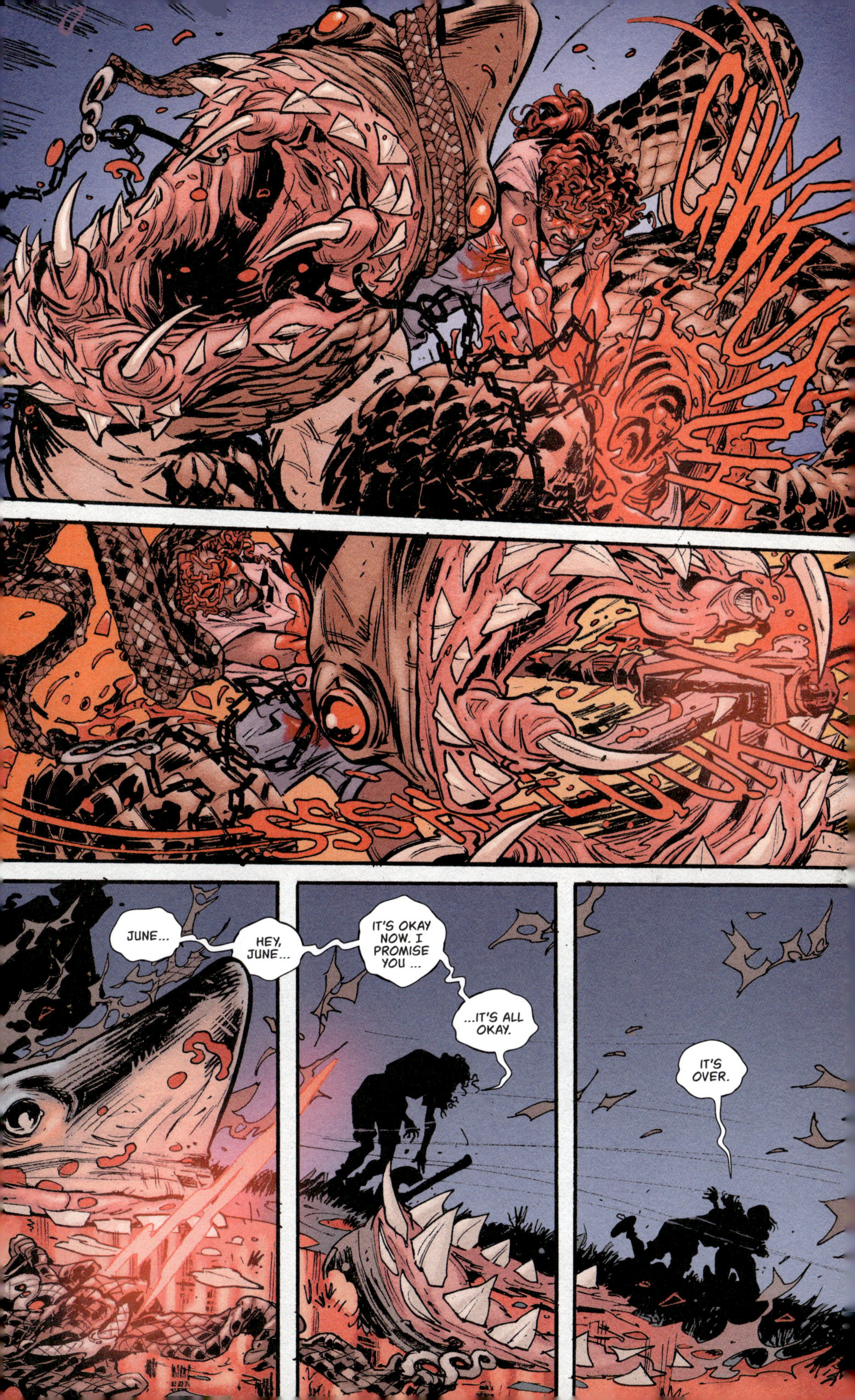
CHKK
SSSHH
JUNE...
HEY, JUNE...
IT'S OKAY NOW. I PROMISE YOU ...
...IT'S ALL OKAY.
IT'S OVER.

THIRTY-NINE MINUTES LATER.

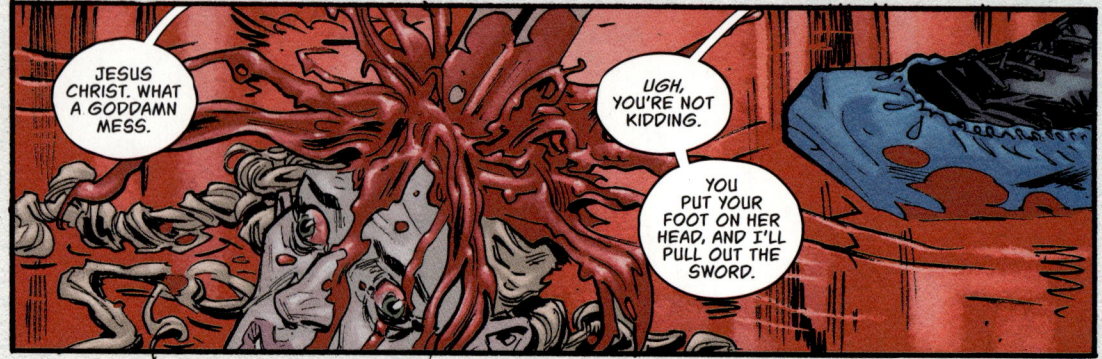

THANKS FOR VISITING **BRODY ISLAND!** A TOP 10 YANK MAGAZINE HIDDEN TREASURE (1980)! SEE YOU AGAIN SOON!

THIS IS AN **OUTRAGE!** I'M THE MAYOR OF THIS ISLAND. I'VE DONE **NOTHING** WRONG.

HOW ABOUT HARBORING **DANGEROUS CRIMINALS?** HOW ABOUT POSSESSION OF **STOLEN GOODS?**

AND I BET EVEN MORE **DIRT** FALLS OUT WHEN WE TURN YOU UPSIDE DOWN AND GIVE YOU A SHAKE.

JESUS CHRIST. WHAT A GODDAMN MESS.

UGH, YOU'RE NOT KIDDING.

YOU PUT YOUR FOOT ON HER HEAD, AND I'LL PULL OUT THE SWORD.

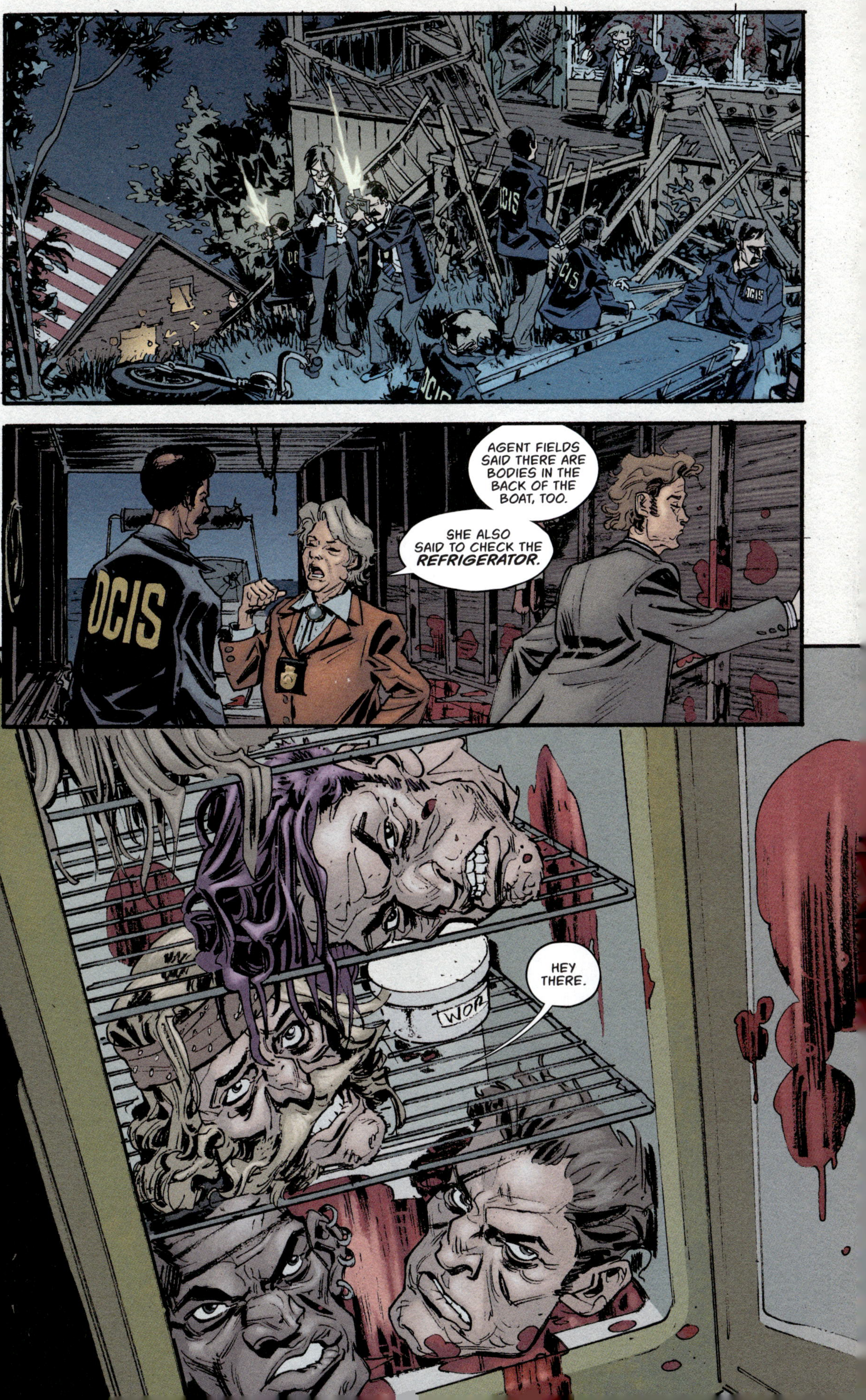
AGENT FIELDS SAID THERE ARE BODIES IN THE BACK OF THE BOAT, TOO.
SHE ALSO SAID TO CHECK THE ***REFRIGERATOR.***
HEY THERE.
DCIS
WOR

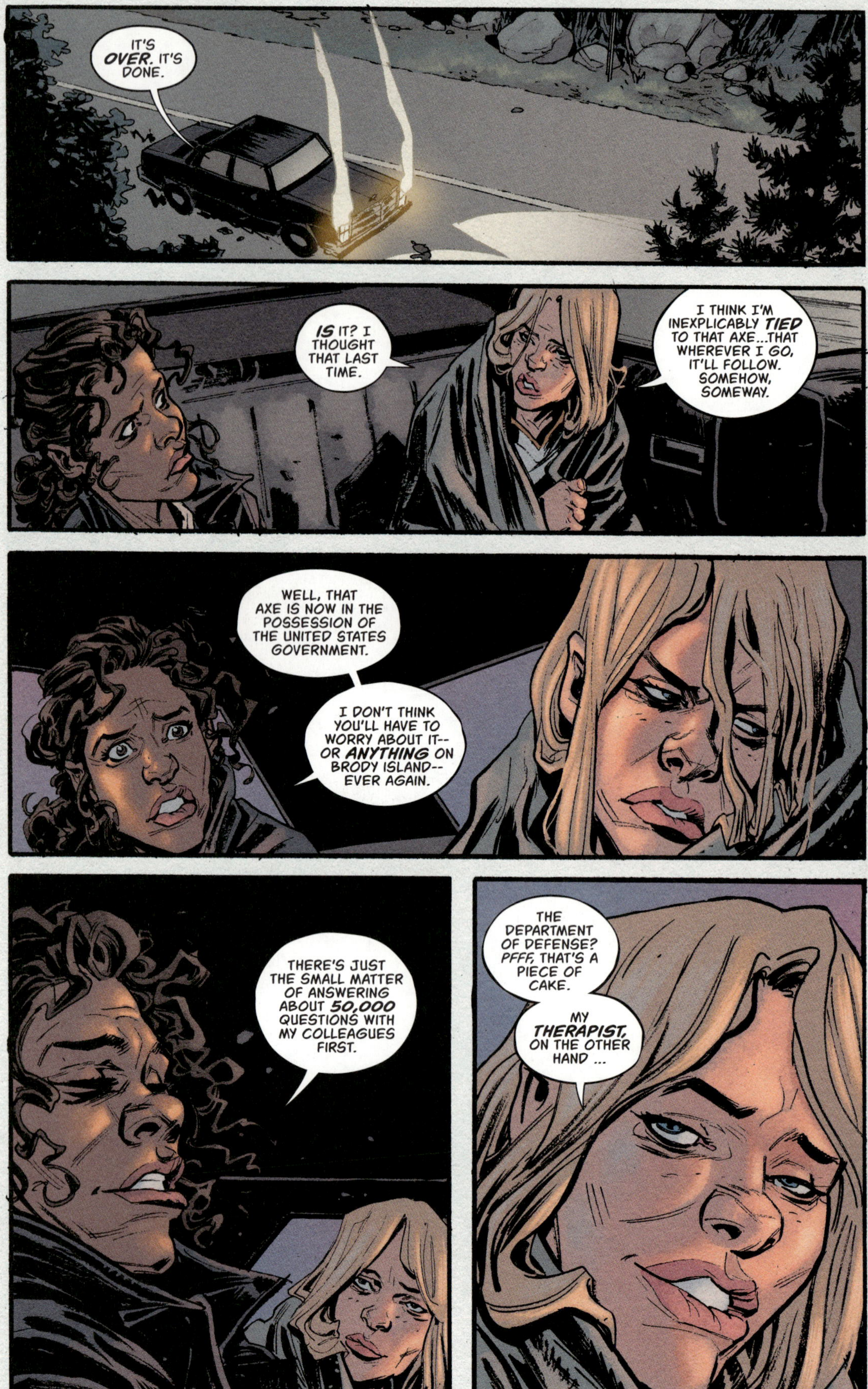
IT'S OVER. IT'S DONE.
IS IT? I THOUGHT THAT LAST TIME.
I THINK I'M INEXPLICABLY TIED TO THAT AXE...THAT WHEREVER I GO, IT'LL FOLLOW. SOMEHOW, SOMEWAY.
WELL, THAT AXE IS NOW IN THE POSSESSION OF THE UNITED STATES GOVERNMENT.
I DON'T THINK YOU'LL HAVE TO WORRY ABOUT IT-- OR ANYTHING ON BRODY ISLAND-- EVER AGAIN.
THERE'S JUST THE SMALL MATTER OF ANSWERING ABOUT 50,000 QUESTIONS WITH MY COLLEAGUES FIRST.
THE DEPARTMENT OF DEFENSE? PFFF, THAT'S A PIECE OF CAKE.
MY THERAPIST, ON THE OTHER HAND ...

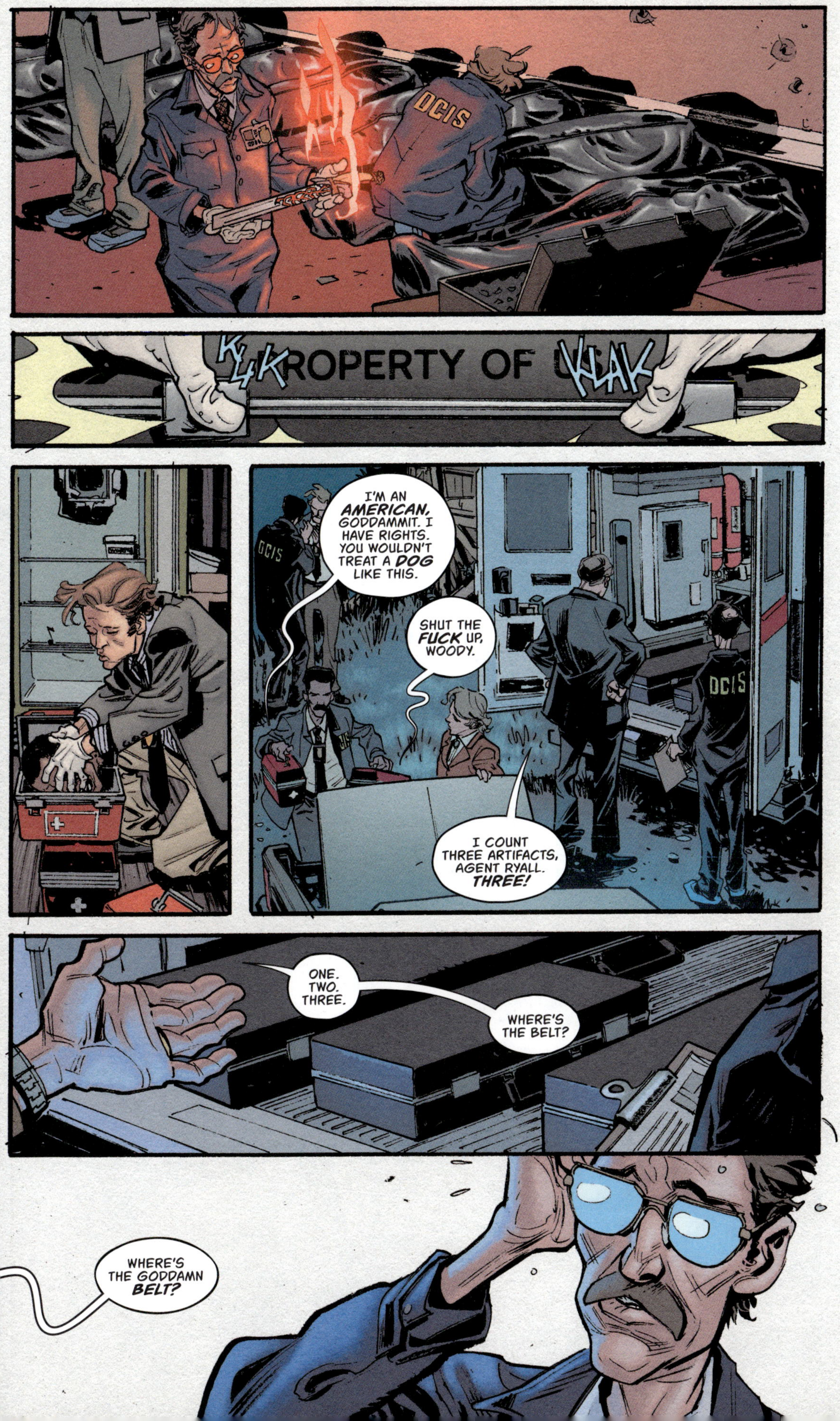

ROPERTY OF
I'M AN AMERICAN, GODDAMMIT. I HAVE RIGHTS. YOU WOULDN'T TREAT A DOG LIKE THIS.
SHUT THE FUCK UP, WOODY.
I COUNT THREE ARTIFACTS, AGENT RYALL. THREE!
ONE. TWO. THREE.
WHERE'S THE BELT?
WHERE'S THE GODDAMN BELT?

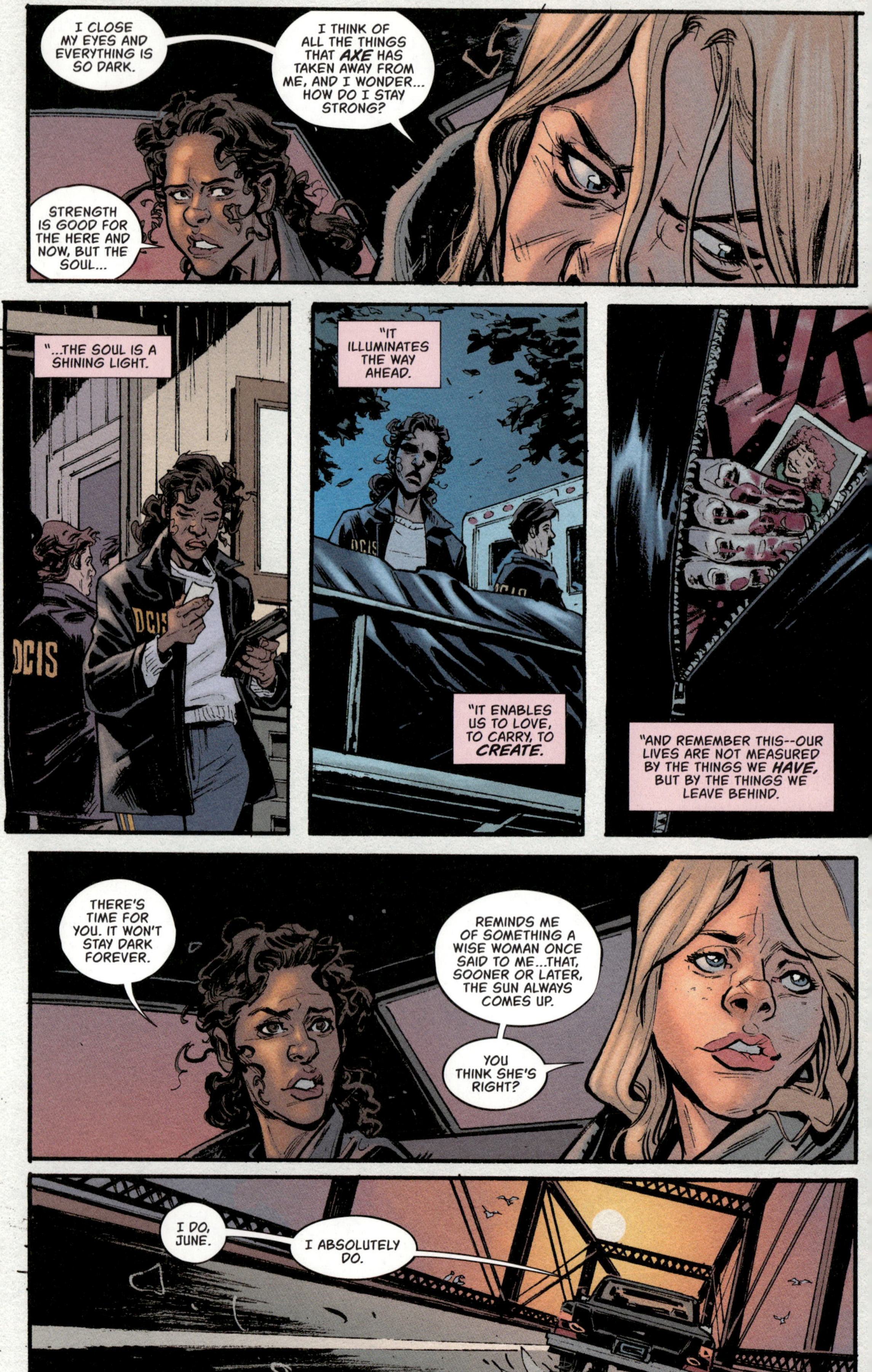
I CLOSE MY EYES AND EVERYTHING IS SO DARK.
I THINK OF ALL THE THINGS THAT AXE HAS TAKEN AWAY FROM ME, AND I WONDER... HOW DO I STAY STRONG?
STRENGTH IS GOOD FOR THE HERE AND NOW, BUT THE SOUL...
"...THE SOUL IS A SHINING LIGHT.
"IT ILLUMINATES THE WAY AHEAD.
"IT ENABLES US TO LOVE, TO CARRY, TO CREATE.
"AND REMEMBER THIS--OUR LIVES ARE NOT MEASURED BY THE THINGS WE HAVE, BUT BY THE THINGS WE LEAVE BEHIND.
THERE'S TIME FOR YOU. IT WON'T STAY DARK FOREVER.
REMINDS ME OF SOMETHING A WISE WOMAN ONCE SAID TO ME...THAT, SOONER OR LATER, THE SUN ALWAYS COMES UP.
YOU THINK SHE'S RIGHT?
I DO, JUNE.
I ABSOLUTELY DO.

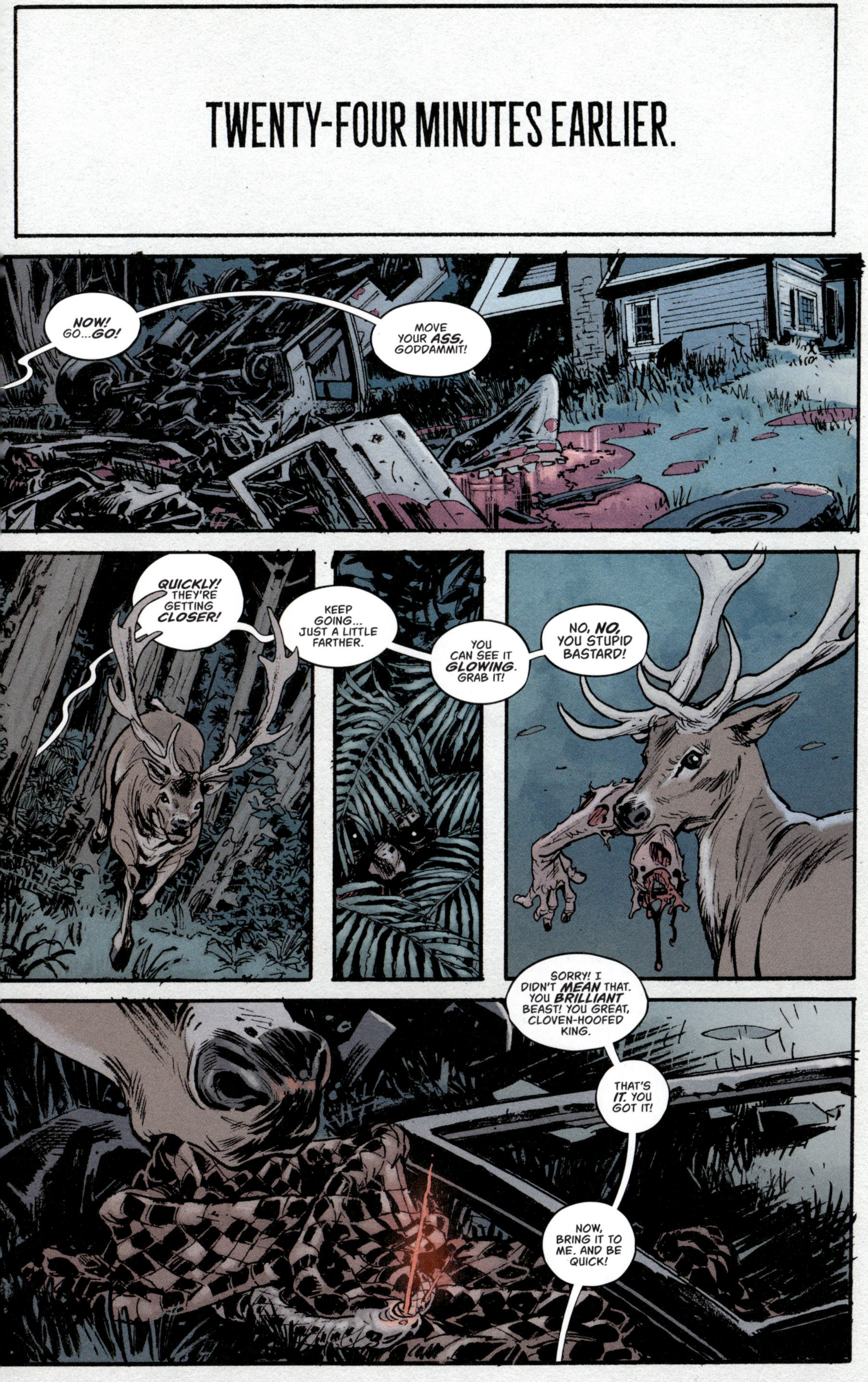
TWENTY-FOUR MINUTES EARLIER.
NOW! GO...GO!
MOVE YOUR ASS, GODDAMMIT!
QUICKLY! THEY'RE GETTING CLOSER!
KEEP GOING... JUST A LITTLE FARTHER.
YOU CAN SEE IT GLOWING. GRAB IT!
NO, NO, YOU STUPID BASTARD!
SORRY! I DIDN'T MEAN THAT. YOU BRILLIANT BEAST! YOU GREAT, CLOVEN-HOOFED KING.
THAT'S IT. YOU GOT IT!
NOW, BRING IT TO ME. AND BE QUICK!

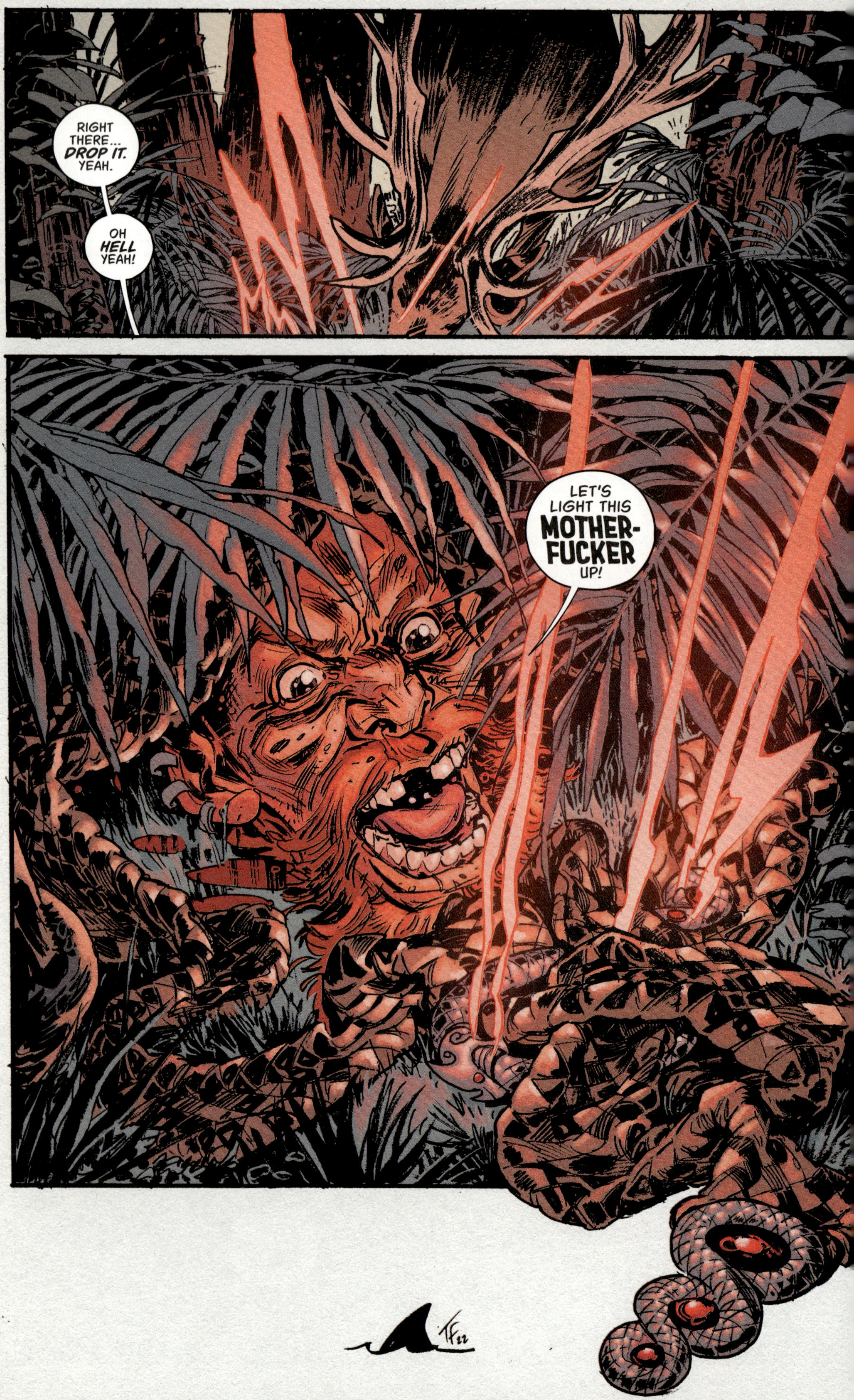
RIGHT THERE... DROP IT. YEAH.
OH HELL YEAH!
LET'S LIGHT THIS MOTHER-FUCKER UP!

REFRIGERATOR FULL OF HEADS

Written by RIO YOUERS Drawn by TOM FOWLER
Colored by BILL CRABTREE Lettered by ANDWORLD DESIGN
Cover by MATEUS MANHANINI Variant cover by JUAN FERREYRA
ANDREA SHEA & CHRIS CONROY Editors

PROPERTY
USA
HUMAN ORGAN

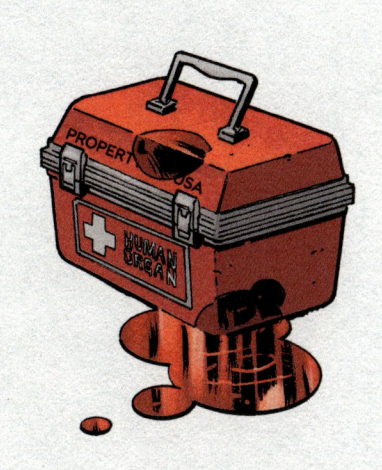

BASKETFUL OF HEADS created by JOE HILL with art by LEOMACS
REFRIGERATOR FULL OF HEADS curated for HILL HOUSE COMICS by JOE HILL

"YOU'D BE AMAZED AT WHAT PEOPLE ON THIS ISLAND WILL DO FOR ME. THEY'D WASH YOUR BLOOD OFF THE WALLS IF I ASKED THEM TO.

AND I WILL ASK THEM TO."

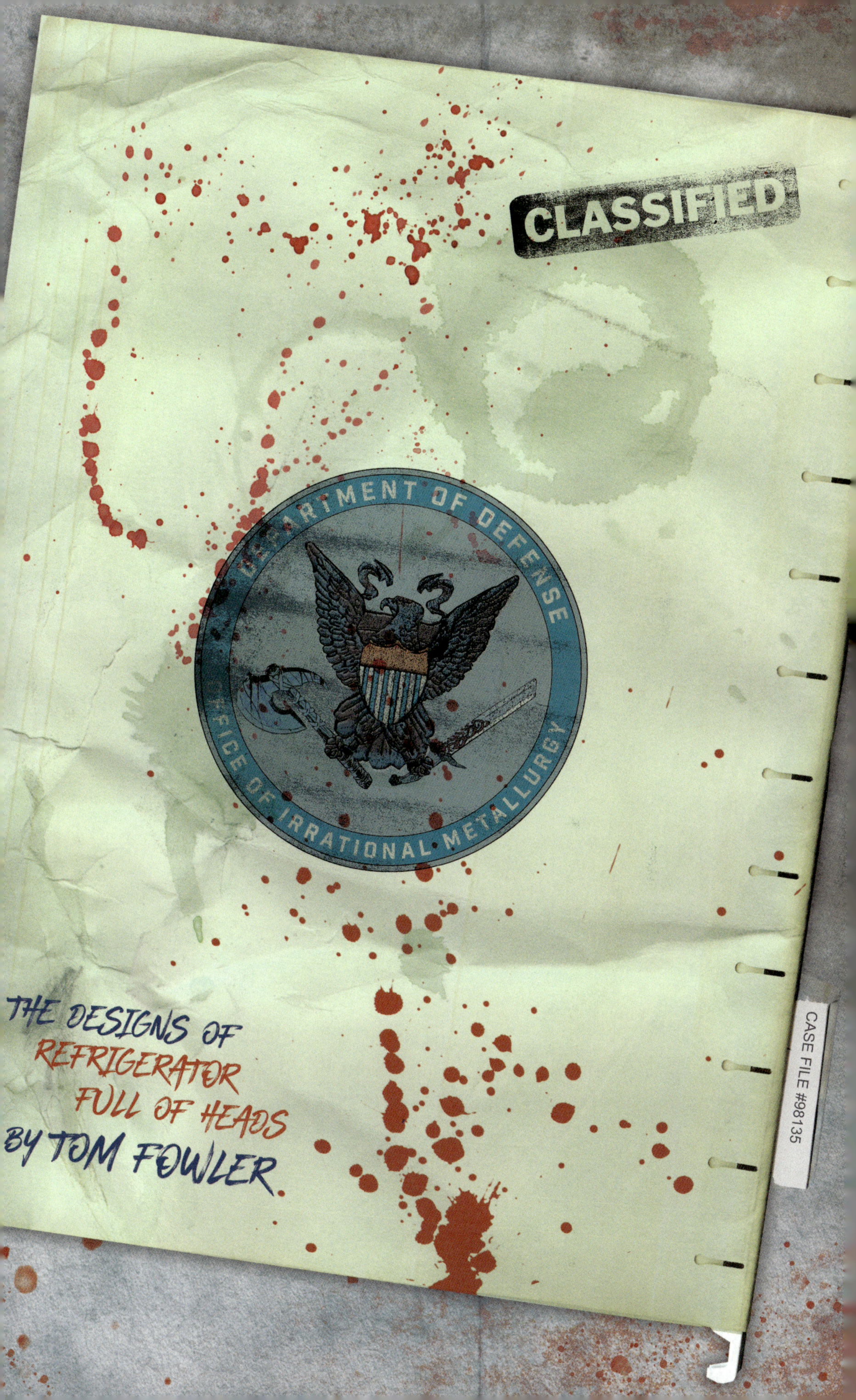
CLASSIFIED
DEPARTMENT OF DEFENSE
FFICE OF IRRATIONAL METALLURGY
THE DESIGNS OF
REFRIGERATOR
FULL OF HEADS
BY TOM FOWLER
CASE FILE #98135

THE AGENTS

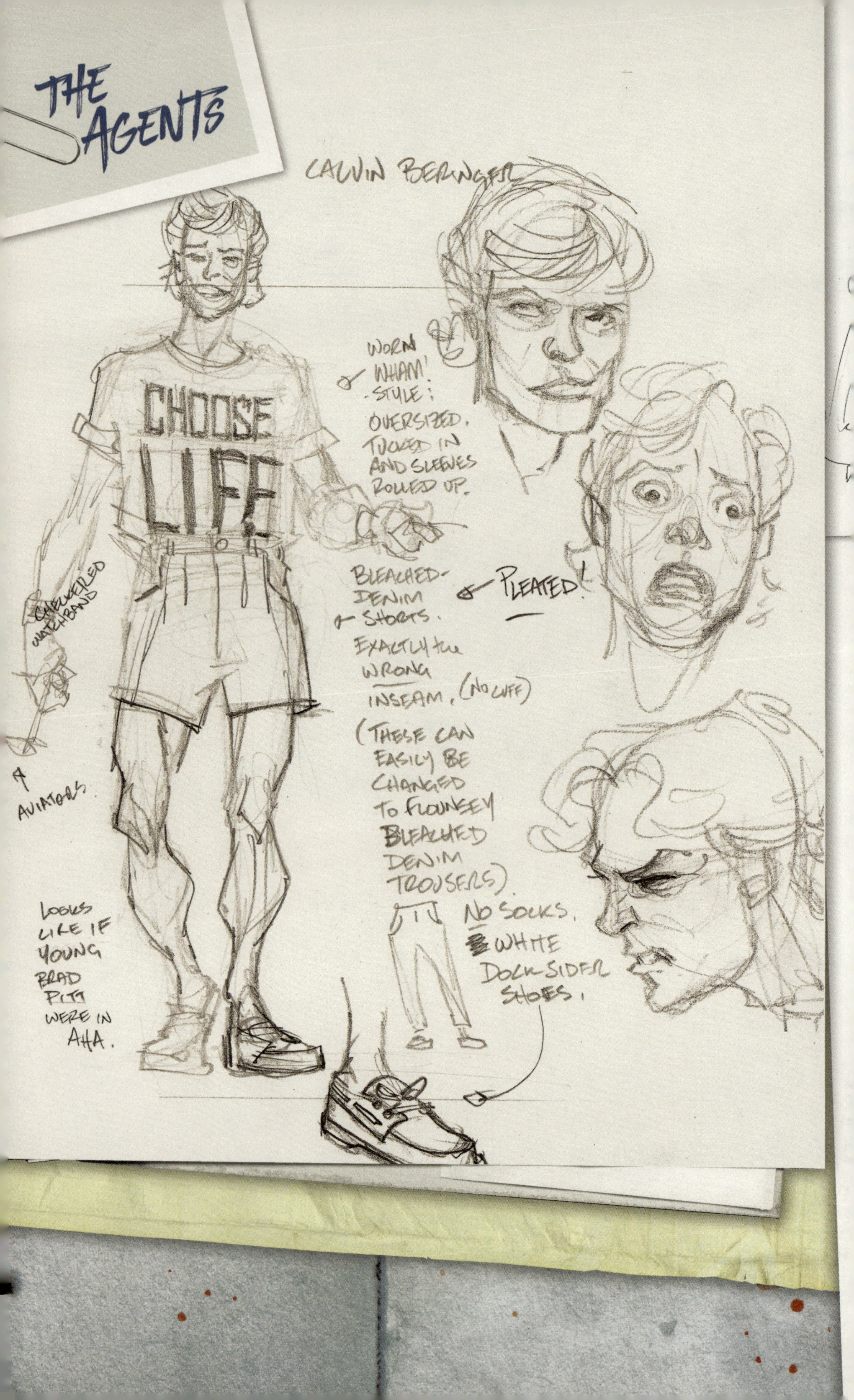
CALVIN BERINGER
CHOOSE LIFE
WORN WHAM! STYLE: OVERSIZED, TUCKED IN AND SLEEVES ROLLED UP.
BLEACHED-DENIM SHORTS.
PLEATED!
EXACTLY the WRONG INSEAM. (NO CUFF)
(THESE CAN EASILY BE CHANGED TO FLOUNSEY BLEACHED DENIM TROUSERS)
CHECKERED WATCHBAND
AVIATORS
NO SOCKS.
WHITE DOCK-SIDER SHOES.
LOOKS LIKE IF YOUNG BRAD PITT WERE IN AHA.

ARLENE will likely spend much of the last 3 issues with a messy (increasingly messier) "getting down to business" ponytail.

Collared button-up blouse with a bright, abstract floral pattern. (Gradually soaked in blood.)

High-waisted light, rolled denim shorts.

Thick white socks.
White Gucci tennis shoes w/ puffy laces.

ARLENE fits.

White-framed Ray Bans (because I hate myself.)

Turquois or aqua semi-sheer oversize crop-top over tight, white(?) tank crop (about an inch of bare midriff.)

Pink(?) pleated shorts

...er ...es 2 ...tte ...eaker ...th chonky white sock.

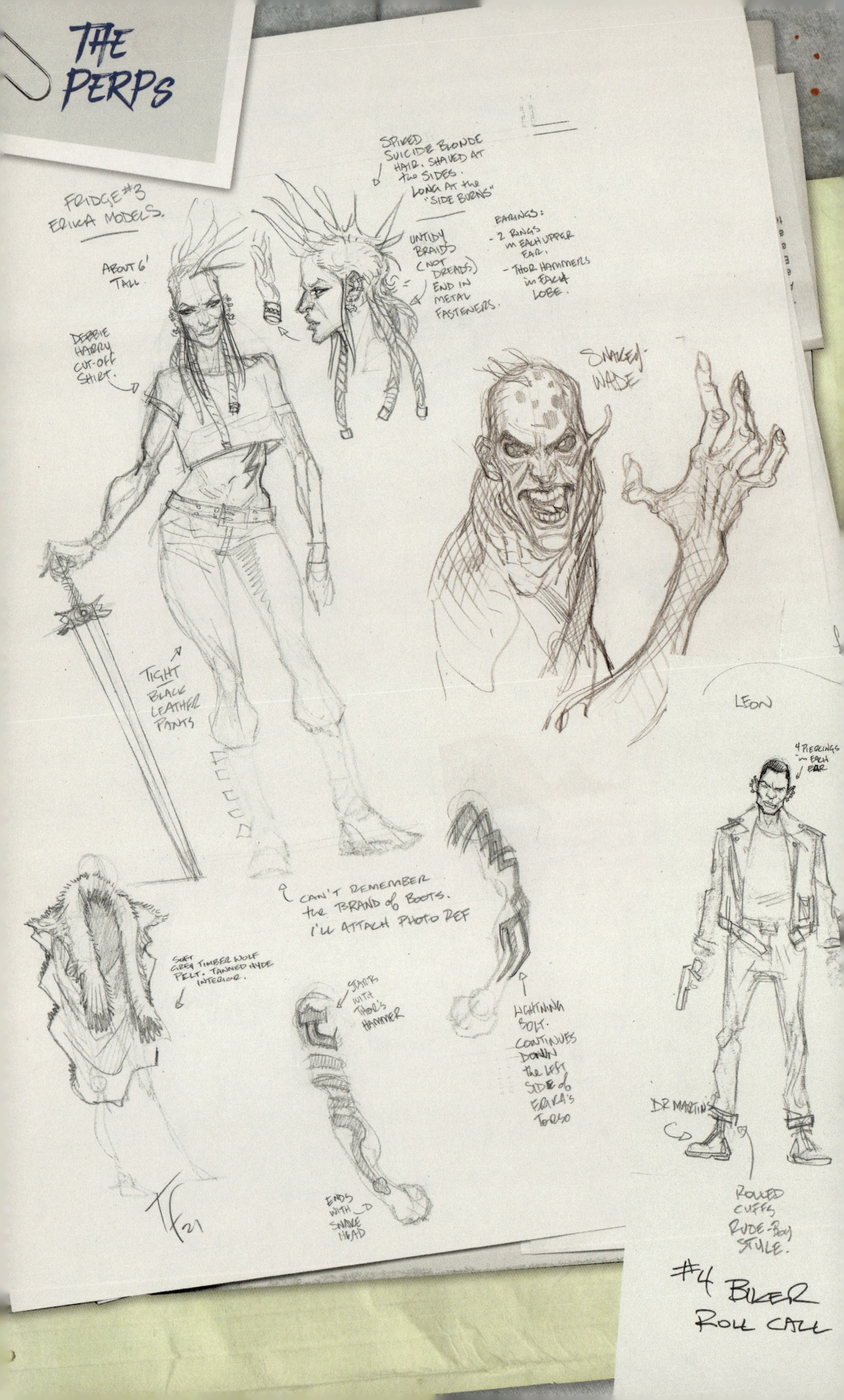
THE PERPS
FRIDGE #3
ERIKA MODELS.
ABOUT 6' TALL
SPIKED SUICIDE BLONDE HAIR. SHAVED AT the SIDES. LONG AT the "SIDE BURNS"
UNTIDY BRAIDS (NOT DREADS) END IN METAL FASTENERS.
EARINGS:
- 2 RINGS in EACH UPPER EAR.
- THOR HAMMERS in EACH LOBE.
DEBBIE HARRY CUT-OFF SHIRT.
SNAKEY WADE
TIGHT BLACK LEATHER PANTS
CAN'T REMEMBER the BRAND of BOOTS. I'LL ATTACH PHOTO REF
SOFT GREY TIMBER WOLF PELT. TANNED HYDE INTERIOR.
STARTS WITH THOR'S HAMMER
ENDS WITH SNAKE HEAD
LIGHTNING BOLT. CONTINUES DOWN the LEFT SIDE of ERIKA'S TORSO
LEON
4 PIERCINGS in EACH EAR
DR MARTINS
ROLLED CUFFS RUDE-BOY STYLE.
#4 BIKER ROLL CALL

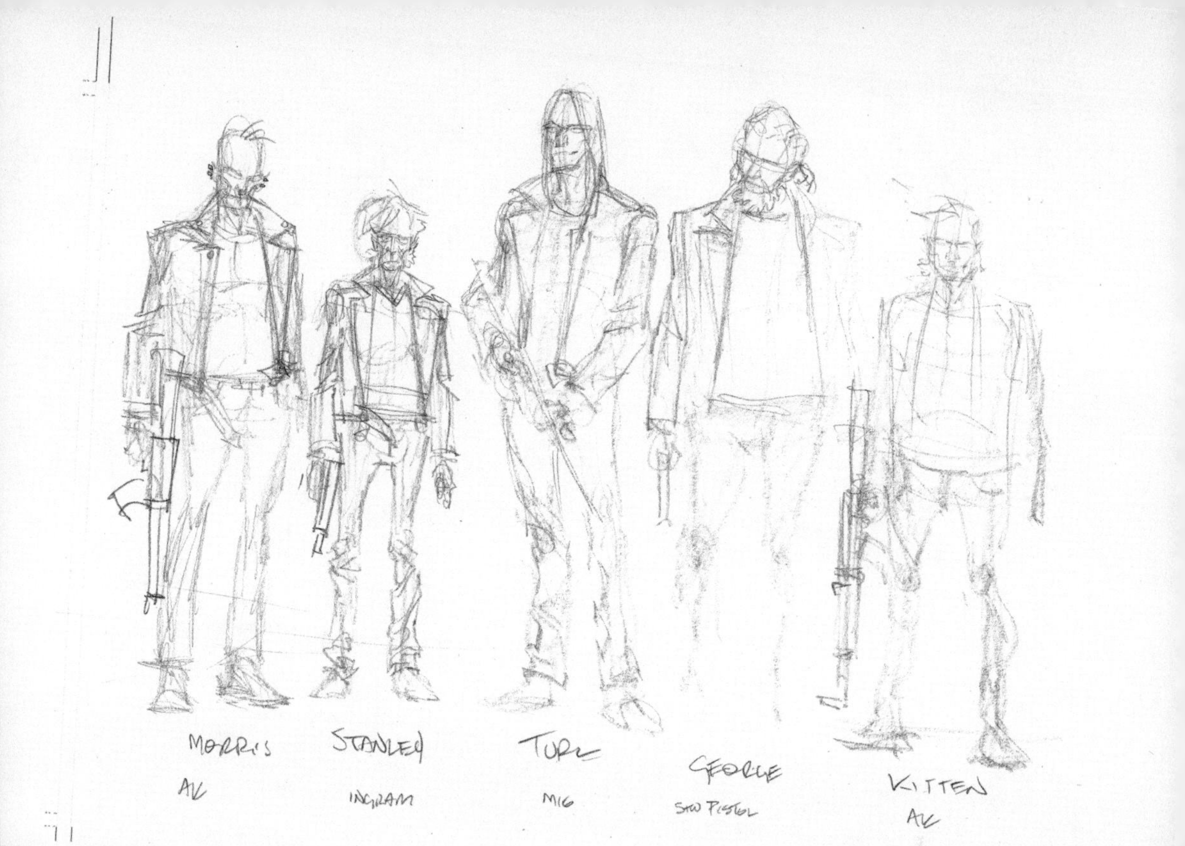
MORRIS
AK
STANLEY
INGRAM
TURK
M16
GEORGE
SAW PISTOL
KITTEN
AK

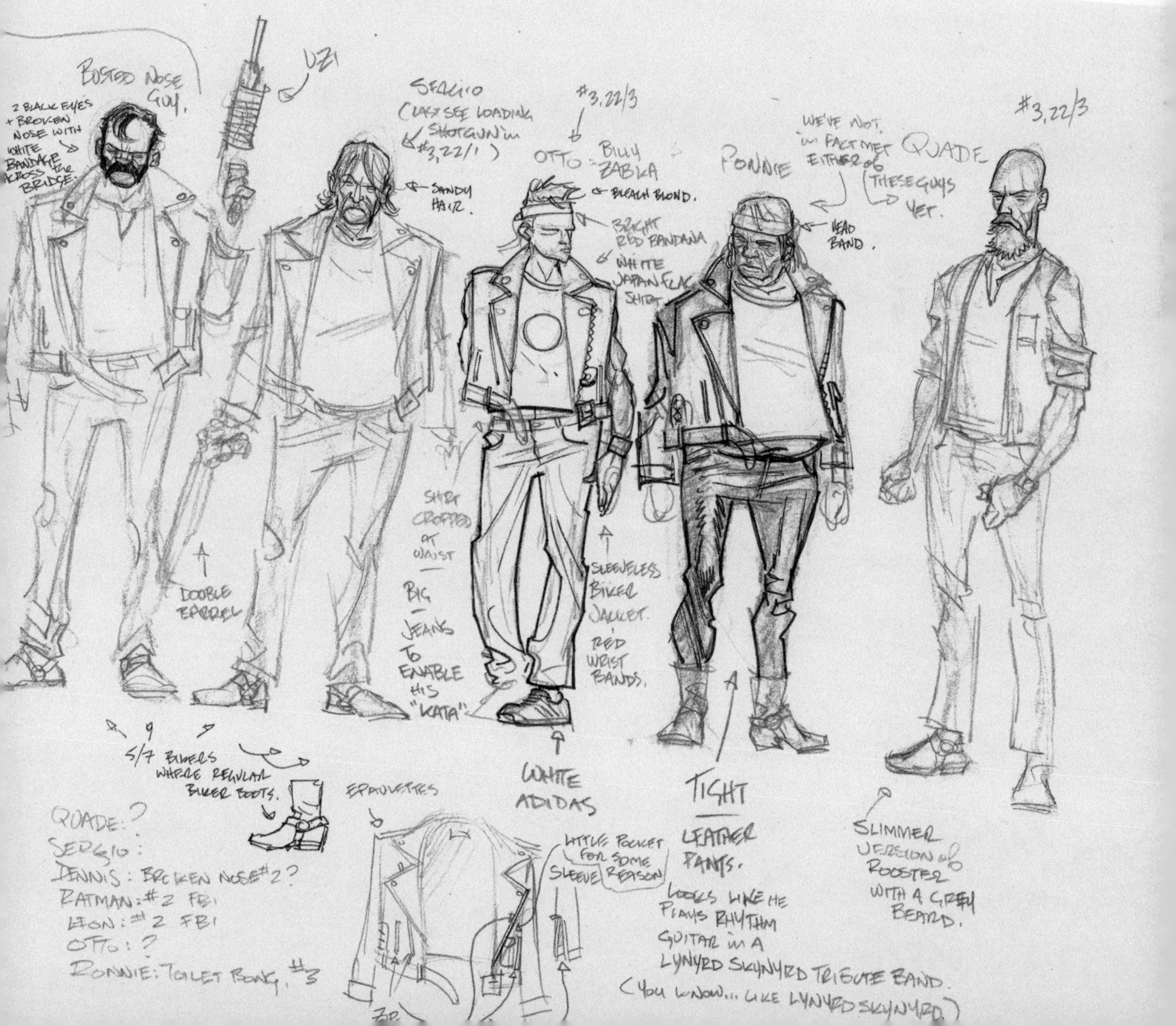
BUSTED NOSE GUY.
2 BLACK EYES + BROKEN NOSE WITH WHITE BANDAGE ACROSS THE BRIDGE.
UZI
SERGIO (LAST SEE LOADING SHOTGUN in #3,22/1)
SANDY HAIR.
#3,22/3
OTTO = BILLY ZABKA
BLEACH BLOND.
BRIGHT RED BANDANA
WHITE JAPAN FLAG SHIRT
RONNIE
WE'VE NOT, IN FACT MET EITHER OF THESE GUYS YET.
QUADE
#3,22/3
HEAD BAND.
DOUBLE BARREL
SHIRT CROPPED AT WAIST
BIG JEANS TO ENABLE HIS "KATA"
SLEEVELESS BIKER JACKET.
RED WRIST BANDS.
5/7 BIKERS WHERE REGULAR BIKER BOOTS.
WHITE ADIDAS
TIGHT LEATHER PANTS.
LOOKS LIKE HE PLAYS RHYTHM GUITAR IN A LYNYRD SKYNYRD TRIBUTE BAND.
(YOU KNOW... LIKE LYNYRD SKYNYRD.)
SLIMMER VERSION of ROOSTER WITH A GREY BEARD.
EPAULETTES
LITTLE POCKET FOR SOME REASON
SLEEVE
ZIP
QUADE: ?
SERGIO:
DENNIS: BROKEN NOSE #2?
RATMAN: #2 FBI
LEON: #2 FBI
OTTO: ?
RONNIE: TOILET BONG. #3

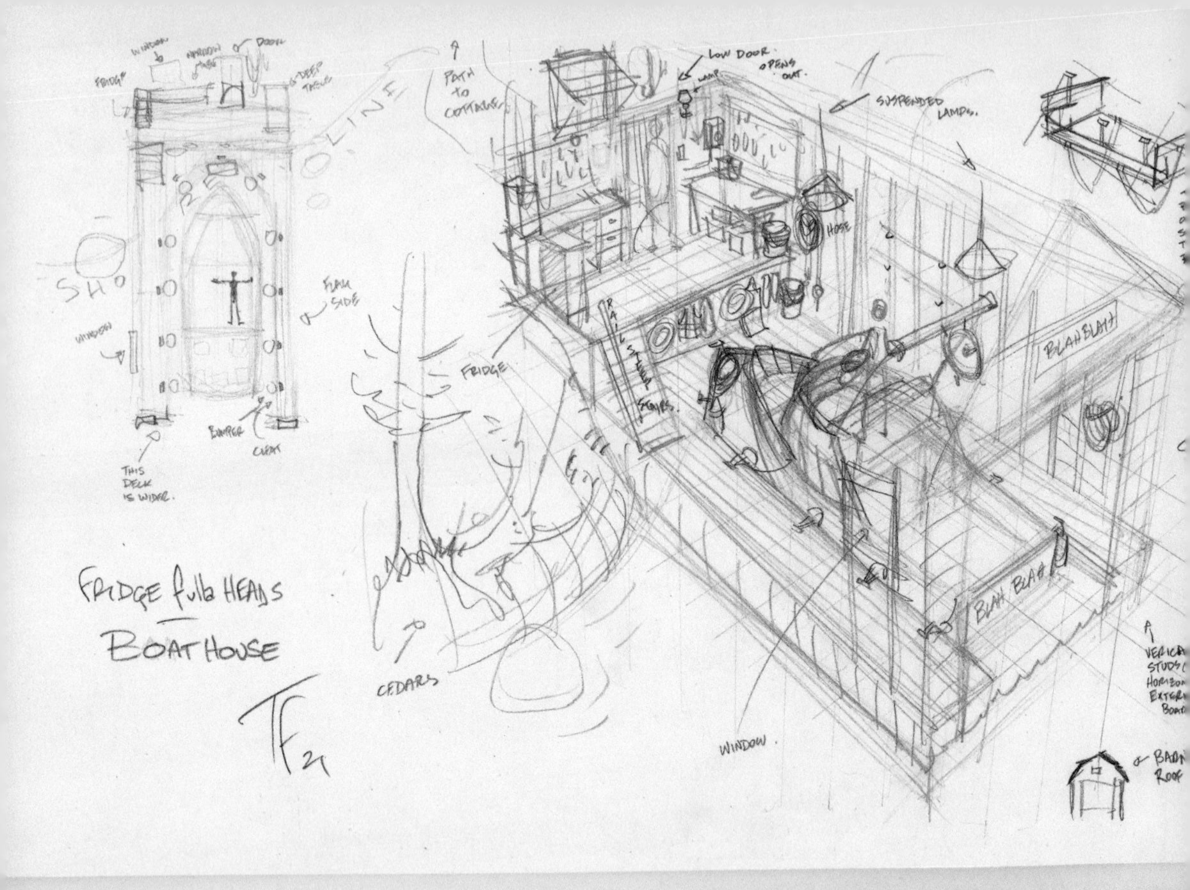
FRIDGE full' HEADS
BOATHOUSE
TF21
PATH TO COTTAGE
LOW DOOR OPENS OUT.
SUSPENDED LAMPS.
FRIDGE
CEDARS
WINDOW
BLAH BLAH
THIS DECK IS WIDER.
BUMPER
CLEAT
BARN ROOF

THE LOCATIONS

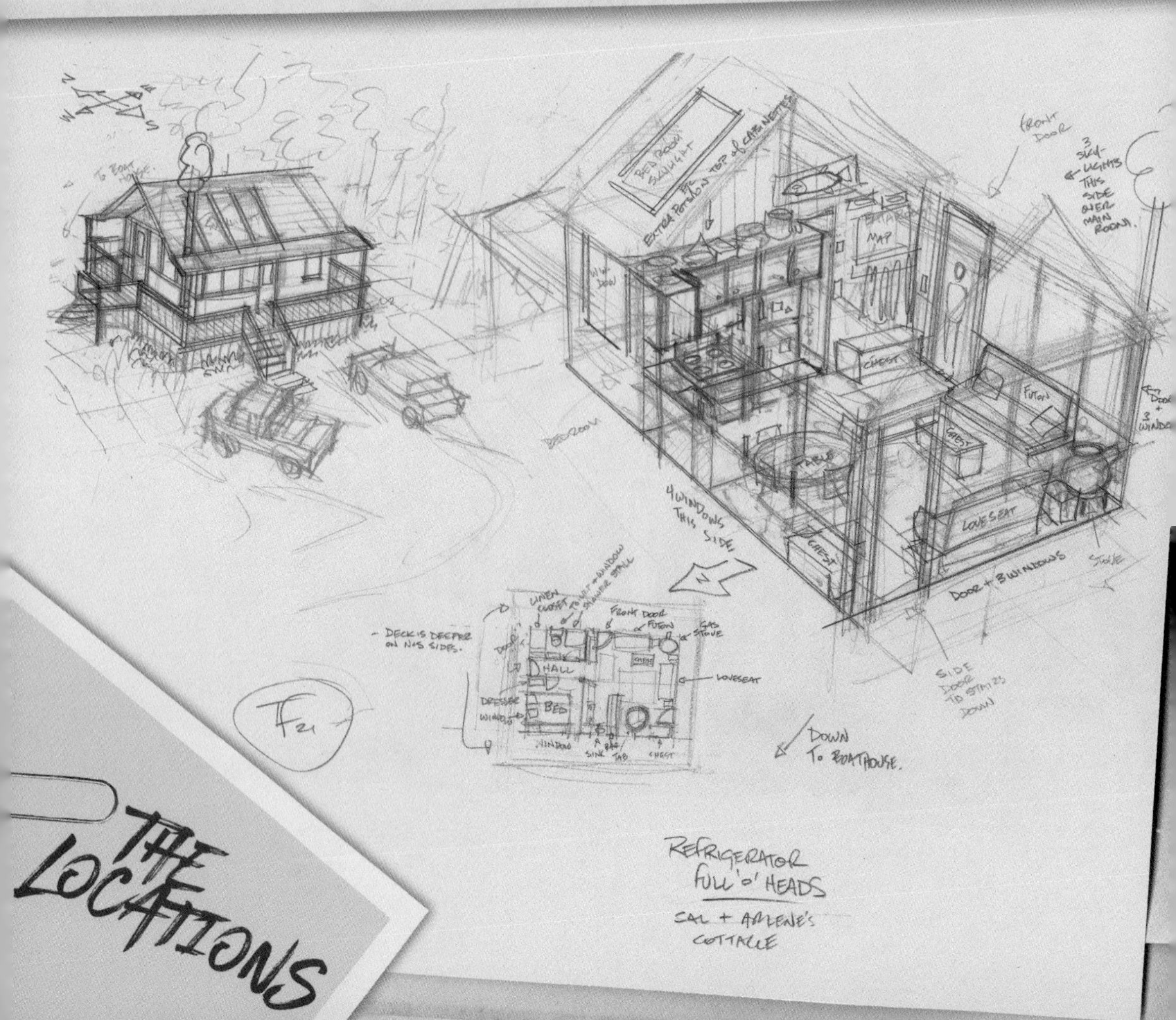
REFRIGERATOR FULL 'O' HEADS
CAL + ARLENE'S COTTAGE
TF21
FRONT DOOR
CHEST
FUTON
TABLE
LOVESEAT
STOVE
4 WINDOWS THIS SIDE
DOOR + 3 WINDOWS
SIDE DOOR TO STAIRS DOWN
DOWN TO BOATHOUSE.
BED
HALL
DRESSER
WINDOW
LOVESEAT
GAS STOVE

THE TARGETS

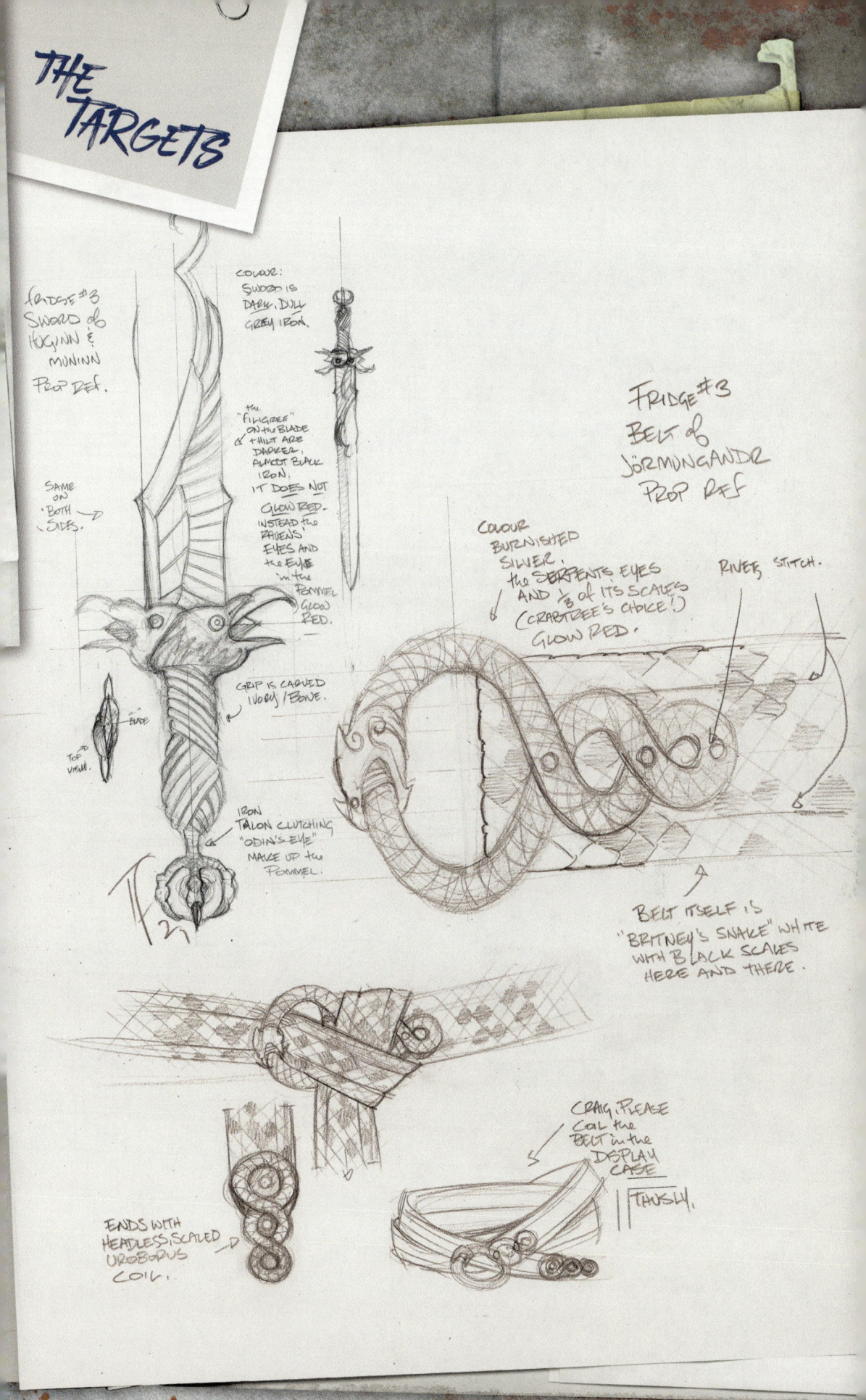

FRIDGE #3 SWORD OF HUGINN & MUNINN PROP REF.

SAME ON BOTH SIDES.

COLOUR: SWORD IS DARK, DULL GREY IRON.

THE "FILIGREE" ON THE BLADE & HILT ARE DARKER, ALMOST BLACK IRON. IT DOES NOT GLOW RED. INSTEAD THE RAVENS' EYES AND THE EYE IN THE POMMEL GLOW RED.

GRIP IS CARVED IVORY / BONE.

BLADE
TOP VIEW.

IRON TALON CLUTCHING "ODIN'S EYE" MAKE UP THE POMMEL.

FRIDGE #3 BELT OF JÖRMUNGANDR PROP REF

COLOUR: BURNISHED SILVER. THE SERPENT'S EYES AND 1/3 OF ITS SCALES (CRABTREE'S CHOICE!) GLOW RED.

RIVET STITCH.

BELT ITSELF IS "BRITNEY'S SNAKE" WHITE WITH BLACK SCALES HERE AND THERE.

ENDS WITH HEADLESS, SCALED UROBORUS COIL.

CRAIG, PLEASE COIL THE BELT IN THE DISPLAY CASE THUSLY.

RIO YOUERS was born after the Beatles broke up but before Jim Morrison died, which makes him old. Damn old. He is the British Fantasy and Sunburst Award-nominated author of *Lola on Fire* and *No Second Chances*. His 2017 thriller, *The Forgotten Girl*, was a finalist for the Arthur Ellis Award for Best Crime Novel. Writing a comic series for DC was a dream come true for Rio, and it's something he tells everyone about, at every possible opportunity, even when they don't ask.

TOM FOWLER is a writer, cartoonist, and illustrator who has worked for a variety of publishers including DC, Marvel, Simon & Schuster, Hasbro, Oni, Valiant, and *MAD Magazine*. His books include *Rick & Morty*, *Venom*, and *The Sandman Universe: Books of Magic*. *Refrigerator Full of Heads* represents Tom's first foray into horror. He liked it. Some in editorial fear maybe too much.

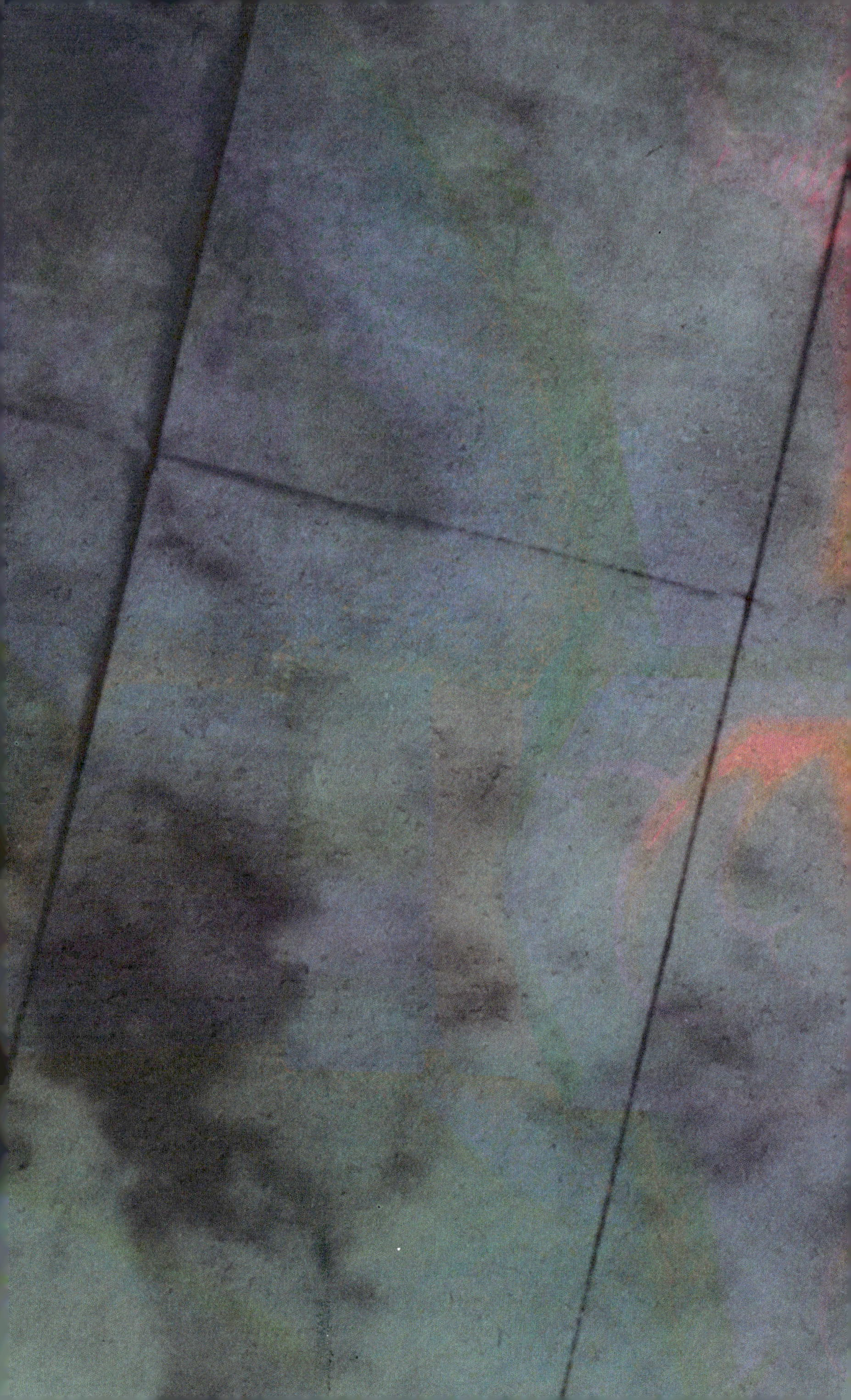